DARK
and
STORMY
KNIGHTS

EDITED BY
P. N. ELROD

ST. MARTIN'S GRIFFIN
NEW YORK

A QUESTIONABLE CLIENT copyright © 2010 by Ilona Andrews. EVEN HAND copyright © 2010 by Jim Butcher. THE BEACON copyright © 2010 by Shannon K. Butcher. EVEN A RABBIT WILL BITE copyright © 2010 by Rachel Caine. DARK LADY copyright © 2010 by P. N. Elrod. BEKNIGHTED copyright © 2010 by Deidre Knight. SHIFTING STAR copyright © 2010 by Vicki Pettersson. ROOKWOOD & MRS. KING copyright © 2010 by Lilith Saintcrow. GOD'S CREATURES copyright © 2010 by Carrie Vaughn. All rights reserved. Printed in the United States of America. For information, address St. Martin's Press, 175 Fifth Avenue, New York, N.Y. 10010.

www.stmartins.com

Library of Congress Cataloging-in-Publication Data

Dark and stormy knights / edited by P. N. Elrod.—1st ed.
     p. cm.
   ISBN 978-0-312-59834-1
   1. Fantasy fiction, American.   I. Elrod, P. N. (Patricia Nead)
   PS648.F3D365 2010
   813'.0876608—dc22

                                        2009046749

First Edition: August 2010

10 9 8 7 6 5 4 3 2 1

CONTENTS

A Questionable Client *by Ilona Andrews* 1

Even Hand *by Jim Butcher* 47

The Beacon *by Shannon K. Butcher* 81

Even a Rabbit Will Bite *by Rachel Caine* 121

Dark Lady *by P. N. Elrod* 157

Beknighted *by Deidre Knight* 205

Shifting Star *by Vicki Pettersson* 245

Rookwood & Mrs. King *by Lilith Saintcrow* 285

God's Creatures *by Carrie Vaughn* 325

A QUESTIONABLE CLIENT

by ILONA ANDREWS

The problem with leucrocotta blood is that it stinks to high heaven. It's also impossible to get off your boots, particularly if the leucrocotta condescended to void its anal glands on you right before you chopped its head off.

I sat on the bench in the Mercenary Guild locker room and pondered my noxious footwear. The boots were less than a year old. And I didn't have money to buy a new pair.

"Tomato juice, Kate," one of the mercs offered. "Will take it right out."

Now he'd done it. I braced myself.

A woman in the corner shook her head. "That's for skunks. Try baking soda."

"You have to go scientific about it. Two parts hydrogen peroxide to four parts water."

"A quart of water and a tablespoon of ammonia."

"What you need to do is piss on it. . . ."

Every person in the locker room knew my boots were shot. Unfortunately, stain removal methods was one of those troublesome subjects somewhere between relationship issues and mysterious car noises. Everybody was an expert, everybody had a cure, and they all fell over themselves to offer their advice.

The electric bulbs blinked and faded. Magic flooded the world in a silent rush, smothering technology. Twisted tubes of feylanterns ignited with pale blue on the walls as the charged air inside them interacted with magic. A nauseating stench, reminiscent of a couple of pounds of shrimp left in the sun for a week, erupted from my boots. There were collective grunts of "Ugh" and "Oh God," and then everybody decided to give me lots of personal space.

We lived in a post-Shift world. One moment magic dominated, fueling spells and giving power to monsters, and the next it vanished as abruptly as it appeared. Cars started, electricity flowed, and mages became easy prey to a punk with a gun. Nobody could predict when magic waves would come or how long they would last. That's why I carried a sword. It always worked.

Mark appeared in the doorway. Mark was the Guild's equivalent of middle management, and he looked the part— his suit was perfectly clean and cost more than I made in three months, his dark hair was professionally trimmed, and his hands showed no calluses. In the crowd of working-class thugs, he stood out like a sore thumb and was proud of it, which earned him the rank and file's undying hatred.

Mark's expressionless stare fastened on me. "Daniels, the clerk has a gig ticket for you."

Usually the words "gig ticket" made my eyes light up. I needed money. I always needed money. The Guild zoned the jobs, meaning that each merc had his own territory. If a job fell in your territory, it was legitimately yours. My territory was near Savannah, basically in the sparsely populated middle of nowhere, and good gigs didn't come my way too often. The only reason I ended up in Atlanta this time was that my part-time partner in crime, Jim, needed help clearing a pack of grave-digging leucrocottas from Westview Cemetery. He'd cut me in on his gig.

Under normal circumstances I would've jumped on the chance to earn extra cash, but I had spent most of the last twenty-four hours awake and chasing hyena-sized creatures armed with badgerlike jaws full of extremely sharp teeth. And Jim bailed on me midway through it. Some sort of Pack business. That's what I get for pairing with a werejaguar.

I was tired, dirty, and hungry, and my boots stank.

"I just finished a job."

"It's a blue gig."

Blue gig meant double rate.

Mac, a huge hulk of a man, shook his head, presenting me with a view of his mangled left ear. "Hell, if she doesn't want it, I'll take it."

"No, you won't. She's licensed for bodyguard detail and you aren't."

I bloody hated bodyguard detail. On regular jobs, I had to depend only on myself. But bodyguard detail was a couple's kind of dance. You had to work with the body you guarded, and in my experience, bodies proved uncooperative.

"Why me?"

Mark shrugged. "Because I have no choice. I have Rodriguez and Castor there now, but they just canceled on me. If you don't take the gig, I'll have to track down someone who will. My pain, your gain."

Canceled wasn't good. Rodriguez was a decent mage, and Castor was tough in a fight. They wouldn't bail from a well-paying job unless it went sour.

"I need someone there right now. Go there, babysit the client through the night, and in the morning I'll have a replacement lined up. In or out, Daniels? It's a high-profile client, and I don't like to keep him waiting."

The gig smelled bad. "How much?"

"Three grand."

Someone whistled. Three grand for a night of work. I'd be insane to pass on it. "In."

"Good."

I started to throw my stink-bomb boots into the locker but stopped myself. I had paid a lot for them, and they should have lasted for another year at least; but if I put them into my locker, it would smell forever. Sadly the boots were ruined. I tossed them into the trash, pulled on my old spare pair, grabbed my sword, and headed out of the locker room to get the gig ticket from the clerk.

When I rode into Atlanta, the magic was down, so I had taken Betsi, my old dented Subaru. With magic wave in full swing, my gasoline-guzzling car was about as mobile as a car-size rock, but since I was technically doing the Guild a favor, the clerk provided me with a spare mount. Her name was Peggy, and judging by the wear on her incisors, she'd started her third decade some years ago. Her muzzle had gone gray, her tail and mane had thinned to stringy tendrils, and she moved with ponderous slowness. I'd ridden her for the first fifteen minutes, listening to her sigh, and then guilt got the better of me and I decided to walk the rest of the way. I didn't have to go far. According to the directions, Champion Heights was only a couple miles away. An extra ten minutes wouldn't make that much difference.

Around me a broken city struggled to shrug off winter, fighting the assault of another cold February night. Husks of once mighty skyscrapers stabbed through the melting snow-drifts encrusted with dark ice. Magic loved to feed on anything technologically complex, but tall office towers proved particularly susceptible to magic-induced erosion. Within a couple of years of the first magic wave they shuddered, crumbled, and fell one by one, like giants on sand legs, spilling mountains of broken glass and twisted guts of metal framework onto the streets.

The city grew around the high-tech corpses. Stalls and small shops took the place of swanky coffee joints and boutiques. Wood-and-brick houses, built by hand and no taller than four floors high, replaced the high-rises. Busy streets, once filled with cars and buses, now channeled a flood of horses, mules, and camels. During rush hour the stench alone put hair on your chest. But now, with the last of the sunset dying slowly above the horizon, the city lay empty. Anyone with a crumb of sense hurried home. The night belonged to monsters, and monsters were always hungry.

The wind picked up, driving dark clouds across the sky

and turning my bones into icicles. It would storm soon. Here's hoping Champion Heights, my client's humble abode, had someplace I could hide Peggy from the sleet.

We picked our way through Buckhead, Peggy's hooves making loud clopping noises in the twilight silence of the deserted streets. The night worried me little. I looked too poor and too mean to provide easy pickings, and nobody in his right mind would try to steal Peggy. Unless a gang of soap-making bandits lurked about, we were safe enough. I checked the address again. Smack in the middle of Buckhead. The clerk said I couldn't miss it. Pretty much a guarantee I'd get lost.

I turned the corner and stopped.

A high-rise towered over the ruins. It shouldn't have existed, but there it was, a brick-and-concrete tower silhouetted against the purple sky. At least fifteen floors, maybe more. Pale tendrils of haze clung to it. It was so tall that the top floor of it still reflected the sunset, while the rest of the city lay steeped in shadow.

"Pinch me, Peggy."

Peggy sighed, mourning the fact that she was paired with me.

I petted her gray muzzle. "Ten to one that's Champion Heights. Why isn't it laying in shambles?"

Peggy snorted.

"You're right. We need a closer look."

We wound through the labyrinth of streets, closing in on the tower. My paper said the client's name was Saiman. No indication if it was his last or first name. Perhaps he was like

[6]

Batman, one of a kind. Of course, Batman wouldn't have to hire bodyguards.

"You have to ask yourself, Peggy, who would pay three grand for a night of work and why. I bet living in that tower isn't cheap, so Saiman has money. Contrary to popular opinion, people who have money refuse to part with it, unless they absolutely have to do it. Three grand means he's in big trouble and we're walking into something nasty."

Finally we landed in a vast parking lot, empty save for a row of cars near the front. Gray Volvo, black Cadillac, even a sleek gunmetal Lamborghini. Most vehicles sported a bloated hood—built to accommodate a charged water engine. The water-engine cars functioned during magic waves by using magic-infused water instead of gasoline. Unfortunately, they took a good fifteen minutes of hard chanting to start, and when they did spring into action, they attained a maximum speed of forty-five miles per hour while growling, snarling, and thundering loud enough to force a deaf man to file a noise complaint.

A large white sign waited past the cars. A black arrow pointed to the right. Above the arrow in black letters was written, "Please stable your mounts." I looked to the right and saw a large stable and a small guardhouse next to it.

It took me a full five minutes to convince the guards I wasn't a serial killer in disguise, but finally Peggy relaxed in a comfortable stall, and I climbed the stone stairs to Champion Heights. As I looked, the concrete-and-brick wall of the high-rise swam out of focus, shimmered, and turned into a granite crag.

Whoa.

I squinted at the wall and saw the faint outline of bricks within the granite. Interesting.

The stairs brought me to the glass-and-steel front of the building. The same haze that cloaked the building clouded the glass, but not enough to obscure a thick metal grate barring the vestibule. Beyond the grate, a guard sat behind a round counter, between an Uzi and a crossbow. The Uzi looked well maintained. The crossbow bore the Hawkeye logo on its stock—a round bird-of-prey eye with a golden iris—which meant its prong was steel and not cheap aluminum. Probably upward of two hundred pounds of draw weight. At this distance, it would take out a rhino, let alone me.

The guard gave me an evil eye. I leaned to the narrow metal grille and tried to broadcast "trustworthy."

"I'm here for one fifty-eight." I pulled out my merc card and held it to the glass.

"Code, please."

Code? What code? "Nobody said anything about a code."

The guard leveled a crossbow at me.

"Very scary," I told him. "One small problem—you shoot me and the tenant in one fifty-eight won't live through the night. I'm not a threat to you. I'm a bodyguard on the job from the Mercenary Guild. If you call to one fifty-eight and check, they'll tell you they're expecting me."

The guard rose and disappeared into a hallway to the right. A long minute passed. Finally he emerged, looking sour, and pushed a button. The metal grate slid aside.

I walked in. The floor and walls were polished red granite. The air smelled of expensive perfume.

"Fifteenth floor," the guard said, nodding at the elevator in the back of the room.

"The magic is up." The elevator was likely dead.

"Fifteenth floor."

Oy. I walked up to the elevator and pushed the Up button. The metal doors slid open. I got in and selected the fifteenth floor, the elevator closed, and a moment later a faint purring announced the cabin rising. It's good to be rich.

The elevator spat me out into a hallway lined with a luxurious green carpet. I plodded through it past the door marked 158 to the end of the hallway to the door marked with the EXIT sign and opened it. Stairs. Unfortunately in good repair. The door opened from the inside of the hallway, but it didn't lock. No way to jam it.

The hallway was T-shaped with only one exit, which meant that potential attackers could come either through the elevator shaft or up the stairs.

I went up to 158 and knocked.

The door shot open. Gina Castor's dark eyes glared at me. An AK-47 hung off her shoulder. She held a black duffel in one hand and her sword in the other. "What took you so long?"

"Hello to you, too."

She pushed past me, the thin, slightly stooped Rodriguez following her. "He's all yours."

I caught the door before it clicked shut. "Where is the client?"

"Chained to the bed." They headed to the elevator.

"Why?"

Castor flashed her teeth at me. "You'll figure it out."

The elevator's door slid open, they ducked in, and a moment later I was alone in the hallway, holding the door open like an idiot. Peachy.

I stepped inside and shut the door. A faint spark of magic shot through the metal box of the card-reader lock. I touched it. The lock was a sham. The door was protected by a ward. I pushed harder. My magic crashed against the invisible wall of the spell and ground to a halt. An expensive ward, too. Good. Made my job a hair easier.

I slid the dead bolt shut and turned. I stood in a huge living room, big enough to contain most of my house. A marble counter ran along the wall on my left, sheltering a bar with glass shelves offering everything from Bombay Sapphire to French wines. A large steel fridge sat behind the bar. White, criminally plush carpet, black walls, steel-and-glass furniture, and beyond it all an enormous floor-to-ceiling window presenting the vista of the ruined city, a deep darkness lit here and there by the pale blue of feylanterns.

I stayed away from the window and trailed the wall, punctuated by three doors. The first opened into a laboratory: flame-retardant table and counters supporting row upon row of equipment. I recognized a magic scanner, a computer, and a spectrograph, but the rest was beyond me. No client.

I tried the second door and found a large room. Gloom pooled in the corners. A huge platform bed occupied most of the hardwood floor. Something lay on the bed, hidden under black sheets.

"Saiman?"

No answer.

Why me?

The wall to the left of the bed was all glass, and beyond the glass, far below, stretched a very hard parking lot, bathed in the glow of feylanterns.

God, fifteen floors was high.

I pulled my saber from the back sheath and padded across the floor to the bed.

The body under the sheets didn't move.

Step.

Another step.

In my head, the creature hiding under the sheets lunged at me, knocking me through the window in an explosion of glass shards to plunge far below. . . . Fatigue was messing with my head.

Another step.

I nudged the sheet with my sword, peeling it back gently.

A man rested on the black pillow. He was bald. His head was lightly tanned, his face neither handsome nor ugly, his features well shaped and pleasant. Perfectly average. His shoulders were nude—he was probably down to his underwear or naked under the sheet.

"Saiman?" I asked softly.

The man's eyelids trembled. Dark eyes stared at me,

luminescent with harsh predatory intelligence. A warning siren went off in my head. I took a small step back and saw the outline of several chains under the sheet. You've got to be kidding me. They didn't just chain him to the bed, they wrapped him up like a Christmas present. He couldn't even twitch.

"Good evening," the man said, his voice quiet and cultured.

"Good evening."

"You're my new bodyguard, I presume."

I nodded. "Call me Kate."

"Kate. What a lovely name. Please forgive me. Normally I would rise to greet a beautiful woman, but I'm afraid I'm indisposed at the moment."

I pulled back a little more of the sheet, revealing an industrial-size steel chain. "I can see that."

"Perhaps I could impose on you to do me the great favor of removing my bonds?"

"Why did Rodriguez and Castor chain you?" And where the hell did they find a chain of this size?

A slight smile touched his lips. "I'd prefer not to answer that question."

"Then we're in trouble. Clients get restrained when they interfere with the bodyguards' ability to keep them safe. Since you won't tell me why the previous team decided to chain you, I can't let you go."

The smile grew wider. "I see your point."

"Does this mean you're ready to enlighten me?"

"I'm afraid not."

I nodded. "I see. Well then, I'll clear the rest of the apartment, and then I'll come back and we'll talk some more."

"Do you prefer brunets or blonds?"

"What?"

The sheet shivered.

"Quickly, Kate. Brunets or blonds? Pick one."

Odd bulges strained the sheet. I grabbed the covers and jerked them back.

Saiman lay naked, his body pinned to the bed by the chain. His stomach distended between two loops, huge and bloated. Flesh bulged and crawled under his skin, as if his body were full of writhing worms.

"Blond, I'd say," Saiman said.

He groaned, his back digging into the sheets. The muscles under his skin boiled. Bones stretched. Ligaments twisted, contorting his limbs. Acid squirted into my throat. I gagged, trying not to vomit.

His body stretched, twisted, and snapped into a new shape: lean, with crisp definition. His jaw widened, his eyes grew larger, his nose gained a sharp cut. Cornsilk blond hair sprouted on his head and reaching down to his shoulders. Indigo flooded his irises. A new man looked at me, younger by about five years, taller, leaner, with a face that was heartbreakingly perfect. Above his waist, he was Adonis. Below his ribs, his body degenerated into a bloated stomach. He looked pregnant.

"You wouldn't tell me what you preferred," he said mournfully, his pitch low and husky. "I had to improvise."

* * *

"What are you?" I kept my sword between me and him.

"Does it really matter?"

"Yes, it does." When people said shapeshifter, they meant a person afflicted with Lyc-V, the virus that gave its victim the ability to shift into an animal. I'd never seen one who could freely change its human form.

Saiman made a valiant effort to shrug. Hard to shrug with several pounds of chains on your shoulders, but he managed to look nonchalant doing it.

"I am me."

Oh boy. "Stay here."

"Where would I go?"

I left the bedroom and checked the rest of the apartment. The only remaining room contained a large shower stall and a giant bathtub. No kitchen. Perhaps he had food delivered.

Fifteenth floor. At least one guard downstairs, bullet-resistant glass, metal grates. The place was a fortress. Yet he hired bodyguards at exorbitant prices. He expected his castle to be breached.

I headed to the bar, grabbed a glass from under the counter, filled it with water, and took it to Saiman. Changing shape took energy. If he was anything like other shapeshifters, he was dying of thirst and hunger right about now.

Saiman's gaze fastened on the glass. "Delightful."

I let him drink. He drained the glass in long, thirsty swallows.

"How many guards are on duty downstairs?"

"Three."

"Are they employed by the building owners directly?"

Saiman smiled. "Yes. They're experienced and well paid, and they won't hesitate to kill."

So far so good. "When you change shape, do you reproduce internal organs as well?"

"Only if I plan to have intercourse."

Oh goodie. "Are you pregnant?"

Saiman laughed softly.

"I need to know if you're going to go into labor." Because that would just be a cherry on the cake of this job.

"You're a most peculiar woman. No, I'm most definitely not pregnant. I'm male, and while I may construct a vaginal canal and a uterus on occasion, I've never had cause to recreate ovaries. And if I did, I suspect they would be sterile. Unlike the male of the species, women produce all of their gametes during gestation, meaning that when a female infant is born, she will have in her ovaries all of the partially developed eggs she will ever have. The ovaries cannot generate production of new eggs, only the maturation of existing ones. The magic is simply not deep enough for me to overcome this hurdle. Not yet."

Thank Universe for small favors. "Who am I protecting you from, and why?"

"I'm afraid I have to keep that information to myself as well."

Why did I take this job again? Ah yes, a pile of money. "Withholding this information diminishes my ability to guard you."

He tilted his head, looking me over. "I'm willing to take that chance."

"I'm not. It also puts my life at a greater risk."

"You're well compensated for that risk."

I repressed the urge to brain him with something heavy. Too bad there was no kitchen—a cast-iron frying pan would do the job.

"I see why the first team bailed."

"Oh, it was the woman," Saiman said helpfully. "She had difficulty with my metamorphosis. I believe she referred to me as an 'abomination.'"

I rubbed the bridge of my nose. "Let's try simple questions. Do you expect us to be attacked tonight?"

"Yes."

I figured as much. "With magic or brute force?"

"Both."

"Is it a hit for hire?"

Saiman shook his head. "No."

Well, at least something went my way: amateurs were easier to deal with than contract killers.

"It's personal. I can tell you this much: the attackers are part of a religious sect. They will do everything in their power to kill me, including sacrificing their own lives."

And we just drove off a cliff in a runaway buggy. "Are they magically adept?"

"Very."

I leaned back. "So let me summarize. You're a target of magical kamikaze fanatics, you won't tell me who they are, why they're after you, or why you have been restrained?"

"Precisely. Could I trouble you for a sandwich? I'm famished."

Dear God, I had a crackpot for a client. "A sandwich?"

"Prosciutto and Gouda on sourdough bread, please. A tomato and red onion would be quite lovely as well."

"Sounds delicious."

"Feel free to have one."

"I tell you what, since you refuse to reveal anything that might make my job even a smidgeon easier, how about I make a delicious prosciutto sandwich and taunt you with it until you tell me what I want to know?"

Saiman laughed.

An eerie sound came from the living room—a light click, as if something with long sharp claws crawled across metal.

I put my finger to my lips, freed my saber, and padded out into the living room.

The room lay empty. No intruders.

I stood very still, trying to fade into the black walls.

Moments dripped by.

A small noise came from the left. It was a hesitant, slow clicking, as if some creature slunk in the distance, slowly putting one foot before the other.

Click.

Definitely a claw.

Click.

I scrutinized the left side of the room. Nothing moved.

Click. Click, click.

Closer this time. Fear skittered down my spine. Fear was good. It would keep me sharp. I kept still. Where are you, you sonovabitch?

Click to the right, and almost immediately a quiet snort to the left. Now we had two invisible intruders. Because one wasn't hard enough.

An odd scent nipped at my nostrils, a thick, slightly bitter herbal odor. I'd smelled it once before, but I had no clue where or when.

Claws scraped to the right and to the left of me now. More than two. A quiet snort to the right. Another in the corner. Come out to play. Come on, beastie.

Claws raked metal directly in front of me. There was nothing there but that huge window and sloping ceiling above it. I looked up. Glowing green eyes peered at me through the grate of the air duct in the ceiling.

Shivers sparked down my back.

The eyes stared at me, heated with madness.

The screws in the air duct cover turned to the left. Righty tighty, lefty loosey. Smart critter.

The grate fell onto the soft carpet. The creature leaned forward slowly, showing me a long conical head. The herbal scent grew stronger now, as if I'd taken a handful of absinthe wormwood and stuck it up my nose.

Long black claws clutched the edge of the air duct. The beast rocked, revealing its shoulders sheathed in shaggy, hunter green fur.

Bingo. An endar. Six legs, each armed with wicked black claws; preternaturally fast; equipped with an outstanding sense of smell and a big mouth, which hid a tongue lined with hundreds of serrated teeth. One lick and it would scrape the flesh off my bones in a very literal way.

The endars were peaceful creatures. The green fur wasn't fur at all; it was moss that grew from their skin. They lived underneath old oaks, rooted to the big trees in a state of quiet hibernation, absorbing their nutrients and making rare excursions to the surface to lick the bark and feed on lichens. They stirred from their rest so rarely that pagan Slavs thought they fed on air.

Someone had poured blood under this endar's oak. The creature had absorbed it, and the blood had driven it crazy. It had burrowed to the surface, where it swarmed with its fellows. Then the same someone, armed with a hell of a lot of magic, had herded this endar and its buddies to this highrise and released them into the ventilation system so they would find Saiman and rip him apart. They couldn't be frightened off. They couldn't be stopped. They would kill anything with a pulse to get to their target, and when the target was dead, they would have to be eliminated. There was no going back from endar madness.

Only a handful of people knew how to control endars.

Saiman had managed to piss off the Russians. It's never good to piss off the Russians. That was just basic common sense. My father was Russian, but I doubted they would cut me any slack just because I could understand their curses.

The endar gaped at me with its glowing eyes. Yep, mad as a hatter. I'd have to kill every last one of them.

"Well, come on. Bring it."

The endar's mouth gaped. It let out a piercing screech, like a circular saw biting into the wood, and charged.

I swung Slayer. The saber's blade sliced into flesh and the

beast crashed to the floor. Thick green blood stained Saiman's white carpet.

The three other duct covers fell one by one. A stream of green bodies charged toward me. I swung my sword, cleaving the first body in two. It was going to be a long night.

The last of the endars was on the smaller side. Little bigger than a cat. I grabbed it by the scruff of the neck and took it back into the bedroom.

Saiman smiled at my approach. "I take it everything went well?"

"I redecorated."

He arched his eyebrow again. Definitely mimicking me. "Oh?"

"Your new carpet is a lovely emerald color."

"I can assure you that carpet is the least of my worries."

"You're right." I brought the endar closer. The creature saw Saiman and jerked spasmodically. Six legs whipped the air, claws out, ready to rend and tear. The beast's mouth gaped, releasing a wide tongue studded with rows and rows of conical teeth.

"You provoked the volkhvi." It was that or the Russian witches. I bet on the volkhvi. The witches would've cursed us by now.

"Indeed."

"The volkhvi are bad news for a number of reasons. They serve pagan Slavic gods, and they have thousands of years of magic tradition to draw on. They're at least as powerful as Druids, but unlike Druids, who are afraid to sneeze the wrong way or someone might accuse them of bringing back human sacrifices, the volkhvi don't give a damn. They won't stop, either. They don't like using the endars, because the endars nourish the forest with their magic. Whatever you did really pissed them off."

Saiman pondered me as if I were some curious bug. "I wasn't aware that the Guild employed anyone with an education."

"I'll hear it. All of it."

"No." He shook his head. "I do admire your diligence and expertise. I don't want you to think it's gone unnoticed."

I dropped the endar onto Saiman's stomach. The beast clawed at the sheet. Saiman screamed. I grabbed the creature and jerked it up. The beast dragged the sheet with it, tearing it to shreds. Small red scratches marked Saiman's blob of a stomach.

"I'll ask again. What did you do to infuriate the Russians? Consider your answer carefully, because next time I drop this guy, I'll be slower picking him back up."

Saiman's face quivered with rage. "You're my bodyguard."

"You can file a complaint, if you survive. You're putting both of us in danger by withholding information. See, if I walk, I just miss out on some money; you lose your life. I have no problem with leaving you here, and the Guild can stick its thumb up its ass and twirl for all I care. The only thing that keeps me protecting you is professional pride. I hate bodyguard detail, but I'm good at it, and I don't like to lose a body. It's in your best interests to help me do my job. Now, I'll count to three. On three I drop Fluffy here and let it go to town on your gut. He really wants whatever you're hiding in there."

Saiman stared at me.

"One. Two. Th—"

"Very well."

I reached into my backpack and pulled out a piece of wire. Normally I used it for trip traps, but it would make a decent leash. Two minutes later, the endar was secured to the dresser and I perched on the corner of Saiman's bed.

"Are you familiar with the legend of Booyan Island?"

I nodded. "It's a mythical island far in the Ocean, behind the Hvalynskii Sea. It's a place of deep magic where a number of legendary creatures and items are located: Alatyr, the father of all stones; the fiery pillar; the Drevo-Doob, the World Oak; the cave where the legendary sword Kladenets is hidden; the Raven prophet; and so on. It's the discount warehouse of Russian legends. Any time the folkloric heroes needed a magic object, they made a trip to it."

"Let's concentrate on the tree," Saiman said.

I knew Slavic mythology well enough, but I hadn't had to use it for a while and I was a bit rusty. "It's a symbol of nature. Creature of the earth at its roots, the serpent, the frog, and so on. There is a raven with a prophet gift in the branches. Some myths say that there are iron chains wrapped around the tree's trunk. A black cat walks the chain, telling stories and fables. . . ."

Saiman nodded.

Oh crap. "It's that damn cat, isn't it?"

"The oak produces an acorn once every seven years. Seven

months, seven days, and seven hours after the acorn falls from the tree, it will crack and grow into the World Oak. In effect, the tree manifests at the location of the acorn for the period of seven minutes."

I frowned. "Let me guess. You stole the acorn from the Russians and swallowed it."

Saiman nodded.

"Why? Are you eager to hear a bedtime story?"

"The cat possesses infinite knowledge. Seven minutes is time enough to ask and hear an answer to one question. Only the owner of the acorn can ask the question."

I shook my head. "Saiman, nothing is free. You have to pay for everything, knowledge included. What will it cost you to ask a question?"

"The price is irrelevant if I get an answer." Saiman smiled.

I sighed. "Answer my question: Why do smart people tend to be stupid?"

"Because we think we know better. We think that our intellect affords us special privileges and lets us beat the odds. That's why talented mathematicians try to defraud casinos and young brilliant mages make bargains with forces beyond their control."

Well, he answered the question.

"When is the acorn due for its big kaboom?"

"In four hours and forty-seven minutes."

"The volkhvi will tear this high-rise apart stone by stone to get it back, and I'm your last line of defense?"

"That's an accurate assessment. I did ask for the best person available."

I sighed. "Still want that sandwich?"

"Very much."

I headed to the door.

"Kate?"

"Yes?"

"The endar?"

I turned to him. "Why were you chained?"

Saiman grimaced. "The acorn makes it difficult to control my magic. It forces me to continuously change shape. Most of the time I'm able to keep the changes subtle, but once in a while the acorn causes contortions. Gina Castor walked in on me during such a moment. I'm afraid I was convulsing, so my recollection may be somewhat murky, but I do believe I had at least one partially formed breast and three arms. She over-reacted. Odd, considering her profile."

"Her profile?"

"I studied my bodyguards very carefully," Saiman said. "I handpicked three teams. The first refused to take the job, the second was out due to injuries. Castor and Rodriguez were my third choice."

I went back to the bed and ducked under it. They'd chained him with a small padlock. Lock picking wasn't my strong suit. I looked around and saw the small key on the dresser. It took me a good five minutes to unwrap him.

"Thank you." He rose, rubbing his chest, marked by red pressure lines. "May I ask why?"

"Nobody should die chained to the bed."

Saiman stretched. His body swelled, twisted, growing

larger, gaining breadth and muscle. I made a valiant effort to not vomit.

Saiman's body snapped. A large, perfectly sculpted male looked at me. Soft brown hair framed a masculine face. He would make any bodybuilder gym proud. Except for the bloated gut.

"Is he preferable to the previous attempt?" Saiman asked.

"There is more of you to guard now. Other than that, it makes no difference to me."

I headed into the living room. He followed me, swiping a luxurious robe off a chair.

We stepped into the living room. Saiman stopped.

The corpses of endars had melted into puddles of green. Thin stalks of emerald green moss sprouted from the puddles, next to curly green shoots of ferns and tiny young herbs.

"The endars nourish the forest," I told him.

He indicated the completely green carpet with his hand. "How many were there?"

"A few. I lost count."

Saiman's sharp eyes regarded my face. "You're lying. You know the exact number."

"Thirty-seven."

I zeroed in on the fridge. No telling when the next attack would come, and I was starving. You can do without sleep or without food, but not without both and sleep wasn't an option.

Saiman trailed me, taking the seat on the outer side of the counter. "Do you prefer women?"

"No."

He frowned, belting the robe. "It's the stomach, isn't it?"

I raided the fridge. He had enough deli meat to feed an army. I spread it out on the bar's counter. "What do you do for a living, Saimain?"

"I collect information and use it to further my interests."

"It seems to pay well." I nodded to indicate the apartment.

"It does. I also possess an exhaustive knowledge of various magic phenomena. I consult various parties. My fee varies between thirty-six hundred and thirty-nine hundred dollars, depending on the job and the client."

"Thirty-six hundred dollars per job?" I bit into my sandwich. Mmm, salami.

"Per hour."

I choked on my food. He looked at me with obvious amusement.

"The term 'highway robbery' comes to mind," I managed finally.

"Oh, but I'm exceptionally good at what I do. Besides, the victims of highway robbery have no choice in the matter. I assure you, I don't coerce my clients, Kate."

"I'm sure. How did we even get to this point? The stratospheric fee ruined my train of thought."

"You stated that you prefer men to women."

I nodded. "Suppose you get a particularly sensitive piece of information. Let's say a business tip. If you act on the tip, you could make some money. If you sell it, you could make more money. If both you and your buyer act on the tip, you both would make money, but the return for each of you would be significantly diminished. Your move?"

"Either sell the information or act on it. Not both."

"Why?"

Saiman shrugged. "The value of the information increases with its exclusivity. A client buying such knowledge has an expectation of such exclusivity. It would be unethical to undermine it."

"It would be unethical for me to respond to your sexual overtures. For the duration of the job, you're a collection of arms and legs which I have to keep safe. I'm most effective if I'm not emotionally involved with you on any level. To be blunt, I'm doing my best to regard you as a precious piece of porcelain I have to keep out of harm's way."

"But you do find this shape sexually attractive?"

"I'm not going to answer this question. If you pester me, I will chain you back to the bed."

Saiman raised his arm, flexing a spectacular biceps. "This shape has a lot of muscle mass."

I nodded. "In a bench-pressing contest you would probably win. But we're not bench pressing. You might be stronger, but I'm well trained. If you do want to try me, you're welcome to it. Just as long as we agree that once your battered body is chained safely in your bed, I get to say, 'I told you so.'"

Saiman arched his eyebrows. "Try it?"

"And stop that."

"Stop what?"

"Stop mimicking my gestures."

He laughed. "You're a most peculiar person, Kate. I find myself oddly fascinated. You have obvious skill." He indicated the budding forest in his living room. "And knowledge to back it up. Why aren't you among the Guild's top performers?"

Because being in top anything means greater risk of discovery. I was hiding in plain sight and doing a fairly good job of it. But he didn't need to know that. "I don't spend much time in Atlanta. My territory is in the Lowcountry. Nothing much happens there, except for an occasional sea serpent eating shrimp out of the fishing nets."

Saiman's sharp eyes narrowed. "So why not move up to the city? Better jobs, better money, more recognition?"

"I like my house where it is."

Something bumped behind the front door. I swiped Slayer off the counter. "Bedroom. Now."

"Can I watch?"

I pointed with the sword to the bedroom.

Saiman gave an exaggerated sigh. "Very well."

He went to the bedroom. I padded to the door and leaned against it, listening.

Quiet.

I waited, sword raised. Something waited out there in the hallway. I couldn't hear it, but I sensed it. It was there.

A quiet whimper filtered through the steel of the door. A sad, lost, feminine whimper, like an old woman crying quietly in mourning.

I held very still. The apartment felt stifling and crowded

in. I would've given anything for a gulp of fresh air right about now.

Something scratched at the door. A low mutter floated through, whispered words unintelligible.

God, what was it with the air in this place? The place was stale and musty, like a tomb.

A feeling of dread flooded me. Something bad was in the apartment. It hid in the shadows under the furniture, in the cabinets, in the fridge. Fear squirmed through me. I pressed my back against the door, holding Slayer in front of me.

The creature behind the door scratched again, claws against the steel.

The walls closed in. I had to get away from this air. Somewhere out in the open. Someplace where the wind blew under an open sky. Somewhere with nothing to crowd me in.

I had to get out.

If I left, I risked Saiman's life. Outside, the volkhvi were waiting. I'd be walking right into their arms.

The shadows under the furniture grew longer, stretching toward me.

Get out. Get out now!

I bit my lip. A quick drop of blood burned on my tongue, the magic in it nipping at me. Clarity returned for a second, and light dawned in my head. Badzula. Of course. The endars failed to rip us apart, so the volkhvi went for plan B. If Muhammad won't go to the mountain, the mountain must come to Muhammad.

Saiman walked out of the bedroom. His eyes were glazed over.

"Saiman!"

"I must go," he said. "Must get out."

"No, you really must not." I sprinted to him.

"I must."

He headed to the giant window.

I kicked the back of his right knee. He folded. I caught him on the way down and spun him so he landed on his stomach. He sprawled among the ankle-tall ferns. I locked his left wrist and leaned on him, grinding all of my weight into his left shoulder.

"Badzula," I told him. "Belorussian creature. Looks like a middle-aged woman with droopy breasts, swaddled in a filthy blanket."

"I must get out." He tried to roll over, but I had him pinned.

"Focus, Saiman. Badzula—what's her power?"

"She incites people to vagrancy."

"That's right. And we can't be vagrants, because if we walk out of this building, both of us will be killed. We have to stay put."

"I don't think I can do it."

"Yes, you can. I'm not planning on getting up."

"I believe you're right." A small measure of rational thought crept into his voice. "I suppose the furniture isn't really trying to devour us."

"If it is, I'll chop it with my sword when it gets close."

"You can let me up now," he said.

"I don't think so."

We sat still. The air grew viscous like glue. I had to bite it to get any into my lungs.

Muscles crawled under me. Saiman couldn't get out of my hold, so he decided to shift himself out.

"Do you stock herbs?"

"Yes," he said.

"Do you have water lily?"

"Yes."

"Where?"

"Laboratory, third cabinet."

"Good." I rolled off of him. I'd have only a second to do this, and I had to do it precisely.

Saiman got up to his knees. As he rose, I threw a fast right hook. He never saw it coming and didn't brace himself. My fist landed on his jaw. His head snapped back. His eyes rolled over and he sagged down.

Lucky. I ran to the lab.

It took a hell of a lot of practice to knock someone out. You needed both speed and power to jolt the head enough to rattle the brain inside the skull but not cause permanent damage. Under normal circumstances, I wouldn't even try it, but these weren't normal circumstances. Walls were curving in to eat me.

If I did cause too much damage, he would fix it. Considering what he had done to his body so far, his regeneration would make normal shapeshifters jealous.

Third cabinet. I threw it open and scanned the glass jars. Dread mugged me like a sodden blanket. *Ligularia dentata,*

Ligularia przewalski . . . Latin names, why me? *Lilium pardali-num, Lobelia siphilitica.* Come on, come on . . . *Nymphaea od-orata*, pond lily. Also known to Russians as *odolen-trava*, the mermaid flower, an all-purpose pesticide against all things unclean. That would do.

I dashed to the door, twisting the lid off the jar. A gray powder filled it—ground lily petals, the most potent part of the flower. I slid open the lock. The ward drained down, and I jerked the door ajar.

Empty hallway greeted me. I hurled the jar and the pow-der into the hall. A woman wailed, smoke rose from thin air, and Badzula materialized in the middle of the carpet. Skinny, flabby, filthy, with breasts dangling to her waist like two empty bags, she tossed back grimy, tangled hair and hissed at me, baring stumps of rotten teeth.

"That's nice. Fuck you, too."

I swung. It was textbook saber slash, diagonal, from left to right. I drew the entirety of the blade through the wound. Badzula's body toppled one way, her head rolled the other.

The weight dropped off my shoulders. Suddenly I could breathe, and the building no longer seemed in imminent danger of collapsing and burying me alive.

I grabbed the head, tossed it into the elevator, dragged the body in there, sent the whole thing to the ground floor, sprinted back inside, and locked the door, reactivating the ward. The whole thing took five seconds.

On the floor, Saiman lay unmoving. I checked his pulse. Breathing. Good. I went back to the island. I deserved some coffee after this, and I bet Saiman stocked the good stuff.

* * *

I was sitting by the counter, sipping the best coffee I'd ever tasted, when the big-screen TV on the wall lit up with fuzzy glow. Which was more than a smidgeon odd, considering that the magic was still up and the TV shouldn't have worked.

I took my coffee and my saber and went to sit on the couch, facing the TV. Saiman still sprawled unconscious on the floor.

The glow flared brighter, faded, flared brighter . . . In ancient times people used mirrors, but really any somewhat reflective surface would do. The dark TV screen was glossy enough.

The glow blazed and materialized into a blurry male. In his early twenties, dark hair, dark eyes.

The man looked at me. "You're the bodyguard." His voice carried a trace of Russian accent.

I nodded and slipped into Russian. *"Yes."*

"I don't know you. What you do makes no difference to me. We have this place surrounded. We go in in an hour." He made a short chopping motion with his hand. *"You're done."*

"I'm shaking with fear. In fact, I may have to take a minute to get my shivers under control." I drank my coffee.

The man shook his head. *"You tell that* paskuda, *if he let Yulya go, I'll make sure you both walk out alive. You hear that? I don't know what he's got over my wife, but you tell him that. If he wants to live, he has to let her go. I'll be back in thirty minutes. You tell him."*

The screen faded.

And the plot thickens. I sighed and nudged Saiman with my boot. It took a couple of nudges, but finally he groaned and sat up.

"What happened?"

"You fell."

"Really? What did I fall into?"

"My fist."

"That explains the headache." Saiman looked at me. "This will never happen again. I want to be absolutely clear. Attempt this again and you're fired."

I wondered what would happen if I knocked him out again right there, just for kicks.

"Is that my arabica coffee?" he asked.

I nodded. "I will even let you have a cup if you answer my question."

Saiman arched an eyebrow. "Let? It's my coffee."

I saluted him with the mug. "Possession is nine-tenths of the law."

He stared at me incredulously. "Ask."

"Are you holding a woman called Yulya hostage?"

Saiman blinked.

"Her husband is very upset and is offering to let us both go if we can produce Yulya for him. Unfortunately, he's lying and most likely we both would be killed once said Yulya is found. But if you're holding a woman hostage, you must tell me now."

"And if I was?" Saiman rubbed his jaw and sat in the chair opposite me.

"Then you'd have to release her immediately or I would

walk. I don't protect kidnappers, and I take a very dim view of violence toward civilians, men or women."

"You're a bewildering woman."

"Saiman, focus. Yulya?"

Saiman leaned back. "I can't produce Yulya. I am Yulya."

I suppose I should've seen that coming. "The man was under the impression he's married to her. What happened to the real Yulya?"

"There was never a real Yulya. I will tell you the whole story, but I must have coffee. And nutrients."

I poured him a cup of coffee. Saiman reached into the fridge and came up with a gallon of milk, a solid block of chocolate, and several bananas.

Chocolate was expensive as hell. I couldn't remember the last time I'd had some. If I survived this job, I'd buy a couple of truffles.

I watched Saiman load bananas and milk into a manual blender and crank the handle, cutting the whole thing into a coarse mess. Not the chocolate, not the chocolate . . . Yep, threw it in there, too. What a waste.

He poured the concoction into a two-quart jug and began chugging it. Shapeshifters did burn a ton of calories. I sighed, mourning the loss of the chocolate, and sipped my coffee. "Give."

"The man in question is the son of Pavel Semyonov. He's the premier *volkhv* in the Russian community here. The boy's name is Grigorii, and he's completely right, I did marry him, as Yulya, of course. The acorn was very well guarded and I needed a way in."

"Unbelievable."

Saiman smiled. Apparently he thought I'd paid him a compliment. "Are you familiar with the ritual of firing the arrow?"

"It's an archaic folkloric ritual. The shooter is blindfolded and spun around, so he blindly fires. The flight of the arrow foretells the correct direction of the object the person seeks. If a woman picks up the arrow, she and the shooter are fated to be together."

Saiman wiped his mouth. "I picked up the arrow. It took me five months from the arrow to the acorn."

"How long did it take you to con that poor guy into marriage?"

"Three months. The combination of open lust but withholding of actual sex really works wonders."

I shook my head. "Grigorii is in love with you. He thinks his wife is in danger. He's trying to rescue her."

Saiman shrugged. "I had to obtain the acorn. I could say that he's young and resilient, but really his state of mind is the least of my concerns."

"You're a terrible human being."

"I beg to differ. All people are driven by their primary selfishness. I'm simply more honest than most. Furthermore, he had the use of a beautiful woman, created to his precise specifications, for two months. I did my research into his sexual practices quite thoroughly, to the point of sleeping with him twice as a prostitute to make sure I knew his preferences."

"If we get out of this, I need to remember never to work for you again."

Saiman smiled. "But you will. If the price is right."

"No."

"Anyone will work for anyone and anyone will sleep with anyone, if the price is right and the partnership is attractive enough. Suppose I invited you to spend a week here with me. Luxurious clothes. Beautiful shoes." He looked at my old boots, which were in danger of falling apart. "Magnificent meals. All the chocolate you could ever want."

So he'd caught me.

"All that for the price of having sex with me. I would even sweeten the deal by assuming a shape preferable to you. Anyone you want. Any shape, any size, any color, any gender. All in total confidentiality. Nobody ever has to know you were here. The offer is on the table." He placed his hand on the counter, palm down. "Right now. I promise you a week of total bliss—assuming we survive. You'll never get another chance to be this pampered. All I need from you is one word."

"No."

He blinked. "Don't you want to think about it?"

"No."

He clamped his mouth shut. Muscles played along his jaw. "Why?"

The TV screen ignited. Grigorii appeared in the glow. Saiman strode to the screen with a scowl on his face. "I'll make it short." His body boiled, twisted, stretched. I shut my eyes. It was that or lose my precious coffee. When I opened them, a petite red-haired woman stood in Saiman's place.

"Does this explain things enough?" Saiman asked. "Or do I need to spell it out, Grigorii?"

"You're her?"

"Yes."

"I don't believe it."

Saiman sighed. "Would you like me to list your preferred positions, in the order you typically enjoy them? Shall we speak of intimate things? I could recite most of our conversations word for word, I do have a very precise memory."

They stared at each other.

"It was all a lie," Grigorii said finally.

"I call it subterfuge, but yes, in essence, the marriage was a sham. You were set up from the beginning. I was Yulya. I was also Siren and Alyssa, so if you decide to visit that particular house of ill repute again, don't look for either."

Oh God.

The glow vanished. Saiman turned to me. "Back to our question. Why?"

"That man loved you enough to risk his own neck to negotiate your release. You just destroyed him, in passing, because you were in a hurry. And you want to know why. If you did that to him, there's no telling what you'd do to me. Sex is about physical attraction, yes, but it's also about trust. I don't trust you. You're completely self-absorbed and egoistic. You offer nothing I want."

"Sex is driven by physical attraction. Given the right stimulus, you will sleep with me. I simply have to present you with a shape you can't resist."

Saiman jerked, as if struck by a whip, and crashed to the floor. His feet drummed the carpet, breaking the herbs and fledgling ferns. Wild convulsions tore at his body. A blink and he was a mess of arms and legs and bodies. My stomach gave up, and I vomited into the sink.

Ordinarily I'd be on top of him, jamming something in his mouth to keep him from biting himself, but given that he changed shapes as if there were no tomorrow, finding his mouth was a bit problematic.

"Saiman? Talk to me."

"The acorn . . . It's coming. Must . . . Get . . . Roof."

Roof? No roof. We were in the apartment, shielded by a ward. On the roof we'd be sitting ducks. "We can't do that."

"Oak . . . Large . . . Cave-in."

Oh hell. Would it have killed him to mention that earlier? "I need you to walk. You're too heavy and I can't carry you while you convulse."

Little by little, the shudders died. Saiman staggered to his feet. He was back to the unremarkable man I'd first found in the bedroom. His stomach had grown to ridiculous proportions. If he were pregnant, he'd be twelve months along.

"We'll make a run for it," I told him.

A faint scratch made me spin. An old man hung outside the window, suspended on a rope. Gaunt, his white beard flapping in the wind, he peered through the glass straight at me. In the split second we looked at each other, twelve narrow stalks unfurled from his neck, spreading into a corona around his head, like a nimbus around the face of a Russian icon. A bulb tipped each stock. A hovala. Shit.

I grabbed Saiman and threw him at the door.

The bulbs opened.

Blinding light flooded the apartment, hiding the world in

a white haze. The window behind me exploded. I could barely see. "Stay behind me."

Shapes dashed through the haze.

I slashed. Slayer connected, encountering resistance. Sharp ice stabbed my left side. I reversed the strike and slashed again. The shape before me crumpled. The second attacker struck. I dodged left on instinct and stabbed my blade at his side. Bone and muscle. Got him between the lower ribs. A hoarse scream lashed my ears. I twisted the blade, ripping the organs, and withdrew.

The hovala hissed at the window. I was still blind.

Behind me the lock clicked. "No!"

I groped for Saiman and hit my forearm on the open door. He ran. Into the hallway, where he was an easy target. I lost my body. Goddamn it.

I sprinted into the hallway, trying to blink the haze from eyes. The stairs were to the left. I ran, half-blind, grabbed the door, and dashed up the stairs.

The blinding flare finally cleared. I hit the door, burst onto the roof, and took a kick to the ribs. Bones crunched. I fell left and rolled to my feet. A woman stood by the door, arms held in a trademark tae kwon do cat stance.

To the right, an older man grappled with Saiman. Six others watched.

The woman sprang into a kick. It was a lovely kick, strong with good liftoff. I sidestepped and struck. By the time she landed, I'd cut her twice. She fell in a crumpled heap.

I flicked the blood off my saber and headed for Saiman.

"You're Voron's kid," one of the men said. "We have no

problem with you. Pavel's entitled. His son just threw himself off the roof."

Ten to a million the son's name was Grigorii.

I kept coming. The two men ripped at each other, grappling and snarling like two wild animals. I was five feet away when Pavel head-butted Saiman, jerking his right arm free. A knife flashed; I lunged and saw Pavel slice across Saiman's distended gut. A bloody clump fell, and I caught it with my left hand purely on instinct.

Magic punched my arm. Pale glow erupted from my fist.

Saiman twisted and stabbed something at Pavel's right eye. The volkhv stumbled back, a bloody pencil protruding from his eye socket. For a long moment he stood, huge mouth gaping, and then he toppled like a log. Saiman spun about. The muscles of his stomach collapsed, folding, knitting together, turning into a flat washboard wall.

The whole thing took less than three seconds.

I opened my fist. A small gold acorn lay on my palm.

The golden shell cracked. A sliver of green thrust its way up. The acorn rolled off my hand. The green shoot thickened, twisted, surging higher and higher. The air roared like a tornado. Saiman howled, a sound of pure rage. I grabbed him and dragged him with me to the stairs. On the other side, volkhvi ran for the edge of the roof.

The shoot grew, turning dark, sprouting branches, leaves, and bark. Magic roiled.

"It was supposed to be mine," Saiman snarled. "Mine!"

Light flashed. The roaring ceased.

A colossal oak stood in the middle of the roof, as tall as

the building itself, its roots spilling on both sides of the high-rise. Tiny lights fluttered between its branches, each wavy leaf as big as my head. Birds sang in the foliage. A huge metal chain bound the enormous trunk, its links so thick, I could've lain down on it. A feeling of complete peace came over me. All my troubles melted into the distance. My pain dissolved. The air tasted sweet, and I drank it in.

At the other side of the roof, the volkhvi knelt.

Metal clinked. A black creature came walking down the bottom loop. As big as a horse, its fur long and black, it walked softly, gripping the links with razor-sharp claws. Its head was that of a lynx. Tall tufts of black fur decorated its ears, and a long black beard stretched from its chin. Its eyes glowed, lit from within.

The cat paused and looked at me. The big maw opened, showing me a forest of white teeth, long and sharp like knives.

"Ask."

I blinked.

"You were the last to hold the acorn," Saiman whispered. "You must ask the question or it will kill all of us."

The cat showed me its teeth again.

For anything I asked, there would be a price.

"Ask," the cat said, its voice laced with an unearthly snarl.

"Ask, Kate," Saiman prompted.

"Ask!" one of the volkhvi called out.

I took a deep breath.

The cat leaned forward in anticipation.

"Would you like some milk?"

The cat smiled wider. "Yes."

Saiman groaned.

"I'll be right back."

I dashed down the stairs. Three minutes later, the cat lapped milk from Saiman's crystal punch bowl.

"You could've asked anything," the creature said between laps.

"But you would've taken everything," I told it. "This way all it cost me is a little bit of milk."

In the morning Peters came to relieve me. Not that he had a particularly difficult job. After the oak disappeared, the volkhvi decided that since both Pavel and Grigorii were dead, all accounts were settled and it was time to call it quits. As soon as we returned to the apartment, Saiman locked himself in the bedroom and refused to come out. The loss of the acorn hit him pretty hard. Just as well. I handed my fussy client off to Peters, retrieved Peggy, and headed back to the Guild.

All in all I'd done spectacularly well, I decided. I lost the client for at least two minutes, let him get his stomach ripped open, watched him stab his attacker in the eye, which was definitely something he shouldn't have had to do, and cost him his special acorn and roughly five months of work. The fact that my client turned out to be a scumbag and a sexual deviant really had no bearing on the matter.

Some bodyguard I made. Yay. Whoopee. I got to the Guild, surrendered Peggy, and filled out my paperwork. You win some, you lose some. At least Saiman survived. I wouldn't get paid, but I didn't end the job with a dead client on my hands.

I grabbed my crap and headed for the doors.

"Kate," the clerk called from the counter.

I turned. Nobody remembered the clerk's name. He was just "the clerk."

He waved an envelope at me. "Money."

I turned on my foot. "Money?"

"For the job. Client called. He says he'd like to work exclusively with you from now on. What did the two of you do all night?"

"We argued philosophy." I swiped the envelope and counted the bills. Three grand. What do you know?

I stepped out the doors into an overcast morning. I had been awake for over thirty-six hours. I just wanted to find a quiet spot, curl up, and shut out the world.

A tall, lean man strode to me, tossing waist-long black hair out of the way. He walked like a dancer, and his face would stop traffic. I looked into his blue eyes and saw a familiar smugness in their depths. "Hello, Saiman."

"How did you know?"

I shrugged and headed on my way.

"Perhaps we can work out a deal," he said, matching my steps. "I have no intentions of losing that bet. I will find a form you can't resist."

"Good luck."

"I'm guessing you'll try to avoid me, which would make my victory a bit difficult."

"Bingo."

"That's why I decided to give you an incentive you can't refuse. I'm giving you a sixty percent discount on my services. It's an unbelievable deal."

I laughed. If he thought I'd pay him twenty-six dollars a minute for his time, he was out of luck.

"Laugh now." Saiman smiled. "But sooner or later you'll require my expertise."

He stopped. I kept on walking, into the dreary sunrise. I had three thousand dollars and some chocolate to buy.

* * *

"Ilona Andrews" is the pseudonym for a husband-and-wife writing team. Ilona is a native-born Russian and Gordon is a former communications sergeant in the U.S. Army. Contrary to popular belief, Gordon was never an intelligence officer with a license to kill, and Ilona was never the mysterious Russian spy who seduced him. They met in college, in English Composition 101, where Ilona got a better grade. (Gordon is still sore about that.)

Gordon and Ilona currently reside in Georgia with their two children and three dogs.

The have coauthored two series, the bestselling urban fantasy of Kate Daniels, and romantic urban fantasy of The Edge, and are working on the next volumes for both.

Visit them on the Web at **www.ilona-andrews.com.**

EVEN HAND

by JIM BUTCHER

A successful murder is like a successful restaurant: ninety percent of it is about location, location, location.

Three men in black hoods knelt on the waterfront warehouse floor, their wrists and ankles trussed with heavy plastic quick-ties. There were few lights. They knelt over a large, faded stain on the concrete floor, left behind by the hypocritically named White Council of Wizards during their last execution.

I nodded to Hendricks, who took the hood off the first man, then stood clear. The man was young and good-looking. He wore an expensive yet ill-fitting suit and even more expensive yet tasteless jewelry.

"Where are you from?" I asked him.

He sneered at me. "What's it to y—"

I shot him in the head as soon as I heard the bravado in his voice. The body fell heavily to the floor.

The other two jumped and cursed, their voices angry and terrified.

I took the hood off the second man. His suit was a close

cousin of the dead man's, and I thought I recognized its cut. "Boston?" I asked him.

"You can't do this to us," he said, more angry than frightened. "Do you know who we are?"

Once I heard the nasal quality of the word "are," I shot him.

I took off the third man's hood. He screamed and fell away from me. "Boston," I said, nodding, and put the barrel of my .45 against the third man's forehead. He stared at me, showing the whites of his eyes. "You know who I am. I run drugs in Chicago. I run the numbers, the books. I run the whores. It's my town. Do you understand?"

His body jittered in what might have been a nod. His lips formed the word "yes," though no sound came out.

"I'm glad you can answer a simple question," I told him, and lowered the gun. "I want you to tell Mr. Morelli that I won't be this lenient the next time his people try to clip the edges of my territory." I looked at Hendricks. "Put the three of them in a sealed trailer and rail-freight them back to Boston, care of Mr. Morelli."

Hendricks was a large, trustworthy man, his red hair cropped in a crew cut. He twitched his chin in the slight motion that he used for a nod when he disapproved of my actions but intended to obey me anyway.

Hendricks and the cleaners on my staff would handle the matter from here.

I passed him the gun and the gloves on my hands. Both would see the bottom of Lake Michigan before I was halfway home, along with the two slugs the cleaners would remove from the site. When they were done, there would be nothing left of the two dead men but a slight variation on the outline of the stain in the old warehouse floor, where no one would look twice in any case.

Location, location, location.

Obviously, I am not Harry Dresden. My name is something I rarely trouble to remember, but for most of my adult life, I have been called John Marcone.

I am a professional monster.

It sounds pretentious. After all, I'm not a flesh-devouring ghoul, hiding behind a human mask until it is time to gorge. I'm no vampire, to drain the blood or soul from my victim, no ogre, no demon, no cursed beast from the spirit world dwelling amid the unsuspecting sheep of humanity. I'm not even possessed of the mystic abilities of a mortal wizard.

But they will never be what I am. One and all, those beings were born to be what they are.

I made a choice.

I walked outside of the warehouse and was met by my consultant, Gard—a tall blond woman without makeup whose eyes continually swept her surroundings. She fell into step beside me as we walked to the car. "Two?"

"They couldn't be bothered to answer a question in a civil manner."

She opened the back door for me and I got in. I picked up my personal weapon and slipped it into the holster beneath my left arm while she settled down behind the wheel. She started driving and then said, "No. That wasn't it."

"It was business."

"And the fact that one of them was pushing heroin to thirteen-year-old girls and the other was pimping them out had nothing to do with it," Gard said.

"It was business," I said, enunciating. "Morelli can find pushers and pimps anywhere. A decent accountant is invaluable. I sent his bookkeeper back as a gesture of respect."

"You don't respect Morelli."

I almost smiled. "Perhaps not."

"Then why?"

I did not answer. She didn't push the issue, and we rode in silence back to the office. As she put the car in park, I said, "They were in my territory. They broke my rule."

"No children," she said.

"No children," I said. "I do not tolerate challenges, Ms. Gard. They're bad for business."

She looked at me in the mirror, her blue eyes oddly intent, and nodded.

There was a knock at my office door, and Gard thrust her head in, her phone's earpiece conspicuous. "There's a problem."

Hendricks frowned from his seat at a nearby desk. He was hunched over a laptop that looked too small for him, plugging away at his thesis. "What kind of problem?"

"An Accords matter," Gard said.

Hendricks sat up straight and looked at me.

I didn't look up from one of my lawyer's letters, which I receive too frequently to let slide. "Well," I said, "we knew it would happen eventually. Bring the car."

"I don't have to," Gard said. "The situation came to us."

I set aside the finished letter and looked up, resting my fingertips together. "Interesting."

Gard brought the problem in. The problem was young and attractive. In my experience, the latter two frequently lead to the former. In this particular case, it was a young woman holding a child. She was remarkable—thick, rich, silver white hair, dark eyes, pale skin. She had very little makeup, which was fortunate in her case, since she looked as if she had recently been drenched. She wore what was left of a gray business skirt-suit, had a towel from one of my health clubs wrapped around her shoulders, and was shivering.

The child she held was too young to be in school and was also appealing, with rosy features, white blond hair, and blue eyes. Male or female, it hardly mattered at that age. They're all beautiful. The child clung to the girl as if it would not be separated, and was also wrapped in a towel.

The girl's body language was definitely protective. She had the kind of beauty that looked natural and . . . true. Her features and her bearing both spoke of gentleness and kindness.

I felt an immediate instinct to protect and comfort her.

I quashed it thoroughly.

I am not made of stone, but I have found it is generally best to behave as if I am.

I looked across the desk at her and said, "My people tell me you have asked for sanctuary under the terms of the Unseelie Accords, but that you have not identified yourself."

"I apologize, sir," she answered. "I was already being indiscreet enough just by coming here."

"Indeed," I said calmly. "I make it a point not to advertise the location of my business headquarters."

"I didn't want to add names to the issue," she said, casting her eyes down in a gesture of submission that did not entirely convince me. "I wasn't sure how many of your people were permitted access to this sort of information."

I glanced past the young woman to Gard, who gave me a slow, cautious nod. Had the girl or the child been other than they appeared, Gard would have indicated in the negative. Gard costs me a fortune and is worth every penny.

Even so, I didn't signal either her or Hendricks to stand down. Both of them watched the girl, ready to kill her if she made an aggressive move. Trust, but verify—that the person being trusted will be dead if she attempts betrayal.

"That was most considerate of you, Justine."

The girl blinked at me several times. "Y-you know me."

"You are a sometimes associate of Harry Dresden," I said. "Given his proclivities about those he considers to be held under his aegis, it is sensible to identify as many of them as possible. For the sake of my insurance rates, if nothing else. Gard."

"Justine, no last name you'll admit to," Gard said calmly, "currently employed as Lara Raith's secretary and personal aide. You are the sometimes lover of Thomas Raith, a frequent ally of Dresden's."

I spread my hands slightly. "I assume the 'j' notation at the bottom of Ms. Raith's typed correspondence refers to you."

"Yes," Justine said. She had regained her composure quickly—not something I would have expected of the servitor of a vampire of the White Court. Many of the . . . people, I suppose, I'd seen there had made lotus-eaters look self-motivated. "Yes, exactly."

I nodded. "Given your patron, one is curious as to why you have come to me seeking protection."

"Time, sir," she replied quietly. "I lacked any other alternative."

Someone screamed at the front of the building.

My headquarters shifts position irregularly, as I acquire new buildings. Much of my considerable wealth is invested in real estate. I own more of the town than any other single investor. In Chicago, there is always money to be had by purchasing and renovating aging buildings. I do much of my day-to-day work out of one of my most recent renovation projects, once they have been modified to be suitable places to welcome guests. Then, renovation of the building begins, and the place is generally crowded with contractors who have proven their ability to see and hear nothing.

Gard's head snapped up. She shook it as if to rid herself of a buzzing fly and said, "A presence. A strong one." Her blue eyes snapped to Justine. "Who?"

The young woman shuddered and wrapped the towel more tightly about herself. "Mag. A cantrev lord of the fomor."

Gard spat something in a Scandinavian tongue that was probably a curse.

"Precis, please," I said.

"The fomor are an ancient folk," she said. "Water dwellers, cousins of the jotuns. Extremely formidable. Sorcerers, shape changers, seers."

"And signatories," I noted.

"Yes," she said. She crossed to the other side of the room, opened a closet, and withdrew an athletic bag. She produced a simple, rather crude-looking broadsword from it and tossed it toward Hendricks. The big man caught it by the handle and took his gun into his left hand. Gard took a broad-bladed axe out of the bag and shouldered the weapon. "But rarely involved in mortal affairs."

"Ms. Raith sent me to the fomor king with documents," Justine said, her voice coming out quietly and rapidly. Her shivering had increased. "Mag made me his prisoner. I escaped with the child. There wasn't time to reach one of my lady's strongholds. I came to you, sir. I beg your protection, as a favor to Ms. Raith."

"I don't grant favors," I said calmly.

Mag entered in the manner so many of these self-absorbed supernatural cretins seem to adore. He blasted the door into a cloud of flying splinters with what I presumed was magic.

For God's sake.

At least the vampires would call for an appointment.

The blast amounted to little debris. After a few visits from Dresden and his ilk, I had invested in cheap, light doors at dramatic (as opposed to tactical) entry points.

The fomor was a pale, repellent humanoid. Seven feet tall, give or take, and distinctly froglike in appearance. He had a bloated belly, legs several inches too long to be proportionately human, and huge feet and hands. He wore a tunic of something that resembled seaweed beneath a long, flapping blue robe covered in the most intricate embroidery I had ever seen. A coronet of coral was bound about his head. His right hand was extended dramatically. He carried a twisted length of wood in his left.

His eyes bulged, jaundice yellow around septic green, and his teeth were rotted and filthy. "You cannot run from me," he said. His wide mouth made the words seem somehow slurred. "You are mine."

Justine looked up at me, evidently too frightened to turn her head, her eyes wide with fear. A sharper contrast would have been hard to manage. "Sir. Please."

I touched a button on the undersurface of my desk, a motion of less than two inches, and then made a steeple of my hands again as I eyed Mag and said, "Excuse me, sir. This is a private office."

Mag surged forward half a step, his eyes focused on the girl. "Hold your tongue, mortal, if you would keep it."

I narrowed my eyes.

Is it so much to ask for civility?

"Justine," I said calmly, "if you would stand aside, please." Justine quickly, silently, moved out from between us.

I focused on Mag and said, "They are under my protection."

Mag gave me a contemptuous look and raised the staff. Darkness lashed at me, as if he had simply reached into the floorboards and cracks in the wall and drawn it into a sizzling sphere the size of a bowling ball.

It flickered away to nothingness about a foot in front of my steepled hands.

I lifted a finger and Hendricks shot Mag in the back. Repeatedly.

The fomor went down with a sound like a bubbling tea-kettle, whipped onto his back as if the bullets had been a minor inconvenience, and raised the stick to point at Hendricks.

Gard's axe smashed it out of his grip, swooped back up to guard, and began to descend again.

"Stop," I said.

Gard's muscles froze just before she would have brought down the axe onto Mag's head. Mag had one hand up-lifted, surrounded in a kind of negative haze, his long fingers crooked at odd angles—presumably some kind of mystic defense.

"As a freeholding lord of the Unseelie Accords," I said, "it would be considered an act of war if I killed you out of hand, despite your militant intrusion into my territory." I narrowed my eyes. "However, your behavior gives me ample latitude to invoke the defense of property and self clause. I will leave the decision to you. Continue this asinine behavior, and I will kill you and offer a weregild to your lord, King Corb, in accordance with the conflict resolution guidelines of section two, paragraph four."

As I told you, my lawyers send me endless letters. I speak their language.

Mag seemed to take that in for a moment. He looked at me, then Gard. His eyes narrowed. They tracked back to Hendricks, his head hardly moving, and he seemed to freeze when he saw the sword in Hendricks's hand.

His eyes flicked to Justine and the child and burned for a moment—not with adoration or even simple lust. There was a pure and possessive hunger there, coupled with a need to destroy that which he desired. I have spent my entire life around hard men. I know that form of madness when I see it.

"So," Mag said. His eyes traveled back to me and were suddenly heavy-lidded and calculating. "You are the new mortal lord. We half believed that you must be imaginary. That no one could be as foolish as that."

"You are incorrect," I said. "Moreover, you can't have them. Get out."

Mag stood up. The movement was slow, liquid. His limbs didn't seem to bend the proper way. "Lord Marcone," he said, "this affair is no concern of yours. I only wish to take the slaves."

"You can't have them. Get out."

"I warn you," Mag said. There was an ugly tone in his voice. "If you make me return for her—for them—you will not enjoy what follows."

"I do not require enjoyment to thrive. Leave my domain. I won't ask again."

Hendricks shuffled his feet a little, settling his balance.

Mag gathered himself up slowly. He extended his hand, and the twisted stick leapt from the floor and into his fingers. He gave Gard a slow and well-practiced sneer and said, "Anon, mortal lordling. It is time you learned the truth of the world. It will please me to be your instructor." Then he turned, slow and haughty, and walked out, his shoulders hunching in an odd, unsettling motion as he moved.

"Make sure he leaves," I said quietly.

Gard and Hendricks followed Mag from the room.

I turned my eyes to Justine and the child.

"Mag," I said, "is not the sort of man who is used to disappointment."

Justine looked after the vanished fomor and then back at me, confusion in her eyes. "That was sorcery. How did you . . . ?"

I stood up from behind my desk and stepped out of the copper circle set into the floor around my chair. It was powered by the sorcerous equivalent of a nine-volt battery, connected to the control on the underside of my desk. Basic magical defense, Gard said. It had seemed like nonsense to me—it clearly was not.

I took my gun from its holster and set it on my desk.

Justine took note of my reply.

Of course, I wouldn't give the personal aide of the most dangerous woman in Chicago information about my magical defenses.

There was something hard and not at all submissive in her eyes. "Thank you, sir, for . . ."

"For what?" I said very calmly. "You understand, do you not, what you have done by asking for my help under the Accords?"

"Sir?"

"The Accords govern relations between supernatural powers," I said. "The signatories of the Accords and their named vassals are granted certain rights and obligations—such as offering a warning to a signatory who has trespassed upon another's territory unwittingly before killing him."

"I know, sir," Justine said.

"Then you should also know that you are most definitely

not a signatory of the Accords. At best, you qualify in the category of 'servitors and chattel.' At worst, you are considered to be a food animal."

She drew in a sharp breath, her eyes widening—not in any sense of outrage or offense, but in realization. Good. She grasped the realities of the situation.

"In either case," I continued, "you are property. You have no rights in the current situation, in the eyes of the Accords—and more to the point, I have no right to withhold another's rightful property. Mag's behavior provided me with an excuse to kill him if he did not depart. He will not give me such an opening a second time."

Justine swallowed and stared at me for a moment. Then she glanced down at the child in her arms. The child clung harder to her and seemed to lean somewhat away from me.

One must admire such acute instincts.

"You have drawn me into a conflict which has nothing to do with me," I said quietly. "I suggest candor. Otherwise, I will have Mr. Hendricks and Ms. Gard show you to the door."

"You can't . . . ," she began, but her voice trailed off.

"I can," I said. "I am not a humanitarian. When I offer charity it is for tax purposes."

The room became silent. I was content with that. The child began to whimper quietly.

"I was delivering documents to the court of King Corb on behalf of my lady," Justine said. She stroked the child's hair absently. "It's in the sea. There's a gate there in Lake Michigan, not far from here."

I lifted an eyebrow. "You swam?"

"I was under the protection of their courier, going there," Justine said. "It's like walking in a bubble of air." She hitched the child up a little higher on her hip. "Mag saw me. He drove the courier away as I was leaving and took me to his home. There were many other prisoners there."

"Including the child," I guessed. Though it probably didn't sound that way.

Justine nodded. "I . . . arranged for several prisoners to flee Mag's home. I took the child when I left. I swam out."

"So you are, in effect, stolen property in possession of stolen property," I said. "Novel."

Gard and Hendricks came back into the office.

I looked at Hendricks. "My people?"

"Tulane's got a broken arm," he said. "Standing in that asshole's way. He's on the way to the doc."

"Thank you. Ms. Gard?"

"Mag is off the property," she said. "He didn't go far. He's summoning support now."

"How much of a threat is he?" I asked. The question was legitimate. Gard and Hendricks had blindsided the inhuman while he was focused upon Justine and the child and while he wasted his leading magical strike against my protective circle. A head-on confrontation against a prepared foe could be a totally different proposition.

Gard tested the edge of her axe with her thumb and drew a smooth stone from her pocket. "Mag is a fomor sorcerer lord of the first rank. He's deadly—and connected. The fomor could crush you without a serious loss of resources. Confrontation would be unwise."

The stone made a steely, slithery sound as it glided over the axe's blade.

"There seems little profit to be had, then," I said. "It's nothing personal, Justine. Merely business. I am obliged to return stolen property to signatory members of the Accords."

Hendricks looked at me sharply. He didn't say anything. He didn't have to. I already knew the tone of whatever he would say. *Are there no prisons*, perhaps. Or, *No man is an island, entire of itself. It tolls for thee.* On and on.

Hendricks has no head for business.

Gard watched me, waiting.

"Sir," Justine said, her tone measured and oddly formal. "May I speak?"

I nodded.

"She isn't property," Justine said, and her voice was low and intense, her eyes direct. "She was trapped in a den of living nightmares, and there was no one to come save her. She would have died there. And I am *not* letting anyone take her back to that hellhole. I will die first." The young woman set her jaw. "She is not *property*, Mr. Marcone. She's a *child*."

I met Justine's eyes for a long moment.

I glanced aside at Hendricks. He waited for my decision.

Gard watched me. As ever, Gard watched me.

I looked down at my hands, my fingertips resting together with my elbows propped on the desk.

Business came first. Always.

But I have rules.

I looked up at Justine.

"She's a child," I said quietly.

The air in the room snapped tight with tension.

"Ms. Gard," I said, "please dismiss the contractors for the day, at pay. Then raise the defenses."

She pocketed the whetstone and strode quickly out, her teeth showing, a bounce in her step.

"Mr. Hendricks, please scramble our troubleshooters. They're to take positions across the street. Suppressed weapons only. I don't need patrolmen stumbling around in this. Then ready the panic room."

Hendricks nodded and got out his cell phone as he left. His huge, stubby fingers flew over its touchscreen as he sent the activation text message. Looking at him, one would not think him capable of such a thing. But that is Hendricks, generally.

I looked at Justine as I rose and walked to my closet. "You will go with the child into the panic room. It is, with the possible exception of Dresden's home, the most secure location in the city."

"Thank you," she said quietly.

I took off my coat and hung it up in the closet. I took off my tie and slipped it over the same hanger. I put my cuff links in my coat pocket, rolled up my sleeves, and skinned out of my gun's holster. Then I slipped on the armored vest made of heavy scales of composite materials joined to sleeves of quite old-fashioned mail. I pulled an old field jacket, olive drab, over the armor, belted it, holstered my sidearm at my side, opposite a combat knife, and took a military-grade assault shotgun—a weapon every bit as illegal as my pistol in the city of Chicago—from its rack.

"I am not doing it for you, young lady," I said. "Nor am I doing it for the child."

"Then why are you doing it?" she asked.

"Because I have rules," I said.

She shook her head gently. "But you're a criminal. Criminals don't have rules. They break them."

I stopped and looked at her.

Justine blanched and slid a step farther away from me, along the wall. The child made a soft, distressed sound. I beckoned curtly for her to follow me as I walked past her. It took her a moment to do so.

Honestly.

Someone in the service of a vampire ought to have a bit more fortitude.

This panic room looked like every other one I've had built: fluorescent lights, plain tile floor, plain drywall. Two double bunks occupied one end of the room. A business desk and several chairs took up the rest. A miniature kitchen nestled into one corner, opposite the miniature medical station in another. There was a door to a half-bath and a bank of security monitors on the wall between them. I flicked one switch that activated the entire bank, displaying a dozen views from hidden security cameras.

I gestured for Justine to enter the room. She came in and

immediately took a seat on the lower bunk of the nearest bed, still holding the child.

"Mag can find her," Gard told me when we all rendez-voused outside the panic room. "Once he's inside the build-ing and gets past the forward area, he'll be able to track her. He'll head straight for her."

"Then we know which way he'll be moving," I said. "What did you find out about his support?"

"They're creatures," Gard said, "actual mortal beings, though like none you've seen before. The fomor twist flesh to their liking and sell the results for favors and influence. It was probably the fomor who created those cat-things the Knights of the Blackened Denarius used."

I twisted my mouth in displeasure at the name. "If they're mortal, we can kill them."

"They'll die hard," Gard warned me.

"What doesn't?" I looked up and down the hallway outside the panic room. "I think the primary defense plan will do."

Gard nodded. She had attired herself in an armored vest not unlike my own over a long mail shirt. Medieval look-ing, but then modern armorers haven't aimed their craft at stopping claws of late. Hendricks, standing watch at the end of the hall, had on an armored vest but was otherwise cov-ered in modified motorcyclist's armor. He carried an assault shotgun like mine, several hand grenades, and that same broadsword.

"Stay here," I said to Justine. "Watch the door. If anyone but one of us comes down the stairs, shut it."

She nodded.

I turned and started walking toward the stairway. I glanced at Gard. "What can we expect from Mag?"

"Pain."

Hendricks grunted. Skeptically.

"He's ancient, devious, and wicked," Gard clarified. "There is an effectively unlimited spectrum of ways in which he might do harm."

I nodded. "Can you offer any specific knowledge?"

"He won't be easy to get to," she said. "The fomor practice entropy magic. They make the antitechnology effect Dresden puts off look like mild sunspot activity. Modern systems *are* going to experience problems near him."

We started up the stairs. "How long before he arrives?"

From upstairs, there was the crash of breaking plate glass. No alarm went off, but there was a buzzing, sizzling sound and a scream—Gard's outer defenses. Hendricks hit a button on his cell phone and then came with me as I rushed up the remaining stairs to the ground floor.

The lights went out as we went, and Hendricks's phone sputtered out a few sparks. Battery-powered emergency lights flicked on an instant later. Only about half of them functioned, and most of those were behind us.

Mag had waited for nightfall to begin his attack and then crippled our lights. Quite possibly he assumed that the darkness would give him an overwhelming advantage.

The hubris of some members of the supernatural community is astonishing.

The nightvision scopes mounted on my weapon and

Hendricks's had been custom-made, based off of designs dating back to World War II, before nightvision devices had married themselves to the electronics revolution. They were heavy and far inferior to modern systems—but they would function in situations where electronic goggles would be rendered into useless junk.

We raised the weapons to our shoulders, lined an eye up with the scopes, and kept moving. We reached the first defensive position, folded out the reinforced composite barriers mounted there, and knelt behind them. The ambient light from the city outside and the emergency lights below us was enough for the scopes to do their jobs. I could make out the outline of the hallway and the room beyond. Sounds of quiet movement came closer.

My heart rate had gone up, but not alarmingly so. My hands were steady. My mouth felt dry, and my body's reaction to the prospect of mortal danger sent ripples of sensation up and down my spine. I embraced the fear and waited.

The fomor's creatures exploded into the hallway on a storm of frenzied roars. I couldn't make out many details. They seemed to have been put together on the chassis of a gorilla. Their heads were squashed, ugly-looking things, with wide-gaping mouths full of sharklike teeth. The sounds they made were deep, with a frenzied edge of madness, and they piled into the corridor in a wave of massive muscle.

"Steady," I murmured.

The creatures lurched as they moved, like cheap toys that had not been assembled properly, but they were fast for all of that. More and more of them flooded into the hallway, and their charge was gaining mass and momentum.

"Steady," I murmured.

Hendricks grunted. There were no words in it, but he meant, *I know.*

The wave of fomorian beings got close enough that I could see the patches of mold clumping their fur and tendrils of mildew growing upon their exposed skin.

"Fire," I said.

Hendricks and I opened up.

The new military AA-12 automatic shotguns are not the hunting weapons I first handled in my patriotically delusional youth. They are fully automatic weapons with large circular drums that rather resembled the old tommy guns made iconic by my business predecessors in Chicago. One pulls the trigger and shell after shell slams through the weapon. A steel target hit by bursts from an AA-12 very rapidly comes to resemble a screen door.

And we had two of them.

The slaughter was indescribable. It swept like a great broom down that hallway, tearing and shredding flesh, splattering blood on the walls and painting them most of the way to the ceiling. Behind me, Gard stood ready with a heavy-caliber big-game rifle, calmly gunning down any creature that seemed to be reluctant to die before it could reach our defensive point. We piled the bodies so deep that the corpses formed a barrier to our weapons.

"Hendricks," I said.

The big man was already reaching for the grenades on his belt. He took one, pulled the pin, cooked it for a slow two count, and then flung it down the hall. We all crouched behind the barriers as the grenade went off with a deafening crunch of shock-wave-driven air.

Hendricks threw another one. He might disapprove of killing, but he did it thoroughly.

When the ringing began to fade from my ears, I heard a sound like raindrops. It wasn't raining, of course—the gunmen in the building across the street had opened fire with silenced weaponry. Bullets whispered in through the windows and hit the floor and walls of the headquarters with innocuous-sounding thumps. Evidently Mag's servitors had been routed and were trying to flee.

An object the size of Hendricks's fist appeared from nowhere and arced cleanly through the air. It landed on the floor precisely between the two sheltering panels, a lump of pink-and-gray coral.

Gard hit me with a shoulder and drove me to the ground even as she shouted, "Down!"

The piece of coral didn't explode. There was a whispering sound, and hundreds of tiny holes appeared in the blood-stained walls and ceiling. Gard let out a pained grunt. My left calf jerked as something pierced it and burned as though the wound had been filled with salt.

I checked Hendricks. One side of his face was covered in a sheet of blood. Small tears were visible in his leathers, and he was beginning to bleed through the holes.

"Get him," I said to Gard, rising, as another coral spheroid rose into the air.

Before it could get close enough to be a threat, I blew it to powder with my shotgun. And the next and the next, while Gard dropped her rifle, got a shoulder under one of Hendricks's, and helped him to his feet as if he'd been her weight instead of two hundred and seventy pounds of muscle. She started down the stairs.

A fourth sphere came accompanied by mocking laughter, and when I pulled the trigger again, the weapon didn't function. Empty. I slapped the coral device out of the air with the shotgun's barrel and flung myself backward, hoping to clear the level of the floor on the stairwell before the pseudo-grenade detonated. I did not quite make it. Several objects struck my chest and arms, and a hot blade slipped across my unscarred ear, but the armor turned the truly dangerous projectiles.

I broke my arm tumbling backward down the stairs.

More laughter followed me down, but at least the fomor wasn't spouting some kind of ridiculous monologue.

"I did my best," came Mag's voice. "I gave you a chance to return what was mine. But no. You couldn't keep yourself from interfering in my affairs, from stealing my property. And so now you will reap the consequences of your foolishness, little mortal. . . ."

There was more, but there is hardly a need to go into details. Given a choice between that egocentric drivel and a broken arm, I prefer the latter. It's considerably less excruciating.

Gard hauled me to my feet by my coat with her spare hand. I got under the stunned Hendricks's other arm and helped them both down the rest of the stairs. Justine stood in the doorway of the safe room, at the end of the hallway of flickering lights, her face white-lipped but calm.

Gard helped me get Hendricks to the door of the room and turned around. "Close the door. I may be able to discourage him out here."

"Your home office would be annoyed with me if I wasted your life on such a low-percentage proposition," I said. "We stick to the plan."

The valkyrie eyed me. "Your arm is broken."

"I was aware, thank you," I said. "Is there any reason the countermeasure shouldn't work?"

Mag was going on about something, coming down the steps one at a time, making a production of every footfall. I ignored the ass.

"None that I know of," Gard admitted. "Which is not the same answer as 'no.'"

"Sir," Justine said.

"We planned for this—or something very like it. We don't split up now. End of discussion. Help me with Hendricks."

"*Sir,*" Justine said.

I looked up to see Mag standing on the landing, cloaked in random shadows, smiling. The emergency lights on the stairwell blew out with a melodramatic shower of dying sparks.

"Ah," I said. I reached inside the safe-room door, found

the purely mechanical pull-cord wrapped unobtrusively around a nail head on the wall, and gave it a sharp jerk.

It set off the antipersonnel mines built into the wall of the landing.

There were four of them, which meant that a wash of fire and just under three-thousand-round shot acquainted themselves with the immediate vicinity of the landing and with Mag. A cloud of flame and flying steel enveloped the fomor, but at the last instant the swirling blackness around him rose up like a living thing, forming a shield between Mag and the oncoming flood of destruction.

The sound of the explosions was so loud that it demolished my hearing for a moment. It began to return to me as the cloud of smoke and dust on the landing began to clear. I could hear a fire alarm going off.

Mag, smudged and blackened with residue but otherwise untouched, made an irritated gesture, and the fire alarm sparked and fizzled—but not before setting off the automatic sprinklers. Water began pouring down from spigots in the ceiling.

Mag looked up at the water and then down at me, and his too-wide smile widened even more. "Really?" he asked. "Water? Did you actually think water would be a barrier to the magic of a fomor lord?"

Running water was highly detrimental to mortal magic, or so Gard informed me, whether it was naturally occurring or not. The important element was quantity. Enough water would ground magic just as it could conduct electricity and short-circuit electronics. Evidently Mag played by different rules.

Mag made a point to continue down the stairs at exactly the same pace. He was somewhat hampered in that several of the stairs had been torn up rather badly in the explosion, but he made it to the hallway. Gard took up a position in the middle of the hallway, her axe held straight up beside her in both arms like a baseball player's bat.

I helped Hendricks into the safe room and dumped him on a bunk, out of any line of fire from the hallway. Justine took one look at his face and hurried over to the medical station, where she grabbed a first-aid kit. She rushed back to Hendricks's side. She broke open the kit and started laying out the proper gear for getting a clear look at a bloody wound and getting the bleeding stopped. Her hands flew with precise speed. She'd had some form of training.

From the opposite bunk, the child watched Justine with wide blue eyes. She was naked and had been crying. The tears were still on her little cheeks. Even now, her lower lip had begun to tremble.

But so far as anyone else knew, I was made of stone.

I turned and crossed the room. I sat down at the desk, a copy of the one in my main office. I put my handgun squarely in front of me. The desk was positioned directly in line with the door to the panic room. From behind the desk, I could see the entire hallway clearly.

Mag stepped forward and moved a hand as though throwing something. I saw nothing, but Gard raised her axe in a blocking movement, and there was a flash of light, and the image of a Norse rune, or something like it, was burned onto my retina. The outer edge of Gard's mail sleeve on her right arm abruptly turned black and fell to dust, so that the sleeve split and dangled open.

Gard took a grim step back as Mag narrowed his jaundiced eyes and lifted the crooked stick. Something that looked like the blend of a lightning bolt and an eel lashed through the air toward Gard, but she caught it on the broad blade of her axe, and there was another flash of light, another eye-searing rune. I heard her cry out, though, and saw that the edges of her fingernails had been burned black.

Step by step she fell back, while Mag hammered at her with things that made no sense, many of which I could not even see. Each time, the rune-magic of that axe defeated the attack—and each time, it seemed to cost her something. A lightly singed face here. A long, shallow cut upon her newly bared arm there. And the runes, I saw, were each in different places on the axe, being burned out one by one. Gard had a finite number of them.

As Gard's heels touched the threshold of the safe room, Mag let out a howl and threw both hands out ahead of him. An unseen force lifted Gard from her feet and flung her violently across the room, over my desk, and into the wall. She hit with bone-crushing force and slid down limply.

I faced the inhuman sorcerer alone.

Mag walked slowly and confidently into my safe room and stared at me across my desk. He was breathing heavily, from exertion or excitement or both. He smiled, slowly, and waved his hand again. An unpleasant shimmer went through the air, and I glanced down to see rust forming on the exposed metal of my gun, while cracking began to spread through the plastic grip.

"Go ahead, mortal," Mag said, drawing out the words. "Pick up the gun. Try it. The crafting of the weapon is fine, mortal, but you are not the masters of the world that you believe yourselves to be. Even today's cleverest smiths are no match for the magic of the fomor."

I inclined my head in agreement. "Then I suppose," I said, "that we'll just have to do this old school."

I drew the eighteenth-century German dragoon pistol from the open drawer beside my left hand, aimed, and fired. The ancient flintlock snapped forward, ignited the powder in the pan, and roared, a wash of unnatural blue white fire blazing forth from the antique weapon. I almost fancied that I could see the bullet, spinning and tumbling, blazing with its own tiny rune.

Though Mag's shadows leapt up to defend him, he had expended enormous energy moving through the building, hurling attack after attack at us. More energy had to be used to overcome the tremendous force of the claymores that had exploded virtually in his face. Perhaps, at his full strength, at the height of his endurance, his powers would have been enough to turn even the single, potent attack that had been designed to defeat them.

From the beginning, the plan had been to wear him down.

The blue bolt of lead and power from the heavy old flintlock pierced Mag's defenses and body in the same instant and with the same contemptuous energy.

Mag blinked at me, then lowered his head to goggle at the smoking hole in his chest as wide as my thumb. His mouth moved as he tried to gabble something, but no sound came out.

"Idiot," I said coldly. "It will be well worth the weregild to be rid of you."

Mag lurched toward me for a moment, intent upon saying something, but the fates spared me from having to endure any more of him. He collapsed to the floor before he could finish speaking.

I eyed my modern pistol, crusted with rust and residue, and decided not to try it. I kept a spare .45 in the downstairs desk in any case. I took it from another drawer, checked it awkwardly one-handed, and then emptied the weapon into Mag's head and chest.

I am the one who taught Hendricks to be thorough.

I looked up from Mag's ruined form to find Justine staring at me, frozen in the middle of wrapping a bandage around my second's head.

"How is he?" I asked calmly.

Justine swallowed. She said, "He m-may need stitches for this scalp wound. I think he has a concussion. The other wounds aren't bad. His armor stopped most of the fragments from going in."

"Gard?" I asked without looking over my shoulder. The valkyrie had an incredible ability to resist and recover from injury.

"Be sore for a while," she said, the words slurred. "Give me a few minutes."

"Justine, perhaps you will set my arm and splint it," I said. "We will need to abandon this renovation, I'm afraid, Gard. Where's the thermite?"

"In your upstairs office closet, right where you left it," she said in a *very* slightly aggrieved tone.

"Be a dear and burn down the building," I said.

She appeared beside my desk, looking bruised, exhausted, and functional. She lifted both eyebrows. "Was that a joke?"

"Apparently," I said. "Doubtless the result of triumph and adrenaline."

"My word," she said. She looked startled.

"Get moving," I told her. "Make the fire look accidental. I need to contact the young lady's patron so that she can be delivered safely back into her hands. Call Dr. Schulman as well. Tell him that Mr. Hendricks and I will be visiting him shortly." I pursed my lips. "And steak, I think. I could use a good steak. The Pump Room should do for the three of us, eh? Ask them to stay open an extra half an hour."

Gard showed me her teeth in a flash. "Well," she said, "it's no mead hall. But it will do."

I put my house in order. In the end, it took less than half an hour. The troubleshooters made sure the fomorian creatures were dragged inside, then vanished. Mag's body had been bagged and transferred, to be returned to his watery kin, along with approximately a quarter of a million dollars in bullion, the price required in the Accords for the weregild of a person of Mag's stature.

Justine was ready to meet a car that was coming to pick

her up, and Hendricks was already on the way to Schulman's attentions. He'd seemed fine by the time he left, growling at Gard as she fussed over him.

I looked around the office and nodded. "We know the defense plan has some merit," I said. I hefted the dragoon pistol. "I'll need more of those bullets."

"I was unconscious for three weeks after scribing the rune for that one," Gard replied. "To say nothing of the fact that the bullets themselves are rare. That one killed a man named Nelson at Trafalgar."

"How do you know?"

"I took it out of him," she said. "Men of his caliber are few and far between. I'll see what I can do." She glanced at Justine. "Sir?"

"Not just yet," I said. "I will speak with her alone for a moment, please."

She nodded, giving Justine a look that was equal parts curiosity and warning. Then she departed.

I got up and walked over to the girl. She was holding the child against her again. The little girl had dropped into an exhausted sleep.

"So," I said quietly. "Lara Raith sent you to Mag's people. He happened to abduct you. You happened to escape from him—despite the fact that he seemed to be holding other prisoners perfectly adequately—and you left carrying the child. And, upon emerging from Lake Michigan, you happened to be nearby, so you came straight here."

"Yes," Justine said quietly.

"Coincidences, coincidences," I said. "Put the child down."

Her eyes widened in alarm.

I stared at her until she obeyed.

My right arm was splinted and in a sling. With my left hand, I reached out and flipped open her suit jacket, over her left hip, where she'd been clutching the child all evening.

There was an envelope in a plastic bag protruding from the jacket's interior pocket. I took it.

She made a small sound of protest and aborted it partway.

I opened the bag and the envelope and scanned over the paper inside.

"These are account numbers," I said quietly. "Security passwords. Stolen from Mag's home, I suppose?"

She looked up at me with very wide eyes.

"Dear child," I said, "I *am* a criminal. One very good way to cover up one crime is to commit another, more obvious one." I glanced down at the sleeping child again. "Using a child to cover your part of the scheme. Quite cold-blooded, Justine."

"I freed all of Mag's prisoners to cover up the theft of his records at my lady's bidding," she said quietly. "The child was . . . not part of the plan."

"Children frequently aren't," I said.

"I took her out on my own," she said. "She's free of that place. She will stay that way."

"To be raised among the vampires?" I asked. "Such a lovely child will surely go far."

Justine grimaced and looked away. "She was too small to swim out on her own. I couldn't leave her."

I stared at the young woman for a long moment. Then I

said, "You might consider speaking to Father Forthill at St. Mary of the Angels. The Church appears to have some sort of program to place those endangered by the supernatural into hiding. I do not recommend you mention my name as a reference, but perhaps he could be convinced to help the child."

She blinked at me, several times. Then she said quietly, "You, sir, are not very much like I thought you were."

"Nor are you. Agent Justine." I took a deep breath and regarded the child again. "At least we accomplished something today." I smiled at Justine. "Your ride should be here by now. You may go."

She opened her mouth and reached for the envelope.

I slipped it into my pocket. "Do give Lara my regards. And tell her that the next time she sends you out to steal honey, she should find someone else to kill the bees." I gave her a faint smile. "That will be all."

Justine looked at me. Then her lips quivered up into a tiny, amused smile. She bowed her head to me, collected the child, and walked out, her steps light.

I debated putting a bullet in her head but decided against it. She had information about my defenses that could leave them vulnerable—and more to the point, she knew that they were effective. If she should speak of today's events to Dresden . . .

Well. The wizard would immediately recognize that the claymores, the running water, and the magic-defense-piercing bullet had not been put into place to counter Mag or his odd folk at all.

They were there to kill Harry Dresden.

And they worked. Mag had proven that. An eventual confrontation with Dresden was inevitable—but murdering Justine would guarantee it happened immediately, and I wasn't ready for that, not until I had rebuilt the defenses in the new location.

Besides, the young woman had rules of her own. I could respect that.

I would test myself against Dresden in earnest one day—or he against me. Until then, I had to gather as many resources to myself as possible. And when the day of reckoning came, I had to make sure it happened in a place where, despite his powers, he would no longer have the upper hand.

Like everything else.

Location, location, location.

* * *

Jim Butcher enjoys fencing, martial arts, singing, bad science-fiction movies, and live-action gaming. He lives in Missouri with his wife, son, and a vicious guard dog. You may learn more at www.jim-butcher.com.

THE BEACON

by SHANNON K. BUTCHER

There were ten rounds in Ryder Ward's Glock, but he was going to need only one.

The Beacon was here in this small, middle-of-nowhere, so-cute-it-made-him-want-to-puke Minnesota town. He could feel the deep, almost inaudible thrumming of its heart.

All he had to do was put one round between the Beacon's eyes and he could go back home to his life, such as it was. At least until the next Beacon summoned him. There was always another one—always someone who needed killing.

He hoped like hell that this time, the Beacon would be an old man.

Daddy? Daddy, wake up.

Ryder shoved the orphaned child's voice from his head and popped a trio of antacids into his mouth. He didn't want to think about his last job—the lifeless body of the last Beacon sprawled on the toy-littered living room carpet. And Ryder sure as hell didn't want to think about the tiny, chubby hand of the little girl trying to shake her dead father awake.

Daddy, are you sick?

He ground his back teeth together and focused on driving through the thickening snow. The sooner he finished this job, the sooner he'd see things were back to normal and he'd be offing old men with only a few good years left. That young man was an anomaly, that's all.

Ryder eased his truck over the icy streets. Snow was falling harder now as the forecasted blizzard rolled in, and even with his windshield wipers on high, it was getting hard to see where he was going. The bump of his tire against the curb told him he was still on the street, though just barely.

He pulled into the alley behind a coffeehouse where the deep beat of the Beacon's heart was the loudest. The alley where he left his truck was narrow and choked with snow. Getting out of here once the job was done was going to be tricky, but nothing he couldn't handle. Just like all the other times.

Since his birthright had kicked in, he'd killed seventeen Beacons, and so far he'd never once been hauled in by police for questioning. Why would he be? There was nothing to tie him to his victims, no apparent motivation for him to do what he did.

When it came to solid motivation for a serial killer, cops didn't tend to buy in to magical birthrights or the inherited ability to locate human magnets for otherworldly evil. If he ever got caught, he'd just tell them the voices in his head told him to kill—it'd be a lot simpler for everyone that way.

Not that Ryder was planning on getting caught. Get in, kill the Beacon, get out. Simple.

He trudged around the building through the snow, guessing he had maybe twenty minutes of daylight left—more than enough time to get the job done and get out of this too-cute town and back to his garage where he belonged, back to engines and wrenches and grease, all of which made perfect sense and didn't burn his guts.

The lights inside the coffeehouse were dimmed by the falling snow, but he managed to find the door and slip inside. Bells tinkled merrily against the glass, announcing his arrival.

Great. So much for stealth.

The smell of fresh coffee and cinnamon filled his nose. The snow sticking to his eyelashes began to melt in the humid warmth. The gust of cold wind he'd let in subsided, allowing the lacy curtains on the windows to settle back into place.

No one sat at any of the small tables or booths. As far as he could see, the place was deserted, but he knew better. He could feel how close the Beacon was—feel a throbbing in the air, as waves of sound too low for a normal person to hear emanated from the Beacon's heart. The sound thudded against his ears, resonated inside his chest. He could tell by the slowly increasing cadence that he was running out of time.

"I didn't think anyone was out in this mess," came a soft, feminine voice through an open doorway behind the counter. "Be right with you."

Ryder froze in place. The Beacon was a woman?

She hurried through the door, drying her hands with paper towels. Her soft brown hair was pulled back in a ponytail at the nape of her neck. A white apron tied around her waist showed off slim curves. She had a wide smile and the sweetest, most angelic face he'd ever seen. He doubted she was even thirty years old.

Too young to die.

How could he pull the trigger and end her life?

How could he not?

Melted snow dripped from his hair and ran down his neck, leaving cold paths of frigid water in their wake. The gun in the holster under his arm burned his skin. His ears were clogged with the sound of his racing pulse.

Ryder stood there, dripping, and as she watched him, her smile began to fade.

"Are you okay? Do you need help?" she asked.

His jaw clenched against the urge to answer her innocent questions. He couldn't speak to her. If he did, it would only make his job that much harder. If he spoke to her, she'd be a real person.

Besides, what was there for him to say? *Hi, I'm here to kill you. I'm sorry it has to end this way. If you don't die, a monster will appear and all the people around you will be eaten.*

No words would make this any easier, for either of them. Best just to get it done and get the hell away from here.

The woman stepped toward him. Ryder unzipped his leather jacket and reached for his gun.

"Did you get stuck in the storm? You're soaking wet." Sweet concern filled her voice, and it was all he could do not to turn around, walk out, and let her live the last few hours of her life in peace.

But what about the rest of this too-cute town? Didn't its residents deserve to live?

The only way that was going to happen was if he put a bullet right between her pretty blue eyes. One woman's life in trade for that of hundreds more. She was going to die tonight. There was nothing he could do to change that. It was his job to make sure she was the only one who had to die.

Ryder cursed his birthright for the millionth time.

"Have a seat," she told him. "I'll get you something hot to drink." She hurried off before he could stop her.

Get a grip. He needed to stop thinking and just do this thing. Get it over with.

A deep sound of mourning rose up from his chest, despite his intent to remain silent. He tossed another pair of antacids in his mouth. He doubted they'd help, but it was something to do with his hands—something that didn't involve pulling out his Glock.

The woman came back moments later, gripping a tall mug in her slender hands. "I made you hot cocoa. I hope you like it." She set it on a nearby table and pulled out a chair for him. "You should sit. You look like you're about to fall over."

Ryder took one step after another, hauling his dripping ass over to the table. He told himself that the shot would be easier to take if he was closer. It had nothing to do with the lure of her caring tone or the warmth of the drink she'd made for him.

He didn't deserve warmth, and he sure as hell didn't deserve her care.

He looked down at the chair she'd offered, then at the steaming mug. He couldn't accept either. Not when he knew what he had to do to her.

"I'm sorry," he said. He wanted to ask for her forgiveness, but he didn't deserve that, either.

He pulled out his weapon and aimed it at her head.

Those pretty blue eyes widened, and her lips parted on a gasp of shock. She stepped back, lifting her hands. They trembled.

"I'll give you whatever you want. There isn't much cash, but it's yours. Please, don't do this," she begged.

"I'm sorry," Ryder repeated. What else could he say?

A loud pounding of footsteps came from the far side of the room. Ryder swung his weapon to the left, aiming it at the noise. A wooden door swung open, revealing a staircase leading up. And a little girl.

"Mama, can I go online?"

The little girl couldn't have been more than seven years old. She had her mother's pretty blue eyes and the cutest pointed chin he'd ever seen. She saw his gun pointing at her and came to a dead stop. The air around her throbbed, beating out a deep, almost inaudible rhythm—one only Ryder and men like him could hear.

This woman wasn't the Beacon.

The little girl was.

Hell, no. He couldn't do this. Let whatever demon was coming have this town. He was going to throw the woman and her kid into his truck and get them out of here.

And go where? The Terraphage would follow the Beacon

wherever Ryder took her. With the roads as bad as they were, he'd have no hope of outrunning it.

If they were going to survive this, he was going to have to make a stand. Kill the Terraphage when it came.

A mocking bubble of laughter rose up inside of him. No one could kill one of those things. Anyone who had been stupid enough to try had failed. The Terraphage was huge, evil, and unstoppable.

Which meant he needed every second possible to come up with some kind of plan.

Ryder didn't see the chair coming at his head until it was too late. He tried to duck it, but the woman's aim was true and the metal leg connected with the side of his skull.

Lights out.

Jordan watched the man crumple to the ground, lifting the chair to strike at him again. Rage poured through her limbs, making her stronger than she would have imagined. She shook with the force of it, clenching her teeth against the need to let out a battle cry.

How dare he point that gun at her baby?

Anne started toward her, but Jordan held up a hand. "Stay back, honey. He's dangerous."

Or he had been. Right now he was limp and bleeding, lying utterly still. Maybe she'd killed him.

Part of her hoped so. A man who would draw a weapon on a child deserved to die.

He was a big man, filling out that worn leather jacket with wide shoulders and a thick chest. His hair was dark, damp, and mussed. Small scars marred the backs of his hands, especially his knuckles. Jordan guessed they were from bar fights or something equally distasteful. Any man who would point a gun at a child wouldn't have hesitated to take out his anger with his fists.

Jordan had never regretted her divorce; her ex was a loser who had never wanted Anne. But for the first time since turning her back on men, Jordan wished she had one around— someone willing to protect her and her daughter from the threat this man posed.

Anne took a tentative step closer. "Mama, that's the man I dreamed about. The one that came right before the monster."

A cold, heavy dread slithered down Jordan's spine. Her daughter's dreams had been getting progressively worse for weeks now, but Jordan thought they'd been making progress. "No, it's not. That's just your imagination playing a dirty trick on you."

"No. That's him. I'm sure that's him. He's even got the same messy hair."

Jordan stepped to the left to block Anne's line of sight. "Just go upstairs and get me that big roll of tape out of the toolbox. We'll talk about this later."

The pounding of little feet told Jordan her daughter had done as she asked.

She kicked the gun out of reach and poked the man's leg with the toe of her shoe. He didn't move. He didn't make a sound. Encouraged by his stillness, she moved closer and poked him in the ribs.

Nothing. He was out cold. Or doing one heck of an acting job.

Anne returned with the duct tape. "Who is he, Mama?"

"I don't know."

"Why'd he have a gun?"

"I don't know that, either."

"What are we gonna do with him?"

Jordan let out a sigh that shook with nerves. "I'm going to tie him up so he can't get away, then call the police."

"I'll call. I know the number."

Of course she did. Jordan had made sure Anne knew how to stay safe. Even though they lived in a small town with nearly no crime, that didn't mean things couldn't go wrong.

The man bleeding on her floor was proof of that.

Jordan prayed the man wasn't acting. She prayed even harder that his appearance wouldn't set Anne back in dealing with her nightmares.

She rolled the man onto his stomach and went to work taping him up nice and tight. He was heavy, and his limbs were thick with muscle, but she was still riding that adrenaline high and managed to get him trussed up, taped from wrists to elbows and ankles to knees.

He wasn't going anywhere unless she let him.

Now that it was safe, Jordan pressed her finger to the side of his neck, feeling for a pulse. His beat strong and steady, and she let out a small sigh of relief. She hadn't killed him.

Whether or not he deserved it, she didn't like the idea of being the executioner any more than she liked the idea of having a dead man lying in her coffee shop.

Jordan heard her daughter tell the sheriff's department what had happened. Her high, sweet voice sounded odd describing something as grim as facing off against an armed intruder.

"Mama, Cindy says she needs to talk to you."

Jordan picked up the gun with two fingers, as though it were covered in acid, and set it on the counter. She took the phone from Anne.

"Hey, Cindy."

Cindy was the dispatcher at the sheriff's station, and they'd gone to high school together. Her voice was rough from years of smoking, but she'd always been calm in the midst of chaos, even during the days of high school drama. "I heard you caught yourself a robber."

Something about the way the man had acted made Jordan wonder if that was what he'd been up to, but there'd be time to figure that out later. "Guess so. When can you send someone to come get him? I whacked him on the head pretty hard."

"The roads are a mess. We've got several injury accidents and no staff to spare. If you're not in danger, it's going to have to wait until we get things back under control."

"We're fine, but he may not be."

"Is he breathing?"

"Yeah."

"That'll have to be good enough. Call me if anything changes. I'll send someone as soon as possible, okay?"

"Sure. I'll be here."

Jordan hung up and saw Anne inching closer to the unconscious man, leaning forward as far as she could without falling over. "Stop right there, nosy. You go upstairs and keep yourself out of trouble while I wait for the police."

"I'm sure that's the man from my dreams."

"And I'm sure he's not. Go on upstairs, now."

"Can I go online?"

"Sure. You know the rules."

Anne nodded and pounded up the stairs, sounding as though she weighed as much as a grown man.

Jordan sat at a nearby table to watch her captive, sipping the hot chocolate she'd made for him. Her hands were still shaking, but at least she'd gotten through the worst of this ordeal.

Anne was safe, and that's what really mattered.

The gunman needed a shave and a haircut. Everything about him screamed bachelor, from his wrinkled shirt to his bad-boy leather jacket to his overworn boots. Still, there was something about him that intrigued her. Maybe that's what Anne felt that made her think she'd dreamed about him.

He was definitely dreamy in a your-mama-warned-you kind of way. Six-feet-and-change worth of walking trouble.

His eyes cracked open and he sucked in a hissing breath.

"Does your head hurt?" she asked him.

"Yeah."

"Good."

He struggled to sit up, but with his hands trapped behind him, he had no leverage.

"I wouldn't bother," said Jordan. "You're tied up way too tight to move."

"Guess so."

"Who are you?"

"Doesn't matter," said the man.

"If it doesn't matter, then tell me your name."

"Ryder Ward."

"Want to tell me why you're here?" she asked.

"Not particularly. What time is it?"

"Why? Got somewhere to be?"

"Anywhere but here if it's nightfall."

Jordan looked outside at the falling snow. She couldn't tell if the streetlights were on or not, but there was enough of a glow outside to know it wasn't full dark. "Not quite."

"We don't have much time, lady," he said.

"The name's Jordan, not lady, and we have all the time in the world until the police show up. Just sit tight and I won't have to knock you out again."

He looked up at her, his dark eyes haunted by something she could only imagine. "I know what this looks like, but I swear to you I never wanted to hurt you. Either of you."

"You have a funny way of showing it. Pointing a gun at someone usually indicates an intention to harm them."

He sighed. Incredibly, his body twisted and he managed to sit up. Sweat had broken out along his hairline at the effort, but it was more than she'd thought he could manage.

Maybe she hadn't tied him up tight enough.

"Your daughter. She's special."

Anger spiked through her veins, making her voice come out in a growl. "Never speak of her again, or I'll be mopping what's left of you off my floor for a week."

He simply lifted an eyebrow at her threat, ignoring it. "She has bad dreams. Nightmares."

Jordan hid her surprise that he knew about the dreams. "All kids do."

"Not like this. Hers are getting more frequent. She sees huge, writhing creatures that want to eat her. She thinks they're real."

How could he know that? Only a handful of people were aware of Anne's bizarre dreams.

"She's right," said Ryder, his voice quiet with regret. "Those creatures are real, and they do want to eat her."

"Shut up," barked Jordan. "You don't know anything about us."

His shoulders fell in defeat. "I wish that were true. I wish I'd never met you or your daughter. I wish I was just a normal guy and that she was just a normal kid, but neither one of us is going to get their wish."

"What is that supposed to mean?"

"It means that our time is up. The creatures from her dreams are called Terraphages. Certain people can call them from wherever it is they live and let them into our world. Those people are called Beacons, and your daughter is one. The fact that I knew where to find her means there's a Terraphage on the way right now."

Mama, that's the man I dreamed about. The one that came right before the monster.

"What a load of crap." Jordan's voice didn't hold nearly as much disbelief as she would have liked.

"You know I'm right. I can see it in your eyes. If I wasn't

right, then how would I know about the dreams? How would I know they're happening more often?"

Jordan had no answers.

"The Terraphage is coming for her tonight. The only way to stop it from breaking through into our world is to kill her. That's why I was here."

"To kill my daughter." Just saying the words made Jordan's stomach clench in sickening anger. How dare he even imagine such a thing? She should kill him now. Tell the police it was self-defense. If he lived, he might try to hurt some other child.

Jordan looked toward the weapon lying on the counter and back at the man. Could she do it? Could she really pull the trigger now that he was a threat?

His gaze skittered away until he was staring down at his boots. "I didn't know she was a kid. It's almost always an old man."

As if that excused murder. "And now that you know?"

He let out a defeated sigh. "It doesn't matter. I can't kill her, so the Terraphage will be here soon to do the job. I've failed, and now this whole town will be dead before sunrise."

"Does that include you?"

"Yeah. It does."

It was the bleak acceptance in his tone that made her believe him. The resignation. "You really believe this is true, don't you?"

"Look, lady, I didn't ask for this job. I don't want it. I hate killing people, but it's better than the alternative—letting Earth be overrun by these things whenever they get hungry.

I'm just glad my part of this mess is over now. Let someone else worry about it for a change. I'm done."

"If what you're saying is true, and something terrible is coming here tonight, then why not kill it instead?"

"Because there's no way to kill it. Others have died trying. The Terraphage is unstoppable."

"Have you ever tried?"

"My grandfather did."

"And?"

"And there wasn't enough left of him to bury. Just mangled pieces of his armor covered in blood. Nearly two hundred people died before the sun came up and forced the Terraphage back where it came from."

"If that's true, then why didn't any of us hear about it? That kind of thing makes news."

He shook his head. "It was years ago. Local authorities chalked it up as a tornado from a storm that came out of nowhere. They kept thinking that eventually they'd find the remaining bits of folks spread out across Oklahoma, but they never did. The Terraphage ate them. It gorged itself on human flesh, wrecked the town, and is going to do so again tonight."

Jordan could almost picture her beloved town torn to ribbons, her friends broken and bleeding. She couldn't let that happen. Especially not to Anne.

"How do we stop it?" she asked.

"Weren't you listening? We don't. We just pray that we're among the first to go."

"So, what? You're just giving up?"

His wide shoulders lifted in a tight shrug. "Looks like.

Besides, if I live, I'll just have to go back to killing other innocents. I've had enough of that to last a lifetime, and there's no retirement option for this line of work."

"I should take Anne and run. Even as dangerous as the roads are, they can't be as bad as whatever's coming."

"You can run. Anne can't. Wherever she goes is where the thing will show up. She's the one drawing it here."

Jordan refused to believe that. She refused to give up and let some beast *eat* her daughter. "There has to be something we can do."

His dark eyebrows twitched in irritation. "I was trying to think of an idea when you bashed me over the head."

"I'm not sorry I did it."

"Gee. Really?" He rolled his eyes. "I suppose we could wait until the last minute. As soon as the thing shows up, you two can run and I'll hold it off for as long as I can. The town will still be destroyed, but you two might make it."

"How can you say that so casually? You're talking about the possible death of hundreds of people, yourself included."

He gave a negligent shrug. "Wrong place, wrong time. Life sucks."

"You're serious. You're going to stay behind and fight this supposedly unstoppable thing."

"Unless you've got some better ideas."

Beneath them, the ground began to shudder. The mug of hot chocolate shimmied to the edge of the table and toppled over, shattering on impact.

The man's eyes widened. "Time's up. It's coming. Cut me loose."

Jordan grabbed the back of a chair to steady herself. "How did you do that? How did you make the floor shake?"

"I didn't. This isn't a trick."

"It has to be."

"So, you think I found some way to rig your building to shake without you knowing it in order to convince you to let me go because I knew before I walked in here that you were going to manage to tie me up? Is that more believable than monsters?"

He had a point. He couldn't have known he'd end up trapped unless he was psychic or had a time machine—neither of which seemed any more plausible than monsters.

"I'm not lying to you," he said. "How could I know about your girl's dreams unless I've been through this before?"

"You could have broken into her therapist's office and stolen the records."

He snorted in disgust. "Why? Why the hell would I do that?"

"I don't know. None of this makes any sense."

The floor trembled again, the motion swelling like the crest of a wave rising from the ocean. Chairs toppled. Dishes rattled on their shelves.

"We're out of time," said the man, his voice tight with urgency.

Jordan didn't want to believe him. She wanted to wait until the police showed up and helped her straighten out this mess. But he was growing more desperate, struggling to stand even though she knew he'd simply fall over again. His powerful body strained to move, making a vein on the side of his head pop out.

"Please," he said, looking right at her, hiding nothing. "Let me try to help. It probably won't make a difference, but at least I won't die lying down."

Whatever was going on, he believed what he was saying. Of course, that could simply mean he was insane.

Beneath her feet the floorboards trembled, cracking as they moved. A large bulge rose up near the stairway as if something below were trying to push its way up through the floor.

Until this moment, Jordan had hoped that all of this was some kind of sick joke. But standing here, watching the floor pulse as if alive, she knew that had been wishful thinking. Something was trying to break through.

She grabbed a pair of scissors from behind the counter and sliced through the duct tape in a matter of seconds, praying she wouldn't regret freeing him.

He ripped the tape from his sleeves, destroying the leather. "Where's your car?"

"In the back alley."

"The tiny POS covered in snow?"

"Yeah."

"Not going to cut it." His hands were free, and he reached into his jacket pocket and pulled out a set of keys. "I'll start my truck for you and pull it up close to the door. It'll get you where you need to go in this snow and do so in a hurry."

Jordan didn't want to leave this man behind to die, but she'd do so in a heartbeat if it saved her baby. "Thanks."

"Good luck, Jordan. You're going to need it."

She sprinted for the stairs, leaping over the protruding bulge, yelling for Anne to grab her coat.

The floor near the stairway had settled again, but it wouldn't stay that way long. Ryder didn't know how long it would take the Terraphage to break through into this world, but he knew for a fact that he wanted to be armed by the time it did.

His Glock was on the counter, but he didn't think that 9 mm rounds were going to do anything more than piss the thing off. He needed more firepower—the kind he kept stashed in the back of his truck, just in case.

Only seconds had passed, but the woman already had her daughter in tow, heading down the stairs.

"Stay there," he ordered them. "You can't leave until the last second, or it'll just come in wherever you are."

"Mama, I don't want to see it," said the girl. "I see it when I sleep. I don't want to see it when I'm awake, too."

The fear in her voice tore at Ryder's heart. He'd never once felt sympathy the way he did for the tiny moppet. He wasn't sure what to do to make her feel better, but he knew he had to try something. "Close your eyes, honey. I won't let it get you."

The woman hugged her daughter closer. "How much longer?"

"I don't know. Never done this before. I need to get some guns out of my truck. I don't know how much good they'll do, but it's the only chance we've got."

"Don't be long."

He wasn't. It took him less than a minute to start the truck, move it close to the door, and gather his supplies. The metal box was too heavy to lift, so he dragged it over the ground, plowing away the snow as he went. Now the girls had a nice clear path to the truck, at least until the driving snow filled it in again. At the rate it was falling, that wouldn't be long, but he didn't think that was going to be a problem. The Terraphage would show up at any moment.

He pushed through the door. Snow billowed into the room, driven by the wind. Ryder shoved the door closed to keep out the chill and to keep Jordan from leaving until it was time. He really didn't want the Terraphage to eat his truck.

"The highway heading west was a parking lot when I came into town," he said. "Don't go that way."

"South?"

"As good a guess as any."

"I've got family down that way. They'll take us in."

The floor trembled, pulsing with a throbbing energy that resonated in time with that coming from the little girl.

Ryder glanced at her, then back at her mother. He lowered his voice, hoping the girl wasn't listening too closely. "Unless I kill it—which isn't likely—I don't know what will happen. I don't know if it will come for her again tomorrow night."

"Then you'd better kill it, Ryder. We're counting on you."

No pressure.

A deep groaning sound rose from the ground beneath the coffeehouse. The little girl crawled up her mother's body, clinging to her like a monkey. "It's coming, Mama!"

"It's going to be okay, baby. This man has come here to kill it."

Anne looked at him, her blue eyes brimming with tears and her pointed chin wobbling. "Really?"

"Really," lied Ryder. "Listen to your mom and this will all be over soon." One way or another.

The floorboards beneath his boots shuddered and bulged, cracking into jagged splinters. Ryder jumped back and flung open the metal box full of weapons and ammunition.

He loaded his .45, a rifle, and a shotgun, set the rifle on the counter, holstered the .45 under his arm, shoved his pockets full of ammo, and aimed the shotgun at the bulge in the floor. "First glimpse you get of the thing, run. Got it?"

Jordan gave a shaky nod and stepped toward the door.

The bulge in the floor moved, sliding toward Jordan like a wave toward the beach.

"Stop!" yelled Ryder, but it was too late. She'd moved too far, and now the Beacon was drawing the Terraphage toward their exit, blocking the way.

The floor beneath Jordan's feet bowed, tossing her back into the room, away from the back door. She hit the wall, taking the brunt of the blow on one shoulder as she shielded her daughter's body.

Shards of wood filled the air and showered down on top of them. Ryder felt the sting of cuts across his face but ignored them. A giant black hole opened up in the floor, and a heartbeat later, the pulsing mass of the Terraphage appeared in the opening.

It was huge, filling one corner of the room. Oily, dark

green skin hung on its jagged frame, leaving visible the oddly jointed bone structure beneath. Six eyes glowed flame orange from deep within its fleshy head, pulsing in time with the Beacon's heart. Saliva poured from its jaws, and inside its mouth—which was wide enough to swallow a small car whole—were hundreds of tiny, serrated teeth angled back toward its throat.

Ryder had heard the stories. He'd grown up with tales of the Terraphage haunting his dreams, but he'd never actually seen one before. He stood there, staring in shock, his mind unwilling or unable to accept what he saw. Fear slithered over his skin until he was shaking. A cold sweat that stank of terror and defeat slid down his ribs.

Now he knew why the warnings he'd heard all his life had been so dire, why he'd been taught to show no mercy—to kill the Beacon before it was too late. The thing that stood before him could not be stopped. It was power incarnate, hunger made manifest. There was nothing a puny human like him could hope to do to win.

"Mama, no," came the little girl's frightened cry.

"Don't look, Anne. Just don't look," said Jordan, her voice a whisper of terror.

As if that would help. They were all going to die now. He knew that. Part of him wanted to fling himself at the thing and get it over with, but the rest of him fought that idea, thrashing in defiance at the notion that he'd give up now. He'd allowed this thing to come here. It was his duty to at least try to stop it.

If he could save one little girl, at least his death would

have some meaning. No one else would remember him or care that he was gone, but Anne might. If she made it out alive.

The Terraphage lumbered forward toward Anne. The girl screamed. Jordan clutched her daughter and tried to push herself to her feet with one arm. Ryder leveled his Mossberg and fired the first slug.

A deafening boom blasted the room, but the monster didn't even rock back. It did, however, turn its focus onto Ryder, which was fine with him. If he got it away from the door, Jordan had a small chance of getting her daughter out of here alive.

"That's right, you ugly fuck," he growled as he took aim at the thing's eyes. "Come and get me."

Ryder fired again. And again. The Terraphage roared in anger, and a tentacle as thick as Ryder's leg shot out toward him.

He flung himself back to avoid it, landing hard on one of the small tables. It collapsed under his weight and he went down just as the razor-sharp tip of that tentacle sliced at him. His head slammed into the floor hard enough to put a light show on display behind his eyelids. He shook it off and instinctively rolled to the side. The muzzle of the shotgun burned his cheek as it rolled with him, but he barely felt it.

As dizzy as he was now, he didn't dare stop fighting the thing long enough for it to refocus its attention on the Beacon.

He pushed to his feet, seeing two of the monsters lumbering toward him, hunched over to clear the high ceilings. His vision was fuzzy but clearing fast. Just not fast enough. The double vision faded and the two beasts coalesced back into one again just as it swiped one huge clawed paw toward Ryder's head.

He ducked as he brought up the barrel of the shotgun to shield himself from the blow. The weapon was ripped from his hands. It slammed into the wall and clattered to the floor, well out of reach.

All he had left was the rifle across the room on the counter and the handgun in his shoulder holster. If the shotgun slug didn't break that thing's hide, the .45 might not even make a dent. He needed to get to the rifle. Fast.

Ryder lunged to take cover under a booth table. He was at the front of the building now, hoping he'd drawn the Terraphage far enough away from the back door.

"Run, baby!" he heard Jordan yell.

Relief sang through his veins. He'd saved the little girl—given her the means to escape.

Just then the Terraphage spun around as if sensing their escape. It let out a high-pitched, hissing howl as it leapt toward the Beacon.

Anne screamed, her terrified voice rising to a deafening pitch that clawed at Ryder's ears. Jordan scooped up her daughter and huddled in the corner, trying to shield the child with her body.

It wouldn't do any good. The Terraphage would gobble them up together, swallowing them whole.

Hell, no. He was not going to watch this happen.

Ryder shot out from under the table, grabbed one of the

chairs, and hurled it at the Terraphage's back. It roared in anger, swinging its lumbering body around as that razor-tipped tentacle shot out at his head.

He lifted another chair and batted it away. The tentacle cut through the wooden seat, leaving the wood singed and smoking at the edge.

Holy shit!

Ryder had always refused to learn to fight in his grandfather's inherited plate mail, and at this moment, he wanted to kick his own ass for not listening. No way was his leather jacket going to stop that weapon from slicing him down to the bone. If it managed to hit something vital, game over.

Behind the monster, Jordan made a run for the kitchen. He prayed there was another way out, and if so, he was going to need to hold the doorway so they had time to get away.

With that thought in mind, Ryder flung the remains of the chair at the Terraphage's orange eyes and made a break for the kitchen. He slid through the opening and slammed the door shut behind him. It was made of wood, nice and solid, but after what he'd seen that thing do to the chair seat, he was convinced it wouldn't hold long.

A stainless-steel shelf stocked with supplies sat next to the door. Ryder grabbed the top shelf and toppled it over in front of the door.

"What are you doing?" asked Jordan. She was breathless, and panic raised her voice an octave.

"Giving you time to escape."

"There's no way out of here."

The door shuddered under the Terraphage's first attack.

"Then why the hell did you run in here?" he demanded. He needed more barriers to pile in front of the doorway. Something—anything to put in the path of that thing.

"I thought we'd be safe in here. It would give you time to kill it."

"Listen, lady. There is no killing it. I tried to tell you that before. You run or you die." He grabbed a sack of flour and piled it onto the toppled shelving. "Is there a window or anything you can use to get out?"

"No."

"Then you'd better start tearing a hole through the wall."

"It's brick."

"Hope you've got some dynamite, then, or we're all dead."

Anne whimpered, making Ryder feel like shit for scaring her more. She already knew she was going to die. He didn't need to make it worse by scaring her more.

Ryder pushed a giant, freestanding mixer across the floor, ripping the cord from the wall. He shoved it onto the sloppy pile, knowing even as he did it that the effort was futile.

Jordan cradled her daughter. Her face was pale as death. "Closest thing I have is a propane tank I use on the grill in the summer."

Ryder froze as the beginnings of a plan slithered into his mind. "Where is it?"

"Pantry." She pointed toward an open doorway.

He ran to the pantry, found the tank. He couldn't tell if it was completely full, but it was their best shot.

"Get in the pantry and stay there," he ordered.

"What are you going to do?"

"Try to drive it back to where it came from." Or at least send it off to find someone else to eat who was less trouble.

"What can I do to help?"

"Pray for a miracle."

Jordan hugged her daughter's trembling body. They were both huddled in the back corner of the pantry, as far away from that abomination as they could get. They couldn't see what was happening, which somehow made things more frightening. If Ryder failed, they'd have no clue the monster was coming for them until it was too late.

"It's gonna eat us," whispered Anne. "Just like in my dreams."

"No, baby. Ryder's going to kill it and we're all going to walk away." The lie didn't sound convincing, even to Jordan's own ears.

"I don't want to die, Mama."

"You're not going to die."

A rumbling roar bellowed out from the monster, shaking the canned goods on the wooden shelves. Anne flinched and tightened her hold around Jordan's waist.

Ryder shouted a violent curse that rang with pain. A gunshot went off. The monster hissed and hit a wall hard enough to topple some of the dry goods from their shelves. A can of green beans rolled toward Jordan's toes.

Anne was right. They weren't going to make it out of here alive, not if Jordan didn't help him.

"Stay right here, baby. I'm going to help Ryder kill it and I'll be right back."

"No, Mama. Don't go."

Jordan cradled her daughter's precious face in her hands. Tears streamed down her pale cheeks, and her blue eyes pleaded for Jordan to stay. "I'll be fine. I promise."

Anne shook her head. "You don't know. You haven't seen what it can do."

"Those were just dreams. You'll see when this is all over that the dreams weren't real."

"The monster showed up like in my dreams. Ryder showed up like in my dreams. We're gonna die like in my dreams, too."

"No. I'm not going to let that happen. You stay here. Stay quiet. I'll be back in just a few minutes."

Jordan kissed her forehead, maybe for the last time. Tears stung her eyes as she soaked in her daughter's face. She didn't want to leave her, but she'd do whatever it took to even the odds against that thing.

"Love you, baby."

"Love you, too," said Anne, her voice weak with fear and tears.

Before Jordan could change her mind, she turned and left.

The shelving in front of the kitchen door was a mangled mass of metal. The bag of flour had burst open, covering everything in a fine layer. Blood splattered the floor, mixing grotesquely with the white powder.

The fight had moved back into the main room of the coffeehouse. She could hear the hissing of the monster and Ryder's acidic curses coming from the next room.

Jordan hurried over the floor, careful not to slip in the flour. She grabbed the knife caddy on her way out, thinking she could hurl them at the beast if nothing else. She wasn't a fighter, but she'd do whatever it took to protect her baby girl.

As she cleared the doorway, she saw Ryder dodge a massive tentacle that shot out from the monster's stomach. The tip of it gleamed red with his blood, as did the claws on one of the beast's giant paws.

Ryder had been injured. He was a strong, fast, capable man. What chance did she have against something as huge and powerful as this?

A panicked gale of laughter rose up in her chest. She fought it down, not wanting to give away her presence. Maybe if it didn't know she was here, she could get in a lucky shot.

Jordan had never thrown a knife before, but she'd seen it done on TV. She grabbed the biggest one she had by the blade and flung it end over end toward one of the monster's eyes.

The handle hit just to the left of where she aimed, bouncing off harmlessly. She hadn't managed to hurt it, but she had managed to get the thing's attention.

Great.

The fiery light in its eyes flared, trapping her gaze. The greasy weight of fear descended on her, pinning her in place. Like a deer frozen in headlights, she was unable to move. She couldn't even breathe. An alien presence slithered into her thoughts, burrowed into her brain like a worm. The world stopped. Time fell away. She heard a hissing whisper buzzing in her ears, telling her hope was futile. Death was easier. All she had to do was hold still and it would all be over. Let it eat her, just as Anne had said.

Poor, sweet Anne. Her baby was going to have to grow up without a mother. If she was lucky enough to grow up at all.

The monster lumbered toward her, growing larger by the second. Jordan tried to close her eyes. She didn't want to see it happen, but she couldn't look away. The monster wouldn't let her. It held her gaze, whispering to her of death and peace.

How could there be any peace without Anne? Who was going to take care of her? She couldn't stand here and let this thing eat her. She had to fight.

The fiery light in the monster's eyes flared brighter, and a searing pain exploded between Jordan's temples. The hissing inside her ears grew louder. Her knees locked. Her body shook under the strain of trying to break free from the monster's hold.

It was close now—close enough to touch. It opened its jaws, and Jordan could feel its satisfaction slithering inside her mind. It knew it had won.

Jordan put the image of her baby's face in her mind and clung to that. Her mind filled with memories of Anne's first laugh, her first step, her first day of school, when she seemed far too little to be away for so long. She'd been so brave that day, wiping away Jordan's tears and telling her she was a big girl now. She'd come home from school devastated that she hadn't learned to read that day, and it had been Jordan's turn to wipe away the tears.

So many happy memories of going to the zoo or watching cheesy movies and making up their own dialogue. Jordan was going to miss so much of Anne's life, but she'd take her baby's sweet smile with her and hold it close, always.

A heavy weight slammed into her, knocking her off her feet. Shock ripped her eyes open, despite her desire not to witness her gruesome death. Instead of the monster, it was Ryder who was on top of her. He'd knocked her out of its path and was now shielding her with his body.

Now that she was no longer looking into the monster's eyes, the hissing whisper was gone from her mind and she was back behind the wheel of her own body. She blinked up at Ryder, trying to shed the lethargy in her limbs and the suicidal haze in her mind. She wasn't sure what had just happened—how it had turned her into a person she didn't recognize—but she knew she wasn't going to let it happen again. No more looking into the monster's eyes.

"Get back in the damn pantry," growled Ryder, then he rolled over and started firing at the thing. It roared in pain and reared back. The tentacle flapped in the air as if trying to swat away the bullets.

"I'm trying to help."

He pushed to his feet, and she could see blood soaking the front of his shirt. Three parallel cuts had torn it to shreds, as well as scoring his skin beneath. "You're just in the way."

"Tell me what I can do to kill it."

"Nothing. We're screwed."

"I'm not letting it eat my baby. We need a plan."

He fired again. The bullets weren't breaking the skin, but they were keeping the thing pinned against the far wall as it batted at them like mosquitoes. "I had one, but it's not working."

"What was it?"

"Get it to eat the propane tank. Shoot the tank and make it explode in the thing's mouth."

"Do you think that would work?"

"Maybe. But it knows the tank's not food, so it's not going for it."

It leaned forward from the wall, only to flinch back when Ryder's gun fired again. Jordan didn't know how many bullets he had in that gun, but they weren't going to last long.

The monster ate people. Maybe if the tank smelled like people, it would eat it. At this point, anything was worth a shot.

Jordan took one of the small knives from the caddy and scored a line on her forearm. Blood welled up from the cut.

"What the fuck are you doing?" demanded Ryder.

She smeared her blood over the tank, painting it a grotesque red. "Up here we do a lot of fishing. You have to put scent on your bait to get the fish to bite."

The Terraphage lumbered closer. Ryder fired again, only this time it didn't back away. "Get back. I'll see if it works."

Jordan scurried back behind the counter. She grabbed a towel and tied it over the wound to slow the bleeding. She couldn't see what was going on, but she could hear the gunshots and Ryder's vile curses rising up every few seconds.

At least he was still alive to curse.

She pushed herself to her feet, hoping to take a peek, and

a few feet away spied Ryder's rifle lying on a pile of spilled coffee beans.

Jordan snatched it up. She was no marksman, but she knew the basics. Point and shoot. Just like a camera.

Ryder tossed the bloody tank at the monster. A snakelike tongue shot out and grabbed it, drawing it into the thing's mouth.

Victory coursed through her. It had worked. The monster had taken the bait.

"Die, fucker," growled Ryder as he fired his handgun at the tank.

The bullet pinged off harmlessly, not even denting it. There was no explosion, not even any flames.

Their plan had failed.

They were all going to die.

Shit! Now what was he going to do? That propane tank was supposed to explode like in the movies. Hell, if Hollywood was to be believed, all he should have had to do was throw a rock at the thing to get it to burst into flames.

But no. He couldn't get that lucky.

The bloody tank rolled around in the Terraphage's mouth as if it were sucking on a piece of candy. Its blistered tongue flickered over it, cleaning away every trace of blood. As distracted as it was by its treat, it wouldn't be that way long.

It would either spit out the tank or swallow it, rendering it invulnerable inside the belly of the beast. Either way, Ryder was still screwed.

A huge boom exploded behind him. He turned around to see Jordan wielding the rifle.

"I can't get a clear shot," she shouted.

Most of the blood was gone. They had only a few seconds left. "Toss it here."

She did. Ryder caught it and charged the Terraphage. The pale tank was barely visible now. It was going down the thing's throat. He had time for only one shot. He stopped, aimed, and fired.

And missed.

The bullet tore into the soft pallet of the Terraphage's mouth. It roared in pain. As its mouth opened, the tank fell to the floor, landing in a puddle of saliva.

His plan had failed. Anne was going to die despite his best efforts.

"Get out!" he yelled over his shoulder. "I'll try to keep it distracted."

Jordan didn't ask questions. She sprinted for the kitchen.

Ryder reloaded the rifle, grabbed the propane tank, and propelled himself into the Terraphage's open jaws.

Jordan raced back through the room with Anne just in time to see Ryder dive into the monster's mouth. She had no idea what he was doing, but there wasn't time to stop and figure it out.

All she cared about was that the door was clear, Anne was firmly in her arms, and they were getting the hell out of here.

She hurried outside, barely feeling the cold. She pushed Anne through the open door of the truck, scurried up onto the wet seat, and gunned the engine. It purred like a cat as she slid over the streets, heading out of town as fast as the tires could carry them.

Ryder was dead. All she could do now was make his sacrifice mean something by getting her baby out alive.

The Terraphage's jaws clamped down hard, crushing Ryder. Something in his leg cracked and pain screamed up his spine, setting his brain on fire. For several precious seconds, all he could do was let the pain wash over him, consume him. He couldn't think. He couldn't breathe, which was likely a blessing. The stench of decaying meat clinging between the thing's teeth was overwhelming.

Finally, he pulled himself together enough to remember his task. He pointed the barrel of the rifle at the propane tank and fired.

He braced himself for the explosion, but none came.

The pressure around him changed, undulating as the Terraphage began to swallow him whole. He tried to hold on to the tank, but it was ripped from his fingers as it slid down the Terraphage's throat first.

A hissing noise filled his ears. A sulfurous, rotting smell filled his nose. Gas. Either he'd managed to rupture the tank or the Terraphage's powerful jaws had.

The dark, hot stench grew until Ryder was dizzy from holding his breath. When he could no longer stand it, he tried to pull in some air, only to find that his nose and mouth had been mashed against the Terraphage's flesh, cutting off any available oxygen. His shoulder and hip joints popped and burned as the pressure around his body increased. Hot, wet muscles shoved him back toward its throat. He tried to fight it, but he was no match for this kind of power. He was along for the ride. The best he could hope for now was to get one quick shot off to ignite the gas in the Terraphage's belly, killing himself so he didn't have to burn to death in its stomach acid.

Lights winked behind his eyelids from lack of oxygen. He was running out of time fast. His hand still gripped the rifle. His arm was going numb, and he had no hope of moving it within the muscular confines of the Terraphage's mouth, but he thought he could move his finger enough to pull the trigger. All he had to do was wait until he was on his way down its gullet before he fired. Anything sooner and the muzzle flash wouldn't ignite the gas.

Dozens of serrated teeth dug into his leg. Hot, sharp pain streaked up his spine. He felt something crack more than he heard it, and another wave of agony washed over him. An involuntary scream exploded inside him, but he couldn't pull in enough breath to let it out. The silent scream coursed through his chest, sapping him of what little strength remained.

Dizziness slid over him, threatening to steal his consciousness. His muscles grew weak and began to tremble from lack of oxygen. He wasn't going to last much longer. He had to do this now.

As the Terraphage swallowed him, his arms slid down its throat first. He tried to pull the trigger, but it was coated with saliva and who knew what else. His finger slipped off. He tried again.

Numbness vibrated through him. Blackness closed down around him until even the twinkling stars in his vision disappeared. His strength faded, making even the small movement of one finger difficult.

Ryder gritted his teeth and focused all his concentration on that one little digit. His finger twitched. The rifle bucked in his grip.

He didn't hear the explosion, but he felt it. Pressure slammed into him like a giant fist. The heat seared his hands and face. He became weightless for a brief instant before he hit something hard. Pain engulfed him, and he could no longer fight its pull. He let go and let the numbing blackness swallow him whole.

Ryder woke up to the feel of a little hand squeezing his. He cracked one eye open and hissed at the brightness of the light surrounding him.

"He's awake, Mama."

Anne. That was Anne talking. He'd know that sweet voice anywhere.

"Careful, honey. Don't hurt him," said Jordan.

As if that were possible. He already hurt about as much as a body could. Every joint ached, and the pain in his leg was enough to tell him that it was either broken or missing completely. He wasn't yet ready to see which.

He forced his eyes open and saw Anne's pretty face beaming down at him. Her blue eyes were glowing with happiness. "You killed the monster," she told him, smiling.

"I did?"

"Yeah. Big-time. You're a hero."

Ryder nearly snorted. Only the thought of how it would make his ribs ache held him back. "You think so, huh?"

"Yep. You even killed the monster in my dreams. They're all gone now."

"That's enough, Anne," said Jordan. "Let him rest."

Ryder squeezed her precious hand before letting her go.

He'd saved her. He'd killed the Terraphage. Not only that, but that low pulse of sound that had once beat in time with her heart was gone. Anne was no longer a Beacon. She was safe—a normal little girl with her whole life ahead of her.

Knowing he had played a part in that felt pretty damn good.

Jordan sat on the side of the bed, taking up the spot left open by Anne's departure. Her fingers were soft but strong as they moved over his palm. "You're going to be okay. Your leg is broken in two places and you have a ton of stitches and a few burns, but the doctors say you'll survive."

"That's good to hear." It would be even better once he got some pain medication, but that could wait for a few more minutes. He didn't want to look weak in front of her, not when she was staring at him as though he'd handed her the world.

"You're a hero," she whispered. Tears shimmered in her blue eyes. "You saved my baby."

The gratitude made him uncomfortable, so he tried to shrug it off. The pain in his joints stopped him from pulling off the whole nonchalant act. "No big deal."

"It is to me. Thank you."

Ryder swallowed down an awkward lump of emotion.
"Sure. Whatever."

"So, what now?"

Three months later, Ryder followed the call of the Beacon to
a small, sandy Nevada town no one would really miss.

The low, nearly inaudible pulse of the Beacon's heart
thrummed nearby, coming from the town's only grocery
store. He wasn't sure who the Beacon would be this time—
man, woman, old, young—but it hardly mattered to him.
Not anymore.

His grandfather's dented plate mail rattled as he walked
into the store. He knew he looked ridiculous, but that was
okay by him. Lying in a hospital bed again wasn't. This time,
he'd come prepared to do battle. Another one of the Terraphages was going to die tonight. The rifle strapped to his back
would help. The explosives would help even more.

There were ten grenades dangling from his waist, and he
was going to need every one of them. And then some.

* * *

Shannon K. Butcher once spent a summer chasing torna-
does with the National Severe Storms Lab in Oklahoma
on an undergraduate research project. A former engi-
neer, she now writes full-time. She lives with her husband
and their son. Vist her at www.ShannonKButcher.com.

EVEN A RABBIT WILL BITE

by RACHEL CAINE

I got a letter from the Pope in the morning mail. Handwritten. I was inclined to shred it, along with the credit card offers and the pleas from charities, but I felt a little guilty. Not because of the sender, but because of the quality of the envelope. They sure don't buy the Holy Father the cheap stuff at Wal-Mart; this was crisp, beautiful linen paper, probably made by hand by some revered, tottering artisan, and there was an embossed crossed-keys seal on the flap. Too nice to shred.

He probably knew that. Which was why he'd sent it and not some officious underling with a cheaper stationery budget.

I shut the door to my small apartment against the fierce Phoenix heat and shuffled over to the kitchen table, next to the window. I moved aside the Dragon's Eye and sorted through things until I found my reading glasses, perched them on the end of my nose, and then ripped open the envelope with a dagger that had once belonged to some king or other. The fat, homicidal one? Well, that described most of them.

Inside, the folded sheet of paper matched the envelope. Another embossed seal on the page and somewhat messy writing that I worked out bit by bit. My eyes aren't what they used to be, and I don't get to use my Italian much.

> *Most honored Lisel,* it read. *Forgive me for not paying you the courtesy of a visit, but it isn't as easy to slip away and pass anonymously these days as it used to be, in the days before television and the Internet.*

Actually, I was just glad he hadn't tried it. The last thing I needed was an ineptly disguised pontiff trailing a mile-wide caravan of paparazzi to the doorstep of my little retirement community.

> *I have been informed that you are shortly to step down from your post as Dragonslayer, after so many centuries of service. I, and the entire world, remain in your debt. You have been a good and faithful servant of the Church and God, and I offer you my personal blessing and thanks as you lay down your glorious burden and pass this mighty responsibility to a new generation.*

There were several things wrong with this. First, I wasn't retiring, I was being made redundant—and thanks, God, or whoever was running the machinery out there, for making me feel even more useless than I already did. Second, it was hardly a "mighty responsibility." Maybe it had been when *I'd* taken the job seven hundred and forty-two years ago; in those days, there had been many dragons alive, all of them deadly and cunning and determined to exterminate as many humans as they could, with whatever means they could find.

Today, there was one dragon left. One. And he lurked out in the sands of the Egyptian desert, comforted by the heat in his bones for the same reason I'd retired to Phoenix. He was old and tired, and he had outstayed his welcome in the world.

Glorious, it was not. It never had been.

I sneered at the Holy Paper and crumpled it into a ball, then threw it at the kitchen trash can. It bounced off the side and skipped across the faded linoleum floor, where it startled my old gray cat, Fidget, into opening both eyes. Fidget batted the papal bullshit around for a few seconds, then yawned and went back to sleep.

I felt exactly the same.

I drained the rest of my first pot of coffee and pulled the Dragon's Eye back to the center of the table. It was a red-tinted crystal ball on a plain wooden stand. It looked like something you could buy in any new age shop, but take my word for it, there's not another like it in the world. I didn't know the origin of it, and I didn't want to know; there was something that deep in my still-superstitious soul I mistrusted.

It knew too much, this orb. It saw too much. I sometimes wondered if there was something on the other end, looking back—if it exposed me as much as the thing I observed.

With a quick, practiced gesture, I put my hand on top of the smooth, warm crystal and felt a hum rise up inside. The crystal clouded, then showed me a flickering confusion of images—vivid ocher sand, hot blue sky, the glitter of crystals in shadow, a burst of flame. Always the sand, blowing, whispering in dunes. Nothing to be seen except the sand, as if he stared at it for hours, mesmerized in much the same way that modern feeble humans stared at their television sets.

So, that duty was completed. Karathrax was still in the desert, as he had been for the past hundred and twelve years and handful of months. I checked every day, but it was pro forma, the work of thirty seconds, and then I went on with my life, such as it was. There'd be no last great epic battle between the two of us. We were old, cranky, and tired, and it was a fucking long trip to Egypt. Or to Phoenix, for that matter. I couldn't see either one of us summoning the will to make it happen.

I started the morning rituals—made more coffee, drank more coffee, sat on the toilet for a while (what? like you don't?), read the morning paper in all its stunning sameness. I don't know why they call it "news." There's nothing new about what happens in this world on a daily basis—I'm not talking about scientific discoveries; those are moderately interesting and a constant source of amazement. No, I'm talking about human nature. As a species, we seem to be unable to learn the lesson of history. When a dog bites us, it's still a shock that dogs bite. Or that man will murder his brother. Or that greed and self-interest and blind hatred are built into our very souls.

I despair.

I was clucking my tongue over the lurid, breathless

accounts of crime when the doorbell rang. *Son of a bitch.* The kid was early. I should have gotten my ass in gear instead of moping around the house like a bitter old woman.

Even though, of course, that was accurate enough.

I looked down at myself—sloppy, fuzzy zip-front robe, flannel pajamas underneath even in the heat of summer, bony feet in grubby fleece house shoes. I'd been planning to dress up a bit, maybe put on something formal for the occasion. The impressive red silk robes given to me by one of the long-dead emperors of China, perhaps. Or something from the papal treasure chest.

Oh, screw it. Who was I trying to impress, anyway?

I shuffled to the front door, checked the peephole, and saw a fish-eye view of a medium-tall young girl. Ridiculously young, it seemed to me, and fashionable. She was smiling nervously, shifting around as if she were thinking of leaving at any second. Sadly, she did not.

I fumbled back the six or seven locks, one after another, forgot the chain, banged the door hard at the full stretch of it, closed it and slipped it off, and finally opened the door fully to gaze upon the new Dragonslayer.

She looked like a goddamn cheerleader. Maybe twenty, if that—fresh out of the petty rigors of high school, glowing with youth and vitality and health and smart-ass attitude. She was wearing a hipster t-shirt with some ironic logo, tight blue jeans, and some kind of cheap-looking sneakers that had probably cost more than my monthly rent. "Mrs. Martin?" she said. She sounded bright and chipper and nervous.

"Get your ass inside," I said. I was still wishing I'd put on the formal robes or something, but the whipcrack of command in my voice was effective without them. The girl scurried over the doorstep, and I slammed and locked it behind her. "What's your name?"

"Ellen," she said. "Ellen Cameron."

"I'm going to call you Ellie. Coffee?"

She looked relieved to have something so normal to agree to, so I tottered off to the kitchen to put on a fresh pot. While it brewed, Ellen stood politely where I'd left her, looking around but not touching. Good. I couldn't stand people who fondled my things uninvited. Not that I'd had any of *that* sort of behavior in the last hundred years.

God, I hated being old. Looking at Ellie, with her fresh, summery youth, made that burn inside me like a blowtorch. When I was her age, I'd had dragon's blood forced down my throat, fresh from a dying beast. It had been a foul custom, but it had rendered me almost as immortal as the dragons. Impossible to get more now, though. The girl would just have to do without.

I brought back the cups and sat the girl at the table. She was a neat, strong child. If not a cheerleader, she'd be a gymnast or a soccer enthusiast. Soccer, I decided. She had an outdoor glow, and gymnasts tended to spend their time inside.

"Right," I said. "My name is Lisel von Haffenburg-Martin, and I have killed four dragons in my time, which is more than any Dragonslayer before or since. Most would-be Dragonslayers die before they feel the breath on their neck from the dragon who's been stalking them. Lucky me, I have survived to retire. Now, I get to train *you* to take my place."

Ellie folded her hands in her lap and did her best to look like a good student. It was a poor attempt, but then the child was hardly out of school. At least she had better manners than most of her contemporaries, I'd give her that. "Do you mind if I ask—" She swallowed hard. "Ask if you ever—if the dragons . . ." She burst out into laughter all of a sudden, and the painfully polite girl disappeared. "Oh, man, this is crazy. You're an old lady, and we're talking about fighting dragons."

"No," I said. "We're talking about *killing* dragons. Not fighting them. This is something else altogether. We're not knights, Ellie. We're not heroes. We're exterminators. Think of dragons as enormous, eternal roaches, and you get a better idea of what it is we do."

"Ugh." Her pert little nose—quite different from my prominent beak—wrinkled in disgust. "But I get to use a sword, right?"

"You must read a great many stupid books," I snapped back. "Of course you don't. Why in the world would you go up against something as fierce as a dragon with a *sword*? Honestly, it takes a man to think of something that idiotic. You kill a dragon with only one weapon."

Ellie started to ask the obvious question, but then I saw her shift sideways. I liked that. She'd be clever and not easy to predict. "You're not talking about real *dragons*, right? Like with wings and scales and *grrrrr*?" She made a kittenish attempt at a predator's face and hooked her fingers like claws. It was moderately amusing.

"Oh yes," I said. "Huge, vicious, fast beasts. They breathe

fire. Their scales are as hard as diamonds. If you catch their gaze, they can freeze you in place for the kill. They're smart, cold, and utterly without mercy."

Ellie thought I was lying. It was written all over her milk-fed, self-confident face. I'd grown up in a grim world, rocks and hard edges, steel and muscle and violence. We'd thought it civilized at the time, but now that I look back on it, it was a savage time, and I'd taken to it like a duck to water.

I couldn't imagine this child surviving half a day in that time, even without a dragon's threat hanging over her. She'd have been slaughtered by the first cutpurse fortunate enough to stumble over her.

"Dragons," I said with cool precision, "can also take other forms. And when in other forms, they are vulnerable, without their natural defenses."

"Other forms," Ellie repeated. I could see that regardless of what she'd been told, whatever papal letter she'd received, whatever counseling from her local bishop, she was sure that I was a batty old lady. "Right. Like—what?"

"A particular favorite of Vixariathrax was to assume the form of a cow grazing in a field. He dispatched four separate Dragonslayers that way. Of course, cows were as common as dirt then." I shrugged, although my shoulder was beginning its daily rhythmic dull ache.

"A cow." Her face was a study in doubt. "Then how did you figure it out?"

"It was the only cow in the field." I smiled slowly. "Cows come in herds, girl. Vixariathrax was a hungry old bugger.

One placid cow, left standing in a field trampled by dozens? Something was definitely wrong."

"How did you kill him?"

"Same way I killed them all," I said. "With cleverness. For him, I shot him from cover. He never saw me coming until it was too late. Poisoned arrows. When he changed back to his dragon form, the poison was trapped inside. He thrashed himself to death out in that field. Took a while, but it was effective enough."

Ellie had gone quiet, frowning. I saw revulsion in her now. "Doesn't sound very . . ."

"Honorable?" I put all the scorn I could into the word. "There's nothing honorable about killing dragons. Nothing brave about it. You put them down, or they kill you. That's all there is to it."

"But—" She licked her lips. "How many are there out there to fight?"

"One."

Ellie opened her mouth, closed it, looked even more reluctant.

"Oh, don't be so squeamish. One's enough," I said. "One dragon has the power to destroy a million people, more if he's grown angry. He's a flying, unstoppable, calculating nuclear bomb. He could destroy a city a day, *every* day, and there would be almost nothing that could stop him once he was going about it."

"They could put him in a zoo or something."

"Zoo," I repeated. "Do you imagine that is a better end

for something so magnificent than a decent death? To be gawked at by thousands, millions, trapped for eternity in a small, inadequate cell? And no zoo could hold him, girl. No *prison* could hold him, for that matter. You could bury him under a mountain and he would dig his way out."

She swallowed. "Modern weapons—"

"They have weapons," I said flatly. "Us. Dragonslayers. We're the weapons, and we're so effective that in two thousand years, we have hunted dragons from thousands down to one. One last, old, lonely, angry dragon. If that distresses you, get your ass out of my chair and leave. I don't have time to train some weak-livered baby sentimental about a killing machine who'd gladly rip *you* apart and pick his teeth with your ribs, if given half a chance." I was not exaggerating. I'd seen it happen to my predecessor, Godric. Harenthrax had taken his time about the dismemberment, starting with pulling away tiny bits like fingers and toes and eating them like appetizers before starting to disarticulate the man's limbs. Godric had stopped screaming only when his lungs failed. I was not sure how long it had taken him to really die after that. I'd grown numb. In the end, I'd fallen asleep, shameful as that was, and woke only when the screaming had stopped.

She got up, the girl, and stood there staring down at me. Her lips pressed into a thin line. "You're a mean old bitch," she said. The sheen of politeness was completely gone. Good. I had no real use for manners.

"Oh, yes, I am all that. 'Old' being the operative word. I survived the worst four dragons could throw at me. I survived politics, wars, husbands, and the death of everything I ever loved. Because I am *smart*. Because I am *ruthless*. If you think that is a character fault, you have no business being a Dragonslayer. You'll be dead before you smell your first whiff of sulfur."

She headed for the door.

"Go on," I called after her. "Be sure to tell God you're an idiot when you get to heaven. Probably tomorrow."

That stopped her in her tracks. "What?"

"The Holy Father handpicked you," I said. "I didn't. I don't get any say in who comes after me, and I'm stuck with whoever they send me. So if you walk away today and don't learn anything, fine, no skin off my ancient nose, is it? I'm retired. I'll be training your replacement tomorrow, and telling him about your suitably gruesome, gory death. Because if I know who you are, most assuredly old Karathrax already knows as well." I picked up the Dragon's Eye—it was surprisingly heavy, about the weight of a good bowling ball—and shuffled over to thrust it at her. She took it, wide-eyed. "There. Consider yourself trained. Now get the hell out."

"But—" She stared at the crystal. "What is it?"

"Your problem," I said. "You don't want to listen to the mean old bitch, fine. Figure it out yourself. Now shoo!"

I shoved her right out the door, slammed it, and started the tedious process of locking it all. Around lock number two, she started knocking tentatively on the door.

By lock number four, she was pounding on it. "All right, all right, stop making such a racket!" I yelled through the door, and unlocked it again. I let the girl in. This time, I left the locks unturned because I might want to eject her, quickly. With force. "Now, are you willing to pay attention?"

"Yes, ma'am," Ellen said, but I read a simmering resentment in her expression, in the tense set of her shoulders. "Sorry. Um, here, could I set this down . . . ?" She lifted the heavy weight of the Dragon's Eye.

"No," I said. "You can stand there and hold that out in front of you, for the next hour. Consider it punishment duty."

And training, for what would come next.

Ellen bit her lip, then stretched out her arms, and almost immediately the shaking began.

I sat down, refilled my coffee cup, and picked up the paper.

She wasn't completely hopeless. For one thing, she wasn't a complainer; I can't abide complainers. She did everything she could to fulfill whatever task I set her, even the impossible ones, and she didn't whine even when she was sore, bruised, cut, exhausted, and ready to drop. I think it became a personal mission for her, to wear me down.

Good luck, little girl. Even as old and feeble as I was now, I was Lisel Dragonslayer. She'd woken something in me, a fierce pride, a desire to stretch myself. I abandoned the old-woman robes and house scuffs; I began dressing in loose running suits, suitable for fighting, and sturdy athletic-type shoes. Velcro closures. Greatest thing in the world.

I started her out training with a staff, because she could do herself the least damage with that, and I could do the most to her without maiming. Fun all around. Ellie was surprisingly strong and fast, but then, I supposed the Pope hadn't just picked her name out of a hat; they had an entire council of researchers working on things like that, identifying potential Dragonslayers, filtering them, vetting them, prying into every corner of their lives. Much easier in my day, when your lord and master pointed a bony finger your direction and said, "Take that one." In my case, my lord and master had been my husband. I'd gotten along better with the dragons, frankly.

Ellie was out of school, and the Church was fronting her family a lot of money—hush money—combined with a dizzying cocktail of faith and flattery. I didn't know if the Pope actually took any of this seriously; they all professed to it, but none of the pontiffs I could remember had ever actually seen a dragon. Then again, their trade was to believe in things unseen. And they'd never tried to cut me out of the papal budget, so far as I knew, which must have meant something significant. Even the Pope has downsized.

I knew, because I asked, that Ellie's family had been promised a million dollars a year for the next ten years, all squirreled away in some Swiss account, with allowances funneling to her parents through some byzantine arrangement of shell companies. It was a pension, supposedly. Both her mother and father had retired from their jobs. Ellie got a stipend that would keep her in anything her heart desired, barring haute couture fighting gear.

I certainly hadn't been paid that excessively, but then, I supposed the standard of living was much lower in my day. I'd never hungered or lacked for shelter or comfort. Same basic thing, I supposed. There was no point in being bitter that the budget for the newer generation was more luxurious than in my heyday.

The training proceeded apace. Ellie took two weeks to reach a mastery of the staff sufficient to convince me to let her graduate to edged weapons. Blade proficiency took a bit longer, but she came every day, training her pretty little heart out . . . first with a dull practice blade against a post, then against me. That was humiliating.

For her, of course.

The fourth time I disarmed her without breaking a sweat, she got a mulish, angry look as she swiped up the fallen sword. "I thought you said you don't kill a dragon with swords!" she spat. "Why do I have to—"

"Because I said so," I interrupted. Sometimes I love being old. "Now shut up and fight." It was the closest she'd come yet to real complaints, and I wasn't surprised; by this time, I'd been a screaming banshee, shouting abuse at Godric like a fishwife at a wandering husband. It was hard bloody work, especially since we conducted our business out in the desert, far from prying eyes and passing motorists curious about what a pair of women might be doing with medieval weapons in the hot sun.

She settled into a fighting stance, with a firm two-handed grip on her sword, and advanced. This time she was a little better; it took me three parries to find an opening, but this time I didn't settle for stripping away her sword; I slammed the point of my weapon hard into her chest, knocking her back to the ground. She lay there on the dusty soil, blinking up at the desert sun, and tears trickled out of her eyes to cut clean lines through the dirt on her face. She was weary, sweaty, and so very young.

I hesitated for a second, then slammed my sword blunted point down into the sand hard enough to make it stand upright and reached down to offer her a hand. She stared at it for a second, gasping for breath, and then gripped it and let me haul her to her feet. Sand showered out of her clothes in an ocher flow and clung to her sweaty skin in clumps.

"You need all your skills," I said. "Strength. Agility. Quickness of body and mind. Discipline. Patience. Ruthless dedication. That is why I'm teaching you. Not how to chop wood with a sharp edge. Any fool can do that."

She thought about what I said. I could see the wheels turning. Over the past few weeks, she'd impressed me as much for her thoughtfulness as for her athleticism, which was considerable. I wondered how bright the girl really was. Brighter than most modern simpletons, I would guess; she questioned everything, accepted nothing without turning it this way and that. One would almost think rhetoric was still a skill possessed by the common man.

I reached in my pack, tossed her a bottle of water, and opened one for myself. We sat in the shade of a spiky bush—one of the few around—and swigged. She didn't speak at first. Neither did I.

Eventually, she said, "The dragon. The one who's left. You haven't told me anything about him."

"You're not ready," I said. "Learning about dragons is the last thing you do."

"Why?"

I almost smiled. She asked why more than any child I'd ever known. "Because I say so."

"Mrs. Martin—"

"Lisel," I said.

Her cheeks colored slightly. "Lisel." It sounded stilted and forced. "Why is knowing about him dangerous?"

"I didn't say it was dangerous. It's distracting."

"Why?" Her huge eyes were fixed on me in challenge.

I surrendered, for the first time. "All right. I'll tell you about Karathrax, but it doesn't mean you can cut your training short to go after him."

"Yeah, I know. Luke had to go back to Yoda, too. No jumping the gun." I had no idea what she was talking about. Her flush deepened. "Sorry. Go on."

"It's not known how old Karathrax is," I said. "He was in the earliest records handed down among the Dragonslayers. What is certain is that he was the cleverest of all of them, and the most patient. He waited once for fifty years, pretending to be mortally injured, simply to destroy the Dragonslayer who wounded him."

Ellie's eyes got even wider. "How many people has he killed?"

"In general? Thousands, certainly. The destruction of several medieval cities was ascribed to Karathrax, as the dragons began to wage a coordinated war against the Dragonslayers. He's been responsible for the death of almost a dozen of us, over the centuries."

"But before you."

"I'm just the last one left alive," I said. "I wasn't the only one when I was chosen. I was one of almost a hundred. By the time Karathrax was the last, so was I."

She said nothing to that. We drank our water in silence, and then she finally ventured, "But he must have done something terrible, right? I mean, not just being a dragon. Something to make us hunt him down like this."

"Are you deaf? I said he killed thousands. Destroyed almost a dozen Dragonslayers!"

"I know," she said softly. "But that's war, kind of. They were fighting for their survival. Why were we killing them in the first place?"

She understood nothing. Nothing at all. The water in my mouth suddenly turned from sweet to bitter, and it was all I could do to choke it down. "Never you mind," I said sharply, and got to my feet. My aches and pains, accumulated slowly over all the centuries, reminded me yet again of the years. "Get up and fight."

Ellie stared at me for a few exhausted seconds, bottle raised halfway to her lips, then deliberately took another drink, replaced the cap, and climbed up with her sword in her hand.

I hurt her a few more times, pushing myself as much as her, and as she drove us back to my apartment, I saw tears cutting silently through the dust on her cheeks. She looked small, tired, and dispirited.

I got out, hefted the equipment bags, and trudged back to my apartment, feeling as sore as she must have been. When I looked back, Ellie was slumped over her car's steering wheel, forehead resting against the leather-wrapped surface. Gathering the strength to drive away, I presumed. It was getting dark, and the clear sky was cooling from hot blue to the icy color of the deep ocean. Stars flickered like glitter thrown by God.

It was dark enough, and she was distracted. I dropped the bag into the grass, removed something from a side pocket, and slipped quietly back down the path, keeping to the blackest of the shadows. I circled the back of the idling car, moved up beside the driver's side, and slowly lowered the gun in my hand to touch the side of Ellie's head.

"You're dead," I told her. I wasn't angry, only a little disappointed. She flinched and looked up. Her eyes were red and running with tears, her face burning with the force of her self-pity. "You think I'm dangerous? I'm an old woman. I'm nothing. Karathrax is your enemy, and he is cold and eternal and clever, and he *will not* have mercy on you. He will steal up on you in the dark, just like this, and end your life. You can be hurt. You can be killed. You understand?"

She did. I saw the fury and hurt slip over her expression, but then it melted away.

She nodded without saying anything.

I slipped the .38 back into the pocket of my running suit and shuffled back to where I'd left the training bag, opened the door of my apartment building, and greeted a couple of my elderly neighbors shuffling along on their walkers.

I needed a drink, a hot bath, and an evening of game shows.

I was in the tub, thinking how nice it was to have steaming, scented water without having to lug heavy buckets to a cauldron, when the bathroom door opened silently and Ellie stood there looking at me. She wasn't crying anymore. She hadn't showered, she hadn't changed clothes, she hadn't even washed the dirt from her skin. She looked a little savage, and in her hand was the gun, which she'd taken out of my training bag, I assumed.

"Bang," she said. "You're dead. See? I can sneak up on people, too."

She closed the bathroom door, and I heard her leave, slamming the door behind her.

I relaxed and let out a long, satisfied breath.

She was ready for the next level.

"This," I told Ellie the next morning, "is Dragonkiller."

I opened up a long wooden box lined with velvet and took out a bow made of carved, yellowing bone. A thick string of sinew dangled from the bottom. I held it in both hands, ceremonially, and handed it to Ellie, who accepted it the same way. Instinct, I assumed. I hadn't made a production out of it, although it was a ceremony of sorts.

A rite of passage.

"It's a bow?" She sounded uncertain. I sighed.

"Of course it's a bow," I snapped. "String it."

"Um . . ."

"Put your weight on it, bend it, and slip the loop over the top into the groove."

She blinked, as if she'd never heard of such a thing—and perhaps she hadn't!—and started to try to bend the thing. It wasn't easy; Dragonkiller had been made for a man's strength. She threw herself into it, though, pushing harder and harder until the form finally began to bend.

She strung the bow.

Panting, she looked at it and smiled. A pure, delighted smile of victory, one I remembered smiling myself, upon a time, as the bow bent beneath my hands for the first time. She looked up at me.

I smiled back. It was not voluntary; there was something so purely triumphant in her that it dragged approval out of me, all unwilling.

I transformed it to my usual scowl as swiftly as I could. "Give it here," I said, and snatched it out of her hands. "Don't think that bending the damn thing makes you a master of the bow."

"I don't," she said meekly enough. "I want to learn. I always thought bows were cool."

She wouldn't think they were when her fingertips were shredded and bleeding, when her inner forearm was raw from the snap of the string. But I approved of her mind-set.

"This bow," I said, "is made of dragonbone, and—"

"Whose bone?" she interrupted me.

"What?"

"Which dragon's?"

I thought for a moment. "Aedothrax," I said. Godric had killed him seventy years before I had been chosen as his apprentice; the bow had seen good service by a dozen Dragon-slayers before and since and had come back to me. "Dragonbone is excellent for these kinds of weapons. Very springy, but resistant. It never breaks."

"Dragons never break bones?"

"Not under normal circumstances. I told you, they are tough bastards."

Ellie nodded, taking in the information with her usual concentration. I pulled the bow back to its full extension, a use of strength I hadn't attempted in years. I only just managed, but I refused to allow the strain to show. I loosened it just as slowly, then handed it back to Ellie and took out a quiver from the other half of the wooden case. In it were a dozen handmade arrows, all of the same dragonbone, tipped in sharp iron with viciously pointed heads. The fletching was a vivid red, as hot as it had been the day I'd stripped and dyed the feathers. It hadn't faded at all.

Unlike me. But then, I hadn't been shut up in a box for a hundred years. It only felt that way.

Ellie reached for it. I pulled it back out of reach. "Not yet. First, you learn to string and unstring the bow. Then we go on to target practice."

"But I want to learn to shoot!"

"Of course you do," I said, and rolled my eyes. "And I'm certain you know nothing at all about it. Your generation is taught nothing that's of any practical use at all, are you?"

"Hey, I'm really good with computers!"

"I rest my case." I nodded at a heavy padded target in the corner. "Fine. I'll let you shoot—*carefully*. Carry that, too. We're going to practice."

Ellie's face screwed up in frustration, but she managed to balance target and bow without much difficulty. I carried the quiver, a folding chair, and the water bottle. Comfort and survival. Let the apprentice do the heavy lifting.

In the car, as we drove out to our usual desert practice area, I found myself saying, "How do your parents feel about your new calling?" *Small talk?* Whatever demonic spirit had just possessed me to make *small talk?* I stared straight forward through the dusty windshield, frowning, appalled at myself.

Ellie, though, responded instantly like a puppy to a pat. "Mom's very devout, so, you know. Just the fact that the Pope actually called the house . . . I mean, even Dad was impressed by that. And the money, of course. Everybody's impressed by money." She sounded a little bitter and ironic about that. I approved. "Mom's worried about me, though."

"You've not *told her*!"

"Oh, no—I mean . . . no. I said I was doing some training. Like Special Forces stuff. Army of God, all that stuff. She won't tell anybody." Ellie fell silent, nervously tapping fingers on the steering wheel. "Hey, Lisel?" When I didn't answer, she swallowed and continued. "Do I get to have, you know, friends? Boyfriends? A life?"

"Can I stop you?" I turned my face away, staring out at the passing desert. The flickering landscape connected to something else, and I changed the subject. "Are you using the Dragon's Eye as I told you?"

"I check it every day," Ellie said. "For about an hour. He doesn't do much, does he?"

"He's old," I said. "And tired."

"But I thought he was clever and dangerous!"

"Oh, he's those things as well. Dragons can lie dormant, consumed by their own affairs, for a hundred years or more, and then suddenly take a notion to destroy half of Chicago. Never assume that lazy equals weak."

"Did you ever make that mistake?" she asked. Which was a very good question, and one I did not want to answer.

"Once," I finally said.

"What happened?"

"London," I said shortly. "In 1666." She gazed back at me with perfect, milk-fed blankness, a placid cow of the new age rich with information and remarkably poor in actual knowledge. "The Great Fire of London."

Then she surprised me with a very small smile. "I thought it started from that guy's bakery. On Pudding Lane."

"And I thought children your age knew only what appeared on your Twitter page about history."

"I didn't say it wasn't on Twitter." She lifted one shoulder in a charming, self-deprecating shrug. "I started reading up on disasters. I figured some of them must have been caused by dragons, right? I wanted to know what I was up against."

I pulled in a deep breath. The child had actually done something intelligent. "The decision to put the blame on poor Master Farriner was made at the highest levels of the court, but actually, the blame rested on me. I'd wounded the dragon, and it had fled to nurse its wounds. I didn't chase. I thought—I thought she had learned her lesson, and would stay well away from humans, at least for a few hundred years." I felt myself drifting on memory, rich and bright. "She was beautiful, Heliothrax. So beautiful. Her scales were the color of twilight, and her eyes blazed like flame. They are beautiful, you know. It's a shame they are so savage."

"So you tracked her down and killed her." Ellie's voice had gone soft and quiet, and her face was turned away from me, wind whipping her hair across to hide her expression.

"Yes," I said. It was the one thing I had ever done that still haunted me. She had been wounded and afraid, and alone of all the dragons I had ever killed, she had transformed herself at the last into a human. A human child, crippled and trembling and weeping. "So many innocent people died in London, even though they didn't keep good counts. There was so much destruction. I had no choice. I had to put her down."

The car arrived at the turnout and bumped off from tarmac to soft, hissing sand. The same track we'd taken dozens of times by now; there was a definite road being formed by the grooves of Ellie's tires. She was silent until we arrived at the training spot and then shut off the engine and listened to the quiet tick of the metal cooling before she said, "How did you know it was her? Heliothrax, I mean?"

"She was the closest."

"What if she didn't do it?"

I sighed. "Does it really matter which of them did it? They were all deadly, all dangerous, all bent on killing us. A response had to be made. I made it."

That shape-changed dragon, looking up at me with a child's tear-filled, burning eyes. Trying to speak but not knowing how, because that was knowledge that Heliothrax had never bothered to acquire.

"I made it," I repeated, and got out of the car to walk stiffly in circles, loosening up my ancient bones and muscles. Ellie opened the trunk, and I began pulling out our training supplies—two folding chairs now, since I had decided she had advanced sufficiently that there was no need to keep her in discomfort when resting. Ample water. A small bag of food, enough to last two days, since I always plan for emergencies. I left the emergency shelter equipment in the car and removed the weapons and training bag.

We began the day as we had all other days—katas to loosen and center, sword practice (at which Ellie was becoming— much to my surprise—acceptable), knives. Then I opened the case that held Dragonkiller, unstrung, and handed the weapon to her to bend and string. I walked out with the target and placed it a child's training distance away.

"We'll start slowly," I said, adjusting the target slightly to be sure it was just so. "Before you touch the arrows, I want you to—"

Something hissed past me, over my shoulder, and buried itself in the dead center of the concentric rings. I dodged aside, breathing hard, and stared at the quivering arrow, the vivid fletching.

I looked back to see Ellie standing, tall and straight and beautiful, bracer on her forearm, plastron strapped to her chest, leather glove on her hand, fitting another arrow to the bowstring.

"Thank you," she said, "for teaching me so well. I admit, there's a certain thrill to it, isn't there?"

She no longer sounded like Ellie Cameron, shallow teen struggling to swim in shark-infested waters.

She sounded like the shark.

Ellie sighted, stretched the string, and released with perfect form, classical as Diana hunting a doe.

The arrow drove into the target within a breath of the first. Ellie methodically drew another from the quiver.

"You're probably wondering right now what's happening," she said. She set the arrow on the string but didn't draw. Her blue eyes were wide and calm and fixed on me. "That's the feeling of every hunted beast, Lisel. The anger, the hurt, the anguish, the confusion. Even a rabbit will bite, at the end. Did you know that? Even the mildest of animals will fight to live."

I had an awful feeling growing in my chest, like a malignancy, like the illness I had avoided all these long centuries. She was right: I was hurt, I was angry, I was afraid and confused. And all I could force from my lips was, "Who are you?"

"You know who I am, Lisel," Ellie said, and smiled. Her eyes changed slowly, blue fading and somehow brightening into the lick of pale flame. "You know."

Karathrax.

I didn't hesitate. I threw myself sideways, behind the archery target, and in the same instant, Karathrax pulled and fired, a snap shot that should have gone wide but would have instead punched through my body if I hadn't managed to get the target in the way. I rolled, pulling the target with me, and got into a crouch. The target was a heavy, awkward shield, but it was better than nothing, and I used it as I ran for the nearest genuine shelter, a heavy cactus that leaned near a dune.

Ellie—no, *Karathrax* (I had to stop thinking of him as a human now) was calmly setting another arrow to the bow-string. In no particular hurry, nor did he need to be. He had trapped me, dissembled *perfectly.*

"When?" I shouted to him. "When did you kill the child?"

"Before she ever reached you," he said. "I kept her alive for quite some time, to learn from her so I could impersonate her appropriately. She's buried quite near here, actually. I didn't eat her."

"Kind of you."

"I've been waiting, Lisel. Waiting for the opportunity to face you and *talk.* Talk as Heliothrax would have, if you'd not slaughtered her without mercy."

I needed to get to the weapons. There was little chance for me, but what there was lay in the weapons cache, the water, the emergency shelter. Karathrax was suited to the desert, and he could shed this human form and assume his dragon form at any time. Once he did, he would be . . . invincible.

I had killed my dragons with cleverness, from concealment, with poisons and treachery. I couldn't take him in a fight, and we both knew it.

But even a rabbit bites.

I needed a distraction, something that would make Karathrax believe that he was on the verge of realizing all his hundreds-of-years-old dreams of destroying me.

Focus, I told myself. *You have weapons you haven't told him about*. That was true; there were levels of training, of ability, that Karathrax had never seen, because he'd believed he'd seen all he needed.

He'd not seen this.

It was the most treacherous and difficult skill I had ever learned, and the most chancy; it required levels of commitment and fearlessness that most never mastered. I had scars from it, many scars, and some of them had been all but fatal.

I closed my eyes a moment, centered myself, and then stood up from concealment. I didn't speak. I needed all my focus on Karathrax.

He didn't wait. Ellen Cameron's slender, tanned fingers tensed, the bow stretched, and I read the tremor in her arm as the muscle began to release.

Timing was everything to this. I'd gained barely enough distance to make it possible, but my concentration, my reaction time, had to be perfect.

No thought.

Nothing but the action.

I felt a sharp sting as my hand closed, just a bit early, on the arrow, and the barbed, sharpened head sliced furrows in my palm and fingers. That was all right. The important thing was to catch *and stop* the arrow, slow it so that if it did penetrate my skin, it would do so shallowly. The blood on my hand would only help sell the illusion, if I had gotten it right.

I had, barely. The arrow was lodged in my chest, sunk in to the depth of perhaps half an inch, but the illusion of it was solid. I screamed, dropped onto my side, curled around the arrow. Blood from my cut hand smeared a gory mess across the front of my tracksuit.

Karathrax waited a long, long moment, then took the bait, walking through the sand and nocking another arrow along the way. He wanted to kill me with the bones of his kin, not something human, like a sword. I understood that.

I played dead, and slowly, with just the tiniest play of muscles, worked the arrow free of my skin. Blood wicked through the cloth covering my chest, vivid evidence of my wound. Even better.

I felt cool relief from the hot sun as Karathrax stood over me, nearly as tall as the towering cactus with its defiant spikes. Ellie Cameron's pink shoe rolled me over onto my back, and I made sure my eyes were half-open, fixed, unmoving.

One more thing I could do to sell the illusion.

I let my bladder loose, the way the dead do. The sharp smell of urine filled the clear desert air.

Overhead, a vulture riding the thermals shifted its course.

Karathrax's eyes were eerie in Ellie's face, merciless and cold. This was the moment of true danger; if he had a doubt, even an instant's doubt, he would simply shoot me again. In fact, if he'd let me train him any further, I'd have trained him to do just that. *Never assume something is dead,* I would have told him. *Never approach without administering a coup de grâce, preferably in the head.*

As old as he was, he might have known that, but as a dragon, he likely had never had to fear much. Only humans. And even then, only a few. His instincts were wired differently. Dragons didn't care whether their prey was alive or dead; the death was inevitable once they began to eat.

I heard the creak as the bowstring relaxed. Karathrax laughed softly.

"Dead in your own filth," he said in Ellie's soft, girlish voice. "What an ignoble end you all find, you humans. I think I'll take your skin for a trophy. I'll use it in my cave, as a rug."

My eyes were burning from dryness, and the urge to blink was almost unbearable, but I abstained until he'd shipped the bow over his shoulder and glanced away to reach for the knife holstered in leather at Ellie's belt. *Ellie.* A child, waylaid and destroyed, purely to provide Karathrax with the appropriate opportunity.

When he shifted to draw the knife, I focused my concentration again to a pinpoint. There could be no fumbling, no wasted motion, no hesitation—I visualized the motion, and then in the next shadow-second I copied it with muscles and will, turning the arrow, dragging it through cloth, and slicing its razor edge deep through the Achilles' tendons on both legs, just above the heels, left vulnerable by cute pink athletic shoes with their appliquéd hearts.

Blood burst out in a flood, and Karathrax/Ellie let out a yelp of pure surprise and shock, wavered, and then I saw the pure horror on the face as the fine, precise engineering of the legs ceased to work. His body toppled, arms flailing, and he lost the knife as he hit the ground face just inches away. I flung myself across him, found the knife, and closed my bloody fingers around the gritty handle.

"No!" Karathrax roared, and I heard all the things he had described in that voice—anger, hurt, anguish, and confusion. *Even a rabbit will bite.*

I was no rabbit.

Karathrax twisted beneath me, and I knew I had seconds to finish this. He could shed this vulnerable human form, fortify himself inside a dragon shell, and though he would carry his crippling injury with him, he would be fiendishly difficult to hurt or kill again.

Our eyes met. I put the knife to the fragile human throat, the girl's throat, Ellie's throat, and I remembered the child, the crying child that Heliothrax had become at the end.

"She was my mate," he said. "You slaughtered the one you call Heliothrax for nothing. For *nothing.* Our females didn't fight. Didn't kill. Didn't burn. None of them did. But you didn't bother to tell one dragon from another, did you? We were all the same threat."

"*You* killed our women. Our children."

"You were prey," he said. "We didn't understand you could think, not for a long time. We didn't understand you communicated. We do it differently, in ways you would never perceive, in color and light. These crude sounds you make, they were beyond our senses. Heliothrax tried, in the end. I watched you kill her."

"And did nothing."

His golden eyes blazed. "I was half a world away! I saw through *her* eyes." Odd. It had never occurred to me that the Dragon's Eye, the orb I looked through, was truly just that— the eye of a dragon. But perhaps it was true.

That reminded me of something. I cut a little deeper with the knife. "How did you deceive me? I saw through your eyes, in the desert. You never left."

Ellie's lips split into a cold grin. "You saw what you wanted to see," Karathrax said. "Desert. It never occurred to you that what you were seeing might have been me in *your* desert. It was a long, cold flight, racing the sun, and I was daring fate, but I knew it was time. Time to end it."

"It is," I said. Yet something in me was howling. Something awful. When Karathrax was gone, something would be missing from the world that would never be in it again.

He killed Ellie.

And I had slaughtered his mate, punishing her on behalf of all dragons, with no more care for who she was or what she'd done than singling out one ant from a colony.

I'd killed so many of them, with poisons. Deception. Treachery. Heliothrax had been the first I'd faced, the first I'd bloodied a sword on, the first I'd destroyed with my own reddened hands.

Karathrax would be the last.

He should have changed by now, I realized. He could have taken on his dragon shape, ripped me apart, crawled away to a bitter healing in a lonely world.

He hadn't.

We stayed that way for a long moment, my ancient enemy and I, and then I said, "Do you want to die as a human?"

"No." Ellie's even teeth flashed in a grim smile. "But I'm old, Lisel. Far older than you. Changing form is a young dragon's game. Changing back is the work of hours for me these days. I don't suppose you'll be polite enough to wait."

I readied the knife.

"But," Karathrax said, "what happens to you, Lisel? When my blood is in the sand, what magic will you have left to sustain you? You've lived all these hundreds of years of stolen time because your life is linked to that of the dragons. Because seven hundred years ago, Godric forced you to drink the hot blood of my sire, Aedothrax, and bound you into the dragon line. Your life is linked to mine. Nothing else now."

I knew he was right. Godric had said so, from the beginning—the dragon's blood would sustain us as long as the dragons lived. Once the last dragon was gone . . .

I took a firmer grip on the knife. "I'll risk it."

"Not a risk. A certainty. You kill me, you die." His eyes darkened back to Ellie's clear blue. "But the same isn't true for me. If I kill you, I go on."

I had taught her too well. Too well.

The girlish right hand, during the distraction of his speech, had drawn a small, hidden dagger, and now Karathrax buried it to the hilt in my side, at the same time shoving me off with all the strength in that small female body. He couldn't walk, but he could crawl, and crawl he did, not away from me, but *toward* me. Pain radiated from the wound in my side, flooding in pounding waves through my body, and my shaking hand tried and failed to remove the knife. It was stuck in bone.

Karathrax took the larger hunting knife away from me. My blood thickened the sand. So did his.

We sat together in silence, and then he reached out and pulled the knife from my side. I screamed, unable to stop, and my vision flared white, then gray.

When it cleared, Karathrax was raised up on his arms, looking down at me from Ellie's perfect, pretty face.

"I hated you," he said. "For hundreds of years, you were the only thing in the world that existed to me. Your death. Your blood. Your suffering."

And it had been the same for me, with him. Enemies to the end. Even long past the point where it had made any sense.

"But now I see you're just an old, tired woman," he said. "Old, tired, and lost."

He slowly lowered himself down, a controlled collapse, and I saw the pupils of his golden eyes growing wider.

"You kill with poison," he said. "Don't you?"

That was what I had been about to tell Ellie, before Karathrax had revealed himself. *Before you touch the arrows, I want you to learn precautions against the poison.* Because every wicked edge had been tainted with it, a poison that felled dragons and humans alike.

It had sliced my hands, as I'd caught it.

It had sliced open the tendons at the backs of his legs. A death sentence for us both.

"I'm sorry," I said, and it came from some secret, true, dark place inside me. "She was magnificent. You were all magnificent. And we were wrong to destroy you. I know that. I knew it then."

And in the end, Karathrax reached for my hand, and we lay in the hot, comforting afternoon, growing cold in the sun together.

"Murderer," he murmured before his eyes fluttered closed.

My heartbeat slowed, slowed, and in the instant before it stopped, I thought, Guilty.

No doubt the Pope would have disagreed.

He would have been wrong.

* * *

Rachel Caine is the *New York Times* bestselling author of the popular Weather Warden series and the young adult Morganville Vampires series. She has another series, Outcast Season, which began in 2009 with the novel *Undone*. In addition, Rachel has written paranormal romantic suspense for Silhouette, including *Devil's Bargain, Devil's Due,* and *Athena Force: Line of Sight* (which won a 2007 RT Reviewers' Choice Award). Visit her Web site: www.rachelcaine.com. MySpace: www.my space.com/rachelcaine.

DARK LADY

by P. N. ELROD

My name is Jack Fleming. I am owned by a nightclub. As a sideline I have been known to help damsels in distress, though in my experience the damsels of the Windy City are well able to look after themselves. Now and then I'll step in, against my better judgment, and attempt to lend a hand; just call me Don Quixote with fangs.

CHICAGO, APRIL 1938

"Myrna," I said to the apparently empty room, "you are the pip."

Myrna wouldn't leave the office radio alone and kept changing the station to dance music when I wanted to hear the sports scores. I'd dial it back, but soon as I sat down, she'd switch to dance music again.

"Five minutes," I said, twisting the knob. "Just lemme listen for five minutes, then pick whatever you like."

She gave no reply until I was behind my desk, then Bing Crosby crooned from the speaker, smooth as butter, the volume twice as high as normal.

"Okay. You win. Just turn it down so I can work."

After a moment, the volume eased. She'd made her point.

Arguing with a dame gets you nowhere fast.

Arguing with a ghost dame who happens to be haunting your nightclub is just plain screwy, but some nights I'm a slow learner.

I could imagine her putting on a smug smile, though I had no idea what she looked like. She'd been a lady bartender killed by shrapnel from a fragmentation grenade during a gang war that began and ended years before I bought the building. The bloodstain marking where she'd bled to death was visible on the floor behind the lobby bar. I'd replaced the tiles a few times, but the stain always reappeared.

Myrna was quirky, but as ghosts go—and I don't have much experience—she was okay. She seemed to like me and my friends, and even helped out at the club's bar, moving bottles around. Sometimes she played with the lights, which was hell when we had a stage show going, but I didn't mind much. She was usually undemanding, comfortable company, just not at present.

Maybe she was bored. I could sympathize. The nights got long for me, too, though I had worldly distractions to keep me busy.

I hammered various keys on my adding machine, pulled the lever, then wrote the result into the correct ledger column. It being Sunday night, my club was closed, and I used the time to check stocks and balance the books. The place was quiet, except for the radio.

Myrna must have changed her mind: Bing's voice faded

and ceased altogether with a soft click. The dial no longer glowed. She'd switched it off, which was odd. I held still and listened, and downstairs in the chrome-trimmed lobby a visitor rapped insistently on the front door.

Someone must have spotted my Studebaker in its reserved slot in the side parking lot and knew I was putting in extra time. A customer would have seen the CLOSED sign and noticed the lights were off. A friend wanting to visit would have phoned so I could leave the door unlocked. My partner and my girlfriend had their own keys, so it could be anybody. Might as well find out what the problem was, and it would be a problem, hopefully not a lethal one.

I'm not being melodramatic. I have aggravated a number of people in Chicago's underworld. My last two years have, to wildly understate things, been harrowing. On my first day in town I ran afoul of some gangsters, which led to my untimely death, which led to a lot of other things that I would rather not go into. The end result put me in this office doing the books on a Sunday night and wondering if yet another mug on the wrong side of the law had plans to ventilate me.

Taking a shortcut, I vanished, sank through the floor, angling to the left, and then re-formed in the lobby with nary a hair out of place.

It's ghostlike, but I'm *un*dead, not dead.

That's spelled v-a-m-p-i-r-e.

Look it up in *Webster's,* but don't take the definitions as gospel. It's given me an edge on life and hard times, and I keep quiet about it. People will forgive you for having Mob associations, but let them find out you visit the Stockyards every few nights to drink blood and it's a pitchfork parade with torches followed by a hammer-and-stake party.

Okay, *that* was melodramatic, but why take chances? What I drank in private was my own business.

The small light behind the lobby bar was on; Myrna liked it that way, but the rest of the space was dim and echoed the rappings of my visitor. I could make out a shape through the frosted-glass windows set in the doors. The height and build indicated the caller was female, and so it proved when I opened up. She was plump, looked as if she'd just come from church in her best black clothes, and under one arm was a paper-wrapped parcel tied with string. She wore a short-brimmed hat, and a thick black veil obscured the top half of her face. A purse dangled from her other arm, which was raised to knock again. She rocked back with a little "oh" of surprise.

"Jack Fleming," she said decisively, taking in my rolled-up shirtsleeves and unbuttoned collar. The day had been warm, or so I'd been told, the night temperate enough to throw open the windows.

"Maybe."

"I'm Emma Dorsey. You don't know me, but I do costuming work over at the Nightcrawler Club."

Good enough. The memory prompt reminded me that I knew her by sight, if not to speak to; I recalled a youngish woman of her proportions floating about backstage with the leggy, giggling dancers. There should be a pleasant face under the veil, a match to her soft voice, and neatly combed hair the same color as her dress.

I motioned her in with a word of welcome.

"What is it, something for Bobbi Smythe?" My girlfriend was a professional singer and might have placed a costume order. If her outfit was so skimpy as to fit inside the parcel, which looked about half the length of a shoebox, then I couldn't wait to see her in it.

"N-no, nothing like that. I need help, and I shouldn't even ask, but I'm scared, and Bobbi's always said you're a straight-arrow guy and . . ."

I let her run on, steering her toward the bar.

"C-could you lock the door?"

I took a quick gander outside to see if anyone was hanging around who might spook her. The street was clear of suspicious characters. I locked up.

The general darkness within was no problem for me, but her human-normal sight and the hat veil limited her view. She finally brushed the obscuring barrier out of the way. She usually wore glasses for her work, but they were gone now, and for the first time I got the full impact of her lustrous dark eyes. Wow. Film stars would kill for big, expressive glims like those.

"Drink?" I asked. Whatever her story, it might require a jolt of alcohol.

"Oh. No, thank you. I don't drink."

"Good habit to get into," I said. I gave her a moment to explain herself, but she was taking in the high ceiling, red velvet curtains, and black and white marble tile floors. Mine was a swank operation, and I was proud of it. "Like my place?"

"I've seen it from the outside, but never been in. It's very nice." She sounded distracted. Her heart pattered fast, and I could smell fear.

"I'll put some lights on, give you a tour."

"Oh! No lights. Please! I'm sorry, I'm doing this badly. I don't know where to start."

"You'll get to it. Let's go to my office. Bar stools aren't comfortable when you're sober."

She made a little "hmm" sound of hesitation but followed me upstairs. The office door was open. It had been shut when I'd vanished from the room. Myrna was being helpful, probably curious, too.

I got Emma Dorsey to sit on my new sofa and pulled up a chair to face her. She perched primly on the edge and fumbled the parcel so it rested on her lap. The way her gloved fingers twitched around like nervous butterflies gave me to understand that she didn't care much for the contents. It was wrapped in plain brown paper, just the way those ads in the backs of magazines promise, and the string was a thick, sturdy twine tied in a bow. No address was visible.

"What do you need help with, Mrs. Dorsey?" I asked.

"Um . . . it's Miss Dorsey, but call me Emma, everyone does, and it's about my boyfriend . . . my fiancé, I mean. I'm still getting used to that." She plucked off her gloves and put them in her purse, then tucked it next to her. No engagement ring, so the change must have been recent.

"Congratulations. Who's the lucky man?"

"Joe Graedon." She briefly pulled in her lower lip, her breath giving a hitch as she waited for a response.

"Don't think I've met him."

"Um . . . yes, you have. He works for Gordy. At the Nightcrawler."

"Lots of guys do."

"You might know him as Foxtrot Joe?"

"Ah." I tried not to give a reaction, but she was watching and saw what she expected.

"He loves me," she said, as though that explained everything.

Love is responsible for nearly every kind of insanity in the world, though greed, vanity, and pure meanness contribute their portion to the general misery. I'm usually in favor of love, the good kind, the kind that's between me and my girl, but Bobbi and I were a match. I couldn't see Emma and Foxtrot Joe passing each other on the street, much less walking hand in hand in the same direction. She was plump and cheery, he was hard edges, as personable and tough as a brick wall, but crazier matches have happened.

He worked collections with Gino Desanctis, who answered directly to Northside Gordy, who ran the Nightcrawler Club and a large chunk of territory in Chicago. Gordy was a good friend of mine, one of the few who knew about the vampire stuff.

Relations sorted, I asked, "What's going on?"

"Joe did something stupid. He did it for me, for us. He's crazy about me, and it's not really his fault, but if I make it right, maybe Gordy won't . . . do anything."

A well-considered euphemism, that. It covered all manner

of mayhem from a severe bawling out to sinking a bullet into the head of an offender as a cautionary lesson to impart wisdom and prudence upon potential offenders.

Gordy was capable of ordering up all kinds of havoc when required, though I never stuck around to watch if I could help it. He also owed me a few favors. Emma might have heard and hoped I could work a miracle for her.

"What did Joe do?"

He'd dropped from sight with money that was not his. When a collector goes missing—along with cash—guys like Gordy tend to get homicidally annoyed. While the gangs had no problem skimming a share off the various businesses of the city, they took a dim and grim view when one of their own skimmed some for himself. Joe's continued employment, not to mention his ability to keep breathing, was in peril.

Collectors worked in pairs so they could keep an eye on each other and not get ideas, but Joe had earned a reputation for reliability, so his boss, Desanctis, let him loose on his own once in a while.

"Then," said Miss Dorsey, "Joe started talking about us getting married and how we didn't have enough money, but I thought we did. I don't need a fancy ring. A plain gold band was good enough for my mother and it's good enough for me, but Joe said he wanted only the best."

It didn't sound right. She was sincere, but none of this tender consideration for a prospective bride went with what I knew about Foxtrot. He had gotten the name from the way he'd roughhoused a slow-to-pay gambler twice his size. The larger man took a swing; Joe took a swing. The gambler staggered back several strangely graceful steps before slamming into a slot machine, which fell on him when he hit the floor. It knocked him out for a week, and when he woke up he didn't remember the debt. He still had to pay it—and for the machine. Joe hung around the hospital and made sure. After that, Joe had only to smile at deadbeats and ask if they wanted to dance.

"It's not like he took the money that was going to his boss," she went on. "He had people put a dollar or more on top of that, and it added up. He wasn't stealing, this was more like getting a tip."

Foxtrot raised a total of eight hundred bucks, which gave me an idea of just how profitable and wide-ranging an operation it was. He'd collected almost a year's pay in less than a week. I was in the wrong business, what with trying to be honest.

"A tip." My tone was completely neutral.

"He did it for me. He's crazy about me. I told him not to, but he just couldn't help himself."

If he was getting tips on top of regular collections, no one would say a word. A few bucks going to Foxtrot was cheaper than a hospital stay.

"Look, if Gordy doesn't know about these tips, then—"

"He *does* know. Someone complained last night to him, now Gino Desanctis has people looking for Joe. That's why I asked you to lock the door. They've been watching my place, I guess to see if he came by. I sneaked out with my landlady's family. They were going to evening Mass, and I just stayed in the middle of them and got on the El. I was going to the Nightcrawler, but I got so shaky and scared. Then I remembered Bobbi talking about how you sometimes helped people, so I took a chance that you might be open tonight. But the place was dark, and then I saw the lights in the upstairs and——"

"What do you need me for?" I could guess, but she'd worked herself up to it, and it wouldn't be polite to take it from her.

"I was hoping you could go with me to see Gordy. I——I don't think I could get the story out with Gordy watching me."

Gordy was intimidating as hell to guys who killed for a living, never mind the effect of his steady gaze on this plump little seamstress. But with or without me, she had a bad night ahead.

"I'll go along for moral support, but understand that Joe's in for it. I can't interfere with how Gordy does business."

"But don't you work for him, too? You ran the club and—and the other things. . . ."

I'd reluctantly filled Gordy's big shoes for a brief and terrible time while he recovered from a case of lead poisoning caught during a botched assassination attempt. "Just the once, and I wasn't in charge so much as a target. Some of those guys still hate me for it."

Desanctis was one of them, but he'd been smart enough not to act on it at the time. He'd kept his distance to watch and wait for me to fall on my face, which didn't exactly happen. He wouldn't appreciate me putting my nose into this, though.

"You think they'll kill Joe."

"I couldn't say." There was a remote chance that they'd beat him to hell and gone and kick him out of Chicago, but I didn't want to get her hopes up. An execution was far more likely.

"But if he gives *back* the money, wouldn't that make a difference?"

"It's not about the money, but the fact he took it in the first place. They can't trust him. Crazy as it sounds, the gangs run on trust same as any other business. If a clerk steals money from the till, they're gonna fire him, no matter if he returns everything."

She looked down, visibly crushed, fingers brushing the sides of the parcel.

"What d'ya have there?"

"Joe left it for me. It was outside my door this evening. With a note. He explained what he did and why and what I had to do. I tried calling him, but I guess he's hiding. It's the money—all of it. He wrote that if I took this to Gordy, it would make things right. He doesn't dare go in himself."

"May I?"

She handed it over with no hesitation, a gleam of hope in her gorgeous dark eyes. I felt bad for inspiring that kind of trust. In my heart I knew hers was a lost cause.

The box felt a little heavy. Even eight hundred one-dollar bills wouldn't weigh much of anything. Maybe some of it was in coin. I shook it, but nothing shifted or clinked.

"Here," she said, pulling the loose ends of the bow. "He told me to wait for Gordy to open it, but you should check—"

The bow did not come undone; the twine slipped an inch and caught. She automatically gave it a strong yank with me reflexively tightening my grip on the box to brace it, and suddenly the string dangled free in her hand, a large metal ring looped fast to the intact bow.

In the space between one of her heartbeats and the next, I glimpsed a slit in the paper where the ring had popped out, and a dreadful understanding jolted me to panicked action. I lobbed the parcel behind the couch and flung Emma bodily through the doorway so quick and hard, she didn't have time to blink.

I can move fast, but even my unnatural speed wasn't enough for me to follow *and* pull the door shut behind. Instead, I used my momentum to slam it closed and vanished just as a hideous flat *BANG* clubbed the room into perdition.

A discharge of countless tiny *things* gusted through the space I'd occupied, the concussion flattening my invisible and formless self against the door, which shifted violently in reaction to the blast. It was like an army of machine gunners firing in unison for just one second. A Thompson can spit a dozen slugs in a single tick of the clock.

I'd been through this before, believe it or not, an experience I'd thought never to repeat.

But it was over. One horrible explosion and dusty silence.

It was safe. I could re-form and go solid.

Any time now.

No hurry.

No hurry at all.

A faint whimper from the hall drew me out of hiding. Emma.

I forced my terrified self to ooze back into solidity.

The office door was wood veneer over thick metal, specially made to keep intruders from breaking in to find me apparently dead on the sofa during the day. The thing was heavy and required an extra-strong metal frame to support the weight.

In the wake of the explosion it hung loose by one twisted hinge, steel showing through where the wood had been flayed off. I made a grab just as it gave and propped it against the wall with no small respect. The door had done its job of protection, just not in a way I could have anticipated.

Emma was facedown across the thin hall rug, moving feebly, glory hallelujah. Bruised and breathless and paralyzed with shock was a *good* state to be in. By the grace of God, an armored door, a four-second fuse, and yours truly having damned fast reflexes, she'd *not* been shredded into a bloody corpse by her fiancé's parting present.

The sheer wickedness of it—and I'd seen more than my share in the last two years—sickened and infuriated me. I wanted to put a fist right through Foxtrot Joe's face. I nearly put one through the wall, but there was enough damage to the joint.

Shaking as well from unspent adrenaline, I helped a violently trembling Emma to the washroom and put her on the toilet seat before her legs gave out. The light was gone, but I kept flashlights in every room in the place. Myrna's predilection for playing with the electrics made them a necessity. I found the one under the sink and clicked it on. I can see fine in the dark, but I need help in windowless spaces like this one.

Emma was drained white, her breathing down to little panicky hiccups. I told her everything was all right, because that's what we both needed to hear, and gave her a glass of water. I had to help her hold it. She got one sip, then turned away, coughing. Wetting a towel, I made her put her head down and eased the towel onto the back of her neck. When I was sure she wouldn't fall over, I went to check the remains of my office.

The walls were pocked and holed, lath and plaster exposed, dust everywhere. The desk was riddled with shrapnel. The lights were out; anything made of glass was shattered. The liquor cabinet in the corner leaked like a boozy Niagara. It hadn't been hit, the concussion had been sufficient.

The sofa was inside out, with stuffing all over. Just as well that I'd vanished. The metal shards of the grenade would have gone right through my body—hellishly painful—but wood was deadly. Even if a piece missed my heart or didn't tear into my brain through an eye socket, I could bleed to death with dozens of splinters piercing my skin.

The two windows overlooking the street had been open to air out the office and had allowed some of the force of the blast to escape. Both swung outward and were wire reinforced and bulletproofed, so they were intact, but the blinds and curtains were shredded. I crunched across the debris-choked floor and checked the neighborhood.

The shops and other businesses were closed and Sunday-night quiet a block either way. There were no residences in the area, so no out-of-place cars or startled pedestrians caught my eye. No watchful bad guys lurked in the false security of alley shadows.

I heard a click from the radio, the sound it makes when you switch it on. The dial remained dark. The speaker had shrapnel stuck in it, and every tube inside the case must now be junk.

"I'll get you a new one, Myrna," I said aloud. "Are you okay?"

Not that I expected a reply, but she had ways of making her presence known.

Nothing. Which worried me.

I'm nuts. There was a live dame in my washroom in need of help, and here I was anxious about a dead one. But Myrna was a friend, even if I had never seen her.

"It was a grenade, honey. That's why I'm asking."

Total silence clotted the room like a physical thing. For a second I thought I'd gone deaf; it was that profound. The temperate air drifting through the windows turned deathly cold and still. I breathed in to speak again, and it was too thick to use. I had to make do with what was left in the bottom of my lungs, and my voice came out high and wheezy.

"Myrna, honey . . . you okay?"

The chill got colder and colder still. Gooseflesh galloped up my arms and pinched the back of my neck. The feeling in the room turned oppressive, the weight of it so great that if my heart could beat, it might have stopped from the excess pressure. I'd never felt *anything* like this from her before. Though fairly immune to cold, I gave in to a sudden shiver.

"Myrn—"

Icy wind howled to unexpected life around me, blowing *outward* through the windows. A terrific cloud of plaster dust and stuffing whipped past, stinging my eyes.

"M-Myrna—calm down!"

Now that was stupid. *Never* tell an angry female to calm down. It just makes things worse. The lady rattled me through and through.

The door, propped at an angle, suddenly shifted and toppled like a tree, making a heavy, oddly musical *whannnng* when it struck the floor. The ventilated desk shifted as though being shoved by an invisible Charles Atlas, shooting broadside across the floor until it slammed the wall behind. My sturdy chair, caught between, broke into sticks.

Papers swirled; I grabbed what I could reach, then gave up and fled before any wood shards got picked up in the storm and started slicing me.

"Jeeze," I muttered, getting out of the line of fire from the gaping doorway. Papers fluttered out and sifted down. All the wind was confined to the office.

The ghosts in movies and plays weren't like this. They moved ponderously slow or stood in place, looking unearthly. Myrna was throwing things around like an invisible, intelligent tornado.

After all this time, she'd finally scared me.

I shouldn't have mentioned the grenade. Considering how

she'd died, she was bound to be sensitive about that kind of thing.

I hustled toward the washroom, thinking to get Emma out until things settled.

She still had the wet towel on the back of her neck and her head between her knees. She began to straighten.

"It's just me," I said. "How you doing?"

"What's all that noise?"

"Wind. Looks like we might get some rain."

She didn't question it and kept her head down, asking if I was all right. I made sure she hadn't broken anything from being pitched out and told her what had prompted the action. She wanted to know how I'd escaped.

"I dove behind the desk. Got lucky."

"B–but a *bomb*? There was a bomb in the box?"

"Not a big one," I said, glad she couldn't see me wincing. If I could still hypnotize people, I'd have eased her right over this part of things.

Myrna must have tuckered herself out: the office-sized cyclone abruptly ceased. The building went silent again, the normal sort, not the pending disaster kind.

"J-Joe left that for *me*? . . ." Emma straightened, tears spilling from her eyes. "He meant for me to take it t-t-to Gordy and *kill* us. . . ."

Another stupid thing to do is to tell a female to not cry. I knew better. My girlfriend was not the kind to turn on the waterworks gladly or often, but she'd taught me how to deal with them. There were five thousand other matters I had to see to before dawn came, but I put an arm around Emma, offering her one end of the toilet tissue to unreel to soak up her tears.

She cut loose, loud and ugly, but I couldn't fault her for it, not one damned bit. I wanted to kill Foxtrot for doing this to her.

Maybe I would.

Emma's initial reaction eased, and she lurched up with determined strength, spun in place, and yanked up the toilet lid just in time.

I'd done my duty holding her while she cried, but Bobbi hadn't said a word about what to do when a lady is being sick. I backed off, glad I didn't need to breathe, and looked the other way. Some instinct told me to start the water in the sink, so I did that, then backed the rest of the way out of the little room.

Right into Gino Desanctis, Foxtrot Joe's boss. He looked as surprised as I felt.

I glared at him, an intruder in my territory and indirectly responsible for Foxtrot. Hardly aware of the action, I slugged Desanctis square in the gut.

He folded and dropped, but he wasn't alone. The two guys behind him surged forward to teach me manners, and I took them out just as quick.

There was a *third* man behind them, but he stayed in place, calmly regarding the rumpus.

"Greetin's to ye, Jacky-lad," he boomed cheerfully. That Irish accent . . .

He flipped open a lighter, the little flame overwhelmed by the gloom of the hall, but enough to show his face.

"Riordan?" I returned, unpleasantly surprised. He was supposed to be a private investigator but was happy enough to ignore the law when it suited his bank account. We'd had a few run-ins, none of them good. The first time we met, he'd broken my shoulder with a tire iron. He had been aiming for my skull. "What the hell are you doing here?"

He held the lighter with a steady hand. Me punching flat three of Gordy's best didn't deserve so much as an eye twitch. He'd seen me cut loose on bigger and tougher guys and not break a sweat. "Those fine lads strewin' the floor are looking for Emma Dorsey."

Riordan had an egg-shaped balding head under a rakish hat, plenty of teeth, and brown eyes topped by arching brows. They gave him an ingrained expression of perpetual naïveté that he wholeheartedly exploited when he thought he could get away with it. In truth, he was as clever-brained as they come, but certifiably insane. If some head doctor locked the Irish bastard in a booby hatch, I'd have been glad to lose the key.

"You're looking for Foxtrot, you mean," I said.

"They are for certain. The lads an' me were havin' such a nice game of billiards when Gino came by wantin' 'em to earn their keep. Seein' that one owes me three dollars and the other owes me four, I'm keepin' an eye on 'em till we finish our game. Have ye seen our Foxtrot?"

"No."

"What about the lovely lady we followed here?" He pulled out a cigarette.

"She's not feeling well. Foxtrot tried to scrag her with a grenade rigged in a box. It was meant for her and Northside Gordy."

Riordan let the lighter burn a fraction longer than needed to fire up his smoke. "So that was the mighty flash and bang we saw from the street. A grenade, y'say? Sure?"

I glanced at the floor where Emma had landed. The twine bow and the ring with its attached pin lay almost at his feet. I pointed at it and at the now quiet office. "What do you think?"

He picked up the twine, then peered in the room. Not much glow from the streetlight came in the windows, but he saw what he needed to see. "Damn. You're one lucky mother's son. The lady's all right?" His tone changed, losing its usual sardonic grate, his accent softening.

"Shaken but in one piece."

"Glad to hear it." He switched back to what I had thought was his normal voice. "Y'say that was her fella's doin'?"

"She thought she was returning the money Foxtrot took. He left her a note to take it to Gordy, but we opened—"

Desanctis lurched from the floor, favoring his bruised middle, and pulled a revolver from his shoulder holster a second short of getting his full balance. I was on him and grabbed the gun away, my hand freezing on the barrel to keep it from turning. He was startled, then swung a fist, but I stepped out of range, too ready pop him again. It had felt good to have a target.

"Oh, now, Gino. Leave the man be," said Riordan, a little sharply. "We're all friends here."

Desanctis put the brakes on, glaring. "You saw it, he busted me."

"This hall's darker than the inside of Satan's arse. He didn't know ye."

I went with his lead. There was more going on here than Riordan looking after his pool hall bets. "I thought you were Foxtrot come to look at the blood."

"Gimme my piece. I'll show you blood." The man was not interested in explanations and clearly not used to coming in second in a fight. I am tall, but on the lean side; he had an inch and fifty pounds on me, all of it muscle. Most guys never challenged that combination; the others rarely lived to regret it. Desanctis was one of those specialists who knew all the finer points about how to turn people into fish food.

"That's *over*, Gino." Riordan's voice had gone ominously low and level, his eyes narrow and razor sharp. He got a surly grunt in reply.

"Keep it put away," I told Desanctis, handing the gun back butt first. "This is my place; only I am allowed to shoot people here."

He snorted contempt and called me a goddamned punk, which was an accurate description, so I let it pass. We were about the same age—late thirties—but I look a lot younger. I've gotten used to hearing "punk" flung my way.

"How'd you get in?" I asked Riordan.

"Picked the back door lock." He inhaled deeply from his cigarette and blew the smoke to one side. "Took a few minutes. That's good-quality brass you got for keepin' out the riffraff."

I accepted the compliment with mixed emotions and vowed to find a locksmith who could install something better. "Thanks for not breaking the door down."

"Seemed best not to irritate the landlord. You've quite the temper, or so I've seen."

There was little point discussing his lack of haste to get inside. He knew something about explosions. If you don't hear screaming afterward, chances are high that no one survived, and you don't want to see what's left.

"I'm thinkin' we should take this news to Gordy, along with the lady," said Riordan.

Exactly what I planned to do.

"We keep looking for Foxtrot," said Desanctis, helping one of his men up. "I'm not running to the boss every time something don't work out. We got the dame. She'll know where Foxtrot is."

Without being too obvious, I put myself between them and the washroom. "If she did, she'd have contacted him by now. He set her up. Guess he thought if she could knock off Gordy, we'd be too distracted to go after him." I'd purposely included myself in matters. It was time. Any bastard trying to kill a nice gal like Emma deserved my personal attention. "But why would he do that for a lousy eight hundred?"

"And Gordy put you in charge." A scornful Desanctis got the second man on his feet. "What does this dump turn that makes *that* lousy money?"

I looked at Riordan. "What'd I miss?"

"Books have been gone over, sums have been added, and stacks of lolly counted and counted again. There's eight hundred *thousand* missing from this month's take, Jacky-lad."

It required a long, still moment for me to absorb that large a sum. Such numbers weren't real. They had to be made up. That kind of money was for governments, not people. I'd known the scale of Gordy's operation was huge, but not that huge. "Jeeze."

"Y'can imagine Gordy's not in the least amused."

He wouldn't show it. Maybe his pale eyes would be a little harder than normal. If Foxtrot had any sense, he'd be on his way to Outer Mongolia and hoping it would be far enough. So much cash explained why Riordan was hanging around. If there was a chance in hell for him to nab some of it . . .

"Come on," said Desanctis. "Let's get the skirt and—"

"Take her to Gordy," I finished. "He'll want to talk with her. Riordan, bring that grenade pin. I'm going to shove it down Foxtrot's throat." I took a step toward the washroom, and my foot caught on something. Emma's purse. It hadn't been there before. Myrna again, now in a helpful mood.

I picked up the little bag and looked in on Emma. She'd set the flashlight on its end on the floor like a candle. She had apparently heard everything and looked anxious.

"You ready to travel?" I asked, voice low.

"Guess I have to be. But those men . . ."

"Are gonna behave. I'll stick by you. If I have to be someplace, you get next to the Irishman out there named Riordan.

He's crazy, but he'll look after you. He's got a soft spot for women."

"I know him. He's kind of scary."

"Right now you need scary friends."

She gave a brief, blotchy grimace, accepted her handbag, pulled on her gloves, and stood straight. Not much height to her, but plenty of poise. I got the flashlight and backed out like a knight making way for his lady.

"Gentlemen," I said, certain none would take exception to the irony, "Miss Emma Dorsey needs a safe escort to the Nightcrawler Club."

Riordan's eyes flickered with amusement as he swept off his hat. "It's my specialty and privilege to be of service to ye, missy. Shamus Riordan, me name is me game, spell it the same."

Desanctis growled under his breath, then spoke aloud. "Where's your boyfriend, Emma?"

"I don't know. That's God's honest truth."

"He ain't hiding in your flat, we checked, so where else would he go?"

She shook her head, glancing at me.

"The lady doesn't know," I said. "You're familiar with how he does business. Where do you think he'd go?"

"We checked those places. He ain't in any of 'em."

"Then figure he's on a train, bus, or car with a hell of a head start. You cover the stations?"

"In this town and all stops between here and both oceans. With eight hundred grand running loose, we got more eyes than J. Edgar Hoover."

"You didn't tell them about the money, did you?"

"Of course not."

"Foxtrot can buy his way past anyone with it."

"That he can," said Riordan, looking pleased.

"You're after the money," I said, unsurprised.

"Why, Jacky-lad, on the life of my sainted aunt Murgatroyd, of course I am. A man can go far and live high forever on that much lolly."

"Until we find you," Desanctis pointed out. He didn't sound worried that Riordan would get anywhere near the cash.

"Well, life's uncertain, Gino. I'd live well for as long as I could. That's all any of us have till Saint Peter whispers in your ear."

It was an impossible quest. Foxtrot had time to put himself anywhere, either to hole up until the initial search slacked off or to get as far away as possible. If it had been me, I'd have hired a pilot and flown south to a whole different continent.

"Been watching Emma's place?" I asked as we trooped unhurriedly down to the lobby.

"We went by to see if she'd join up with her boyfriend," said Desanctis.

"Why didn't you talk to her sooner?"

"Dames are funny when they're gone on a guy. They clam up no matter what you do to 'em. It was a better bet to have her lead us to him."

Emma's hand, which was on my arm, tightened its grip. I did not ask how Desanctis came by his information about women. I'd already slugged him once tonight and didn't need a fresh excuse.

"The delay gave Foxtrot a big head start," I observed.

We reached the lobby floor, and Desanctis rounded on me. "What are you saying, Fleming? You think I *wanted* that bastard to run off? My head's on the block for this."

He might lose his job and get sent somewhere disagreeable as punishment, but Gordy was a fair man—in his own way. He wouldn't order Desanctis put down without a compelling reason. Good help's hard to find, and the man was good at his job.

"Why did she come to you, anyway?" he wanted to know.

"Emma needed someone to get her in to see the boss."

"Maybe you're helping the two of them lam it out of here."

"Yeah, that makes perfect sense what with that grenade nearly killing us."

"Neither one of you's got a scratch. Maybe you set it off on purpose."

"Gino, why would I blow up my own office? How could that possibly help either of them escape?"

He had no answer. While he was good at collections, it was a job that did not require much brain.

The light behind the lobby bar was still on. I'd had the idea that electricity for the whole building was gone. We took the curved hall into the main room and found the lights on there as well.

"Who else is here?" Desanctis wanted to know.

"Just us."

"Someone put those on. We didn't."

"The building's got electrical problems, always has. Ask anyone."

The floor tables were stripped of their cloths, with chairs stacked on them upside down. They gave the huge room a forlorn appearance. The fixed tiers of booths arranged in a rising horseshoe shape with the open end toward the stage looked more normal. All they needed were people, but there was no show tonight. The stage was dark, its empty boards thick with sullen shadows. I was aware of every mood of this place, and it didn't like being closed.

Our footsteps created hard echoes from the black and white tiles, turned hollow as we crossed the wood dance floor, then resumed hard again. A service door on the other side of the stage took us to a wide hall. It gave access to the basement, backstage dressing rooms, and wide double doors to the alley.

"Why didn't you guys come in the front?" I asked.

"Didn't want to get noticed," said Riordan. "We saw the great boom, left a lad on watch for cops, and Gino kindly got the back open."

"There's a guy? I didn't see him."

"He's in the doorway of the haberdasher's shop across from ye."

I stopped short of pushing forward to the outside. "No, he isn't."

"The streetlight doesn't reach. Deep shadow."

"Riordan, I'd have seen him. I took a look out the office window after the boom. He wasn't there."

Desanctis shoved past. "So what, he moved. Come on."

The lights flickered off-on, just the once. Myrna's communication was limited, but that was her way of sending up the alarm. I stayed put, and Riordan and the others hung back with me, looking uneasy. Desanctis held the back door and watched us watch him for a long moment. He glanced either way in the alley.

"No one's here," he stated.

I transferred Emma's hand to Riordan's arm. "How 'bout I check and make sure?"

"We'll both check." Desanctis took the direction leading to the street, I went toward the parking lot. Two vehicles were there: my still-new Studebaker coupé and next to it what was probably his car, a blue Hudson.

Both had flat tires: driver's-side front on mine, passenger front on the Hudson.

Crap.

Feeling vulnerable, I ducked between the cars, probably in the same spot where the vandal had crouched with something sharp. He had efficiently cut off our means of escape, barring a footrace out of here. The mental picture of our little group sprinting along in full rout, getting picked off one by one by a pursuer shooting from cover, I could blame on a too-vivid imagination. That was not going to happen, but once the thought crossed my paranoid mind, I couldn't shake it.

I didn't care to attempt changing a flat until long after this party left the neighborhood—which would be soon. We were only temporarily stuck. A phone call to Gordy would bring in transport and as many armed mugs as he deemed appropriate. He wouldn't mind.

First, I needed a quick look at the street.

Back to the wall, I eased along, checking everything in my angle of view, my hand twitching, missing a reassuring weight that should have been there. I kept a gun in my office, hadn't thought to bring it along, and I should have. Yeah, I know, I'm a big bad vampire, but Chicago's a rough town. Even the undead need an edge. That damned grenade must have knocked all sense out of my noggin. There were no windows on this side of the club. I could ooze my way through the bricks to get in and raid the top desk drawer, but it would be easier to borrow a gun from Riordan. He always carried more than one.

The shop doorway was indeed empty. A narrow alley divided the opposite block; the ash cans crowding it would make good cover. Half a dozen other doors and nooks offered shelter and were within shooting range. Until now, I'd never thought about the exterior of my club in terms of attack and defense.

I put my head around the corner, letting myself fade from full solidity. My sight dimmed, but in this state a bullet would pass harmlessly through my skull. No one fired, but I did spot what looked like a drunk taking a nap in the club's entry. He was right under the red awning that ran from the door to the curb. I wouldn't have been able to see him from the office window.

Still slightly incorporeal, I drifted toward him; my legs were moving, but I was really floating silently over the sidewalk.

Reaching the shadow under the canopy, I went solid to check for a pulse. The man was limp as wet laundry, but alive. Someone had coshed him good.

He wasn't Foxtrot Joe.

He was positioned so that when the front door opened, he'd fall back and in, blocking the way and providing a distraction. Someone must have thought we'd come out this way. I whipped around, alert to threats, but nothing happened.

Having completed his half-circuit of the building, Desanctis barreled up, face red with fury, his gun out. I put my finger to my lips and hastily signed for him to get down, but he wasn't interested. He kept moving, heading toward the parking lot and rounding the corner. His ripe and heartfelt swearing carried, signaling that he'd found the flat tires.

I had my keys and opened the front door and, with a grim sense of déjà vu, dragged in the casualty. The other time, the guy being dragged had caught a bullet in his leg, so I wasn't experiencing the same kind of life-and-death panic. I was pissed off.

"Heads up, Myrna, we got more trouble." I pulled my burden out of the way so he wouldn't be stepped on accidentally.

I'd had an extra phone installed behind the bar, a fancy one. Punch a button you get my office, punch another and you can make an outside call. It was past time to let Gordy know what was going on. If Foxtrot was hanging around, we might have a chance of grabbing him.

But the phone was dead, its line ripped from the wall.

That wasn't Myrna's style; Foxtrot must have found a way inside. But why? If he had the money, then why risk himself? I checked the lobby's alcove phone booth and found it had also been sabotaged. The receiver lay on the floor, trailing a short tail of cut wire.

Drawing a breath to curse, I caught the scent of human blood hanging in the still air. A second breath, mouth open . . . I could almost *taste* it. Fresh, mixed with sweat, the distinct sour tang of fear, and, above all, *immediacy*—he'd been here scant moments ago.

No hiding places in the lobby; I would have noticed anyone taking cover under the naked tables and stacked chairs and had already been behind the bar.

Going still, I listened, sifting out the breathing of the unconscious man, the distant sounds of city traffic, Riordan holding forth on the other side of the building, the creak as wind played on the awning outside, the clock above the bar ticking, my watch a tiny counterpoint to it . . .

For the barest second, I caught the rasp of air against vocal cords. It took more effort to pin down a direction for that faintest of whispers . . . but I got him.

He was in one of the restrooms. The closer of the two, the ladies' lounge. It was just past the bar, and if you cracked the door, you could see a good section of the front. He'd taken out the front man, left him as a decoy. While we were busy with him, Foxtrot could sneak up behind. The ambush was meant to be *inside,* not out. So why hadn't he tried for me? Was he waiting for the others?

Desanctis barged in, pausing right in the line of fire to snarl something at me, but I launched at him. We hit the hard marble tile in front of the bar with bone-bruising force a hair ahead of the flat crack of a gunshot. The bullet snapped into a wall on the other side of the room but missed us, and that's all that mattered.

I was okay, but it knocked out his air. The single-minded idiot tried to bring his gun around. I slammed it fiercely down and clapped a hand over his mouth, hoping he'd take the hint. He couldn't move, was struggling to breathe. I took my hand away and signed for him to be quiet.

He wheezed and nodded, finally figuring out more important things were going on and that he'd better pay attention.

"Foxtrot's here, hiding in one of the johns," I murmured.

A flash of wide-eyed disbelief, then Desanctis looked ready to pop a blood vessel. Teeth showing, he started up, but I grabbed him back.

"He's in too good a spot, he'll scrag us both. There's a service door for the janitor. I'll get in that way, come up behind him. You stay put. Make him think we're both out here."

He grunted cooperatively. I hurried toward the curving hall to the main room, while he hunkered down at the end of the bar to cover the lounge door. As soon as he turned from me I vanished, changed course, and floated right past him, a necessity since there was no such service entry. Desanctis might have felt a deadly chill as I went by. Unable to see in this form, I had to bump and bumble along by memory and the awareness of solid shapes between me and my goal. This was a stool, that bulk to the right was the bar, skim along a vertical plain of wall on the left, and for the love of Mike *don't* miss the door.

I found it and slipped quickly under the threshold crack and in. My hearing was limited; I couldn't locate Foxtrot by sound, so I cast about with what should be my arms, a blind, invisible monster trying to find its prey before anyone else got hurt.

He was on the floor just inside, right where I'd have been. This close and I could hear his quick, labored breathing. I set myself and went solid, and he was too surprised to react when his gun was suddenly yanked away.

His back propped against the wall, he held the door open a few inches with one outstretched leg. He shifted and the door shut automatically, cutting off most of the light. There was some glow seeping through the red-tinted windows, enough for me, but he'd be blinkered. Just as well; I didn't want him noticing how the mirrors here kept missing me.

I tried a reasonable tone. "All right, Foxtrot, game's over—"

He flopped on one side, throwing his right arm wide to grab. I backed away and smelled fresh blood again, a lot of it, mixed with the sharp, sweet odor of cordite from his one shot. The red color of the window glass made it difficult to see, but his middle was soaked. He held his left arm tight there, panting with pain. His voice was slurred and rushed. "Who izzit?"

"Jack Fleming."

He grunted disgust and stopped trying to find me. "Na' dead."

"In so many words, not quite." I was being strangely polite to him, considering the dirtiness of the grenade trick. His wounding puzzled me, and tardy alarm bells only I could hear went off inside my thick skull. I cursed while pocketing the gun and grabbed him under the arms to drag him out of the way, exactly as I'd done for the fellow in the lobby.

He did not resist. " 'f tha' bas'ard's hurt her . . ."

"She's fine, Joe." I eased him down flat, got towels from a cupboard under the sinks, and pressed a wad of them to whatever damage he'd taken. "Hold it there, can you do that?"

He made no reply, responding by dropping a bloody arm over the makeshift dressing. "Emma . . ."

"Keep quiet."

I opened the door and called out to Desanctis, "It's clear, Gino, I got him."

Desanctis was already in the hall, striding forward, gun raised, which I did not expect, which was damned stupid, but I faded just as he fired. It was such a near thing that I felt the sharp passage of the slug tugging with miserable familiarity through my chest, and it was enough to startle me into vanishing completely.

Dimly, I heard the door thump shut.

Damnation.

I went solid, listening. Desanctis was just on the other side, certainly doing the same thing, reluctant to try the door until he was sure he'd gotten me. It was dark for him; the disruptive flash from his gun would have prevented him from seeing me wink out. I shoved hard on the door to knock him silly, but he skipped back and fired three times right through at chest height, and *that* did the trick.

I dropped like a bag of sand, nerve and muscle in shock from the bullets' passage. The lead shattered bone, seared flesh, and I'd have screamed had there been breath. Instead, I made an ugly choking sound down in my throat and thrashed like a fish. I should have vanished, but something short-circuited things. Blood flowed out front and back, weakening me. I had to vanish to heal or—

Damned wood.

The door was made of pine panels, soft, splintery pine.

My fingers raked over the holes in my chest, clawing for the slivers that had to be there. I pulled one clear but remained solid, still bleeding.

How many more?

They were like little daggers. I had to get them all, but if they were too small or if fragments had tattooed themselves under my hide . . .

Desanctis hauled open the door. I frantically rolled out of the way of his next shot.

It was nearly pitch dark for him. I could use that—

He flicked on the light, revealing the whole appalling mess of what seemed like gallons of blood smearing the black and white tiles, Foxtrot Joe helpless on his back over there, me fumbling desperately to get one slick hand on the gun in my pants pocket, knowing I'd be too late.

Desanctis showed teeth in the bright, ferocious grin of a man who's won everything—

Then one of the heavy chrome bar stools slammed into his shoulders and head like a cannonball.

It knocked him sideways with swift and hard and decisive force. The grin was still on his mug as he hit the inside wall and slithered down, stunned.

The stool clattered metallically on the hall floor, and the door closed again.

I scrambled over to get his gun, but he was in no shape to notice.

My panic-driven strength fled, leaving behind a terrible and mounting exhaustion. I pulled more damned splinters from my skin. Daggers, hell, they were like hot needles, or maybe it was the damned bullet holes that tore another breathless scream from me.

But the instant I dragged a finger-long shard clear, that comforting gray nothingness swept me into a soft, painless haven.

It takes only a moment to heal, and then I'm all right.

Physically.

The rest of it, the recovery that may or may not come when you have to face the ghastly fact that another two-legged predator has tried to remove you from life, takes longer. Much longer. You wonder what's worse, someone murdering you in the heat of rage or coldly blotting you out simply because it makes things easier for his own nonstop and futile strivings to continue.

And I was no better; I had murdered as well. My reasons seemed good enough at the time, but it is a certainty none of them would have convinced my victims.

Maybe it's the ones who don't have a reason that sickens you the most. They carry a darkness that no one can understand. You ask why and get a shrug, and it is the truth. They don't know themselves.

Desanctis, though, knew exactly what he was doing.

Bastards like him leave behind damage that can't be stitched up by a doctor or even a supernatural edge. Parts of my soul were still in tatters from my murder two years ago.

But I can forget that when I'm like this, a ghost but not a ghost.

It is so *good* to be free of a solid body, free of gravity, free of outraged nerve endings, responsibilities, homicidal lunatics, dames in distress, and all the other insane annoyances associated with the farce of living. One of these nights I would vanish and never come back.

But not tonight. I had to get help for Foxtrot. The men who came with Desanctis might be in on things with him. Emma had to be taken somewhere safe. . . .

Solid again and on my feet, I started for the door, but it was yanked open, and by great good fortune for us both, I did not blow a hole in Shamus Riordan's head.

He gaped and pulled back, startled by something other than the gun I'd taken, probably the look on my face. It could not have been reassuring.

Thankfully he was at the wrong angle to see the mirrors,

though he did finally become aware of Desanctis and Fox-trot.

"What a riot you've had, Jacky-lad. Where'd they get you?"

"It's not my blood." I could hear the fast pounding of his heart. I shouldn't be noticing things like that, but hunger sharpened my already excellent senses. Lingering adrenaline would keep me going for a little while, but I'd have to replace what the bullets had taken, and soon. Tunnel vision would come next, then— "What'd you say?"

"Are they dead?" Riordan asked, his voice louder.

"Not yet."

"Where's that girl?"

"Emma's gone?" I asked stupidly.

"She's with me mates. I meant the other girl."

My brain began working. I was in a mood to accept the uncanny. "You didn't throw that bar stool, did you?"

"Now why would I bother when I've a perfectly good shooter?"

True. He held a pipsqueak .22 semiauto, the kind that requires good aim and doesn't make a lot of noise.

"You *saw* a girl?"

"Just a glimpse when I rounded the corner. Me an' the lads heard shots. I told 'em to get Emma out of sight, then came runnin'. A bit late, it seems."

"What'd she look like?"

"Little thing, didn't seem big enough to be throwin' furniture about."

"You've no idea."

"Where is she?"

"Look after Foxtrot. I'll call a doctor and get Gordy over here."

The bar in the main room was also equipped with a fancy phone, this one functioning. I hit the button for the outside line, dialed with a shaking and bloodstained finger, and had a quick, urgent chat with Gordy at the Nightcrawler Club. I told him a doctor was required and why, and that bringing along armed muscle would be a good idea and not to trust anything Gino Desanctis said.

"No problem," Gordy replied, and hung up.

My friend was not much for words, but an expert at getting things moving. He knew I'd answer his questions when the time was right.

Before distractions started piling up, I ducked into the storage area under the main room's tiered seating. It held bar supplies and other odds and ends, and set in the back wall was a hidden door only I knew about. I vanished and reappeared on the other side, fumbling for the light switch.

Sometimes I'd spend the day in this lightproof sanctuary. It had the necessary comforts: an army cot with an oilcloth liner holding my home earth, spare clothes, emergency cash, and books to read in the last hour before the rising sun shut my body down.

I'd recently added a small refrigerator and blessed my extravagant foresight.

Inside were beer bottles with cork stoppers, not the usual

caps. Some months ago I'd cut down my trips to the Stock-yards by siphoning cattle blood into bottles and keeping them cold. It didn't taste as good or last long, but it was a godsend now.

Two bottles left, both at the foul edge of drinkability. I downed them like an alkie just in from Death Valley. If the need got bad enough, I'd have lapped the leavings on the washroom floor. As the cold red stuff flowed sluggishly through my starved body, I was glad not to have been reduced to that humiliation. Still, it was better than assaulting any of the hapless humans under my roof.

All right, with Desanctis I'd have made an exception.

Considering what was in store, he might prefer having his blood drained by a starved vampire than to face Northside Gordy.

I shed my punctured and alarmingly blemished shirt, got a replacement, and emerged from the storage room. One of the two men who had come in with Desanctis was behind the bar and gave a guilty start. He'd been examining the beer taps.

"Where's the boss?" he wanted to know.

"That crazy Irishman's looking after him. Where's Miss Dorsey?"

"She's hiding in the basement with my pal. What's going on?"

"Nothing much. Gordy's on his way over with the cavalry. We're to sit tight."

He looked relieved, and I liked his reaction. It saved me

from punching him flat again. I switched on the tap pump and invited him to serve himself. His mood improved. I could sympathize; nothing like a drink to make you feel better.

I cleaned up in the deep sink behind the bar and pulled on the shirt.

At the basement door, I called down, and the second guy came out with Emma. She was pasty and frightened. I invited the other man to join his partner for beery refreshment and walked her around to the lounge. Riordan had its door propped open with the bar stool. Desanctis, who was still not fully awake, was trussed hand and foot with cut-up towels.

Emma stopped short. "What's happened?"

"Your fiancé's off the hook," I said.

"What do you mean?"

"He didn't leave you the grenade. Gino Desanctis did."

"He—" Unlooked-for hope flooded her face. "Joe didn't . . . ?"

"Maybe Joe skimmed money to buy you a nice ring, and maybe that's what gave Gino the idea to use him to take the fall for a bigger theft. Joe didn't try to kill you. He's been trying to save you."

"That's exactly it, missy," Riordan called from the lounge. He sounded cheerful.

We looked in. Riordan knelt over Foxtrot Joe, pressing a towel to the wound.

Emma gave an alarmed cry and rushed over. Joe was just this side of consciousness and feebly took her hand. She stroked his hair and whispered to him, tears running down her face.

Riordan grinned up at me. "All the world loves a lover, right, Jacky-lad?"

"Looks it."

"Help him!" she shouted at us. "Can't you help him?"

"A doctor's on the way," I said. "Any minute now."

"He'll be fine, missy," Riordan assured her. "I've seen worse that got better. Give him a week and you'll be dancin' at your weddin', sure enough."

She moaned and kissed Joe's forehead, murmuring to him. He smiled at her, and I recognized the look that transformed his hard face: true love. Who'd have thought it?

Riordan continued keeping pressure on the damage as he spoke to me. "Oh, the things I've learned from this patient, y'wouldn't believe, Jacky-lad. Seems our Gino shot this fine fella, an' let on he was goin' to do away with the lovely Emma, too. That didn't sit well with Foxtrot. He played dead, then somehow got himself out of wherever it was Gino stashed him to rot in peace. Poor Joe was supposed to disappear for good, y'see."

"Taking eight hundred grand with him," I said. "Gino gets it all and keeps his spot as collector. He should have stopped there and not gotten cute with the grenade. With Gordy dead he must have thought he could move up to the big office."

"The threat to his lady love kept our Foxtrot goin'. He cabbed over to our Emma's, an' followed Gino following her. Poor lad was on his last legs. Lucky for him you twigged to Gino's game. Just how did that come about?"

"If Foxtrot was guilty of the theft, he had no reason to be here. Gino looked pretty damned surprised about it. He wasn't concerned about you getting near the cash, either. Wrong reaction."

Riordan snorted. "A sad underestimation of my talents."

"It makes sense if Gino's the only one who knows where the money is. Gino had to kill Foxtrot, and then kill me to shut me up about it. The money stays missing for good."

"Lucky for you that little slip of a thing lent a hand. Who is she? Where is she?"

"Her name's Myrna, and she's shy. I wouldn't go—"

The lobby door opened and a skinny guy with a doctor's bag hurried in. He had two other guys with him and a stretcher. They started for the man I'd dragged in earlier, but I called them toward the ladies' lounge.

Without fuss they went to work and shoveled Foxtrot into a beat-up panel truck. It had the name DUCKY DIAPER SERVICE in faded letters on the sides, along with a winking cartoon duck wearing a diaper. Maybe it was someone's humor at work, it being a not-too-subtle reference to cleaning up other people's crap.

Emma Dorsey climbed in the back to take over pressure duty and to hold Foxtrot's hand. As an afterthought they packed in the guy he had coshed, then drove quickly away.

Just as their taillights winked around the corner, twin beams from another large vehicle swung into the street, followed by three more large cars. I recognized Gordy's new armored Cadillac in the lead. Things were about to get much, much worse for Gino Desanctis.

"What a night," I muttered.

The small light behind the bar, the one Myrna liked having on all the time, flickered as though in agreement.

A week later, in my refurbished office, I finished attaching the antenna to Myrna's new toy. Fifty feet of wire had been strung across the roof of my building by a guy who knew how to do that kind of work. The end of it snaked in through special holes drilled down through the ceiling—elaborate, but the reception would be outstanding.

I'd promised her a radio, said that it was hers and hers alone, and she could play whatever she liked whenever she liked.

I was still humbly grateful about the timing of that thrown bar stool.

She had the best Zenith floor model I could find, guaranteed to pick up foreign broadcasts on its shortwave band. The wood cabinet had a rich, honey-smooth finish, and the speaker was larger than any other in the shop. Open the back and you'd see a cone-shaped covering around the speaker itself, sort of like a lumpy bullhorn. You adjusted it to fix the bass sound to fit the size of the room, or something like that. I'd read the directions some other time.

I plugged it in.

The thing came to life with an enthusiastic hum. After it warmed up, I fiddled with the dial and put it on a station playing dance music. It sounded damned good, almost as though you were there.

Gordy had been generous. For saving his life, since I'd been careless enough to explode a grenade meant for him, he sent over an army of carpenters and janitors to clean up my club and restore the office. A friendly guy from a furniture store called me one night and said I was to come over to take my pick of his stock; any friend of Gordy's was his friend, too. He even sounded glad about it.

I didn't protest, accepting it all as Gordy's version of a modest thank-you gesture.

Foxtrot Joe, since he had tried to stop Desanctis, albeit for his own reasons, got to keep the money he'd skimmed but was told to quietly leave town and not come back. Emma wanted him to meet her parents; her dad had a tailor shop down in Springfield, and he was not averse to offering a job to his future son-in-law. Foxtrot was not averse to accepting it. He knew a little about bookkeeping.

Riordan slipped away when no one was looking, which was no surprise. The fact that Desanctis was missing his watch, wallet, and car keys might have had something to do with it. At some point, the flat tire on the snazzy Hudson had gotten fixed, for the car vanished from my parking lot, never to be seen again. Riordan continued driving a battered Ford, claiming with a grin to know nothing about the theft. He stopped by once to ask after Myrna, but I put him off.

He said he couldn't fault me for keeping her to myself, describing her as a darlin' little thing with dark hair. That's all the detail I got, and I couldn't ask for more or I'd have to tell him she was a ghost, and that was none of his business.

How was it that he'd seen her and I'd never had a glimpse? I'd done reading on the subject. Some people could see ghosts and others could not, and the ones who do don't always know it isn't a living person. Riordan might be psychically sensitive and unaware of it. There's plenty of stories about the Irish having the inside track on that stuff.

Or maybe when it came to the psychical I was just color-blind. Or ghost-blind. Being a vampire gave me no edge, apparently, but it didn't bother me much.

Desanctis . . . I never found out what happened to him, and that was fine with me. Gordy ran the dark side of his operation with an arctic-cold efficiency. There are aspects of it I did not need or want to know about, which he respected. The missing money turned up, and how they got Desanctis to talk I also did not need or want to know about.

I sat behind my new desk, looked over the substantial receipt for the radio, and wondered if there was a way I could put it down as a business expense.

Just as I dropped the receipt into the file, the dance music ceased, there was a hiss of static, and then the voice of an announcer reading sports scores filled the air.

"Myrna," I said to the apparently empty room, "you are the pip."

* * *

P. N. Elrod has sold more than twenty novels and at least as many short stories, scripted comic books, and edited several collections, including *My Big, Fat Supernatural Wedding* and *Strange Brew.* She's best known for the Vampire Files series, featuring undead gumshoe Jack Fleming, and would write books more quickly but for being hampered by an incurable chocolate addiction. More about her toothy titles may be found at www.vampwriter.com.

BEKNIGHTED

by DEIDRE KNIGHT

She'd nearly freed him on three separate occasions, coming so close that she could practically touch the mail of his armor. Even now, her fingertips trembled with the eager compulsion to feel its burnished surface. To see the gleam and shine of it as she sliced her knight free from the puzzle's complex design.

A poor cut had ruined the piece's geometry on the first occasion; a wrongly mounted image had felled them on the second. Most recently, he'd vanished from beneath her paintbrush as if never existing within the scene at all, victim of some misapplied hue or ill-timed flick of her artist's hand.

Amateur mistakes, all.

That was before she'd solved her own riddle: that real gold was necessary for creating the intricate puzzle box this task required. Such rare, liquefied bullion wasn't available on the open market, not without a permit from the Artistry Union. (And they couldn't have just *any* puzzle maker freeing immortal captives, now, could they? Imagine the dangers to organized society!)

Unfortunately, permits from the labyrinthine, bureaucratic halls of the Union came down the pike only one way—by greasing the Artistry Czar's palm with some serious coin. Money she definitely didn't have. Heck, she didn't even have enough in savings to impress the lowly Fiber Arts Subczar.

Anyway, the point wasn't the ever-tangling administration of the U.S. government, but rather that she didn't have the kind of bucks required to obtain usable Templar-grade gold. It was like realizing that a drowning man needed saving—but that first you'd have to use your Nikes to hop to Mars for a rope.

The only way to get her mitts on that gold, she'd finally realized, was to sell a bit of her own freedom in exchange for *his*. She would have to do what had always been unthinkable to her sleep-till-noon-and-work-when-you-feel-like-it mindset. Acquire a patron.

Eerily enough, she landed one almost immediately once she committed to the decision. Spookily fast, given the creeping hands of Artistry Union time, where just filling out paperwork for basic requests could take months. The patron application, however, was apparently greased with hot wax, so slippery smooth that her new benefactor arrived at her door within twenty-four hours of her request. She'd landed the beneficent assistance of one Claude Edwards. Now that imperious name, she was certain, *should* belong to a governmental czar, if not to someone from the twisted corridors of history itself.

She'd been under his thrall since he'd appeared at her

workshop almost two weeks ago, that bloodred velvet pouch dangling from his fingertips, swinging like a hypnotist's pendulum. The tassel tangled in his grasp as if he were working a marionette, wheedling it back and forth in his magnetic hold. He'd stood there, with his smoky blue eyes and exotic skin, like some wise mage bearing gifts, as if one of him were enough to do the work of all three famed magi.

From the first, suggestive promises dripped from his tongue, as liquid and entrancing as true Templar gold would be, she was certain. "I have what you require," was his opening seduction gambit. That haughty half-smile of white teeth against dusky skin was the second pearl. "I have in my grasp everything that you seek."

She hadn't mentioned specifics on the application.

"That's saying a lot if you knew what I want, mister." She folded her arms right beneath her breasts, knowing that her size D French bra would appreciate the added lift for effect. "I want a lot of things."

"No desire should be too much for a woman of your talent," he answered in a silky whisper. "Or beauty." He bowed slightly, a sort of almost gesture that left you wondering if it had happened at all.

She slid her gaze up and down his expensively suited body. He had the lean look of a barely restrained panther, the kind that some jet-setting heiress would collar with diamonds. He was also the type of guy who would make a woman, particularly an artist, into another collectible, so she made sure to objectify him as a sort of preemptive strike.

She slid her gaze up and down his form once again. "Most

of the things I want, sir, don't come packaged in thousand-dollar suits. Or looking fine as you do. Just saying."

Except patrons, some teensy, obnoxiously logical voice reminded her. *You are looking for someone exactly like this man.*

He patted the front of his jacket, smoothing it elegantly. "Three thousand dollars," he corrected in *precise* British English. Since preciseness was obviously high on his priority list. His smile widened, one dark hand poised against his jacket in explanation. "Savile Row."

"I love London." She sighed dreamily in response, unable to help herself from the demiswoon. It was, after all, her favorite city on all of God's good earth.

"London." He sighed in kind, clearly indulging her appreciation. "It is my home." He gave another little nonbow, making her blink to be sure she'd not imagined it. "I could take you there. Perhaps. If we arrive at a mutually beneficial arrangement. I believe you would appreciate such a journey."

She stood taller and stared shrewder. "Look, how can I help you?" She gestured over her shoulder toward the workshop's interior. "I'm kinda busy, you know. Clients to please, jobs to do."

His smile faded, and his tone became businesslike. "None as important as mine."

"You're awfully vain." Damn, why had she swooned over London? Talk about credibility erosion.

"Your task remains incomplete. This haunts you. Especially at night. When you dream." His voice was low, as hypnotic as the noise machine she used in an effort to hold the nightmares at bay. "I bring a solution."

He dangled the pouch higher, forcing her gaze to its heavy velvet. Blood crimson, like liquid rubies, the color magnetized her gaze—when it wasn't slipping upward to meet his own moody eyes, smoke blue and turning down at the corners in a perpetually melancholy expression.

She stood in the open doorway, blinking at the bright Charleston sunlight. Two blocks off the river and the midday sky reflected bright, piercing rays. She'd spent the morning huddled over her worktable, squinting under artificial illumination as she worked her saw, swirling a pattern she called "sea wave" into her latest box. Close as she'd get to the ocean this summer, at least with as hard as she perpetually worked. She'd finished the painting itself last week, but it was the cutting of the pieces that could be most problematic.

"So, Mister Savile Row, what do you want with a lowly artist like me?"

"You have no idea what I have here, do you?" He seemed affronted, shocked that so far his sideshow temptations hadn't lured her into his scheme.

She gave an offhand shrug. "Starbucks? If I'm lucky." She pointed at the crimson-colored pouch. "But I don't think they've figured out how to pour liquid coffee into a little satchel like you've got there. Caffeine-laced scones would work, though."

"Didn't bring any with me from England, I'm afraid," he replied, the edges of his thin lips turning up slightly. So did the edges of his crisp accent, just enough to betray impatience. An indication that despite all his heady promises, he considered her simply a means to an end. A trifling, pesky insect that he couldn't quite be bothered to squash.

"Then I've got it." She leaned against the door frame, propping her wire-rimmed glasses atop her head. "And I know, it's a really genius leap on my part, but . . . you're a puzzle collector."

His too-thin smile expanded and he moved closer, the movement as languid as his graceful way of speaking. Lifting his fingertips, he swung his velvet pouch closer and closer to her eyes, the motion counting off time itself like a cosmic metronome.

His voice was husky low as he said, "I've brought you what every poor Artistry Union member craves."

Her gaze flicked back and forth, tracking the bag's motion; her throat tightened compulsively. Sanity demanded that she break the spell; temptation dragged her deeper beneath the undertow of the man's magic.

She swallowed again, trying to blink. "I'm not . . . that poor."

Back and forth, heavy. Filled. Weighty. "Not that rich, either, *Anna.*" A hint of Middle Eastern colored his pronunciation of her name. A touch of it; one red drop of paint falling into clean white. A total alteration to the purity of the hue.

He moved right up against her, the heat of his body radiant. "But not rich enough for what you've been chasing, either. Not for what I can provide freely. Abundantly." He leaned two inches closer, lowering his melodic voice. "You can almost touch him, can't you, Anna."

She reached a shaking hand, ready to seize hold of the

velvet satchel, but it swung right out of her grasp, vanishing. She searched the ground, his hands, but saw nothing. Desperation swamped her in a heartbeat. "I want it," she admitted in a rush, almost ashamed, but not quite. "Yes, you're right. I need it. Very much."

His white teeth flashed in a sudden broad smile, a rich contrast to his moody skin. Beautiful. He was absolutely stunning, just like that bag of his.

"Hold out your hand, Anna," he murmured, and she didn't bother to wonder—just as she hadn't earlier—how he knew her name. Or why he felt he could pronounce it with that bedroom voice and feline gaze. Then again, he'd come to her workshop, received her application. That had to be the reason he seemed so familiar with so many details about her, didn't it?

She complied, extending a palm with almost childlike obedience. At once, her hand was filled, the heavy sack even weightier than she'd imagined.

She laughed, staring at the satchel in pure wonder. "This can't be. Nobody's had access to this stuff for years." Despite her demurral, she could feel the solid, burning strength of the metal slipping inside the velvet, the way it coiled and moved like a living thing. A snake hissing its twin temptations of beauty and knowledge. She shifted the bag, yearning to feel the substance of it, her fingertips already painting, swirling, designing . . . even though she wasn't at her easel yet.

"Those with enough money have always held it in their hands." He took hold of her palm and very deliberately ladled the heavy pouch's contents into her palm. The slithering, living gold came more alive the moment it made contact with her skin.

"Feel it. This is only a small quantity. I can provide this and more, as much of it as you require. As much as you'd ever dream of wielding with your brush or tasting with your artist's tongue."

She allowed the substance to coil about her palm, loop about her wrist, to twine between her fingers.

"It recognizes what you are, Anna. The artistry of your hands cries out to it; see how it responds to you, how it yearns to be touched."

"This isn't real." She turned her hand, watching the way hundreds of unexpected hues and subtleties gleamed in the midday light. "I must be dreaming now. That's what this is. Just another one of my whacked-out nightmares."

"Are you afraid?" He seemed genuinely affronted, stepping through her doorway and into the dark interior of her studio. When had he taken position just inside the frame?

"I don't believe it." She reached her free left hand and drew her eyeglasses down onto the bridge of her nose, studying the substance more closely.

"Living gold. That's what all the legends call it," she observed, watching the thick substance band about each of her fingers, forming swirling rings.

"You are holding that very thing."

"They also say that Templar-grade, liquid gold can drive the artist mad. Did you know that, too?"

He walked all the way into her parquet-floored hallway, studying the intricate paintings she'd applied across her floor.

"Lovely," he observed, staring down his nose at the patterns. But he didn't answer her question.

"Or maybe you just think a little madness is good for the artist's soul?" She followed him inside, closing the door with her bare foot. "That we should be inspired."

"No, you are incorrect." He turned and looked at her, seeming very somber. "I am aware of the insanity side effect, yes. And no, I do not think any artist should suffer thusly."

She stared at her hand, only then aware that she'd begun petting the gold with an absent gesture as they spoke. "Then why offer it to me? I didn't mention what I needed in my application to the union."

He cocked his head. "Application?"

"Yeah, you obviously got hold of my patronage app, right? I mean, that's why you're here. How else would you know my name?" She bobbed her head impatiently; every bit of conversation pulled her away from studying her new possession.

"I do not know of any application."

Her heartbeat quickened, and in reaction, the gold shimmied right up her forearm, escaping inside her shirtsleeve. "Then . . . why are you here? Who sent you?"

"The one you seek." He gave a full bow this time, lingering in the position. "I serve him, as you do." Finally he rose to his full form, smoothing a hand over the front of his suit.

"Look," she said, peeling the gold from around her upper arm and clumping it into her fist. "I'm a free agent. That's how it's always been; that's why applying for a patron was a big thing. I don't serve anybody."

"No?" He lifted a significant eyebrow. "You have made no pledges?"

Three failed tries. Three broken promises. Yeah, she'd been serving him for months now, allowing him to winnow his way into her dreams and paintings and thoughts.

"So tell me one thing. Why are you willing to trust me with something so precious?" She cradled the gold in both palms, walking toward him. She'd just give it back and forget the man who stalked her mind's dark alleys.

Except the stranger's answer changed everything. Altered the odds, tilted the gaming table.

"Simple," he answered, British accent melting into something far more ancient and foreign. "I want to free him, too."

As soon as Claude left, a heavy wave of exhaustion overcame her, the kind that had your eyelids closing no matter how determined you were to continue working. Anna left the studio area of her apartment, dragging herself toward the bedroom, already half-asleep before she collapsed onto the bed.

She had never been one to nap.

Her mother always said she was born with an extra helping of energy, wired with enough stamina to dedicate herself to her many artistic passions. Although puzzle making was the greatest of those, she also created stained glass by commission, dabbled in weaving and intricate crochet, and piddled away her spare time by tiling mosaics.

As she rolled onto her side, the somnolent sound of the noise machine nailed her into sleep, the dream already reaching out to claim her.

It was different this time; she realized that at once, even as she remained fully cognizant that she *was* dreaming. Previously, the knight had been in scenes straight from some tapestry or medieval book of hours. Not now. She was cocooned in darkness, and she heard him breathing somewhere in that black space.

"Where are you?" she cried out, not that she expected an answer. The knight never spoke aloud, although he was very expressive with his eyes and gestures. His silence seemed a prison of its own, almost as if words were forbidden to him. "I can't see anything."

Heavy, labored breathing answered her, and extending both hands, she felt around herself tentatively. The slick, damp surface of stones met her fingertips. They were slimy, wet, and cool to the touch, and she began shaking. Her knight was in danger. He had to be; otherwise, they'd be in another downy meadow or flowery field, azure sky expanding overhead.

The rattle of heavy chains split the darkness, a rumbling moan following in the wake of the sound. She moved forward, feeling about her as if she were in some hellish version of blindman's bluff.

"I'm coming. I'll find you," she tried to reassure him, only to hear another soulful moan.

Her right foot hit chilling iron, and she dropped to her haunches. Feeling the links of chain, she could tell they were encrusted from years of use. She felt her way toward him, using the iron as a guide.

His hot breath hit her face, a panting heat of desperation

as he clasped her shoulders. Without being able to see his eyes or read his expression, she didn't understand what he was clearly begging of her.

"Tell me," she urged, reaching toward him. She felt a sweat-slicked chest, smelled the heavy odor of captivity all over his skin. "I don't know what you need!"

I am not allowed . . . to speak.

"You just did. Now."

Inside . . . you. Only. By . . . my will.

"Then do it again."

Grimy fingers felt her face, her jaw, her mouth, more desperate and aggressive than he'd been in any of the previous dreams. She mirrored the gesture, trying to absorb him, to comprehend what he needed. "Tell . . . me," she whispered, feeling the heat of her own tears as they rolled down her face.

Freedom. Life.

He released her, shoving her backward, and for a dim, black moment she would have sworn she heard the rustle of fur. The click of nails upon decaying stone.

But then there was only piercing light and the drone of her noise machine.

Claude insisted on overseeing every moment of her work as she handcrafted the costly puzzle he'd commissioned, and although it should have made her nervous to have him seated just beyond the penumbra of light, studying her with his shrewd gray blue eyes, she found his presence oddly soothing. The illogic of that effect, how counterintuitive it was to his physical demeanor and shady behavior, didn't even bother her.

Her new patron revealed few secrets as to his own provenance, and she was fine with that fact, but not with how closemouthed he remained about her knight. With the painting nearly complete, she grew frustrated with his lack of communication.

"Look, Claude, I need to know who he is," she said, studying the scene on her easel. It was an image of a dazzling, armored knight battling a lion—just as he had requested. It was also a radically different painting from the one she'd created on her three previous attempts to free the warrior.

Claude had been very detailed in his specifications for the puzzle's image. From the man's golden hair—to be applied with the Templar bullion—to his height and weaponry, to the other knights watching his display of gallant bravery. Even in his description of the open Bible that a monklike figure held, standing off to the far left side of the display. His insistence upon twin deer appearing in the far background only made her laugh. Talk about medieval stereotypes; Claude produced them in spades.

"What are the deer really doing?" she asked at one point, but he merely inclined his head.

"They are part of our scene, Anna. Would you deny them entry?"

As long as nobody in the painting sat in a deer stand, her southern girl soul was fine with including the creatures. So she worked at the canvas day after day, compliant as she fulfilled each of her money man's specifications.

Now, all that remained to finish the painting was to apply the Templar gold to her knight's armor, and if the gleam of his radiant hair was any indication, he would be truly breathtaking once she finalized the piece.

"He is magnificent," Claude murmured, his accented declaration filled with wonder. Admiration.

And something much darker that caused her to turn and face him.

"Not what you expected?" she asked, sliding her wire frames atop her head.

Claude's gray blue eyes were fixed on the knight, widening, then narrowing. "He is . . . alive. Is he not?"

"In some world. I guess." She folded both arms across her chest, not caring that they were covered in paint and that she'd get her smock even dirtier. "Who is he? Like I said, it's time you told me what I'm involved in here."

Claude kept his eyes locked on the representation. "You will have your answers, Anna. Keep working," he answered, exactly as he had from the beginning.

"His name. That's fair," she insisted, tossing her dark ponytail over her left shoulder. "With all he's put me through? Totally fair."

Claude stepped back out from beneath the lights, reclaiming his place in the shadows. "In due time. First, you must finish. It is time to apply the gold."

There was a rustling sound from his seat at her work desk, the brush of velvet against rough hardness, and suddenly she was holding the satchel. He'd kept it from her except for that one hour when he'd instructed her to use gold for the knight's hair.

"Yes," Claude whispered in her ear, brushing up uncomfortably close behind her. "It is definitely time. You want him."

She'd never really thought about the mysterious man that way, not until that moment. A challenge? Yes, he'd been that. A puzzle within an ever-expanding enigma? That, too. She made her trade and living by creating mysteries, even unsolvable ones. No wonder she'd been drawn by the temptation of freeing her knight.

But she'd never actually desired the nameless knight. Until Claude murmured the suggestion, lured her into the web like the spider he was turning out to be.

"I . . . no," she said firmly, even though she'd begun shaking inside. "I just want to know who the heck he is. I need that."

"You need to touch him. I've sensed it from the beginning." Then Claude laughed, drawing fingertips along the exposed flesh of her forearms, pressing behind her. "I'm quite aware of the dreams, remember."

"I've never wanted him in my dreams," she insisted, swatting his hands away from her body.

"Are you so sure, Anna? You must recognize his physical allure by now." He remained behind her, heatedly close, threatening.

They'd passed the point of safety on that very first day, and she'd felt his iron control ever since—but been unable to fight it. Yes, she desired the knight, but it took Claude to bring that fact to life. Now that he'd uttered it, the need and craving speared through her center just as it had for Templar gold itself.

"I . . . I shouldn't. Not him." She tried to sidestep out of Claude's easy grasp, needed to break free, but he shadowed her from behind, clasping her shoulders and mooring her to that spot.

"Yes, you should. It is decreed."

She squirmed in his liquid hold. "Decreed? By who? Shit, Claude, you're getting too spooky even for me now."

"Do you think he chose you by accident? For this task of yours? A knight's duty?"

She shook her head. "I really . . . don't know."

"When did the dreams begin?"

She didn't even have to think about that question. The date lived inside of her, solid as concrete. "A few days before Christmas."

"Ah, and so many months later, they continue. They heighten. His call upon you increases . . . which is why I came now. He spoke to you first on the winter solstice, Anna. And he must be freed—the puzzle must be completed—by just before midnight tomorrow. The summer solstice. It will be another eight hundred years of captivity if you do not succeed."

"Is that how long he's been—"

"Midnight. Tomorrow, Anna," he answered, and turned toward the studio door. "I will return long before."

"What? You're leaving?" She extended the velvet bag in

her palm, feeling the gold's shifting, vibrating weight within. Already the precious metal was responding to her, reacting. "I have to paint his armor. You've been totally specific about everything until now."

Claude paused at her door, a paper thin smile forming on his lips. "You will work his freedom by your own hand," he replied quietly, and with yet another almost bow, he turned to leave.

"What is your name?" Anna asked the knight on the canvas. She stood staring at the painting, wishing that he were as alive as he'd sometimes been in her night visions.

Silence reverberated throughout her studio, only the hum of the air conditioner filling the void.

"If only you could answer me," she whispered, stepping closer to the painting. She lifted tentative fingertips and touched the brush of blond hair that swept across his shoulders. "For some reason, your name is very important to me. But even Claude won't give up your secret."

Closing her eyes, she touched the hard metallic paint, lightly teasing her fingers over the raised surface. She imagined what it would be like to stroke the man's flaxen hair if he were real; wondered if it would be soft or coarse.

It would be as smooth as satin, she realized. She knew it in the core of her being.

Yes, she wanted him, and powerfully. Claude had dipped his own brush deep into her soul and revealed that hidden truth, one she'd been trying to escape ever since the first dream.

The knight never spoke during those nighttime visitations. He beckoned, he implored, he charged . . . usually with the sheer intensity of his eyes. They were gray blue, just like Claude's. Perhaps her patron was some descendant of the mysterious man?

With her own eyes still closed, she stroked his painted hair once again.

And swore she felt the Templar gold come alive, right as his voice traipsed across her skin and soul. *Caution, Anna. He is a dangerous man.*

The sound was husky, heavily accented.

She jolted backward, stumbling as her eyes flew open. But only the painting stood before her, still propped upon her easel.

"Oh, my God." She blinked, raking a loose tendril of hair out of her eyes. "I did not just imagine that."

Silence; the rumble of the air conditioner shutting off; the soft meow of her cat, Cézanne, from the bedroom.

She sucked in several deep breaths, working to calm her rapid heartbeat. Still, no matter how long she stared at the canvas or at the knight himself, she knew she'd heard him speak to her. Not in some dream, but here. Now.

All right, all right, she coached herself. *What were you doing when he talked? You were touching him.*

Stepping forward, she pressed her eyes shut again and lifted a shaking hand to feel the raised surface of the paint. "Talk to me. Please. I need to know more about you."

A purring answer vibrated through her mind. *He is a devil.*

She shook her head, still touching the painted surface of her knight's body. "No, that's not true. He's trying to free you."

For his own purposes.

"But you've wanted freedom. You've begged me for it."

Her eyes flew open, and there he stood. Well, "stood" was far too generous a description for his stance. The knight shimmered in the air, wavering off the canvas into a multi-dimensional, ghostly form and then resetting himself within the painting's context anew.

"Come back!" She pressed desperate fingertips against the canvas. "Tell me what I don't know. What does Claude want from you? From me?"

The figure flickered slightly beneath her hand, rising until, for a brief moment, she felt the heat of his armor, the physical strength of his body. *Claudius seeks to possess me.*

"How? How can I stop him?"

His answer was eerily simple, stark as the painting displayed before her.

Prepare the gold, Anna.

A sharp knock at her door caused her to drop the heavy velvet bag that she still clutched in her hand.

"That's probably him," she whispered at the canvas, but no further instructions came forth. "If I paint you, what happens? If I finish, are you free?"

Another knock, even more impatient than the first.

She backed away from the work, not wanting to take her eyes off the knight; terrified of the man who demanded her attention with his harsh knock.

Finally she composed her face into a mask of strength and calmness, emotions she definitely didn't feel. She could feel her naturally pale Irish American skin flushing hot and tried to will away those betraying red splotches.

Claude stood beyond the threshold, and as soon as she cracked open the door, he pushed past her to the interior.

She placed her right hand on her hip, working to seem in charge. "I thought you were leaving."

"I did," he answered cryptically, gliding far past her.

"Yeah, like ten minutes ago. Tops."

"I forgot something very important." He sauntered toward the painting, inspecting the image. It hadn't changed at all physically—yet for her it had altered completely in the past few moments.

Anna's heart slammed in her chest because Claude must have known that the knight was trying to warn her. Why else would he have returned so quickly and unexpectedly? Somehow, damn the man, he suspected that she'd been interacting with their knight.

She cleared her throat, strolling toward Claude with forced casualness. "Something wrong about the image?"

"I did not forget the painting, Anna." He tossed her a narrowed glance and then looked slowly toward the floor. "But *you* have forgotten your gold. Dropped so casually? I am shocked that you'd dishonor something so precious."

She swallowed, bending to retrieve the bag. "I was painting, and I, uh . . . set it down."

"Then why does the gold cry out?" He pointed toward the satchel, and she clutched it against her breasts protectively.

Only then did she hear the soft, muted cries coming from within the bag itself.

She untied the lace and reached gently inside the bag, taking the gold within her palm. At once the complaining sound stopped, replaced by the rhythmic hum of satisfaction. "I'm sorry," she murmured to the substance, watching it spread about her wrist. "I was working."

"Working? Are you certain?" Claude demanded, the words rough and accusatory. It was the first time he'd ever spoken to her impolitely. Something in his entire demeanor was transformed. Even his accent had thickened.

"You're the one who told me that tomorrow's our deadline." She walked toward the burner that she'd used to heat the first application of gold. "I've got to heat this up so I can get busy."

"I will remain here while you paint," Claude said, unbuttoning his suit jacket.

"So what was it?" she called to him, turning on the burner.

Claude did not answer, so she prompted him further. "You said you forgot something."

He settled at her desk as if he owned the workshop, relaxing into her chair. His mercurial gaze was fixed on her as he formed his fingertips into a thoughtful temple. "I forgot his nature," he said coolly. A blinding white smile formed on Claude's lips. "And I underestimated *yours*."

The melted gold flowed off her paintbrush in all its living, powerful glory, just as it had when she'd applied the texture to her knight's hair. The metal moved across his armor with the same undisguised joy it had expressed in her palm, as if bringing the man to life were the substance's sole destiny. Its one true purpose.

As she applied the last bit, Claude moved close behind her. "It is nearly midnight," he purred against her ear. She shivered at what seemed to be a concealed threat, that hint of something much darker beyond what his words conveyed.

"We have a full day for this to dry and for me to cut the pieces." She studied the image before her, blinking at the way it gleamed with what appeared to be supernatural energy.

"The puzzle must be completed by midnight tomorrow. You must not miss the mark, Anna. Do you understand?"

"You told me that already." It was one of the only definite answers or facts he had supplied during the past days. "But why is the solstice so important?"

"He was trapped on the summer solstice hundreds of years ago. Your completion of his puzzle will finally free him."

"He will . . . what? Just emerge?"

Claude slid a heavy hand along the nape of her neck, sweeping her long dark hair to the side. His fingertips were soft, those of a man who had never used his hands for dirty work. Maybe he'd only ever manipulated others, just as he'd done her.

Maybe he wants something darker with my knight, she considered, feeling Claude's fingertips clasp about her neck.

"Careful, Anna," he warned, his grip firm yet light. "Remember whom you serve."

"Him. You said I serve *him*." She gestured at the painting. "That you do, too."

He bent down, pressing his lips to her exposed nape. "I have served him for the duration of his captivity. You are the one who will free us all when you finish the puzzle."

She sidestepped, and he released her easily. Facing him, she pointed an accusatory finger. "I won't finish unless you tell me the whole story."

Claude smiled slowly. "Go to sleep, Anna. Perhaps your answers await you there."

She stared incredulously. "I can't believe your nerve. I'm telling you I won't finish if—"

"Oh, you will finish. I am certain," he said, still smiling thinly. "You want him too much now to be denied."

The sudden pull of desire came over her anew, coiling through her whole body. Demanding that she touch the knight physically, not just stroke his painting or dream of him. He'd spoken to her earlier—perhaps Claude was right. If she slept again, she might know more about him, might understand his sinister warning from earlier.

"You are very tired, are you not?" Claude asked, tilting his head sideways as he studied her.

And that same blanket of exhaustion she'd felt the first day overcame her at once, leveling her and pulling her down into the darkness before she could take a single step toward her adjoining bedroom.

She entered the painting itself this time. Never, not once in any of her previous attempts, had anything so material— so supernatural—occurred. Drawing in quick breaths, she glanced about the scene, unsteady as she tried to gain her bearings. As she studied her surroundings, she saw that she stood to the right of the knight as he held out his sword to-ward the lion, which roared in agitated complaint.

"Go on! Kill it," she yelled because the lion had turned its green, feline gaze upon her. Those eyes were deadly, yet the knight did not move.

But the lion did.

"Now would be a very, very good time to do your thing," she screamed, stepping backward. Her bare foot caught on something, and she stumbled, falling onto the grassy field, which put her nearly eye level with the lion as it rushed her.

She opened her mouth to scream, but the lion was on top of her, jaws open. Lifting protective hands to her face, she started to scream but was shocked by what the creature did next.

A warm, rough tongue began lapping her on the cheek, then the nose. All the way down her face and neck, nuzzling her.

"What the . . . ?"

The truth hit her then: some elemental structure of her own painting had altered, changing the knight trapped in-side. He was no longer the one in the armor but had become the lion itself. The same big cat that was now affectionately licking her all over, a supernatural manifestation of her own little kitty, Cézanne. But this killer was no tabby cat.

You heard claws against stone in your dream that first day that Claude arrived, she reminded herself. *The knight must have trans-formed then, briefly, as well.*

She slid hands around the lion's powerful neck, feeling

the warm lushness of the creature's fur. His mane was thick and soft, and she found herself stroking him all over just as he blanketed her with such sweet affection.

You are very close, he whispered within her. *Near to freeing me.*

The words rang inside her center, unspoken yet keenly felt.

"You warned me against Claude. What am I supposed to do? Finish the puzzle?"

I will protect you from him. But you must . . . heed my instructions. Trust . . . me.

She slid hands deeper into his fur, petting him just as she would Cézanne, unsure what else to do except treat him like a giant house cat. For one long moment, he rumbled in deep, satisfied reaction. Then she said, "You're a freaking lion, man. What happened to you being the knight in the painting?"

He burrowed his heavy head against her breast. *Claudius has claimed my form. He believes his will to be nearly dominant over mine now.*

"Is he wrong?" She worked her fingers through his thick mane. "You're not even human anymore."

I am as I have always been. The true slayer.

"Tell me your name," she insisted, holding his heavy body even closer. "It's all I've ever asked or wanted out of this. To know who you are."

He lifted off her, staring down with stark eyes. *To hold a man's name is to hold him captive. Claudius knows that truth above all others.*

"I want to free you. You know that. You've always real-ized that. Surely you trust me by now?"

He backed away, opening his mouth with a roar as he turned toward the knight. Only then did she realize that the other figure was frozen. Dark hair, dusky skin, murderous expression. The knight was now Claude. Her lion stared up at the paralyzed figure, baring his sharp, gleaming teeth in a threatening expression.

He turned back to face her, his words moving inside of her mind and soul. *If you learn my name, Claudius could use it as a weapon against you,* he explained. *The very speaking of it has slain much stronger knights than you.*

She shook her head firmly. "I'm not a knight. . . ."

He moved forward and nuzzled her one last time, breath hot against her cheek. *Finish the puzzle . . . and I will finish what Claudius began in me so many years ago.*

She held the saw in her hand, wielding her "sea wave" pattern. As her favorite design, it had seemed most appropriate for her knight's task. They'd been forced to wait until the evening to begin cutting the pieces, the gold not fully dry on the canvas until then.

Although Claude paced, growing increasingly impatient, she'd warned against how disastrous rushing might prove, reminding the man of her previous failed attempts. As those last hours ticked off, the gold slowly drying, Claude had nearly lost his impenetrably cool composure.

As she worked beneath the light now, nearly finished

with the design, he hovered much too close beside her. She paused, saw in hand, and glared up at him. "If I make a mistake, the whole thing'll be botched."

He inclined a slight bow, backing away from her table. "As you say, Anna. You are the expert in this matter." But then he gestured toward the clock that hung over her desk. "Still, allow me to indicate the time. We are fifteen minutes from the solstice."

She bent almost eye level with the puzzle, squinting as she moved the saw. "And I'm no more than a minute from being done. That leaves plenty of time."

And then what? she wondered, panic seizing her as she recalled her knight's warnings in that final dream. He would battle Claude for his very soul, apparently. Where would that leave her?

The tool made a dull, buzzing sound as it reached the edge of the puzzle, and she turned it off, staring down to examine her handiwork. It was a splendid, rare piece, without a doubt. Perhaps her greatest work ever. If she'd wanted, she could have sold it for tens of thousands of dollars, an almost unimaginable sum, really, when you considered the rare Templar gold involved.

Setting the saw beside her on the table, she stared down at the burnished pieces. They seemed to grow more luminous with every passing second, in fact, and she glanced at the work light, wondering if the reflected light was creating the effect.

"You are done?" Claude's words were breathless, excited. "The puzzle is completed?"

"See for yourself." She rolled her chair back from the table, allowing him access.

Claude bent over the table, and she'd have sworn he was panting slightly. "He's stunning. You are a master of your craft."

"He's still inside the puzzle," she pointed out, hating how fast her heart had begun beating. A creeping sense of dread fell over her. Definitely not the lion from her dream. "It's minutes until the solstice. How do we free him?"

"We must break apart the pieces now, scramble the image." Claude reached toward the edge of the puzzle, but she stopped his hand.

"Don't touch it."

Claude stood upright again, studying her through narrowed sea gray eyes. "He was first ensorcelled within a chess set. Did you know that?"

She shook her head. "I know nothing. You made sure of that."

"You knew enough to set about painting him. To realize the Templar gold was necessary."

She shrugged, not wanting to tip her hand as to how intimately she and the knight were attached. "Call it a lucky guess."

"From the chess set, I nearly freed him, but he moved into an illuminated Bible, of all things." Claude laughed heavily. "*That* didn't last long."

Slowly she broke apart the first piece, the lower left corner, and then hesitated. "I'm not sure about this."

Claude reached past her, blocking her from the puzzle with

his large body. "This task, truly, should be mine. He must not have a way of reentering the image once he emerges."

"Would he want to?"

"Sebastian Fray has a talent for many violent acts, especially moving from one image to the next."

A name! Finally. She was certain that Claude had used it intentionally, too. That he was preparing some sort of trap—perhaps for her or more likely for Sebastian himself. But she had her knight's name; all she'd wanted to know, really, or so she'd believed. Now she knew that her desire ran far deeper, was an unquenchable thirst to free a doomed and captive man.

"When you put it that way," she said, "it doesn't sound like *Sebastian* cares too much for freedom."

Claude didn't answer, focusing instead on disassembling the puzzle. The pieces formed a shimmering mound beneath his palms as the last bit fell from his grasp. "He is complete."

That declaration seemed particularly perverse considering that the puzzle she'd painstakingly created lay in broken bits. She was about to remark on that fact when a humming, electric energy began, emanating from the work itself.

A swirling, living image began to take shape within the air, an amalgam of puzzle pieces that seemed to be alive. With a gasp, she looked at the table, but the small heap of cut work remained intact. No, whatever multidimensional tableau was emerging, it breathed with a life all its own, imbued with a dark, otherworldly essence that literally burned the air around her.

She tried to back away but found herself enthralled.

Captivated. Even when she heard the lion's roar, she remained manacled to the floor of her studio as if unseen hands gripped her ankles.

Sebastian became fully solid before she could gasp. Pure gold rippled across his fur, as shimmering and alive as the Templar bullion that had animated him after long captivity. One word said it all: magnificent.

With a ravenous sound, her lion tossed back his head, the mane of vibrant fur standing on end; his eyes were no longer the smoky blue of his human self, but rarest green, filled with shifting hues and accents.

Why didn't Claude ask me to paint Sebastian just like this? some stupid part of her terrified mind wondered.

That was before she noticed the collar, barbed about Sebastian's leonine throat, studded into his fur with sharply faceted diamonds and rubies and emeralds. Claude tightened the rein with a snap, inciting a harsh snarl, one that seemed to come from the heart of the beast.

"Yes, there you go," Claude murmured to the cat in his hypnotic, smooth voice. "You were made for this, Sebastian. To kill. To hunt. I know how you've missed it."

Sebastian's eyes narrowed on her, his jaws snapping as he rumbled a voracious roar.

"There now. There," Claude whispered, walking toward her, leash in hand. "I am here to oblige your basest instincts, knight. Here she is. Your first kill of many."

"No. He's not like that," Anna said, backing up against her worktable. "He isn't what you're saying."

Sebastian snapped his jaws in denial, leaping toward her,

but Claude snapped hard on his leash. "Not yet," he murmured. "It's all in the timing. Midnight, Fray. Midnight."

The solstice. What dark magic did Claude plan to work at the stroke of that hour?

Claude dropped to his knees, raking his hands across Sebastian's mane and fur. "Calm for now, old friend. Patience. Ah, but that never has come easily for you."

"Sebastian, you can still control your own destiny," she told him in a slow, soothing tone. "He only controls you if you allow it."

Claude spun to face her, shadowy, gorgeous features transforming into something terrifying. Scales formed along the sides of his jaws and neck; horrible jaws elongated. "Did he tell you that he sold himself to me? To do my bidding?" he asked, still morphing into something hideous and terrible that was caught between man and dragon.

"He is not your prisoner," she insisted, shaking so hard that the words came out in half gasps. "He has free will."

"This knight, this once brave Templar, sold his freedom for the very gold you used to bring him back to life. Greed overtook him. Ah, and then it was so easy to wield him by my own hand. To make him mine again, as he always should have been."

"You made him a killer."

"I turned him to his true nature. Darkness. Made him like me."

"You're a devil." She jutted out her chin, determined to appear strong. "He told me, earlier. Described exactly what you are."

Claude only laughed in reaction, scales changing hue across his features, humanity nearly vanishing. "I merely gave him what he wanted. As I did for you, Anna. You sought to free him, and now he is unleashed. Well"—he gave the long yoke around Sebastian's neck a jerk—"at least as far as we can trust him until midnight."

Anna stared at the clock over her desk. Only two more minutes until the summer solstice, but she was out of ideas, short on strategy. Yet something kept whispering through her mind, a hidden clue that Sebastian had murmured to her in his last desperate bid to hold on to freedom.

Gold. Something to do with the gold.

Melt me. That's what he'd said, and it hadn't made sense, still didn't.

Now, in the rush of the moment, she swore she heard his voice in the hidden reaches of her mind.

Return me to my metal state!

"Sebastian," Claude commanded, his voice that of true ownership, "kill her. Now. I sense the hunger in you. Hundreds of years and you've not tasted life. How you must have missed the feeding."

"He won't touch me," she countered, almost believing what she said. Cautiously she glanced away from the lion, using her peripheral vision to search for the puzzle pieces. They lay scattered on the floor, the gleam of gold sparkling.

The slap of that long leash bit into the lion's fur, red forming where the barbs struck his golden hair. "Sebastian. Sebastian Fray. Heed my commandment."

The cat's nostrils flared as his eyes narrowed. The clicking of his claws punctuated the silence between them all, and Claude allowed the leash some slack. The lion padded closer toward her, bloodlust evident in his eyes.

To own a man's name was to own his will. He'd said something like that to her in that final dream, she suddenly recalled. That's why Claude kept using it, over and over. He owned Sebastian's freedom because he owned the man's name.

"Sebastian," she said with forced calm, "you won't hurt me. Don't, *Sebastian*."

"He has no care for you now," Claude told her with a hollow laugh. "Don't bother trying to appeal to him."

The lion halted midstride, blinking at her and then turning his massive head toward Claude as if awaiting an order. An explanation as to whom he should heed.

"Take her," Claude murmured, sounding almost like a lover. "We will be powerful again, the two of us as one. You once let me hand you the world. Kill again and it shall be true forever."

The lion turned ravenous eyes upon her, pouncing before she could take a breath. She fell beneath his massive body, going down onto the floor with a hard crack of her skull. Blackness engulfed her, the sinewy threat atop her body wavering with that darkness.

Burn me . . . melt . . . Anna. You are the one to save me. . . .

With a shove, she thrust at the massive beast, but he was dead weight; she might as well have sought to push a felled oak tree off her. But then, seemingly remembering his better nature, Sebastian reared away with a guttural cry.

She seized that moment and began sweeping her palm along the hardwood, scrabbling for even one piece of painted Templar gold. As she scooped up a handful of shimmering pieces, she kicked the table that held the burner, and it went crashing to the floor.

Events happened with that drawn-out pulse of only one or two heartbeats that lasted a lifetime. Claude was dragging on the leash; Sebastian was snapping his jaws at her, overtaken with the need to kill.

And she was hurling the few golden pieces she could grab right into the flame.

I sold my soul for that gold once. Destroy it . . . me. Free me.

Claude rushed forward, seizing hold of both her wrists. "He is mine!" he snarled, but he moved too late. The gold began bubbling and hissing against the wooden floorboards.

The clock struck midnight then, ringing its antique chimes. Claude shoved her aside, taking hold of the leash once again.

But Sebastian vanished from the space between them. Gone, dissolved as effortlessly as he'd seemingly emerged from the puzzle. Claude rounded on her, eyes beady red and scales massing across his enlarging form. Leathery appendages fanned out from his back, scaled like wings but covered in barbs.

A devil. Truly.

And now he would kill her, she thought numbly, but she would never let him own her, not the way he'd owned Sebastian.

"Do you know how many years I've sought him?" His

words bubbled like the melting Templar gold. The sound was dry and chafing, and she pictured a parched brook filled with dry stones. . . . The voice of hell itself.

But another voice murmured in her ear. *I am free, and for that, I thank you humbly. But your knight's duty is not finished.*

Sebastian was alive somehow, still. Was he in the remaining bits of her puzzle?

I am free. But you must vanquish this evil.

"I . . . I . . ." *I'm not a knight!*

This is your destiny; ours together. Look to the gold that bought my soul.

The dragon beast that she might have called Claude—if she were being generous—advanced upon her with a menacing curl of lips over distending fangs.

It took every bit of strength inside her soul, but she searched around her for Sebastian's gold. And there it was, slithering. Snakelike. Enlarging so boldly that she shrieked. The gold that previously had purred beneath her touch began morphing into something as voracious as the beast who stalked toward her. Was the precious metal merely an extension of Claude's will? Was it not obedient to Sebastian, after all?

Except the metal wasn't finished with its fiery transformation. It rose off the floor, as alive as she was; forming into a gleaming sword, it flew into her hand.

She didn't bother thinking or hesitating; she grasped its heavy weight and rose upward, plunging the weapon into the center of the beast's chest. It swiped deathly claws at her, and she ducked backward, shoving the sword deeper into its body. The sword made a vibrating hum, the same pleasured sound the gold had made in her palm, and seemed to assume the task on her behalf.

She dropped to her knees heavily, watching as the sword forced its own way deeper into the creature's chest. Until the monster fell, blood gurgling from between its thin, monstrous lips.

Until, like Sebastian, the devil vanished entirely, protruding golden sword along with it.

She spent the next week praying for a dream or a sign—any instruction at all as to what she, a strange latter-day female knight, was supposed to do. Surely Sebastian wanted her to mop up the proverbial mess. The studio remained as it had after that last battle moment: a bloodstain on her floor, a scorched mark nearby, the burner overturned. The puzzle pieces sat on her work desk, heaped in an incomplete mound, missing several bits of canvas—and all of the gold she'd applied.

After the seventh dreamless night, she sat at the table, switched on the light, and began working the pieces back together.

"Okay, nothing to be scared of," she reassured herself. Truth be told, she was terrified to assimilate the scene again, unsure of what image the puzzle might now reveal.

So she worked very slowly, methodically, fitting each swirled line back together. It became apparent early on that the picture was indeed altered, but she forged ahead, refusing to flinch or doubt. When she finished, three pieces were missing—the ones she'd tossed into the flame—but that wasn't all that had vanished.

A knight stood in the field, brandishing a sword in his grasp, but the lion was no more. She stared down, wishing she could see Sebastian's face, praying that he was truly free.

That was the last time the heavy blanket of sleep overcame her. Laying her head atop the assembled puzzle, she closed her eyes, vaguely aware that the clock on her wall chimed three.

She felt his touch before she saw him or even heard his voice. A warm, strong hand took hold of her shoulder, turning her toward him. Sebastian's eyes were golden for the first time, his gaze lighter than it had ever been in any dream or painting.

He smiled, reaching a hand to her cheek. "You wield a sword with the strength I knew you possessed," he said admiringly.

She flung herself against his chest, crying for the first time since the odyssey had begun. "Sebastian," she murmured, relieved simply to speak his name. "You're free now?"

"From Claude's control, yes." He slid an arm around her back, holding her close.

"I don't understand. You're not . . . what? Not truly free?"

"So long as he could summon me, I was a killer," he said, pressing a kiss against her temple. "You've saved me, Anna. My very soul."

"Then come out of the puzzle!" She pulled back slightly, beseeching him with her eyes. "We can be together now, finally. I have so many questions, so much to tell you."

He stroked rough fingertips along her cheek, caressing her, his expression melancholy. "Ah, and so many kisses I would have for you, Anna," he murmured. "So many. But, alas, it shall never be."

She pressed her cheek against his chest, felt the strong, steady beat of his heart. He was real, human. "But you said I freed you." She wrapped both arms about him. "I feel how alive you are."

He tilted her chin upward, forcing her to look into his eyes again. "Anna, you completed your knight's task with true bravery. But your work is not quite done."

She shook her head. "I did everything you asked."

He lowered his mouth and kissed her, his lips soft and warm. Then he murmured his final instruction. "Burn the other pieces."

Shaking her head, she cried, "But you can't emerge if I do."

He smiled wistfully. "To remain in exile is my freedom, Anna. A freedom you've given me."

"I'll paint you again. I'll find another way—"

"You won't remember. When you burn the last piece, you will dream all of this away. Including this kiss."

He captured her mouth much more roughly than before, deepening the kiss for long moments. The kiss seemed to span as a bridge between eternity and their two hearts; it lasted that long, became that powerful.

Finally he pulled back, stroking her cheek. "I'd rather you remembered that."

"I will remember, because I'm going to find a way to let you live in the real world. Freely."

"Claude turned me into a killer; my soul for that gold, those were our terms. Living here, in the in-between, is the only way to keep my murdering lust at bay. You must burn the pieces to set me free eternally. If you care for me truly, you will complete this one last task."

She opened her mouth, ready to fight and scream and claw for his everlasting salvation, but the dream was yanked away.

Lifting her head, she stared down at the worked pieces, and her tears began to flow in earnest. Because he asked, she would oblige—as she had from the very first time he'd appeared in her dreams. But the pain knifing inside her gut was almost more than she could bear, to know that she was going to make him a captive for eternity, rob him of his one whisper of freedom. In the end, he'd wanted not to be released from captivity, she understood now, but rather to perform one last heroic task: rid the world of Claude and his evil.

She turned the piece in her palm, staring at Sebastian's blond hair, the metallic weight of his armor; she could practically feel his arms closing about her again. Holding her, steadying her.

He'd performed his final act of bravery, she resolved, and so could she.

Standing wearily, she swiped the tears from her cheeks. She moved to light the burner, several jigsaw bits already in her hand.

Staring down, feeding those pieces into the fire, she suddenly wondered what they even were. And why her soft cheek felt chafed, as if by a man's beard, her lips swollen as if kissed.

She turned one last puzzle piece in her grasp, catching the dull hue of a knight's armor. Odd, she thought, it seemed to be missing a color, a vibrant hue. What was it? she thought, staring down—and realized it was absent something *golden*.

With a shrug, she tossed that final fragment into the flames and thought she heard the most absurd, irrational sound as she did so. A lion's roar.

* * *

Deidre Knight began her writing career at age nine and has been writing in one form or another ever since. After nearly a decade of working with Knight Agency clients, she made her own literary debut with *Parallel Attraction*. Her Gods of Midnight series opened with *Red Fire*, followed by *Red Kiss*, with more titles on the way! Check out all her works at **www.deidreknight.com**.

SHIFTING STAR

by VICKI PETTERSSON

Skamar left her so-called Mediterranean-style apartment as she always did: after first sniffing the air to make sure there were no mortals about. She knew who her neighbors were, had watched them coming and going through the small peephole of the front door, and had even observed the older, professional woman upstairs leave a coffee cake on her doorstep. Perplexed, Skamar had mentioned the strange deed to her creator, Zoe, and was told it was a way to welcome her to the neighborhood. So Skamar had eaten the cake in one sitting—God knew her brand-new physical body needed the nourishment—and returned the cake plate to the woman's doorstep before sneaking away.

The only person Skamar hadn't been able to avoid was the man in 117B. He wasn't always there, but he was annoying enough—and, she knew, *interested* enough—that it seemed that way.

"Morning, sunshine," the man said again today, pointedly regarding her copper red hair. His ubiquitous coffee cup steamed fragrantly, his feet were propped on the patio railing, and his otherwise handsome face was marred by a shit-eating grin.

She'd have snarled that Skamar was Tibetan for star, not sun, but she never furnished her proper name to anyone. That was like giving permission to use her personal power, and she'd worked too hard to allow that.

"Vaughn," she said stiffly, because *he'd* given his name freely, insisting she use his first. *Vaughn Rhett.* His obvious attraction crept over her amplified senses and was a heady combination attached to that slim build and open face. It made her skin crawl.

"Join me for a cup of coffee?" he asked, as always.

"No." She only acknowledged him at all because she wanted to keep a low profile. It was the same reason she walked from the complex rather than soared. A redheaded woman circling like an eagle overhead would certainly attract attention. And the Tulpa, she thought, glancing at the crucifixion wounds in her wrists, would easily pinpoint her then.

"Just one?" Vaughn gave her that killer smile again, and his warm, dry scent pulsed over her to pool in her gut. "It's French pressed."

Skamar clenched her teeth and sped up. What the hell were you supposed to feel when someone so clearly wanted to stick his tongue down your throat? It would be so much better, she thought, if the man merely meant to stick a knife in her gut. She'd know exactly what to feel, and do, about *that*.

"You're going to join me for coffee one day, sunshine," he called after her, voice filled with such teasing laughter that it actually did remind her of the sun. "I promise you that."

But by the time she exited the parking lot and hit the wide stretch of Flamingo Road, thoughts of Vaughn, the scent of his coffee and interest, and his meaningless promises dropped away. She stood taller, awareness expanding. Her body temperature was already marrying with the biting December air, a skill not unlike a chameleon's ability to change color . . . and one specific to tulpas. As she walked, Skamar turned her mind to Zoe Archer and why her creator would summon Skamar in daylight hours, and to such a public place.

Yet an uncomfortable tingle, similar to what Skamar had felt under Vaughn's clear gaze, rode the nape of her neck. Her first instinct was renewed annoyance at a fleeting wish for a cup of joe.

Her second was to duck.

The Tulpa's frustrated cry arched banner red above her as she kissed pavement, and he halted in the next second, redirected midair, and sprinted back while she still sprawled. His flesh was molded into a thin, wiry, unassuming form today, but that was for mortal benefit. Snarling, she countered the steel-spined demon that lurked beneath.

He'd caught her fresh. Maybe he didn't yet know that her biorhythms had taken on mortal flow once she'd achieved permanence in this world. How would he? He was still unnamed, only a half-realized entity, forced to describe who he was—the Tulpa—by what he was—a tulpa. Sure, his followers had to call him something, but it would never afford him the formidable kick of power she enjoyed with a given name.

So their next collision had Skamar's fist blasting through

his false visage, surprise spreading over a face that distended so far it should have cracked. Impermanence made the fucker hard to fight, but he still grunted and fell back. Before his features could rearrange themselves into the correct places, her fist plowed through his chest, penetrating all but the last thin membrane.

His scream was a mourner's wail, though to Skamar it was a lover's sigh. Unsurprisingly, he reverted to what had become his standard MO—ambush and retreat—and the wind cut in sharp whistles around their bodies. Panicked, the Tulpa glanced up at the empty expanse of baby blue sky, but Skamar knew he wouldn't risk the small sonic boom triggered whenever they set to flight. Not in the middle of town. Those in Vegas's underworld would converge in minutes, and neither of them wanted to face off against each other *and* their respective troops.

So they angled close to the closed restaurants and office buildings, leapt to rooftops in straight vertical shots, and ran the narrow walking paths like drag racers. When the distance actually lengthened between them, Skamar knew the Tulpa's followers—worshippers whose energy could be summoned at will—had been ordered to gift him with thoughts providing greater speed.

But the gift, the energy, came at a price.

Halting, she hefted a boulder the size of her skull and launched it at his retreating form. The rock plowed into his neck, distending his head so far forward that it hung like a loose tooth off its last thread of gum. Knocked to the ground, he rolled, and Skamar broke into another sprint. Yet the

Tulpa—somehow able to think despite near decapitation—allowed the rotation to propel him forward, and he resumed running. When the distance again increased and he disappeared onto Desert Inn Road, then around the Wynn Resort, Skamar slowed.

That's okay, she thought, breathing hard. She'd learned something new of him. The fool had given up power for speed, and that was knowledge she could capitalize on. Every encounter aiding that was a success. And though she was now late for her meeting with Zoe, she had to smile at the memory of the Tulpa running from her, head literally held in his hands.

Ten in the morning and the Valhalla Hotel's pool was already busy, with music more suited to a nightclub pulsing from hidden speakers and bikini-clad cocktail waitresses ferrying morning mimosas and Bloody Marys to hotel guests. Some, Skamar noted as she followed the perky blond attendant across the expansive deck, had clearly not slept for nights. She squinted against the pool's reflection, amazed that even in the winter, even at Christmas, tourists thought lounging around a pool in Las Vegas was a hedonistic pleasure. The pools were heated, and the guests might feel like rock stars, but really . . . the outdoor Christmas tree was absurd.

"Ms. Belie is just over there, in the VIP cabana." The blonde smiled back at her as they wound through a maze of marble pools, saunas, and outdoor showers. A row of elevated cabanas loomed above the lounge area like the tents of Roman generals. And in the last, reclined like a goddess, was a woman with a general's steel spine. Zoe Archer.

"Ms. Belie?" Skamar said with a raised brow, dropping into a chair opposite Zoe when the attendant had gone. "Why didn't you just choose Ms. Conceal this time? Ms. Disguise, Ms. Pretense?"

Zoe always used some variation of the definition—Sham, Beard, and Twist being favorites. And she did it because . . .

"It's more fun this way." She waved a manicured hand in the air, sending the soft scent of spiced gardenias and warm vanilla wafting Skamar's way. And after giving up her family, a life among the agents of Light, and all her powers with it, Zoe took her fun where she could get it.

"The Tulpa attacked again this morning," Skamar said, noting Zoe had the poolside look down pat. Tanned limbs, a trim blue bikini, and a wide-brimmed straw hat over a long blond wig. In contrast, Skamar's own thrift-store black and spotlessly pale skin clearly marked her as a poolside neophyte. "Ambushed me right outside my complex. Not what I would call fun."

"You didn't have to come," Zoe said, sipping an icy red cocktail.

Ruthlessly unemotional. Typical Zoe. Skamar allowed a wry smile, remembering what it was like to live in the coiling gray matter of that one-track mind. To expect sentimentality from Zoe was to expect the sun to set in the east. She might appear pampered on the outside, drinking her frozen cocktails and nibbling on a fruit platter, but her actions and thoughts were as focused and militant as Skamar's.

"You wouldn't call unless it was important," Skamar conceded, leaning back, though she *didn't* have to come. She was no longer a thought-form, a doppelgänger birthed via the fierce concentration of Zoe's mind. No, now that she was named, and a full-blown tulpa—willful, conscious, immutable—she was the most powerful being in the valley. Yet resisting Zoe's call was still difficult. If Skamar were a magnet, Zoe would be sheet metal.

Zoe responded by tossing her a manila folder. After catching it midair, Skamar pulled out three photos, each of a preteen girl smiling with some degree of uncertainty. Personal information was stapled to a sheet on the back. "The Shadows are abducting girls of a certain type. A certain age."

Skamar looked up. "It could be coincidence."

"No. The Tulpa is looking for *her*."

She wouldn't say Ashlyn's name. It was still a secret in Vegas's underworld, the only thing protecting the child from it and the warring factions of Shadow and Light battling for the city's soul.

Yet soon, thought Skamar, *everyone* would know who Ashlyn was. "Her second life cycle? She's begun?"

Zoe shook her head. "Not yet." But her tone said, *Not long.*

Agents on both sides of the Zodiac could pass as mortals when young, but puberty kick-started the pheromones that acted as a siren's call to their enemies. This marked the second phase, or life cycle, of their development and was the most vulnerable point in a young agent's life. Once Ashlyn's hit, she might as well paint a bull's-eye on her chest. Everyone would know she was Zoe's granddaughter . . . and the Tulpa's.

And if *he* found Ashlyn, he would raise and train her as

Shadow, using her against the troop Zoe had been raised in. The Light. "So you want me to protect her?"

Zoe immediately scoffed. "The way you two brawl? You'd only lead him directly to her." Yet she backtracked immediately, knowing the way the words would strike Skamar. "It's not criticism. You're more powerful than he is, smarter, too—"

"Stop complimenting yourself." Because Zoe had created her that way.

Zoe smiled, but only briefly. "With a little more time and experience, I have faith you'll prevail, my dear Skamar."

Skamar detested the pride that shot through her chest. She shouldn't care what anyone thought, even the woman who'd spent a decade birthing her—thinking her—into existence.

"No, I let that bastard get his hands on her once . . ." Zoe trailed off, and Skamar knew exactly which memory she was fingering. She'd almost lost her daughter *and* granddaughter to their common enemy. "I'll do the guarding this time. Actually, I'm already doing more than that."

A wispy smile threaded Zoe's lips, and an unexpected emotion struck Skamar—green and sharp. She shunted it aside before it could bloom into scent.

Zoe pointed a finger back at the photos. "But they need to be found."

Skamar shrugged. "Let the Light take care of it."

"They can't know about her. Not yet."

Because the Light would be just as anxious to use Ashlyn. Zoe was fed up with the women in her family being used . . . a sentiment Skamar understood and shared. Yet she clenched her jaw and tossed the folder with the girls' photos on the end of Zoe's lounge chair. This quest would interfere with her pursuit of the Tulpa. "They're mortal."

"I'm mortal," Zoe snapped, leaning forward, eyes fired. "And so is my daughter, the one who *named* you, and almost lost her life so you might have limitless power."

"She did it for a child, not me." Which was still unfathomable to Skamar. Joanna Archer had given up all supernatural powers for one mortal soul. What a waste.

"But *you* benefited."

Skamar looked away. Zoe thought their obsession with killing the Tulpa was joint, but Skamar's was different. When she was first birthed from Zoe's mind in physical form, it had been as a doppelgänger, with the ability to mutate into different shapes. The precariousness of her state had frustrated her then. The inability to hold one shape for long had made her feel insignificant, like a ghost. But in some ways it had been freeing, too. Skamar now looked back on that time as someone else might look back on a carefree childhood. Maybe she'd wanted too badly to believe Zoe when she said becoming a full-blown tulpa would make Skamar the most powerful being alive. Maybe she'd been too greedy.

Because while claiming this mortal flesh had indeed provided her with the benefits of permanence—energy and power an unnamed being like the Tulpa could never tap into—its shortcomings were equally potent. The Tulpa— another being who'd walked into existence as a doppelgänger and knew what it was to be untouchable—had bested Skamar briefly and used her new body against her. She swallowed hard as she remembered him driving iron ties into her wrists and ankles before hanging her from a lightning rod and setting her up beneath a roiling sky. For all her strength, she'd been utterly helpless to free herself.

And that pain now stalked her dreams. The first time she woke with a pounding heart and sweat-soaked sheets, she was clear out the apartment door before realizing she wasn't being chased. Not by anything more than memories, at least.

Her paranoia, too, was off the charts. Thus her avoidance of neighbors, small talk with strangers, and even something as simple as a cup of coffee with Vaughn.

Especially a cup of coffee with Vaughn. Because she might be new to the whole flesh-and-bone thing, but she'd watched these mortals long enough to wonder openly at the messy emotions that routinely marred their lives. So what if the blue heat in a man's eyes suddenly made her stomach plummet into her knees? Or if his mouth, when not quirked in humor, looked like a beautiful destructive force? Feelings for another person were an unnecessary chaos. Intimacy gone bad would only open her up to more pain, more fear.

Fuck that.

But Zoe was right about Joanna. She *had* saved her from crucifixion, so that's why Skamar finally nodded.

But she would also continue to hunt the Tulpa. It was the only way she knew to combat the night sweats and remembered fears. And when she caught that sadistic, mutable fucker? She'd string him up as he'd done to her. She'd let him rot so slowly that he'd sit as close to death as anyone could and still remain alive. Then she'd patch him up, nurse him back to near health, and do it all over again. Then the leader of the Shadows, too, would know pain and fear and paranoia.

He would know *intimately,* she thought as she stood, what it was to be touched.

An early spring wind kicked at Skamar like a hard leather boot, though winter still laced the air, lending it icy force. Physical discomfort had taken some getting used to upon claiming her corporeal form, but she tried to look on the bright side. Having to consider her clothing made her blend more naturally with humanity, and she was confident she looked like any other tourist as she patrolled the Boulevard. Though she was admittedly missing the yard-long pink plastic margarita cup. Yet once she'd entered the site of the first victim's abduction—a giant mall centering the infamous Las Vegas Strip—it seemed all she really needed to do to blend was wander aimlessly . . . and buy a bunch of crap she didn't need.

The place was decked out like the North Pole had puked on it, Skamar thought, making her way to the food court. It was there, claimed the newspapers, that a Caucasian man had approached the counter of McGee's Muffin Shop, ordered a lemon-poppyseed pastry, warmed, before yanking the owner's daughter, Lilly, from behind the counter. Some eyewitnesses claimed he'd then leapt a glass balustrade to drop thirty feet before disappearing, and the police hadn't been able to decide whether they should ignore those onlookers altogether or look at them most closely.

So the muffin shop, now considered a crime scene, was cordoned off and dark, and mothers of young children steered their offspring from the storefront as if abduction were an infectious disease. Therefore Skamar hadn't long to wait for an opportunity to leap the counter and disappear into the back room.

The giant stainless-steel mixers were clean, the countertops wiped. It was orderly for a place so abruptly deserted. Yet beneath the scents of flour and sugar—and a particularly noticeable half-open tub of hardening blueberry muffin batter—Skamar still recognized human. The most obvious one smelled of whittled wood, a signatory male scent, though one laced with peppery shock. Skamar dismissed it and ferreted out the other, one as faint as soft, boiled ginger. That had to be Lilly's.

Shutting her eyes, Skamar memorized the hooks and nuances in order to track the girl later. When the door handle next to her began to twist, she jerked back to awareness and thought briefly of bolting back over the counter . . . but why give the mortals another far-fetched story? Besides, the ID cards Zoe had provided included one for a licensed P.I. She'd just tell the shop owner that one of the other families had hired her. Any man desperate to find his missing daughter wouldn't question that.

Yet it wasn't the owner who flicked on the lights and startled at the sight of her. Skamar was dumbfounded, too. Of all people, her annoying neighbor was the last she expected to see.

"What the hell are you doing here?" he asked in as unfriendly a voice as she'd ever heard. As if he had a right to question her.

Skamar flashed her license. "I should ask you the same."

"Brass trumps paper." Vaughn flashed his badge. "Now answer the question."

"A cop?" was all she said, letting her arm fall. "You have a job?"

"You can complete actual sentences?"

Her eyes hardened, but so did his. This was a different Vaughn from the one who undressed her with his gaze each time she passed his balcony. This one was a cool opponent, and perversely she liked it. She also thought she could use it.

"You're the lead detective, then?" she asked, gaining a mere perfunctory nod. "I was hired by the Brundage family to find their daughter. Maybe we could work together?"

That flat cop's gaze met the suggestion as enthusiastically as a cat met water. Yes, Skamar thought. She liked *this* Vaughn very much. "Does that mean you have something useful to add to the investigation, or would I be the only one contributing to this working relationship?"

"I've just started," she admitted with a tilt of her head. "But I'm good, dogged . . . and I was born to hunt the people who do this."

He didn't answer immediately, frowning as he looked around and then shuddering as his eyes fell on the bin of batter. The odd moment passed quickly, though. "You mean the monsters."

She smiled briefly. "That's exactly what I mean."

Eyes narrowed, Vaughn considered her a moment longer,

then offered up his own thin smile. "The third victim was abducted while sleeping. I'm headed to her house now if you want to come along."

Skamar nodded her thanks, so relieved he'd agreed that she didn't worry too much about why. Maybe he was suspicious and wanted to keep her close. Maybe it was another way to angle in for that damn cup of coffee. Whatever, Skamar thought, following Vaughn from the shop. She'd find a way to work it to her advantage. And the unusual step of working with a mortal might prove a good tactic. Busting through the Tulpa's defenses via his front door hadn't produced results, but maybe she could slip through the back this way. If she was really lucky, she might even catch him sleeping.

They were allowed into Debi Truby's bedroom by parents so grief-stricken, they looked like the walking dead. Skamar had never scented so sharp an anguish before, and she wondered how such a little person could be so firmly anchored in a family that her absence set them all adrift. Debi's father floated inconsequentially from room to room, and her mother looked as though she'd been yanked up at the root.

Meanwhile, this new Vaughn pointed out that there was no sign of struggle, forced entry, or unfamiliar fingerprints, which told Skamar little in the way of anything new. She confirmed that Debi was exactly Ashlyn's age and that her youthful scent was impossible to distinguish from an initiate's. That's why the Shadows were casting such a wide net. They'd probably hold the girls until they started menses, returning them, memories erased, once it was clear they weren't Ashlyn. Then again, they might just kill them.

But puberty varied from child to child, so Skamar couldn't help wondering how many years Debi's parents would have to walk the world in panicked despair. Or how many families would be fractured this way before the Shadows ended their search.

The unknown clearly bothered Vaughn as well. As they drove to the second crime scene, a schoolyard, he gnawed on his fingernails, gaze distant.

"These are crimes of opportunity," he finally said out of nowhere. "These girls aren't stalked. That's usually a solo endeavor, and I'm certain there's more than one person in on this. Maybe a cult . . . yet there's no ritual, no social connection. Just similar looks."

"And their birthdays," Skamar added. He was so earnest that she felt compelled to help. She didn't have a lot, but she knew that much. "They're all born within months of each other."

Vaughn frowned, made a note of it on his pad while driving, then sighed as he pulled into the school front's horseshoe drive. They slipped through a narrow opening in the fence, where they stared out over the blacktop. Skamar could almost hear the echo of children's laughter in the darkening yard.

"Why's this so personal to you?" The question earned her a sharp look, but she only inched closer, genuinely curious about what she was scenting. It was an old emotion, dry but still cloying, like the cold ash of incense. "Don't take offense. I'm good at reading people. These cases are touching you in a way others haven't."

Vaughn's gaze locked on the gently swaying tetherballs, and his jaw clenched. "Remember when you were a kid, around nine or so, and you started playing chase with the opposite sex? It was both terrifying and exhilarating . . . though you didn't really know why."

Since she'd had no childhood to speak of, Skamar's nod was a lie.

"The first girl I let catch me was named Anna. She had long brown hair and always wore those plastic barrettes. You know, the ones with bunnies on them? She smelled like blueberry gum, and I can still remember her laugh when she pressed her lips to my cheek. She said she wanted to taste my freckles. Then she raced off, left me standing with my mind in a full buzz."

Skamar said nothing, mesmerized by the idea of this man as a freckle-faced boy and knowing now why he'd gone so still in the bakery. *Blueberries.*

"She was taken the next year from in front of her house. Nobody ever saw her again, not alive, and I would stare at her empty desk every day, remembering how she looked hunched over her work, hoping she'd just walk in the classroom, wearing those plastic barrettes, maybe say that she had just gotten lost."

He looked down, biting the inside of his mouth, then back up at the sky, lost in his memories.

"That summer I went to the library, got permission to use

the microfiche, and found her school picture alongside her obituary. I looked at that image staring back at me, and I swear I could fucking smell the blueberries."

Skamar swallowed hard. "So it's a quest for you? Like those medieval knights, fighting to protect the innocent?"

Zoe's mind had been filled with those stories. She loved them, which was ironic because a former superhero shouldn't wish to be saved by someone else. But Zoe had. She'd longed for it even while taking steps to save herself.

"Don't joke about this." Vaughn pushed away from the fence.

"I'm not," Skamar replied, placing a hand on his arm to stop him, forcing him to look her in the eyes. She slid her fingertips down his arm, then led his to the scarred divots in her wrists. "I—I could have used a knight once myself."

Vaughn froze before that hard expression fractured. Then he gave her destroyed arms a gentle squeeze, and Skamar sucked in a surprised breath. She'd revealed the scars for his sake, to show that bad things happened and it was impossible for him, a mere cop, to be everywhere at once. But the dizziness that shot through her was surprising . . . and it was also unwanted. Okay, so his story about a girl who'd died long ago touched her. But she couldn't let his softheartedness do the same. That would be dangerous for them both.

"Do you have plans tonight?" he suddenly asked, still holding her wrists.

The question had Skamar blinking twice. She pulled away, but Vaughn's grip tightened. "I'm not asking for a date. We can't patrol the whole damn city at once, but we can be in the most likely places these girls are targeted. The Festival of Lights is tonight, and there'll be an enormous teen presence. The Jameson Brothers are playing at eight."

Skamar remained silent, having no idea who the Jameson Brothers were.

"We'll stand out less if we go together," Vaughn explained under her steady gaze. "Follow the girls who most fit the profile and see if anyone else is doing the same."

She frowned. It was a long shot, though no more remote than canvassing the entire valley in hopes of stumbling upon some random abduction. "How many teens did you say will be there?"

"A few hundred. All screaming and giggling, probably at the top of their lungs."

Skamar winced, and the teasing man she first knew, the one who visually undressed her from over his balcony wall, showed his face. Odd, but this time she almost didn't mind. "C'mon," he said, "you were a teen once. You remember what it's like."

Skamar had never been a teen and remembered nothing of the sort—not giggling with friends, not chasing boys in the schoolyard, not even blueberry gum and plastic barrettes. But she did remember hanging from a lightning rod like a sacrificial offering, and she was willing to try anything she could to reconcile that. "I'll be at your place at six."

The Festival of Lights was a month-long event, and while the first three weeks were a cacophonous celebration of family, the last one—and the last night in particular—belonged wholly to the valley's teen population. It was held outdoors, on a refurbished ranch, because despite the carols being sung about sleigh bells and winter wonderlands, December in Vegas was relatively mild. The cold weather wouldn't really strike until the new year, so the light jackets and festive scarves were mostly for fashion's sake.

After excusing himself, Vaughn momentarily left Skamar in front of a faux North Pole, where a Santa smelling of peppermint and vodka was taking pictures with groups of girls too old be sitting on his lap. Skamar took the opportunity to scan the crowd without being watched by Vaughn or burdened by making small talk. She was still in search mode when he returned with a pastry, which she glanced at as if it were an alien life form.

"We're here to work," she said, crossing her arms.

"We're here to blend," he corrected, nudging her with something called a churro. She studied the stick of fried dough and cinnamon sugar, twisting it in her hand before taking a tentative bite. The warmth, the sugar, and the surprising cream-filled center had her eyes winging wide, and she looked up to find Vaughn watching her with a soft, amused gaze. It wasn't the knowing look he shot her from behind his apartment balcony or the hard glaze that assessed her work. It was new, and when he reached up to wipe sugar from her lips, she found she couldn't hold it and dropped her head.

Then he surprised her yet again. The steam from the coffee cup he'd been hiding warmed her face, and she jerked back, causing his amusement to turn into full-fledged laughter. "I told you we were going to share a cup of coffee, sunshine."

His cockiness made laughter well in her, too, so she reached for the cup, muttering as she brought it to her mouth. "Stop calling me that."

"What should I call you, then?" he said, angling again for her name.

She only narrowed her eyes, but when he linked her arm through his, she didn't pull away. His size gave the illusion that he was the stronger of them, she reasoned, and his body heat and the low rumble of his voice were a relatively pleasant duet accompanying an unpleasant task.

So they walked arm in arm, threading through enough teens that the hormones practically flattened the air molecules. As Vaughn had predicted, most were giggling girls, clustered and texting, hair-tossing and bouncing with more energy than twelve-week-old puppies. At one point, a piercing chorus of squeals went up so close to Skamar that her eyes actually crossed. But the uniformity in scent made it simple to ferret out the aberrant one . . . and it was one Skamar knew well.

"What is it?" Vaughn asked, feeling her stiffen. He followed her gaze to a man standing near the fence, a protective arm draped over the shoulders of a glassy-eyed girl. Her head was hidden beneath a thick brown ski cap, and their coloring was so alike that anyone who didn't know better would take him for her father.

The ability to change shape and form was so convenient, Skamar thought, stepping forward. Too bad for the Tulpa that his black slush aura was always the same.

"It's Debi," she whispered. The Tulpa was obviously us-

ing the girl as cover while he canvassed the crowd for another victim. He knew, then, that she wasn't the one. And if
the Tulpa was attending to the matter personally, Zoe was
right. He was hunting their granddaughter.

"I see him." Vaughn spoke too loudly. The Tulpa's gaze
rolled as though his head were riveted to his shoulders. He
noted and dismissed Vaughn, and fastened his attention on
Skamar. With a twitch of his lips, he angled the girl away,
and they headed in tandem toward the main stage.

"Break up," she ordered Vaughn, but he was already pushing through the tight pods of pubescent girls, all seemingly
on a mission to slow him down. The warm-up band had just
taken stage, and the singer yelled for everyone to raise their
hands. Amid the excited screaming, the Tulpa lifted his own
hand as he turned to grin at Skamar. Then he slipped around
a vendor's stall sparkling with lights and ornaments and disappeared.

Skamar knew the Tulpa was expending more energy than
usual on this new physical form and was further limited by
having to drag along a mortal. This knowledge—along with
the phantom smell of blueberries and the memory of Debi's
shell-shocked parents—had Skamar zigzagging like a speed
skater through the tightly packed crowd. If she got to him
before he found a solitary spot, she could separate him from
the girl . . . and take a shot at doing the same with his life.

A small clearing on the asphalt lot and a large burst of speed
put her within arm's reach. Being forced to drag Debi along
unobserved had slowed him significantly. Perhaps he *should*
have held on to his strength, she thought wryly. Yet he dodged

when Skamar leapt, elongating creepily to slide behind a wall of portable toilets. Laughter greeted Skamar even before she whipped around the corner . . . as did a harsh, unmistakably canine growl. Yet halting abruptly, she saw no one but the Tulpa, now pulling Debi into an unyielding headlock. The girl didn't protest or even blink, though her face was quickly turning red.

"Let her go."

"Since when do you care about anyone or anything but my demise?" His dark eyes, fastened on her face, had gone as black as his aura.

"I care about many things," Skamar lied, inching forward. "Not that I'd turn down the opportunity for a little payback."

"Still sore about that little crucifixion prank?" The features on his face shifted, shimmered, then resolidified. Despite his pleasant tone, he was expending a lot of energy. "It was a lark, I was just having a bit of fun. It would be so much more convenient if you just *got over it*."

Skamar took a step forward, testing him. "I'm not here to make life easier on you."

"Another way that we're shockingly alike." He whistled, and the ground next to Skamar's feet moved.

She jumped at the sight of a greyhound, slight and wiry . . . and completely translucent. It glistened now that it was moving, undulating in pearly waves like all doppelgängers. Greys weren't known for their aggressive natures, but canine wardens loathed anyone connected with the Light. And as Skamar had been created in the mind of a former agent of Light, she was certainly that. The dog snarled, baring teeth as long as crystalline spikes, its mouth bubbling with opalescent saliva.

She had time only to think how clever it was to create a warden doppelgänger before the Tulpa spoke. "*Bandit . . . kill.*"

And he named his creature right in front of Skamar, the same way she'd been named and afforded additional power . . . and with the same effect. The beast's body was instantly inked, and it lunged at Skamar with a speed only she possessed.

"Motherfucker!" A bullet followed Vaughn's cry, fired so close that Skamar's ears rang with the aftershocks. It entered the newly created hound, and the creature yelped . . . then grew a good three inches all around. However, the interruption gave Skamar the opening she needed, and she leapt at Bandit while yelling at Vaughn to hold his fire.

The dog's gaping mouth was level with her face, and Skamar shoved her hands inside of it to yank the impossibly sharp incisors in opposite directions. Bandit yelped as she ripped apart its hard palate. Then she bit into the hound's neck, jerked her head, and tore out its larynx. She kept ripping with her teeth, literally consuming half of the animal—and its magic— because the only way to kill a tulpa, even a canine one, was to turn its own magic against it. Thus only another tulpa could do that.

Skamar's vision swam, her mind clouded, and time leapt forward in the strange stop-motion jerks of battle-born fugue. Using the animal's magic, she dismembered its energy and form, and when she'd finished, the body lay in pieces around

her, the thought that had created his spirit was only memory . . . and the Tulpa and Debi were gone. Cursing, she began to rise before remembering Vaughn.

The cop was no longer standing. Shock had leached the
color from his skin, and he was slumped against the last blue
portable. Witnessing the object of his lustful fantasies feasting
on the blood of a mutant hound was apparently more than
he'd expected to see. And, she noted coolly, at some point
between firing that bullet and when she'd cracked the last
bone in Bandit's body, Vaughn had repositioned his gun, setting its sights on her.

Their eyes met, and Skamar rocketed forward. After knocking aside the weapon, she lifted Vaughn clean from his feet, to
propel him into a pickup at the lot's edge. She crowbarred his
neck until his feet began to kick like an upturned beetle's—
still lots of life in the limbs, though no amount of scrambling
would allow escape.

"Get it all out," Skamar rasped, pushing on his stomach
so that the last of his breath wheezed from his lungs. She
then wiped Bandit's blood from her chin, put her mouth to
Vaughn's—beneath eyes widening in horror—and began
to suck.

Mortals were so ignorant, thinking the soul lived in the
eyes. The soul lived in the breath, threaded to the heart and
mind in invisible strings, which pulsed with ethereal life.
Skamar tugged on the brightest of these and was surprised at
how little time it took to lift the memory of the last few
minutes. Vaughn gradually relaxed, and she slowly lessened
her hold, finally allowing life-giving inhalations to alternate

with the small cocktail straw sips she still used to pull that memory clean.

Vaughn shifted, which she allowed because it was expected. His body and mind would create a new story for how and why they got there. The human mind was so weak that it was easily altered. Or maybe, she thought, frowning as she pulled away, it was that strong. All shifting, adaptable beings had to be, right?

Yet what Skamar didn't expect, and somehow still allowed, was to be pulled close again. The new story developing in Vaughn's strong/weak mind was clearly a romance. His mouth fastened on hers this time with a dizzying warmth, an enveloping she'd never before felt yet somehow still welcomed. She returned the kiss, her first, with a shocking urgency. In spite of that, or maybe because of it, she pulled away. Licking now tingling lips, she warily eyed Vaughn . . . who eyed her mouth dreamily.

"How did we—" But he broke off abruptly, putting a hand to his mouth and coming away with blood.

"He punched you," she lied, flushing. Hey, she wasn't the one who'd turned the memory cleanse into a kiss!

But it was already forgotten. Vaughn startled again, then fumbled his phone from his pocket. Face already expectantly grim, it fell further as he read the text, and Skamar didn't have to be told why.

She sighed. "Where?"

"A park in Centennial Hills. The girl's father tried to intervene this time. It looks like he was attacked by a dog, of all things." Vaughn squinted into the sky, searching for a memory as he canvassed the stars, before shaking his head. "Isn't that strange?"

Skamar just nodded, stood, and turned away to hide her bloodied clothing. Touching her hand to still-tingling lips, she thought, Yes. It was all very strange indeed.

The latest victim's name was Theresa, she'd been born within two months of Ashlyn, and her father was mad with grief. He screamed and ranted about mutant hounds until the nurses held him down and sedated him by force.

Meanwhile, the police were just as frustrated. Vaughn fumed about lacking funds and manpower, and Skamar listened with her usual detachment, wondering if this was what "life" was all about. What was the point of opening yourself up to people or caring about things if they could eventually be used against you? Why even have a child if her potential absence resulted in a crater being carved in your chest?

She posed a softer version of this question—one that didn't make her sound as if she didn't understand the mortal state— to Vaughn when he finally fell silent.

"Because it can be so good, too," he said, though he looked pained as he said it. "Knowing that the worst might someday happen doesn't mean you avoid the risk of loving someone. It only means you seize the good when and where you can."

Was that what she'd felt in that darkened parking lot? While stinking of warden blood and having just taken a life, was that what she'd inadvertently done? Was that why Zoe's daughter, Joanna, had willingly offered up her life for a mortal child's? And mostly, Skamar wondered, Was it worth it?

She studied Vaughn. He certainly believed so. Funny how when she looked at him now she saw not his physical weakness, that fragile humanity, but his strong spirit, which seemed directly related to that belief. She could suddenly see how in the simplest of things—an invite for a cup of coffee, a small flirtation, a kiss—he seized his life as fervently as she clung to hers. Seizing life . . . and choosing good.

Skamar was still preoccupied by this when she joined his undercover unit the very next night. They were outfitting a female cop so young-looking that only her scent gave her away as a mature woman. Yet mortal girls verging on puberty were olfactory blank spots in the mind, just like the initiates born in underground sanctuaries and raised to fight on either side of the Zodiac. Therefore this plan to plant the officer in the audience during an evening magic show— where a magician would oh-so-conveniently pick her for his disappearing act—was flawed from the beginning. The Shadows would never fall for it.

The one thing it did have going for it was the proximity to another gathering of teens. Yuletide Magic raised money for underprivileged children while easing the social consciences of parents who otherwise seemed hell-bent on spending an insane amount of money on plastic trinkets for their offspring. Yet Skamar remained skeptical.

"This isn't going to work," she muttered as Vaughn jerked at the neck of his rented tuxedo.

"Why not?" he asked, frowning at his bow tie. It had been her idea for him to pose as an amateur magician, ostensibly to draw the girls close to him and possibly the kidnappers as well. In reality, she wanted only to keep him out of the way. The run-in at the Festival of Lights two nights earlier had shaken her—even if Vaughn didn't remember any of it. She wouldn't want anyone that close to the Tulpa. Never mind a man in possession of a surprisingly kind heart, dry scent, and lips that made hers tingle.

"Too obvious a setting," she lied, as there was no way to explain about the decoy cop's scent.

"Ah, sunshine," he said, grinning as he pulled a springy bunch of colorful flowers from his tuxedo pocket. He offered them to her. "All you have to do is believe in magic."

Skamar crossed her arms until he tucked the flowers away, though her heart skipped a couple of beats and her mouth quirked at one side when he shot her a roguish wink. Be careful, she found herself thinking.

Frowning, she wondered where that particularly *human* worry had come from, and turning away, she almost missed the Shadow entirely. As the bait took to the stage and the undercover officers fanned out about her, Skamar saw Dawn, a petite, unremarkable-looking woman . . . except that she was also the Shadow Gemini. She was speaking with a girl perched at the audience's edge, gesturing animatedly to an exit door. Whatever she said made the girl's eyes pop with excitement, and though no more than five feet from the nearest undercover cop, their body language indicated they were together. Dawn shepherded the girl toward a door leading backstage, and just as they gained the threshold, she shot Skamar a sweet smile over her shoulder.

Skamar glanced over to see if Vaughn had noticed, but he

was now surrounded by half a dozen children who wanted him to hop inside his Plexiglas box, pull the curtains shut, and make himself disappear. It was clear *that* disguise had backfired.

Meanwhile the plant was onstage, ostensibly being hypnotized, and all other eyes were fixed firmly on her. It didn't matter. Skamar was the only one who could keep Dawn from escaping anyway.

She raced through the door and gained the backstage area in time to see the girl yanked behind an arching black scrim. Using the darkness to cover her unnatural speed, Skamar instantly closed the gap between them. Braced for attack—by a warden, by other waiting Shadows, maybe even by the Tulpa—she wasn't ready for a conversation. But Dawn stood across the vast expanse of the stage, one hand holding a knife to the girl's throat, the other muffling her sobs.

"My friends and I want to show you a little magic trick," Dawn called out in a singsong voice.

Skamar laughed harshly. "You mean you and your invisible friends, Dawn?"

"Better than mortal ones," Dawn said, offering up her own harsh laugh. "Especially at a magic show. I mean, it's just so easy to make them go *poof!*"

Then both Dawn and the girl dropped from sight, a trapdoor swinging shut above them. Skamar ran, intending to give the door one hard stomp, but she came up short, Dawn's final words—and the accompanying grin—finally reaching her mind and stopping her heart.

After bolting back to the theater, she nudged aside surly

teens and offended parents to stand in front of the glass magic box. Vaughn was gone, the curtains were pulled shut, and the whole box vibrated with energy. Swallowing hard, Skamar grasped the tassel at the box's side and pulled open the curtains.

A warden as giant and black as hell's gaping mouth lunged at her, banging against the Plexiglas front with rabid fury. Screams erupted behind Skamar as the dog rocketed into the glass. Ignoring the chaos behind her, she reached for a note taped to the box's front. A single word was spelled out in block letters on Valhalla Hotel stationery, one that brought back such an intense memory of pain that she actually sagged.

Valhalla was where. Vaughn was who. Now was when. As for the what? The Shadows weren't making her guess at that: "CRUCIFIXION."

Crumpling the note in her hand, Skamar bolted.

Skamar didn't own any weapons. Shadows were immune to them, so knives and guns were more irritants than deterrents, and the Tulpa was impervious to all weaponry—even the magical ones crafted for Zodiac agents. Skamar couldn't complain about that too much since she shared the immunity as a tulpa, but it was also why she had to take on the Shadows, and whatever trap they'd set, all alone.

Besides, the thought of something happening to Vaughn because of her was suddenly unacceptable. It set off such a panic in her chest, it was as if her lungs had grown wings. She had to stop it or—yes—die trying.

So Skamar skirted slot machines, floor attendants, and oblivious patrons of the Valhalla Hotel and Casino and followed the meaty, furred scent of Shadow wardens into the heart of the property. When she passed the twenty-four-hour café, the girls' scent joined the hounds', causing her heart to skip a beat. She rounded the gift shop, one of four, and felt a mental punch as Vaughn's scent was added to the mix. The olfactory triptych was impossible to miss—a rabid fury matched only by a throbbing fear.

The scents led into a showroom, the grandest she'd ever seen, and home to one of those freaky acrobat shows Vegas visitors couldn't get enough of. Multileveled pools and water features pitted the room's center, and as it was obviously the show's "dark" night, the Coliseum-like theater was empty.

Yet there was still a show going on.

Deep drums pounded through the cavernous room, while refitted spotlights blazed upon the platforms suspended above two pools of water. One held the four girls—bound and cowering in the rounded middle, facing drowning if any of them even wobbled. Their pool had been blackened into shimmering opaqueness.

The other platform held Vaughn Rhett. He was suspended over a sparkling blue pool, though he faced exactly the opposite problem in his potential death. Lifted to his toes by a makeshift series of pulleys and levers, he would suffer crucifixion if his platform suddenly gave way. And though Skamar didn't move, didn't even blink, something inside of her screamed. Her palms also began to sweat as she recalled the acute ache ratcheting up her arms from the giant nails the Tulpa had driven into her wrists. Her calves cramped up reflexively, and she closed her eyes, swaying as she remembered her ribs pressing against her lungs in a slow suffocation. Her normally sharp mental admonition to pull it together might as well have been a kitten's plea.

"Decisions, decisions."

Her eyelids flipped open, and her gaze landed on the ringmaster to this wet, twisted circus. The Tulpa stepped onto the walkway separating the two pools, surrounded by three doppelgänger hounds, their bodies shimmering and frothing, refractive and nauseating. When Skamar said nothing, the Tulpa grinned and took a bow.

"Choose platform A and you'll save four innocent, albeit relatively useless, lives. My pets, then, will have to feast on something else." He placed a hand on the flat head of the nearest warden. It growled liquid menace. "Choose the second, and you'll save only one life—though one that's been trained to save many."

Skamar said nothing. She was trying to still her shaking hands, hidden behind her back.

"No choice!" Vaughn's voice was strained as the rope around his neck drew tighter. "Save the girls!"

He didn't realize his words made her decision more difficult, not less.

The Tulpa smiled. *He* knew it. "Well, it's a conundrum either way. I'll leave you to it."

He began to turn, and Skamar acted out of instinct. Letting out a battle cry, she dove not for Vaughn or the girls, but for the Tulpa. Yet even as she flew forward, he rocketed straight into the air, yanking at ropes he'd had concealed behind his back. The platforms, one attached to each of his wrists, twisted from the pools. The girls fell. Vaughn screamed.

Unable to cease her forward motion, Skamar could only drop to the walkway where the doppelgänger hounds lunged, all three striking at once. Skamar's screams spiraled throughout the theater as the drumbeats increased, syncopated with the girls' terrified cries and, just as they hit the water, the Tulpa's booming laugh. "Permanence must be a bitch."

Skamar was too busy working a jaw full of luminous razors from her left calf while shielding her throat with her other hand. Yet the wardens were almost impossible to see in the reflected light of the tanks, eerie undulations appearing through their not-flesh. A strange sensation began to overtake her, one she'd only smelled on others before but recognized immediately—pure, sharp panic.

When the third hound took a chunk from her back, she arched forward and knew the next would claim her heart. Ironically, it was that sharp pain of teeth piercing skin that brought Skamar back to her senses. She hammered one snarling beast on its head, less to fend it off than to anoint it, naming it even as it regained its balance. "Dasher!"

He shuddered, the forced moniker giving him form as Skamar whipped around, kicking the second. "Dancer!"

The third animal again found her back. "Prancer!"

The power of permanence rippled through them, just as it had done when she'd turned from doppelgänger into a full-blown tulpa. It gave them the same momentary pause she'd had, too, and in that moment she launched herself backward. When they continued their midair attack, the wild snaps of the first two dogs found each other instead. Too far gone with battle lust, and too newly born in their permanent state, they writhed madly, tearing at each other's bodies.

Meanwhile, Skamar propelled the third dog, so recently existing in a liquid form, into the giant tank of water where the girls had already sunk. Release and relief came immediately, and as the third hound lost its breath and life to the black liquid, she dove past the pooling of her own blood to search out the drowning girls.

Blindly, she flailed around until grabbing rope, or hair, or something that wound easily about her hands, then used her legs to thrust herself and the girls straight out of the tank. She dropped the gasping girls on the center platform and braced for the Tulpa's counterattack, only to find the cooling bodies of the hounds destroyed by their own magic.

And then she looked up.

The sensation of flying was an afterthought. She was back on the ground so fast, a tortured man cradled in her arms, that the girls were still sputtering on hands and knees. But Skamar forgot them for now. How odd, she thought, removing the rope from Vaughn's neck, that the Tulpa hadn't missed a trick. After all, she wouldn't have expected a patently unreligious being to remember the spear in the side.

Though Vaughn's larynx was crushed, his neck hadn't snapped, leaving him to bleed out slowly, as the Tulpa had no doubt intended. Holding the man, Skamar thought of the boy who'd once borne kissable freckles. Tearing up, she could almost smell blueberries. "You did it, Vaughn. You saved those girls. Just like one of those medieval knights."

She didn't know if it was the small white lie or her tears dropping to his face that did the trick, but his eyes fluttered open long enough to reveal recognition touching his gaze. "Your . . . name . . ."

It wasn't even a whisper, only his lips moving, but she read them and whispered back, "Skamar. It means star."

And he somehow managed to reward her with a full smile, though the shockingly brave look twisted quickly into an anguished wince. Then as she held him, as she cried for the first time ever, her fragile knight died.

Skamar hadn't opened the door to the apartment in days, never mind left it, so when she allowed Zoe in—and even that had taken a few moments of dull, uninterested consideration—her creator winced at the smell, and then in sympathy. It was the latter emotion that made Skamar want to slam the door shut.

Zoe, in yet another pretty if nondescript disguise, perched on the rented sofa's side. "So, the Tulpa thinks he's won. That you've gone into hiding . . . injured, licking wounds, beaten."

"I don't care what he thinks." Though she did, of course. Thought created reality, and the Tulpa's mind was a dangerously fertile place. But even the idea of facing him was too much effort right now.

"He's still after my granddaughter."

Skamar clenched her jaw, not looking at Zoe. "Well, I don't know how to kill him. Obviously."

Zoe repositioned herself in front of Skamar, who—deeming it too difficult and pointless to move—had simply sunk to her knees just inside the door. Grasping those knees, Zoe squeezed. "Just because you're born for a particular task doesn't mean you don't have to work at it, or that it doesn't come with a price. In fact, if you're really born to do something, chances are you'll die doing it, too."

"Great." As ruthlessly unemotional as always. This time Skamar didn't smile.

Zoe reached for her shoulders. "But meanwhile, you have to *live*."

"I don't even know what that means!" Skamar pushed away from Zoe's touch, even though there was nowhere to go. "You never taught me that, Zoe! All I know is that the first person I opened myself up to in this world is dead because of me. And you know what? They all die! They're all weak and fragile and . . ."

"Mortal?" Zoe asked quietly.

Skamar clenched her jaw so hard, she thought her teeth would crack. "If that's life, if *this* is it . . ." She motioned around at the crappy apartment, but more important, the sorrow stinking up the air, a pain surely even Zoe could scent. If this was life, she continued silently, she wasn't sure she wanted it. Even for the chance to kill the Tulpa.

"This isn't life," Zoe said, taking Skamar's face in her hand and forcing her gaze. "*This* is experience."

"What's the difference?" Skamar muttered, trying to shake the touch away.

Zoe held on, her smile bittersweet. "Experience is what happens when you don't get what you want in life."

Skamar was mortified when her face crumpled. "It hurts," she whispered.

For just one moment, only one, she'd given herself over to something good, and look what had happened. She shook her head. "How do you do it?"

Zoe answered with a question of her own. "Would you rather it never happened? That you'd never met a human who made you want to open up? That either he or you hadn't existed?"

No. Somehow she couldn't wish that.

"You did the best you could," Zoe said, then swallowed hard and bit her lip. "How about allowing me to try and do the same?"

Skamar frowned, only belatedly realizing what Zoe was asking. "Let you in again? No." She shook her head. "My mind is my own now."

Zoe inclined her head. "Yes, but that doesn't mean you can't lean upon others. Let someone else take the reins for a while."

Give up even more power? Even more control just for the opportunity to share the burden? Depend on someone else to thrive? Open, even a fraction, to *love*?

"I don't want control over you, Skamar," Zoe said, misinterpreting her silence, though she'd have been right enough only days before. "I want to give you a moment of peace. I feel . . . somehow responsible."

"For sending me after those girls?" Skamar shook her head, thinking of the families, their tearful reunions . . . the scent of blueberries. No. She knew now that it had been the right thing to do.

"No." Zoe bowed her head. "For birthing you into a world already waiting to cause you pain. It's a mother's shame."

It was the first time Zoe had ever admitted feelings for her beyond ownership, and Skamar was so shocked that she didn't pull away when Zoe took her hand. And after another moment, she leaned against Zoe—strong against the weak—and eventually closed her eyes and gave herself over. One moment wouldn't hurt anything, right?

And then there was the familiar feeling and scent of Zoe moving around in her mind. She relaxed into the meditative rhythm, the reassuring words—affirming, positive, and, when the one-way conversation turned to that of the Tulpa, positively homicidal.

"I'm so proud of you, Skamar," Zoe said in conclusion. "Now rest, dear."

Yes, she thought, drifting off as Zoe let herself out. She was going to need all the energy she could get if she was to continue this fight. And while still unwilling to give up her life for others, maybe—just maybe—she could *live* for them. Giving a fair shot to good people was a worthwhile pastime, right? It was something she could pursue in Vaughn's honor.

When she wasn't hunting the Tulpa, of course.

* * *

The *New York Times* and *USA Today* bestselling author of the Signs of the Zodiac series, Vicki Pettersson was born and raised in Las Vegas. She still lives in Sin City, where a backyard view of the Strip regularly inspires her to set down her martini and head back to the computer. Check out the latest at www.vickipettersson.com.

ROOKWOOD & MRS. KING

by LILITH SAINTCROW

"I need to kill my husband."

Rookwood set the bottle of Scotch on his desk with a precise little click. His teeth were tingling, and he regretted climbing out of bed, not to mention agreeing to meet her so close to dusk. He hadn't had time for his daily jolt of red stuff. "I think you've got the wrong man, lady."

Rookwood's rent was due in a week. He was on his last legs as far as funding went. It was foolish to turn away work, even this kind; but when possible, he preferred to err on the side of caution.

She had money, too. Real money. Her shoes—high-end walking numbers—the fashionable gym-toned slimness, French manicure, and the haircut gave away the size of her bank account, but upper-middle-class suburbia was all over her. There was one like her in every minivan in America. This one had nicer breasts than most, big brown eyes, long, glossy brown hair, a pink T-shirt, and jeans. All she needed were 2.5 kids and a golden retriever to finish the picture.

"Not according to Detective Molstein." She leaned

forward a little. That long brown hair fell over her shoulder. She used expensive shampoo. Something with cloves in it.

Damn you, Mole. What did I ever do to you? Rookwood couldn't settle in the chair behind the desk just yet. Instead, he looked up at the window with its thick iron bars. Rain slapped at the glass, and the night sighed as traffic on Lombard sent splashes of headlight glow through the lattice of blinds. "I don't care who sent you, lady. You've got the wrong man."

Her lips parted, and the flash of pearly-sharp white in his peripheral vision was all wrong. A burning smell slid across his nose, a tang under her brunette spice.

No wonder the inside of his mouth was tingling. If she smelled like that, there was only one possible explanation. Rookwood's weight sank onto his right leg, his entire body subtly braced. *This is either what I've been waiting for or very bad luck.*

"You don't understand, Mr. Rookwood. My husband . . . he's already dead." Her shoulders slumped. "Detective Molstein believed me. He said you'd help me."

He half turned, facing her. Her manicured hand pulled down the scoop neckline of the T-shirt. Her bra was plain and white, the strap cutting into her shoulder, and the deep, glaring red purple bruise on the upper slope of her left breast was as plain as it could be. There were two holes in the middle of the bruising, white and worn-looking.

She was shaking. Her eyes looked even bigger with tears filling them, and his heart thumped twice. This was what he'd been waiting for, it and bad luck at the same time.

Rookwood dropped his rangy frame into the chair behind

the desk. Paper crackled and rustled as he poured her a jolt of Scotch and wished he could take a slug of something strong himself. The sensitivity in his canines retreated a little, but his tongue found the sharp places before he took a deep breath and forced some calm. "All right. Pull your shirt up, ma'am, and tell me everything."

Her name was Amelia King. Thirty on the nose, settled in the suburbs with a husband and a house. They were planning on kids, and she spent her time being the good little wifey, shopping and keeping the house—and herself—trim and clean. Hubby contented himself with making money as a lawyer with Briggs, Fann, and Chisholm.

Mr. King was an up-and-coming criminal defense tightrope walker, successful enough that he was looking at making partner soon.

Which meant he would have security access to the office building downtown. Rookwood's eyebrow rose a little, but he didn't say anything. That was probably, he realized later, his mistake.

He should have come clean with her from the beginning.

But by that point she was crying openly. It wasn't much—a slow trickle from both big, brown, bloodshot, and dark-circled eyes. Her makeup was good, but it couldn't hold up to that constant leak.

She had no idea anything was wrong until the afternoon she returned from grocery shopping and found out hubby had come home early for once, and in a big way. He'd hung himself with his belt over the banister. Hell of a job he did of it, too. Broke his neck and everything.

Three nights after the funeral, after Amelia had cried herself to sleep again, he'd come back.

"There was a tapping at the window." She shivered. "I thought I was dreaming."

The rain swept Rookwood's window restlessly. His teeth ached, and the bottle of Scotch looked really good. The thought of the canister of red stuff in his minifridge looked even better. "Let me guess. You saw him floating outside. Just bobbing up and down like a balloon."

"You . . ." Amelia swallowed dryly. She didn't ask how he knew. It was a stupid question, and maybe she realized it. "It was his eyes." The color had drained from her face, shadows under her cheekbones turned her gaunt.

"They glowed red." Rookwood leaned back in his chair. "Are you a churchgoing woman, Mrs. King?"

Her hands tightened in her lap. "No. We were married in front of a judge."

He waited. An unnecessary detail like that meant there was more to the story. He had trouble keeping his pulse even and steady. *This is it. Don't scare her off. Play this one right, Rookwood.*

The traffic outside made wet, shushing noises, and car light ran over the room in waves. The green-shaded lamp didn't light more than a pool on the desktop. Her eyes glittered a little in the gloom, slowly leaking tears.

Each one was a fresh little nugget of guilt, for him. It was hard to sit still when he wanted to pace.

"My mother was Catholic," Mrs. King amended slowly. "I thought of going to a priest, but . . ."

"But hubby's already bitten you, and you didn't ask too

many questions the first time he came in the window. Naturally. Because he's your husband."

The first surprise was that her chin came up, and the second was the flash in those brown eyes. "What's that supposed to mean?"

Uh-oh. The front legs of his chair thudded down on the floor. He scooped up a pad of paper and a pen he was fairly sure would work. "Write down the cemetery he's in, location of the grave, and his exact name—first, middle, last. The fee's ten thousand. Half now, half when he stops showing up at your window."

Her hands moved nervously. She didn't say a goddamn thing about the money. Instead, she went right for the throat. "Will . . . that . . . make the dreams go away?"

"What dreams?" Rookwood asked, but he knew. The same dreams that rocketed around inside his skull every time he settled down on his cot. The red-tinted, hot, squirming little dreams that filled his mouth with saliva and the fresh copper tang, instead of the pale, dead substitute he held the Thirst off with.

God, yes, he knew. Did she want the bad news now or later?

Later, Rook. After she's paid you.

She shook her head. "If you're going to treat me like I'm stupid—"

His entire mouth ached, and the crackling in his jaw was clearly audible. He leaned forward into the desk lamp's glow, knowing it would etch the shadows on his face even deeper. It would gleam along the lines of the sharpening, lengthening canines and fill his eyes with a flat, reflective shine. He hadn't had his daily dose, and she smelled good—except for the edge of burning to the scent of woman, perfume, and red salt copper.

The edge of burning that tainted his own smell.

His lips peeled back from his teeth. She choked on whatever she'd intended to say next. Under the splash of car tires outside was a nervous, high thudding; it was her pulse tearing through the air of the room and touching his sensitive eardrums.

His mouth ached fiercely as he pulled the Thirst back, the rope he held it on fraying as the sun slipped away over the horizon. His canines retracted, too, his jaw crackling once again. When he was sure he wouldn't cut his tongue on the sharp edges, he spoke. "The dreams don't ever stop. But if my . . ." The words stuck in his throat. "If my *treatment* is successful, they won't get any worse—and neither will you. That I can promise you, Mrs. King."

Her rib cage almost fluttered with sharp, sipping breaths. The sweat along the curves of her throat stood out in diamond drops. Her shirt was now damp, and the fresh wave of clove-tinted scent about knocked him sideways.

He'd always wondered what would happen if someone with his particular problem came along. It would be a key to the bigger problem, of course. But he'd wondered what the Thirst might do.

"Am I going to look like . . . that?" She stared at him as though he'd just done something obscene.

Well, he just *had*. Hadn't he?

"I don't know." He pressed his fingertips together. His mouth didn't want to work right, wanted to slur the words around as if he were drunk. The Thirst pressed its sharp prickles against the inside of his throat. Soon it would spread over his whole body, and only the red stuff would make it retreat. "But I'll give you some advice. Get some raw meat from the supermarket and suck on it. The bloodier the better, or tell your butcher you want blood for blood pudding. It's the only thing that kills that feeling in your throat, and it quiets the dreams down, at least for a while. And that's all you're getting for free, Mrs. King."

Yeah, he was a son of a bitch. But he wasn't going to lose any sleep over it.

Shady Hope Cemetery and Remembrance Home wasn't hallowed ground, for all they buried people here and spoke empty words over them. Hallowed ground would have made the dead sleep a little more quietly.

As it was, anything could rise from these graves. In the last six months, Rookwood had gained a thorough education in just how weird and fluid the borders between life and undeath were and an even more thorough education in how someone who didn't mind a little weirdness could possibly make a living around the edges.

But this was the prize. This was the thing he'd been waiting for since that night of blood and screaming and Chisholm's fangs in his throat.

As soon as he stepped on the grounds he smelled it, the dry burning rat-fur reek of particular contamination. He'd grown used to the varied and insanely ugly smells drifting across his nasal receptors at the slightest provocation, ever since he'd fought off—

Don't think about that. You're on a job, you've taken the nice lady's money, let's get this dog-and-pony show started.

Caution was called for. It could be a trap.

He stayed where he was, boots planted solidly on wet concrete. Behind him, the yellow-painted bar that was supposed to keep out cars and people rattled in the rain-soaked wind. His sweatshirt jacket was already soaked through.

The cold meant nothing. He was used to it. He still ran at a perfect 98.6, but external changes in temperature had ceased to matter as the Thirst got stronger. Tiny increments of burning inched through him every day, nibbling at the edges of his sanity.

That was another mental road he didn't want to go down. Instead, he decided the cemetery was safe enough and got to work.

Amelia's hand-drawn map was exact, committed to memory, and destroyed. He'd also spent a little time looking at satellite photos of the cemetery's green mournfulness. It would have given him the shivers to see how anyone with a laptop and a connection could cruise the city, but the things no satellite photo would show were still safe.

Like the thing he was hunting. Or the things that had made the widow's dearly beloved into a monster.

The grave was right where she'd said it would be. He read the name in the wet, dim glimmer, a nice white marble headstone. The widow certainly hadn't skimped.

Rookwood stood a good three or four feet away from where the corpse's feet would rest and sniffed deeply at the wet air.

The smell was fading. Mr. King was out visiting. When he came back home, he'd find a surprise.

A faint smile clung to Rookwood's face, his flesh stiff against the bones. He took the last few steps forward, set the edge of the shovel against the wet turf, and began to dig.

The first faint gray streaks of dawn found him showered and in dark sunglasses, parked in a nice suburban neighborhood. Led Zeppelin was pouring out life through the speakers of his rusted Cadillac. It was a good car, but stood out like a sore thumb here in the land of minivans and SUVs. Still, it ran like a dream. And with the mods under the hood, he could outrun just about anything. He couldn't quite beat the devil, but it was close.

He waited for "Dazed and Confused" to moan out its last few beats and later thought that if he'd just gone to meet the widow a little earlier, instead of at dawn as agreed, everything would have turned out differently.

The newborn edge of morning sun was struggling up over the rim of the earth, peeking through scudding clouds, as he slammed the car door and hitched the duffel bag onto his shoulder. Jeans, army jacket, boots—he didn't match the neighborhood, either. It made his back itch. He was used to blending in.

In his slices of the city, that kept you alive.

Rookwood scooped the paper drink carrier off the roof

and set out for the widow's front door. The daylight, weak as it was, was a painful glare even behind the shades.

Nice house, white with two stories, green shutters, and a good lawn. Looked as if she'd planted primroses early this year and lavender a few years back. That was good. One lavender bush was worth ten or twelve crucifixes when it came to the—

Rookwood stopped, frowning.

The cedar green front door was open a crack. He couldn't have seen it from the street, but six feet from the door it was a wrong note in the newborn symphony of day.

"Shit," he muttered, and strode up the walk. He hit it with the palm of his free hand, and the door jerked, stopped halfway on its arc by something soft.

Amelia King lay on the floor in the hall. The door had hit her on the head, and her long, glossy brown hair was tangled. She was paper white, in a tattered gray T-shirt and shorts that she probably slept in, and if he hadn't been able to hear the faint whisper of her struggling pulse, he might have thought she was dead.

The entire house reeked of ash and undead. *Jesus Christ. What the hell's this?*

But he knew. The bait had been taken, sooner than he'd thought.

He pushed the door closed and locked it, then knelt at her side. The coffee went on a tiny, spindly decorative hall table. The vase that had probably been sitting there last night was on the floor. He could see how she would have blundered into it, knocking a spray of dried flowers to the floor and smashing something china blue to flinders.

She was taking in little shallow breaths, her lips blue and the rest of her chalky.

"Fuck." The duffel unzipped with a screaming sound, and the insulated chill-pack crumpled aside as he grabbed the plastic bottle. Three or four quick shakes to get everything mixed together, and he checked her teeth. There wasn't time for a transfusion, but if she wasn't far enough along yet—

Reflex snapped her sharp white teeth together, and he almost lost a fingertip. Rookwood snatched his hand back and grabbed her jaw. He jammed the nozzle between her blue lips and gave the bottle a gentle half-squeeze.

"Come on, kiddo," he whispered. "Come on. It's instinct, don't fight it. Come on."

She went rigid for a moment. Some shred of human decency was fighting for its life, and he found himself wishing it would win and hoping it would lose at the same time. Even when it was clinging to survival, there were some things the human animal wouldn't do.

Like drinking the red stuff. He'd given up wondering if it made someone better or worse to get rid of the idea that there were some things you wouldn't do even to survive.

Her lips fastened on the bottle and she guzzled greedily. The sharp points of her extended canines punctured the plastic and she tilted her head a little. The burning smell got stronger as the cold red fluid slid down her throat.

"That's a girl. . . . Good girl." But his eyes scanned the

hall. He slid the sunglasses off carefully, blinked a few times, and found it was bearable. Visual acuity was a boon at night, but not so good inside a house with the lights on.

She made a choking noise. Her eyes flew open, and he grabbed her, shoved the spout of the bottle in as far as it would go, and *squeezed*. She swallowed most of the rest in a huge painful gush, then feebly tried to push him away.

"Quit it. This'll stop the Thirst." He gave the bottle another squeeze, and it burbled in her throat. Her arms stiffened, then she gulped and pushed at him again. Her pulse came back, the doors of her heart slamming solidly shut and then thudding open.

It was damn near miraculous.

"When was he here?" He restrained the urge to shake her. "When, goddammit?"

The bottle fell away from her mouth, hit the polished hardwood floor. Her lips were still cyanotic, but she blinked and an unhealthy flush crept up her cheeks. "What?"

"When did he come back?"

Sense returned to her dark, swimming gaze. "I was asleep. On the couch." The gray T-shirt gaped open, torn over her chest.

Rookwood felt the urge to look down. Those breasts were worth a peek or two, even if she did have suburbia all over her. But wherever his gaze wandered, all he saw were the bruises and the fang marks. There was more than one set, and he wondered how many she had on other parts of her body. The ones on her right breast looked fresh, the edges not worn away and whitened. There was a pin-thin scraping along the border of one perky little nipple, as though a fang had slipped.

Rookwood realized he was staring at her chest. It gave him a funny unsteady feeling, as though he'd been caught peeking in her window.

Christ. Bruised all over; and hubby wasn't too happy last night, either. He tore his eyes away, carefully watched her nose instead, her eyes, the sharp, pearly teeth. Her canines had retracted. A good sign. Her irises were still brown, too—no threading of reflective crimson. And her smell was only tainted, not dipped in the ash and buried. He let out a shaky half-breath.

The widow was proving to be full of surprises.

"There was . . . he was . . . he was *angry*. Furious. He came in and . . ." The shakes hit her, and Rookwood let up a little on her shoulders. His thumbs wanted to move, little soothing motions, but he pushed the urge down. "God. *God.*"

God doesn't help, babe. If He did, we'd be in a better position down here. "I owe you a partial refund." The words scorched his throat. "I didn't think he'd've prepared a place here. Most of the young ones don't think that far ahead." *Still, they're organized here. Other towns, they can't even cooperate enough to wipe their asses.*

Here, they were in a nice, neat little hierarchy. It was an evolution he was hoping wouldn't spread.

Her hand flew up. For a split second he thought she was going to slap him, but instead her fingers clapped over her mouth and she began to scrub at her lips, weakly, as if something there burned her.

A lump in the middle of Rookwood's chest was doing funny things. Like aching. It wasn't the Thirst, it was something else entirely. Amelia King looked up at him, and she peeled her fingers away from her mouth long enough to surprise him again.

"He's in the basement," she whispered. "You shouldn't be here. If he finds out I've hired you, he'll . . ."

She was probably about to say "kill me" but must have realized how that would sound. Ridiculous on the one hand, terrifying on the other. Or maybe she was about to say "kill you" and stopped.

Stopped dead. A grim smile touched Rookwood's lips. His face felt wooden.

"It's day, and he's a newbie. He can't do a damn thing. *We* can, because we're only halfway to where he is." Reciting the rules to a woman was a new experience, and one he discovered he hated. But duty called. "The basement. Is there bare dirt down there, or concrete?" Bare dirt would be problematic, but this was the burbs. He was betting on concrete.

Her eyelids fluttered. She swallowed audibly, and her lips were slowly losing the blue tinge. "C-concrete. But—"

I didn't have time for a transfusion, dammit. She's only halfway instead of all the way because I did the best thing possible. He wished his conscience would believe it and leave him alone. "I didn't think he'd come back here. I thought he'd be caught out in the dawn." He was repeating himself, didn't care. "Go upstairs. Take a shower. By the time you're done, I'll have everything fixed down here. Okay?"

Amazingly, she laughed. It was a thin, hysterical sound.

"Go *upstairs*? Are you out of your *mind*?" She grabbed at the front of his faded green jacket with surprising strength, and Rookwood instinctively shifted his weight back. "Listen to me. *Listen*. He wasn't alone."

He lost his balance and thumped down hard, his teeth clicking together as his ass hit the floor. His pulse leapt like a fish going after a juicy water bug. "How many?"

"J-just one. The two of them. You have to leave—it's his *boss*." Then, the crowning absurdity: "He's a *partner*."

All the better. He couldn't believe his luck. "Which one? Briggs or Chisholm?"

She stared at him as though he'd lost his mind. He supposed it wasn't too far from the truth. "You . . ."

"Fann doesn't leave the offices, I know that much. Which one is in the basement with him, Briggs or Chisholm?"

"How did you—" Then she shut her mouth over the question, knowledge leaping behind those dark eyes. He wasn't sure if that was a good thing or a bad thing. It was looking as if Amelia King were too smart by half. "Who the hell are you, really?" Flatly, calmly, and her mouth turned into a tight line.

How do I even begin explaining? "Just call me a knight in busted armor, lady. I'm here to do some cleaning up."

She didn't want to take a shower, but the ruin of her T-shirt convinced her to get changed. He should have started while she was upstairs and had it halfway done by the time she came back down.

Instead, he had her stove going and eggs sizzling in a

pan. The morning had turned out fine, sun up and patchy fog burning off. The kitchen was bright, open, airy, and indefensible thanks to all that glass—French doors were a security nightmare. He'd already barred the door down to the basement with a long, half-dried vine of wild rose and three silver dollars as well as a splash of holy water. Nothing undead was going to come through there, especially up into a sun-drenched kitchen.

His shades were back on, and he didn't like how glad he was that they hid his eyes. "You need some protein," he said when he heard her breathing in the doorway to the hall. "Eggs go down easy. So does toast. Other stuff, not so much."

Mrs. King apparently didn't want to talk about breakfast. "I want to know exactly what's going on here."

Isn't it obvious? I'm fixing your problem for reasons of my own, not just because you paid me. "I brought you a latte. It's on the counter. I figure if you don't want it, I'll add some chocolate and drink it myself."

"I don't want fucking *coffee*. I want some answers."

"Okay." He slid the eggs out of the pan and onto a blue china plate. The toaster obediently popped up the last two slices of bread he'd found in the kitchen. Her fridge was almost empty. She probably had other things on her mind than grocery shopping. "They're a small club. They have to be, because if they spread, they would suck a city dry in a short time. Nature's got her own way of making sure the predator doesn't overpower the prey completely. And you told me what law firm he worked for. He must've been a bright one, and ruthless, too."

The fight didn't go out of her, but she deflated a bit. "Robert *was* very good at his job. I don't see how that—"

"They look for the bright ones, the hungry ones. You start out as a daylight henchman, and if you're ruthless and lucky enough—or if you have something they want—you get offered more." He spread some of the health-conscious soy margarine crap on the toast, sliced it neatly into quarters, and turned around with the plate in his hand. "They invest a lot in each serious protégé. Whoever was with him was probably the one to bring him into the fold. Was it Briggs or Chisholm?"

She had to clear her throat before her voice would work. "It was Harry. Harold Briggs."

"If it makes you feel better, they left you for dead this morning. The sunlight coming in from the window over the door would have hit your dead body in midafternoon and made sure you didn't rise tonight." He set the plate on the tiled breakfast bar with a precise little click and dared to look up at her. "Eat something. I'm going to go down into the basement and fix this problem for you, and then—"

"What exactly are you going to do, Mr. Rookwood?" She folded her arms, not mollified in the least but willing to listen. She wore a white button-down shirt, jeans, and a fancy pair of flip-flops. She'd buttoned the shirt up all the way, though, but the casual look she was going for wasn't quite working. Her mouth was too tight, and the marks of strain around her eyes robbed her of easiness.

She had the sleeves all the way down and buttoned, too. He wondered again how many marks she had. Usually the new ones fed from only one place. It was only the ones who wanted to hurt who found fresh flesh to bite each time.

Or maybe she'd been passed around a little. It wasn't uncommon. What woman would talk about it, if she had been? Provided she lived to talk about it.

Still. Careful and cautious had saved his life before. Getting all worked up over this widow was a bad idea. "I mean I am going to find out if the older one is still awake and moving around—a daywalker. If he is, I'm going to shoot him first, then ram a stake through *his* chest and cut off his head. Then I'm going to find where your husband's sleeping, and ram a stake through *his* chest and cut off his head. Once the spinal cord's severed, the body will turn to dust in a few hours. Then I make sure no more of them can take up residence in your basement and warn you to sell your house soon. I maybe take a look at some of your husband's paperwork, and then I'm on my merry way."

"And then what?" She didn't even look at the plate between them, eggs congealing and toast turning into a slab of cold overprocessing. He didn't blame her and tried not to look at the way sunlight picked out chestnut in her hair. "What am I supposed to do?"

"I'd suggest leaving town. If Chisholm and Fann find out you're still alive, you're going to have problems." His stomach rumbled unhappily. If she wasn't going to go for the eggs, he would.

Maybe after he finished up downstairs.

"And that's *it*?" That quick, hurtful intelligence in her big, beautiful browns was like a missing manhole cover—a man could drop into those eyes and break an axle easily enough.

"This is what you paid me for. I'll refund a quarter of the fee for your trouble." It was the least he could do, and he hated that, too. "I'm going to be leaving town soon myself. Once I've done what I set out to do."

"Which is *what*? Who are you, really?"

Explaining to her wasn't getting him anywhere. "I'm the man you hired to get rid of your dead husband, ma'am. Now if you'll excuse me, I'm going to get to work. You might hear some noise and smell some funky stuff, but it'll be over soon."

Stairs. God, but he hated open-frame wood stairs. Down one step at a time, the UV handheld not shaking and the modified .45 steady in his other hand. The column of blue light from the UV cut the gloom, and the smell was enough to make him think of retching before his nose shut down. It still coated the back of his throat and touched the place where the Thirst lived. The shades were safe in a pocket, his eyes adjusting to the gloom.

Out here in suburbia the houses had yards to insulate them, and down in a basement half-underground . . . nobody would hear the shots. *Don't worry about that. Keep your mind on your work; this is the oldest one you've gone after so far, and they're tricky. Very tricky. And if he gets loose somehow and gets back to Chisholm . . .*

It was a pointless worry. With the sun up, both of the things were trapped here in the basement. They couldn't leave.

It didn't mean Rookwood would survive a tangle with a daywalker in a dark basement, without sunlight on his side. Best to be cautious. But God, how he *hated* open stairs like this.

He paused halfway down. The basement was open and dark as a new grave, a line of white banker's boxes stacked down the side near the stairs, all of them labeled in a clear schoolgirl hand. Some pieces of furniture under sheeting, standing dumb and quiet under the lash of blue UV when he slid the light across them. A couch, looked like. Maybe a desk. A rocking chair. Another bulky object, looming at the far end.

The fine hairs on the back of his neck rose. Rookwood swept the light one more time, decided not to shift his weight. He was waiting.

Of course, the only place for them to hide—the *logical* place—was behind the stairs. The husband would be insensate from before dawn to just after dusk, but Briggs was much older. He could easily be a daywalker. He wouldn't be able to stand the UV or a flood of sunlight, but he could very well—

The sound was very slight, a rustle of fabric against itself. Rookwood dived, twisting in midair as the stairs shattered. He'd prepared for this, having taken down a load of the red stuff before dawn as he sat in his Cadillac. It burned in his veins as the Thirst pulled at his body. The red tide crawled up his vision, and he landed jarring hard on concrete, arm up and the UV burning a smokelash stripe across the creature's face. The gun spoke, a deafening roar.

Anything less than a .45 didn't have any stopping power. The hollow points would mushroom and spread a load of tiny silver grains at the same time, and if he hit anything in the core, the resultant damage could bleed one of the beasts out in seconds.

Smoke. Reek. The gush of black, brackish fluid that passed for their blood, pattering down and *burning* like acid where it splashed. The gun went skittering, because the thing landed on him, claws out. The UV scorched wherever it touched, but it wasn't enough, it just maddened the red-eyed, humanoid *thing* that snarled, crouching, over him. It was unholy strong, too, another hot gush of its blackness splashing his clothes as he *squeezed* its wrists, the Thirst a red sheet over everything and the rest of him snarling back. The sound was an animal vibration in the lowest reaches of his gut, and he hated it even as it gave him the strength to force the Thing's ancient, rotting arms away, keeping the claws from his throat.

They started to go quick when the shell was breached and the old bad stuff in them leaked out. He heaved up, but the Thing shoved him back down. His head bounced on concrete, and the Thirst slipped.

The Thing's head exploded. The sound was massive, incredible, to match the stink. The disintegrating body slid over to the side, bubbling with foulness where silver grains burrowed into unholy flesh.

What the hell?

Rookwood lay on the floor, stunned and breathless. The burning sludge blinked out of his watering eyes, and he saw Mrs. King. Her lips were pulled back in a feral grimace, and she was clutching his .45 with stiff, outstretched arms. Tears slicked her cheeks, her eyes blazed, and there were spatters of black, smoking foulness all over her white shirt.

She dropped the gun. Rookwood flinched. It would be just his luck for the damn thing to go off.

There wasn't any time to thank her. The Thing, its mutilated head crawling with smoking ick, scrabbled against the concrete, its claws leaving spark-strike scratches. The stake ripped away from the outside of Rookwood's right thigh, Velcro straps giving with a tearing sound, and he rammed it through the Thing's chest.

It was a good thing she'd blown its head off. Otherwise the death scream might've made her pass out or something. As it was, Amelia King was sobbing. The Thing twitched, and she made a miserable, frightened sound, stumbling back and almost falling on the broken stairs.

How the hell had she got down here? Jesus.

"It's okay," he managed through a throat gone dry and sand raspy. "Relax."

She swallowed hard, gulping at air gone close and foul. "Which one? Which one is *that*?" The words broke on sucking gasps of air, but she didn't look ready to faint just yet.

Good for you. "It's not your husband. I'm pretty sure it's Briggs." He checked the Thing carefully, moving his eyes over the Brooks Brothers suit, finding the gold-and-opal signet ring. The stone was cracked and discolored. "Yup. It's Briggs. I wonder . . ."

But he didn't say what he wondered. There was no point.

Instead, he tugged the kukri out of its sheath. The blade gleamed, a clean silver dart. The kitchen—and sunlight—was very far away, but the trickle of illumination down the broken stairs was enough to make him feel a little better. He scooped up the UV, checked it, and was even more relieved when it was still working. God bless quality construction.

"What are you going to do?" She sounded very young, but she hadn't thrown up yet. She was dealing with this better than he had his first time out.

"Cut off what's left of his head, babe." He didn't sound sarcastic, just tired. "Then I'm going to look for your husband." And he was pretty sure he was going to wonder, the whole time, how she'd got down the stairs—and why she'd pulled the trigger.

The widow was turning out to be just *full* of surprises.

"Do they always scream like that?" She hunched her shoulders. Pale, rainy sunlight through kitchen windows flooded her hair, now tangled and not so glossy. She looked a lot less suburbia and a lot more terrified.

And she hadn't fainted when the Thing that had been her husband had let loose its dying wail.

Rookwood taped down the bandage. He'd heal, but there was no point in irritating the wound. He uncurled his arm, and the white glare of gauze against his biceps tinted itself faint pink. Claw marks stung like hell, and he was glad he didn't seem to ever get infected. "Every one I've killed."

She swallowed audibly. "How many have you . . . killed?"

I was a cop eight months ago, babe. This is a new line of work for me. "Enough to be a professional." His shirt was torn, and as he shrugged back into his jacket, he saw that it was also torn, but not as badly. "Listen, Mrs. King—"

"It's Amelia," she said flatly. "How long have you been doing this?"

The time for those questions was when you first met me, you know. But she was a civilian. Still, she'd come down to the basement and blown the head off a daywalking old one. She was made of stronger stuff than most civvies.

But then he thought of the bites all over her. The more he thought about it, the more he thought a new one wouldn't play with her like that. Which made the widow a question mark.

Still, he hated himself for what he was about to do. "Long enough. Look, you should go to a hotel or something. Don't come back here, unless it's during the day. Even then you probably shouldn't come back. They have human bodies to do their dirty work, you know."

"For Christ's sake, this is my *home!*" Her hands on the kitchen counter were white-knuckled. The two paper cups of coffee were probably cold by now, but they smelled good to him. Almost as good as she smelled. The burning tang on her had faded a little.

It wouldn't go away completely, but most probably the one who'd bitten her was dead. If she didn't get bitten again, she'd probably be okay. And when she died it would be a true death.

Of course, there was always the alternative. If what he was thinking was right, he'd probably end up shoving a stake through her and lopping off her pretty head as well.

It wasn't a comfortable thought. Especially when his eyes drifted down of their own accord behind the shades and touched the shape of those bitten breasts under the spattered white shirt. What was a woman like this doing wasting herself as a housewife? Did he even want to ask?

Of course not.

"Stay here and die, then." The kukri was clean; he slid it back in its sheath. The stake was strapped to his thigh again, hawthorn wood easily shedding acidic corruption. "Or get bit again, maybe by Chisholm or another one of their protégés." He felt low and dirty even as he said it.

"I hired you for—"

"You hired me to kill your husband. He's dead. Anything else is extra, and I'm busy." He checked the gun again. The spare ammo in his jacket pockets was a negligible weight. "Enjoy your coffee."

He turned on his heel, scooped up his duffel bag, and was halfway down the hall before he heard her footsteps behind him. Staggering just slightly.

"What am I supposed to *do*?"

It was a forlorn little cry, and he almost stopped.

But his work wasn't done. He sped up, heels jabbing the hardwood, and crunched through the remainder of the vase in the hall.

Outside, the cool, rainy air was a balm to his burning

cheeks. He made it to the Cadillac, dropped into the driver's seat, and was gone before she could come out in her yard and start yelling. Not that he thought she would—Mrs. King wasn't the type.

But if she did come out, he wasn't sure his resolve would hold. There was a suspicious blurring in his eyes, and Rookwood wasn't sure how much more he could hate what he was about to do—or himself.

The house crouched, one window glowing gold. Someone was up late, probably sitting in the kitchen. He didn't get close enough to look.

Rain flirted down, kissed the leaves of trees planted when this housing development was put in. It touched the wide sidewalks, drenched the thirsty lawns, dripped from eaves, and gurgled in gutters. There was no drone of traffic as there was in the city, just the sea-sound of the city in the distance and the occasional rolling breaker of tires on wet asphalt closer.

The rain didn't matter. He stood or crouched easily, moving only enough to keep himself flexible. The night breathed, full of damp dreaming.

The neighbors had both had dinner. Someone brought garbage out across the street behind him. But the widow's house stood, closed and self-contained as the woman herself.

Rookwood waited. She'd come home before dusk, in a silver SUV, and didn't open the garage but carried plastic and paper bags inside with her shoulders up, hurrying. Since then, just the light in the kitchen, mocking the gathering and fallen night.

Lights turned off in the houses around hers. A dog yapped a few yards away until someone yelled, *"Max, get in here!"* A series of happy yips, then a door closing and more silence.

The neighborhood prepared itself for sleep. Rookwood lifted the flask to his mouth, took another swallow of the red stuff. The problem wasn't with it being cold or the flat copper tang to it.

The problem was how good this pale substitute tasted. And how good he could imagine it coming straight from the vein.

His nape tickled. He eased farther back into the shadows, melding with them, his pulse and breathing smoothing out into an imperceptible hum under the ambient nighttime noise. Quiet as a mole in a hole.

It had taken him two months to get his pulse under control. It was worth the work.

The widow's house was like a sore tooth. His gaze kept drifting across it. What was she doing in there? What had she brought home? Had she made any phone calls?

Do your job, Rookwood. He was barely breathing under the dripping fringes of some kind of evergreen. He almost stopped blinking, his pulse struggling with the iron grip of training, instinct whispering that it would be soon, very soon.

He still almost missed it. A shadow flitted over the roof, a quick, lizardlike movement. A faint tinkle of glass breaking, almost lost under the rush of rain, half swallowed by the cloak of fetid silence suddenly drawn choking close around the white walls and green shutters.

He moved. Slippery, squishing grass underfoot, getting

up a good head of speed. Spatters of rain broke against his face. The UV in one hand, its light stuttering on as his thumb flicked, the gun in the other, he streaked for the French doors with only a slight squelching sound betraying his position.

And *hit,* hard, the glass shivering away in fragments and long swords. The noise was incredible, a crashing through the silence the Thing had pulled close around the entire house, and he saw the short white blond hair, the blue eyes, the expensive business suit, in flashes before Rookwood's gun spoke and Chisholm's arm flicked, throwing Amelia King across the kitchen and into the wall as though she weighed less than nothing. She slid down the wall in a queer boneless way, leaving a huge dent behind, and the hot red fury bubbled up under Rookwood's skin.

The Thirst screamed as he hit the Thing with a bone-crunching thud. Fell, his head clipping the tiled counter, and the gun tracked the Thing as it loomed over him, snarling. Five bullets, their sound blurring into and over one another. The UV slashed across Chisholm's face. Smoke burst free.

He looked again into the face of the Thing that had made him, and its mad blue gaze dug into the inside of his skull. It bent down, its snarl ripping across violated air, and he saw a thick, broken wooden dowel protruding from its chest.

I didn't do that. Confusion fought with the Thirst, and instinct jerked his hand with the UV up again. Smoke boiled through the kitchen, bubbling black flesh rising. At night, when they dropped their shield of humanity, the light hurt them. During the day, they never dropped that mask. Maybe it was a survival mechanism—

"I wondered what happened to you." Chisholm's voice, a rich baritone. He reached up, plucked the wood from his flesh with clawed fingers. The mask of humanity was back over the face of the Thing that glutted itself on suffering, and if not for the stripes of bubbling black tissue across his chiseled features, you wouldn't guess he was a terror as ancient as darkness itself. "Baited a little trap, did we, Rook?" Chisholm dropped the sharpened dowel. It clattered on the floor.

Rookwood raised the gun, the Thirst screaming inside his veins. *Kill kill kill!* it yelled, pushed, screeched. *Kill it, kill it now!*

"How's Fann?" he croaked through a dry-burning throat. "Legs grown back yet?"

Amelia King moaned shapelessly. Rookwood forced himself to stare up at Chisholm. *Steady. Pick your shot. Four bullets left. Didn't hit him, worse fucking luck.*

"Your ridiculous little crusade." Chisholm sighed. He was popular in a courtroom, in a nightclub, with the ladies. Courtly, even.

But the ones who wouldn't be missed knew what he really was. The trouble was, they didn't know until too late—and they couldn't tell anyone from beyond the grave.

Nobody except Rookwood.

Rookwood's hand tightened. Chisholm smiled. It was a gentle, paternal smile, the fangs curving down to dimple his chin, the black-charred stripe across his face tingeing with red at the edges as it healed. Fann was the oldest, Briggs was the most adept at using people—but Chisholm was the most dangerous. And now Rookwood had him right in his sights.

"It's not too late to belong to the night, Jeremy." Again that soft, paternal tone. Patient. Loving. "All can be forgiven. I marked you because you're one of us, deep down. You know it."

He's afraid. Of me. It was like a bath of ice water. "Fuck you," Rookwood snarled, and squeezed the trigger.

The gun spoke. Chisholm moved with the inhuman speed of the damned—but not fast enough. The bullet tore into his chest, mushrooming, and a huge black blotch appeared.

The Thing's scream shattered glass, and Rookwood fired again, hit it *again.* It scrabbled away, still screaming, and smashed through the ruin of the French doors, more glass shivering free.

Got him! Savage joy filled his chest. He struggled to his feet. The Thirst burned, plucked at him. *Go now. Hunt him down. He's bleeding bad.*

He glanced over. Amelia King lay slumped against the wall, her glossy hair tangled and matted with bright blood. She was crumpled like a doll thrown carelessly by a child.

Go! Go and get him! He'll go to ground, you can mark the spot and wait for dawn. Then you can put a stake through his fucking heart and cut off his head and be free.

Six months of training, three of lying in wait for just this chance. He'd just flushed the monster out of hiding, and now here he was hesitating.

Amelia King surprised him again. Her eyes opened. Her throat was smeared with blood, and she blinked, dazed.

Oh, goddammit. He bit her. I'd bet money on it. Probably not for the first time, either. But that dowel in his chest . . .

Rookwood surprised himself this time by reaching down. His hand closed around her shoulder—why had he dropped the gun? That was a fool's move. "It's okay." The words cut through the Thirst. "You're safe."

She scrabbled back from his touch. Drywall dust puffed down, snowdust in her hair and over her blood-spattered blue T-shirt. The blood was amazingly red, and his fangs slid free. The bones in his jaw crackled as he wrestled down the Thirst.

She gulped. "Bait." It was the voice of a child caught in a nightmare. "You used me as *bait*."

"I'm sorry." Pale words for the guilt that twisted inside his ribs, tearing at tender tissue. "Amelia—"

"Molstein's dead." Sense came back into her eyes. She scrabbled back even farther, pressing herself against the wall, and clapped a hand to her bleeding neck. "They killed him. Last week before I came to you. *I was bait for you, too.*"

"I knew that," he heard himself say. "Don't worry about it." It was too much to hope for, that one betrayal would balance the other. "Just stay here. I'll be back in a little bit."

She closed her eyes. Her throat worked as she swallowed. He supposed they should both be grateful she was bitten and halfway there. If she'd been safe and uncontaminated, she'd be broken inside. Bleeding to death internally. As it was, her pulse was strong and she looked all right. Pale, but all right.

"You tried to stake him." Rookwood's fingers fell away from her shoulder. "Right?"

"Dowels from the hardware store. Didn't work." She coughed, a lonely, tired sound.

Get after him. If he gets to a safe place, he'll come back tomorrow night and kill her. He rose, scooping up his gun, and she sighed.

"Good fucking deal." His tone was harsher than it needed to be, with the Thirst burning in his throat, spreading down his chest. "Next time use hawthorn. It's the only thing that works well enough to immobilize them. Stay here, I'll be back."

He reloaded as he stepped out into the night. Wet wind slapped him in the face. Chisholm's passage was a drift of reek against the damp, and Rookwood gathered himself. The last flask of red stuff burned against his lips; he swallowed as he ran. It scorched all the way down, and the Thirst snarled. It wanted him to go back and sink his teeth in the bleeding woman, put *his* mark on her throat instead of the other bleeding hole of contamination.

And there were other things he thought he'd left behind wanting to be done, too. No time for them, either. But maybe . . .

He finished gulping and stuffed the flask back in his pocket. The UV was out, and the gun, and he pulled on every inch of more-than-human speed he could gather.

Out here in suburbia, there were even parks. In the city, it would have been a chase across rooftops and through alleys, dodging crowds and sliding across neon. Here there were fences, covered swimming pools—in this wet, cold part of the country, they were ridiculous status symbols—and the freeway like a giant artery.

The reek was flagging by the time he got to the park. He had to double back twice, cutting across fences, struggling through wet underbrush, and cursing. If this were his part of city, he'd know every back alley and sight line, every potential hiding place.

As it was, he almost stepped straight across the little depression in a soccer field. The Thirst jerked him back just in time, avoiding the clawed hand that shot up out of the wet turf.

Brought to bay at last, Chisholm dropped all pretense of humanity. Gone was the smooth courtroom baritone, the neatly combed shock of glossy white hair, the waxen, charming smile. This was the Thing without its daylight mask, its canines long and razor sharp, black sludge dribbling down its chin, and the sodden rags of its expensive suit flapping as it climbed out of its death hole.

He hadn't expected the Thing to have so much pep left. It was still bleeding heavily, the grass smoking as ichor splashed. It crouched, a glassy squeal rising from its foul, bleeding lips. The UV lashed across it, a whip of light. More thin black blood bubbled.

It hit him hard, a last desperate gambit, claws slicing in through cloth and flesh, tangling with his ribs. Agony roared through him, but he was prepared, months of fighting in dark corners and hunting around the edges boiling down to undeniable instinct that had jerked the hawthorn stake free and—

It thudded *home*. His aim was true.

Rookwood lay flat in the mud, the Thirst burning all through him like alcohol fumes. The stab wounds between his ribs ran with red agony. Chisholm's body began to vaporize itself, shredding under the lash of water. Stinging needles of rain peppered both of them, living flesh and dead, rotting sludge. The silver had done its work, poisoning and breaking up the fabric of Chisholm's ancient body. The hawthorn was doing the rest.

Rookwood coughed twice, rackingly. Spat to clear his mouth. The stake quivered in his numb hand.

It took two tries to heave himself up, shoving aside the rotting thing. The rain was a baptism as the Thirst retreated into its deep hole, snarling with each step. Hot blood trickled its fingers down his rib cage. Nothing vital hit. Or so he hoped.

Do it quick, just in case.

The stake was hissing, the wood twitching as what was left of the one who had bitten him jerked slightly. There might have been some life left in the disintegration, but the hawthorn immobilized it. Hate rose bright and sweet in Rookwood's throat.

The kukri sang free of its sheath. The thing twitched.

"You bit the wrong cop, Chisholm." His voice sounded strange even to himself. The soccer field was a long, flat dance floor, rain flinging itself down in needle streaks. He lined up the kukri. It flashed down in an arc of silver, and the head was hacked free. More twitching as nerve death took the body, and Rookwood tilted up his face to the rain.

It was over. Finally over.

Except it wasn't. He wiped the water out of his eyes. Hot trickles had threaded his cheeks. They were different from the scorching trails of blood down his ribs, soaking into his jeans. They vanished under the intensifying rain, curtains of it suddenly pounding the field and his shoulders, slicking his hair down.

Amelia. I promised to go back.

He owed the widow an explanation, at least. And to tell her she was free.

But what if Fann's bitten her, too?

He told himself not to worry about that just yet.

Rookwood cleaned off his kukri. The hawthorn stake slid free of the sludge of corruption, the slurry no longer even recognizably humanoid. The veil over the night retreated. And he felt like himself again for the first time in six god-damn years, since Chisholm had first handed him an envelope of cash and the whole dirty seduction had begun.

Yes, he owed her an explanation. And maybe something more.

The sob caught him by surprise. He bent over, his arms wrapped tight over his belly, the claw marks stinging as they slowly closed. Rookwood locked the sounds behind his tight-clenched teeth, hunched like an old man over the smear of rotting tissue killing the grass underneath it, open eyes staring sightlessly at the crystal gilding of rainwater on every surface.

It wasn't crying, he told himself. It was relief. There was no weakness in relief.

But he did not believe it.

The widow's house blazed with light in every window. As soon as he stepped through the ruin of the French doors again, he knew something was awry.

His boots crushed the carpeting in the master bedroom upstairs. Clothing was pulled out and scattered, a smudge of faintly tainted blood on a white coverlet. Her window faced south, blinds yanked up and scratch marks on the sash outside.

It must have been the very window her husband had bobbed outside, pleading to be let in. His wet skin chilled at the thought.

She wasn't upstairs, or down, or even in the cellar, where the aroma of corruption lingered. The silver SUV was gone, and a mug lay shattered on the kitchen floor. It was a blue-glazed coffee cup, in pieces.

Shit. I told her to stay here! He checked the rooms again, but she was completely, utterly gone.

Any chance he had of breaking the office building down-town had vanished with her, too. God*damn* it. Her husband must have had a security pass and key codes, but his desk was open and she'd left paper scattered on the floor. There went his chance to get the last of the bloodsuckers. Six months of work and an almost botched operation.

Well, it wasn't as if he didn't have time.

Before he left, then, he turned off the lights. He stood for a few moments in her dark kitchen, looking at the imprint of her body on the broken wall. She was damn lucky to still be alive.

I was bait for you, too.

He hoped this wasn't her last surprise.

He'd known Molstein was gone. There was nothing in the papers, but Rookwood still had a few contacts left on the force. His old partner had disappeared, last seen at midnight outside a deli on Thirty-fourth.

Two blocks away from Briggs, Fann, and Chisholm's offices.

Rookwood went home and eyed the Scotch on his desk, put it away.

The Thirst retreated. It didn't go away, but with Chisholm gone it didn't taunt his every waking moment. He actually felt halfway decent and could hold down cooked steak and cheese again.

He needed a jolt of the red stuff once a week instead of every day. He prowled his office, and some of the widow's money went for rent. He was in the clear.

Cases trickled in. A poltergeist on Seventh Street, a collection of dry cleaners being extorted by a gang of werewolves, a man looking for his vanished lover. The last case had nothing weird about it, straight-up breakup work. The lover didn't want to be found, but Rookwood kept the money anyway.

He kept hearing her in the back of his head. *I was bait for you. . . . You don't understand, Mr. Rookwood. . . . Do they always scream like that?* That glossy hair, and the way her lips pulled back from her teeth when she shot Briggs in the head.

It took another rainy night, cars shushing by outside his window and the bottle of Scotch singing from the drawer he'd hid it in, before he realized what her last surprise might be. The newspaper lay open on his desk, the local section barely glanced at before something caught his attention and he froze, staring at the black-and-white print:

". . . since the closure of Briggs, Fann, and Chisholm early last month, after a fire that gutted their offices."

The article was about a sudden dearth of criminal defense lawyers and a rash of arson involving their offices. It didn't take a genius to figure out most of them weren't on vacation or visiting Aunt Mabel. Of course, the real story wouldn't be in the papers, but there was enough between the lines to sit him bolt upright in his chair, the taste of copper in his mouth and his pulse racing like a stock car.

Holy shit. His hands turned into fists. *She learns quick.*

Five minutes later he was out the door, sliding through the wet neon light. He hailed a cab at the corner, sat in a fug of cigarette smoke and fogged windows, and tipped the driver too much as he climbed out on Twenty-third.

The office building was a shell of itself, yellow crime scene tape fluttering. Rookwood stood across the street with his heart in his mouth, staring at the wreckage.

Yes, a quick learner. He wondered how she'd taken care of Fann—the old boy was tricky, and even without his legs he was a formidable opponent.

So formidable Rookwood had been working the best way to get at him inside his fortress-building. The same building that was a charred shell right now.

Goddamn, girl. What did you do?

Of course the widow would have visited the offices during the day. Of course she would know the layout and have her husband's access to the keypads, the magnetic keys, the state-of-the-art systems. Of course she'd be allowed in as the wife of an almost partner, and she'd get past the daytime body-guards because of her scent of burning.

She'd probably come back and taken care of Fann early. He wouldn't put it past her.

There was nothing to do here, but he poked around any-way. The reek of corruption had faded, and the Thirst didn't tingle, warning him of danger.

He caught another cab back home. Dawn was coming up as he put his key in the lock and paused.

The door was unlocked.

Had she been waiting for him to go downtown? He hadn't even felt someone watching.

His office held a ghost of perfume. Rich, brunette, with a tang of ash. On his desk, placed precisely in the pool of yellow light from the lamp, was a fat white envelope. He peeked in—five thousand in crisp hundred-dollar bills. And a note, on paper that smelled like her. The same clear schoolgirl hand she'd used to label the map to her husband's grave.

Mr. Rookwood,

Enclosed please find the remainder of your fee. I hope things are even between us now. I have learned a lot since we last spoke. I think I will be continuing the work.

Sincerely,
Amelia King

P.S. Thank you.

"Goddamn," Rookwood whispered to his empty office. "God*damn*."

There was no reply except the rain.

* * *

Lilith Saintcrow was born in New Mexico, bounced around the world as an Air Force brat, and fell in love with writing when she was ten years old. She currently lives in Vancouver, Washington, with two small children and a houseful of cats. Her Web site is www.lilithsaintcrow.com.

GOD'S CREATURES

by CARRIE VAUGHN

Cormac waited in the cab of his Jeep, watching each car that pulled into the rest area on I-25 north of Monument. So far, none of them looked like the one he was waiting for. A lot of truckers stopped here, with a few road trippers thrown in, all shapes and sizes. McNeill would stand out, when he made his appearance.

Forty-five minutes after he was due, the aggressively souped-up pickup truck veered off the freeway and came up the lane. It had oversize tires, lights on the rollbar, a gun rack—empty for now—in the back window, and a Confederate flag sticker on the bumper. McNeill was that kind of asshole.

Cormac stepped out of the Jeep; McNeill saw him and swerved to park a couple of spots down. The guy climbed out of his truck and dropped to the ground. He was tall and stocky, wearing worn jeans and a flannel shirt over a white tee. He shoved his hands in his pockets and pretended he wasn't cold in the winter air, but he was shrugging and tense, trying to keep warm. Cormac waited for him.

"You're supposed to be keeping your head down," Cormac said flatly, prodding on purpose, knowing it would piss McNeill off.

"What? My head's down." He looked around, frowning, appearing smug because there weren't any cops in sight. "What's your problem?"

"Registration sticker on your plate's expired. That's like waving a flag at the cops," Cormac said, nodding toward the back end of the truck.

"And I don't give a fucking cent to an illegal government." He pulled himself straighter, as if he were daring Cormac to make a big deal out of it.

Yeah, McNeill was one of those. Didn't seem to care that the cops wouldn't get you on the weapons stockpiles or the conspiracy charges. They nailed you on back taxes and traffic violations. You covered your ass on the little things as the price of doing business. But that was why McNeill was a go-between and Cormac did the heavy lifting.

"What's the job?" Cormac said.

He'd gotten a call two days ago. A rancher he'd worked with before had some trouble—Cormac's kind of trouble. They both knew McNeill, who spent a lot of time traveling around the state, so he sent McNeill with the details you didn't talk about over the phone and the down payment. McNeill didn't know what exactly Cormac did. He probably assumed he was some kind of hit man.

Which was mostly true.

McNeill went back to his truck and returned with a manila envelope, which he handed to Cormac. He took only a brief look inside, finding a page of description and a business-sized envelope, thick with cash. There'd be ten hundred-dollar bills. He wasn't going to count it out in the open, but he did pull out a bill and hand it to McNeill for payment.

"Thanks," McNeill said, shoving the hundred in his pocket. "Good luck, man."

Cormac had already turned back to the Jeep.

He arrived at Joe Harrison's ranch in Lamar early the next morning. The old man was waiting for him on the front porch of the ramshackle house. The two-story building was probably close to a hundred years old. It needed a new roof and a coat of paint at the very least. But with a place like this, any extra money the family earned went right back into the ranch. The barns and fencing would get repairs before the house did.

"Thanks for coming," Harrison said as Cormac left the Jeep and walked down to shake his hand. The rancher was in his sixties, his face furrowed and weathered, tough as leather from spending his life raising cattle out here. The kind of guy who was more at home with barbed wire and baling twine than a comfortable chair and a TV set.

"Let's take a look," Cormac said.

Harrison opened a gate in the fence, and they rode in Cormac's Jeep, straight across the prairie for about three miles. Harrison navigated by landmarks, pointing to show Cormac the way.

"There, it's right there," Harrison said finally, and Cormac stopped the Jeep.

Harrison led him to a spot where stands of scrub oak followed the contour of the hills, bordering the open plains. A carcass lay here, partly sheltered by the wind, flattening the grass. About a week old, Cormac guessed. The steer, a typical rust-and-cream-colored Hereford, had been savaged, its gut ripped open from sternum to tail, its face and tongue torn out, its throat flayed. Scavengers had been through since then—scraps of hair and bone radiated out from the remains. Most of what was left was leathery skin and hair over a rib cage and a leering, ragged skull.

"The second one's about a mile that way," Harrison said, pointing again. "And we had another one just last night."

They returned to the Jeep and drove east a mile or so. Cormac didn't need directions this time; he spotted the vultures circling overhead. When he pulled up near the spot, a pair of coyotes ran off, then hunkered down in the long grass, waiting to return to their meal in peace.

The other carcass had been dried out and picked over; it hadn't smelled like anything. The rotten, bloody stink of this one hit Cormac as soon as he left the Jeep.

"The others looked just like this one?" Cormac asked Harrison, who nodded. The rancher winced, turning his face away from the stench.

This one had been gutted like the other. Savaged, but not eaten. Guts and organs spilled out, pink flesh glistened on bones. The scavengers had had a meal handed to them. The weather was too cold for flies, which would have been swarming.

This was why Harrison had called him. They weren't dealing with a predator that killed because it needed to eat. This was a pure killer, and it was only a matter of time before it attacked someone. Cormac had seen this pattern before. A beast like this might start out with the best of intentions. It might flee to a distant wilderness, where it would kill a few rabbits or maybe a deer with no harm done. But then it would start to slide. It couldn't stay away from civilization forever. It would still have the bloodlust, but it wouldn't bother fleeing. Inhibitions would fail; it would struggle to keep from hurting anyone, but someday it would slip. It would attack livestock. Then it would finally give in to instinct and kill the human beings it hated because it was no longer one of them.

Cormac had to find the thing before that happened. Full moon was still a week off, but that didn't matter when one of them went bad. They could change anytime they wanted and did mostly when they lost control.

"You have any idea who's doing this? Anybody notice any strangers around here? Someone who might be camping out? Or has someone in town started acting funny?"

"If I had any idea who it was, I wouldn't need to call you," Harrison said, frowning.

Cormac stepped around the kill, looking for tracks, for the pattern of wolf pads as big as a man's face, with the matching puncture marks of claws. The winter had been dry so far, and the ground was rock hard. He might not have seen anything among the carpet of dead grasses, but werewolf claws were sharp, and he found the little holes in the ground, as far apart as his spread hand. He threw his keys to Harrison. He'd left his rifles in the vehicle but had a semiautomatic handgun in a shoulder holster, hidden under his leather jacket. "I'll meet you back at the house."

"What did you find?"

"Give me the afternoon, I'll let you know."

Harrison drove off in the Jeep, and Cormac followed the tracks.

The wolf could have run for miles. Cormac might be hiking all day—or at least as long as he could keep following his quarry. But for the first couple of miles the trail was clear; he found prints from one stride to the next, and on. The thing was headed in a straight line. Straight for home.

He reached the edge of the property, where Harrison was waiting at the Jeep. Cormac waved at him and kept going. The immense wolf tracks followed the ranch's dirt driveway, then paralleled the highway, back toward town.

So it was someone from town, not some recluse cut off from civilization. That made it worse. This was civilization gone amuck. A werewolf could only follow instinct, which would drive it back home, wherever that might be. A monster might kill its own family and not even know what it did. Cormac had to find it first.

Brick-dry prairie along the highway gave way to empty, weed-grown lots, dirt roads, then cracked pavement, then sidewalks. Weeds gave way to lawns and welcoming rows of houses with porches, screen doors, and family cars outside. This all gave Cormac a sense of foreboding, because he was still following the same tracks, sparse now but sure in their direction: the puncture marks of claws in garden soil, torn-up tufts of grass. He'd lose the trail on pavement but find it again after hunting along the margins of lawns. The trail was straight enough that he wondered if he'd find a man at the end of it, staring back at him with a wolf behind his eyes.

What he found, when the prints and claw marks ended, was an oblong of pressed earth against an old brick building—the kind of shape a person might have made if he'd curled up and gone to sleep right here. The building was big, three stories, probably built around the turn of the last century. It might have been a schoolhouse. Why had the wolf come here?

There were no human footprints to follow; the distinctive claw marks had disappeared. Finally, he lost the trail.

He expanded his search, took in the area. The tall brick building seemed to be the center of a complex. One of the other buildings was definitely a school, like the kind built in the 1960s—low, one story, a flat roof, a grid of windows. Construction paper artwork was hung on the windows in one classroom.

Across a lawn stood another antique building, this one with a high, peaked roof—a steeple with a cross on top. He went around to the front and read the stone marker there: Saint Catherine's.

This was a Catholic church and school.

He preferred the jobs where the wolf was an outcast who fled to the wilderness—no witnesses.

At the end of this, he'd have to kill someone. There'd be

a body, and the cops didn't take "He needed killin'" as an excuse. He could try to tell them the thing was a werewolf, but the end result wouldn't be much different. Prison, psych ward, same thing.

The fewer people saw him lurking around, the fewer people he talked to, the better. He needed to keep it so that the people who did spot him wouldn't be able to point the cops at him. When the body turned up, Harrison wouldn't turn him in. Harrison understood.

Cormac walked along the street, passing the school's grounds and trying to get a feel for the place. He walked by only once, normal, as if he had someplace else to be. Several buildings made up the complex, including a couple of homey brick blocks that seemed to be dorms. Around back was a sports field, and a group of girls in matching gray sweatshirts and green sweatpants played soccer. Maybe aged fifteen to seventeen. So, girls' boarding school, high school. It was a Saturday; they wouldn't be in class. There looked to be a couple of adults out with them, women in sweatpants and jackets. During the week there'd be teachers as well and a priest and staff for the church. They'd live on campus, too. In fact, behind the church he spotted what must have been the rectory, a small, square clapboard house attached to a meeting hall.

The werewolf could be any of them. A hundred possibilities, at least. He didn't know where to start.

When he was done with his quick survey, he cut back a couple of blocks, made his way to the highway again, and returned to Harrison's ranch. Dusk was falling.

Joe Harrison must have seen him coming through a window and met him on the porch.

"You get it? Is it dead?" Harrison said.

Cormac didn't nod or shake his head, didn't say yes or no. "I'm working on it. Wondered if you could tell me anything about the Catholic school up the highway."

"Saint Catherine's? It's a reform school. All girls. Full of troublemakers."

"Really? I didn't see any fences."

Harrison chuckled. "Look around. Where are they going to run off to?"

"I tracked your killer there," Cormac said.

"You think it's one of them kids?" The rancher donned an eager, hungry look.

Cormac frowned, hoping it wasn't. He didn't want to have to go shooting a kid. "I guess I'll have to find out."

Harrison shook his head. "Wouldn't that just figure?"

"You know about any rumors, any suspicions about anyone there? Hear about anything odd?"

"They're Catholics," he said with a huff, as though that explained everything. "You know somebody's always talking about the priest there, if you want rumors."

Cormac rubbed the back of his neck and looked to the distance, to the flat horizon. The sky was deep blue, turning black with the setting sun. "That's not a lot of help."

"I'm just telling you what you asked for. Hey, how long's this thing going to take? When am I going to be able to let my herd graze again?"

"I'll let you know when it's done. By the full moon for sure."

"That's a week away."

"Sure is. But I'll finish when I finish." He turned away.

"I wish Douglas was here working on this," Harrison called after him.

Douglas was Cormac's father. Harrison had known him— that was how he'd known to call Cormac.

Cormac didn't slow down. "Yeah. Well. You got me instead."

He kept watch on the ranch through the night; the were-wolf might return to where it had found easy pickings before. Harrison had penned up the cattle since last night's attack, and the animals crowded the corrals, milling and murmuring unhappily. Cormac kept walking the plains around the ranch house, covering half a dozen miles over the course of a couple of hours. He didn't see anything. He didn't even get that crawling feeling on his neck, as though something were watching him. It was just another cold night.

In the morning, he reclaimed his Jeep and found a ratty motel at the edge of town, where he talked the desk clerk into letting him have a room early. The clerk gave some bullshit about the rooms not being clean, but Cormac counted only three cars in the lot and at least two dozen rooms. Places like this didn't have check-in times, he told the guy, and paid cash in advance.

He brought his weapons case into the room and looked over his collection one more time. A revolver, two semi-automatics, a shotgun, and a pair of rifles. The revolver was mostly to show off. He wore it when he needed to cop attitude, when a potential client expected the tough guy, the Old West gunslinger. And the boxes of ammunition for each of them: 9mm silver rounds for the semis, silver filings in the shotgun shells, and so on. If he couldn't take down the quarry with this, he likely couldn't take it down at all. He'd never needed more than this. He also had a Bowie knife with silver inlay. The bone handle was worn. His father had told him it had belonged to *his* grandfather. His family had been doing this a long time, apparently.

He couldn't be sure; his father hadn't finished telling him all the stories when he'd died, when Cormac was sixteen. Harrison was right: it ought to be his father out here doing this.

After a quick shower and a change into some slightly less grungy clothes, Cormac went to church.

He hadn't been to church—any kind of church—since he was in high school and living with his aunt and uncle. They were some flavor of born-again Christian, and services had involved sitting on hard metal folding chairs in a plain room— rented office space—listening to fire-and-brimstone lectures. He hadn't been back since he went out on his own. He'd never been to a Catholic church at all. He used the tools, of course, holy water and crosses, when he had to. But they were just tools. Any God he believed in wasn't like the one most preachers talked about.

The service had already started when he arrived. He stepped softly and found a seat on the bench in back. No one seemed to pay any attention to him. The church smelled of old wood, melted wax, and incense. The architecture was maybe a hundred years old, lots of dark wood, aged and smooth. The benches—pews—might have been mahogany, but there were pale scuff marks around the edges, where generations of bodies had banged into them. Pale stained glass decorated the tall windows along the walls.

He had a good view of the congregation: a hundred or so girls in front, identical in pressed uniforms; a bunch of plain folk from the town; the priest in a white cassock, standing in front, leading a prayer; and nuns, maybe a dozen, in prim black dresses, sitting in the rows with the girls. Their heads were bare—short and simple haircuts for the most part, no veils—which surprised him. He'd expected them to look the way they did in the movies, with the weird hats and veils.

There were altar girls instead of altar boys. Probably students from the school. Cormac didn't know there was such a thing as altar girls.

During communion, everyone stood, filed down the central aisle, faced the priest with hands raised, accepted the host, and marched back to their seats. Cormac was able to look at nearly every person there. Sometimes he could spot a werewolf in human form just by looking. The way they moved, the body language—more canine than human, hunched over, glaring outward, walking as if they had a tail raised behind them. The gleam in their eyes, as if they'd kill you as soon as look at you. Ones who were losing control, like Harrison's cattle killer, had a harder time hiding it.

He didn't spot anyone who made him suspicious.

The service ended, and the priest and altar girls processed

out as the congregation sang, accompanied by one of the nuns playing a piano that sounded tinny in the big space. The congregation followed, filtering down the central aisle and two aisles to the sides. Cormac made his escape as part of the crowd. He lingered at the corner of the church building, watching. He still wasn't getting a sense off anyone. In his experience, werewolves didn't do well in crowds. They sometimes lived in packs of their own kind but didn't cope well around normal human beings. They saw people as prey. A werewolf wouldn't go to church and be part of a crowd like this, unless his absence would be out of the ordinary and noted. He'd followed the tracks back to town—this wolf was trying to hang on to normal. Maybe he was here and hiding really well. Maybe Cormac would have to stir things up a bit to flush him.

But not right here. Not right now.

He was about to walk away, back to his Jeep and the next part of his plan, when he caught sight of someone coming toward him. One of the nuns. He felt a completely irrational moment of fear. Too many stories about nuns in the collective unconscious; he wasn't even Catholic. It wasn't a mistake— she'd broken from the lingering crowd and came toward him.

Tall, solid, with short gray hair and soft features, jowly almost. She might have been as old as the priest and had the air of an aunt rather than a grandmother. Stern, maybe, rather than kind. Someone who had spent a lifetime bullying girls at a reform school, rulers smacking knuckles and all. But he was letting stereotypes get the better of him again.

He supposed he could have just ignored her and walked

away. What was she going to do, run after him? But the last thing he wanted to do was raise suspicions. It wouldn't cost him anything to find out what she wanted.

"Good morning," she said when she stopped in front of him, hands folded before her, pressed to her skirt.

"Hi," he said, then waited for her to say what she wanted.

"We like to welcome visitors who might be new to the parish," she said. "I wondered if I could answer any questions for you, about the parish or the town."

He probably shouldn't have been instantly suspicious of anyone who showed him the least bit of friendliness. Some people might accuse him of paranoia. But the woman wasn't smiling.

"I'm just passing through, ma'am," he said.

"Oh? Where are you headed?"

He couldn't blame her for looking a little confused there. Lamar wasn't really on the way to anywhere else.

"Denver, eventually," he said.

"Ah. Well then. I hope your travels are safe."

Cormac left. She continued to watch him; he could just about feel it.

Back at his motel room, he slept for a few hours, getting ready for another long night. He dreamed; he always dreamed, vague images and feelings, a sense of some treasure just out of reach or some danger just within reach. That if he was just a little faster, just a little smarter, he could make everything— his life, his past—better. He usually woke feeling nervous. He'd gotten used to it.

Later that afternoon, just before business closing time, he

found a butcher shop in town and bought a few pounds of a low-grade cut of beef, bloody as he could get it. At an ancient Safeway, he picked up a five-pound bag of flour.

Around ten P.M., well after sunset, when most folk were heading to bed—when someone else might be trying to sneak out—he returned to the school. At the edge of the campus, along the trail of claw prints he'd followed back from the ranch, he staked out the bait.

A wind blew in from the prairie, almost constant in this part of the state, varying from a whisper of dry air to tornado-spawning storms. Tonight the breeze was occasional, average. Cormac marked it and moved across it, away from the meat he'd hung from a low branch on a cottonwood. The wind would carry only the meat's scent, not his. The hunter scattered flour on the ground underneath the meat, forming a thin, subtle layer. If the wolf ran away, this would make it easy to track.

He went across the street and found a place near a dusty, unused garage, a hundred yards or so away, to hunker down. He let his gaze go soft, taking in the whole scene, keeping a watch on the bait and the paths leading to it.

Time passed. The moon rose, just a few days from full. However much the werewolf might resist the urge, might control itself until then, at the full moon it would be forced to come out. Then Cormac would have it.

Midnight came and went, and the wolf never showed up to take the bait. It must have satiated the bloodlust on the cattle. It was being careful, now.

After a couple more hours of waiting with no results, he

dismantled the trap—took down the meat and brushed his boot across the flour until it was scattered and ground into the dust and lawn. Covering his own tracks.

The sky was black. It was that time of night when streetlights—and even this town had a few—seemed to dim, unable to hold back the dark. In just a couple of hours, the night would break, the sky would turn gray, and the sun would rise pink in the east. He'd stayed up and watched it happen enough nights that he could almost set his clock by the change in light. But right now, before then, the night was dark, cold, clammy. Three A.M. had a smell all its own.

He switched off the headlights as he slipped into a parking space in front of his room. The motel was a one-story, run-down strip, a refugee from 1950s glory days, with peeling white paint and a politically incorrect sign out front, showing a faded screaming Indian holding a tomahawk: the Apache. All lights were out, the place was dark, not a soul awake and walking around. No witnesses.

Cormac set foot on the asphalt and hesitated. He listened to instinct; when his gut poked him, he trusted it. Something wasn't right. Something was out there. Slowly, he pulled the rifle from under the Jeep's front seat.

There wasn't anyplace to hide out here; the land around the motel was as flat as a skillet, with no trees, only a few buildings, and the motel itself. The two-lane highway stretched out in either direction straight and empty. Cormac didn't hear footsteps, breathing, a humming engine, nothing. He didn't see a flicker of movement except for grasses touched by a faint breeze. He had no sign that anything was out there, except for the tingling hairs on the back of his neck screaming at him that something inhuman was watching.

It thumped onto the roof of the Jeep, slamming the vinyl, rocking the whole vehicle. Cormac ducked, hitting asphalt, as the oversize wolf skittered across the roof and leapt to the ground in front of him.

The door to the Jeep was still open; Cormac jumped inside, scrambling backward, and slammed it shut as the wolf crashed into it on its next attack. Its front claws scraped against the window, digging against the slick surface, snapping at the glass with open jaws and spit-covered teeth.

The damn werewolf had tracked him. No—it hadn't even needed to track him. The Apache was the cheapest motel in town. It just had to lie in wait.

It hadn't made a sound, not a growl or a snarl. It had just pounced, ready to rip him apart. On its hind legs now, it was as tall as the Jeep, larger than a natural wild wolf, because it weighed as much as its human form—conservation of mass. A wild wolf might be around a hundred, hundred twenty pounds. A big werewolf would be close to two hundred. This one was maybe a hundred sixty, hundred eighty. However large it was, however shocking it was to see a wolf as tall as his Jeep, this wasn't the largest he'd ever seen. Not a two hundred pounder. It was thin, rangy. It had speed rather than bulk. Its coat was mostly gray, edged with beige and black. Prairie colors.

The werewolf backed off a moment, then sprang at the Jeep again, crashing full force into the window. The glass cracked.

Cormac couldn't stay in here forever. And he wasn't going to get a better shot than this. He fired.

The rifle thundered in the closed space of the Jeep, rattling Cormac's ears to numbness. The glass of the driver's-side window frosted with a million cracks radiating from a quarter-sized hole in the middle. The wolf had vanished.

He couldn't hear a damn thing, and he wasn't willing to bet he'd blown the thing's head off that easy; he couldn't spot any blood. He looked around but couldn't see much, lying back across the front seats, peering out the remaining windows, mostly into sky.

After rolling to his knees, he broke out the driver's-side window with the muzzle of his rifle, dropping a rain of glass outside, and looked out. Shards of glass glittered across the asphalt. He didn't see the wolf. Definitely didn't see blood. Which meant it had ducked and run. Making his life harder.

He made a quick three sixty, looking out every window, hoping to see where it had fled. Werewolves were fast, but he should have seen something, a flash of movement, the low lupine form dashing madly to safety. Otherwise it was still here, hiding low and out of sight next to the Jeep. He wasn't going to go outside until he knew.

Even if he did manage to kill the thing in a head-to-head fight, facing it down meant risking getting bitten or scratched, which was as good as dead as far as Cormac was concerned. No sense in taking stupid risks; that was the trick.

He started the engine and backed away. Right away he heard a thunk against the side and saw what he was hoping for—the wolf scrambling away from the vehicle, turning tail, and running across the parking lot.

The other trick was realizing werewolves didn't generally take stupid risks, either. Instinct told them to flee when a hunt stopped being easy.

Cormac shoved open the door, stepped out, took aim with the rifle, and fired. The wolf disappeared around the side of the building.

"Damn," he murmured. He'd have known right away if he'd even clipped the wolf. All he had to do was clip it. The silver in the bullet only had to touch the monster's blood to poison it, killing it in a matter of moments. That wolf hadn't slowed down. Cormac had just plain missed. He could kick himself. He didn't miss very often, even when his target was running.

But he'd flushed the thing into the open. That was something. The game wasn't over yet.

The engine on the Jeep was still running, and Cormac got in and headed back toward the Catholic school. Maybe he could run the thing down. Not to mention he didn't want to be around when the cops arrived to investigate the gunfire. Assuming they did. He glanced in the rearview mirror, and the motel was still dark. No lights had turned on. He had to smile—small town on the plains, random gunfire in the middle of the night, and nobody bats an eye. They probably thought it was some kid out shooting street signs. Good enough.

★ ★ ★

He couldn't hope to follow the wolf in the Jeep—the beast traveled overland, in a straight line. Cormac had to stick to streets. But that was okay. The sun had started to rise. Monday morning the school would be busy, just starting its day. Good. Easy for Cormac to tell who was missing then.

He was too close to identifying the wolf to worry much about his low profile. Parked in his Jeep, he watched the campus come to life, girls in their uniforms spilling from the dorms in clumps—packs, almost—hanging around on the lawns, filing into the classrooms.

Then came his turn. He kept the rifle under the seat, automatically felt for the handgun under his jacket, and headed toward the newer school building, where most of the activity was. He scanned the faces quickly, efficiently, recognizing many of them from the church service yesterday. His wolf was around a hundred and seventy pounds, and he searched his mental catalog for anyone he'd seen who fit that description. That ruled out most of the students. But a number of the adults were that size. It would all depend on who was missing, who was away, sleeping it off.

He entered the school and made his way down the main corridor, knowing he was out of place here; his skin crawled as people looked at him, stared at him, identified him as a stranger. Wasn't anything he could do about that, so he concentrated on the job at hand. He walked up and down the hallway once, glancing through the windows in classroom doors, marking faces, noting rooms that didn't have a teacher in them, making a mental checklist of other staff members he ought to be looking for—administrators, even janitors. He hadn't seen anything definitive, nothing that worked on his gut feeling. In a sense, he was trying to prove a negative here, trying to prove an identity by its absence. He had to make sure. He couldn't be wrong when he pulled the trigger.

The building had a lobby, and he waited there while the last of the morning crowd came in and made their way to their classes. A few of the nuns were also teachers—he noted them. Also noted that he didn't see the nun who'd spoken to him yesterday. But maybe she wasn't a teacher. He also hadn't seen the priest. At least, not until he went back outside, where the man was waiting for him on the sidewalk out front.

Out of his cassock now, the man wore plain black trousers and a black shirt with a clerical collar. As Cormac left the building, the priest caught his gaze and started toward him. Cormac could have avoided him, turned around or just walked away. But he'd just as soon hear what the guy had to say. He looked to weigh about a hundred and seventy.

Cormac waited, and the priest stopped in front of him. "You must be the visitor Sister Hilda told me about. I'm Father Patrick." He didn't offer his hand. Neither did Cormac, who only nodded a greeting. The priest didn't seem to mind that Cormac didn't say his name. "You seem to be looking for something," he said.

Cormac kept it straightforward. "There's a wild animal been killing cattle out east of here. I tracked it here. You see anything? Hear anything?"

"And here I was, hoping you were looking for redemption."

In spite of himself, Cormac chuckled. "No. Not yet, anyway."

"Maybe someday, then."

In fact, Cormac was pretty sure he wouldn't make it that far. It didn't bear thinking on. "So I take it you haven't seen anything? If the thing's bedding down around here, you ought to be worried. All these kids around."

Father Patrick gave him a quizzical look. "It's that dangerous?"

"Yeah, it is. I think it'll kill anything in front of it."

"You make it sound like a monster," Father Patrick said.

"Yeah, that's about right."

"And why is it up to you to hunt it? You aren't with the Department of Wildlife, I suspect."

"No, sir. Look, I won't take up any more of your time—"

"Not at all." The priest made a calming gesture with a hand. Like a saint in a religious painting. "But I would ask you to consider letting this go. I'd hate to have to call the police about a trespassing violation."

Cormac just smiled. He'd heard shit like this a hundred times before. "I'll get out of your hair, then." He started to turn away.

"Also consider, that even a monster is a creature of God, and God does take care of His own," the priest said.

Cormac looked at him. "You believe in a God that creates monsters? Monsters who murder?"

"We don't get to choose God. We don't get to make God. God makes us."

He knows, Cormac thought. Or maybe . . . But he couldn't

have been the werewolf; the timing was off. He wouldn't have had enough time to shift back to human, to dress and appear so calm and put together. At least, Cormac was pretty sure he wouldn't have had enough time.

"You know who it is," Cormac said. "You know *what* it is. Then you know it's a devil, a demon——"

"And we're all God's children," Father Patrick said firmly. "I'm going to make that phone call now."

Cormac walked away.

It could be the priest. If he'd been a werewolf a long time, if he had the experience, maybe he could shapeshift that quickly and appear so calm just an hour after attacking Cormac, after getting shot at. But Cormac wasn't sure that made any sense.

Something screwy was going on here. Cormac didn't care what the old man said, he had to take care of it. He had to make the kill soon, because the full moon was approaching and he had a feeling that would be too late. That monster this morning wasn't a creature of God; it was a pure cold killer. A child of Satan. Didn't matter what kind of fancy theology you dressed it up in.

Someone was lounging on the hood of his Jeep. One of the students—an honest-to-God Catholic schoolgirl in a knee-length plaid skirt, cardigan, crisp shirt, and maroon tie, the knot hanging loose, about halfway down her chest. Her black hair—dyed, probably—was in a ponytail, with loose wisps hanging around her face. She was looking away at something and seemed to be chewing gum.

This place was too damn crowded, and too many people had seen him already.

Cormac was practically in front of her when she decided to look at him.

He made the automatic assessment: she was older, maybe seventeen, and full-grown. "Big-boned" was the polite way of describing her sturdy frame. Not quite big enough to be the wolf from last night. But he had to acknowledge the rather predatory look to her. She definitely didn't seem afraid of him.

"What's your story?" he said, resting his hands on his hips.

"I was framed," she said. "They weren't my drugs."

Chuckling, he looked away. "You out here scuffing up my Jeep for a reason?"

She gave the Jeep a long, pointed look. Pale mud caked the wheel wells, the paint job had gone from olive green to pale green over the years, and rust spots had broken out across the hood, where the paint had been dinged by rocks and hail. Not to mention the shot-out window.

"I heard you talking to Father Patrick. And . . . I don't know. I shouldn't even be here." She slumped away from the Jeep and started to walk away.

"Hold on there," Cormac said. "What have you seen?"

She glanced nervously toward the school and bit her lip—a physical expression of the tension he'd been feeling since he arrived. So it wasn't just him. "The other kids tell ghost stories. They talk about hearing noises—howling, banging on the windows. When I first got here, I thought it was just the usual thing, they're always trying to scare the new girl. But they don't go out at night. This is my third boarding school, and I've never been to one where kids didn't break curfew. But here, they don't. They're scared."

"You know that for sure?"

"Yeah. And it's not just them. No one goes out at night. It's the kids who double-check the locks on the doors and windows. We've all heard the noises. The sisters say it's bears or coyotes. But I don't think that's what it is."

"And what do you think it is?"

She ducked her gaze. "It's crazy."

Cormac gave a wry smile. "People always say that to me. Something killed some cattle on a ranch ten miles or so out, and it wasn't coyote or bear. I tracked the thing back here. I think it may be living around here, and I think it's not going to stay happy just killing livestock."

The fearful look in her eyes showed shock but not surprise. He had a feeling he could have said the word "werewolf" and she wouldn't have been surprised.

"I'll get it," Cormac said. "Whatever it is."

"Okay. Good," she said. Her smile was nervous. "I should get back—"

"Hey," he said before she could scurry away. He had a bad idea and hated himself for even thinking it. "Would you mind doing something for me?"

He'd asked the girl to walk across the campus at midnight. That was all. Back and forth between the dormitory and the old school building, across the longest stretch of lawn, slowly and leisurely. She'd looked at him as if he were crazy, and Cormac hadn't wanted to defend himself. He wasn't crazy, just driven. And he lived in a different world from that of most folks, a world where monsters like vampires and werewolves existed.

Which was, in fact, one definition of crazy.

But Cormac had promised he would be there, that he wouldn't let anything happen to her. And that he would fix whatever the trouble was. He tried to tell himself that even if something did happen to her, it was a small price for getting rid of the werewolf. He didn't ask for her name on purpose.

But he was nervous. He'd never worked with live bait before. Not intentionally.

He left the Jeep, plastic sheeting taped over the driver's-side window, at the motel. It would be too hard to hide, and the werewolf would recognize it right off. Easier to sneak around on his own. But without the Jeep he didn't have an escape route.

It was all in the setup. No reason he'd need an escape route, unless this went south. Really far south.

The open lawn separated the campus's buildings from the street. A few trees, towering cottonwoods for the most part, with some maples scattered around and a few clumps of shrubs made up the landscaping. Not a lot of cover available. A long sidewalk led from the street to the church doors, and a couple of tall, well-trimmed shrubs served as a sort of gate at the end of the sidewalk. Cormac settled here with his rifle. The spot offered a view of the lawn and was down-wind from most of the campus. The werewolf wouldn't be able to smell him.

He arrived early and waited there for more than an hour. All the lights in all the buildings went off at ten P.M., except for a porch light over the door of the church. A faint light was visible within as well, over the altar, filtered through stained glass. Cormac supposed the door to the church was unlocked, if tradition held. Maybe that would be his escape route. Ironic.

Midnight came, and he didn't see anything. The girl might have decided not to help him after all. He couldn't blame her. He'd give it another half hour, then go looking for the monster himself. He had to be able to flush out the werewolf some-how. Quietly, he flexed his legs and arms, stretching in place to keep the blood flowing, to keep warm.

There she was. He recognized the dark figure by the shape of her ponytail. Out of the uniform, she wore torn jeans and hugged a short leather coat around herself, hunched over as if cold or fearful. She stomped down the walk aggressively, as though she had something to prove. Cormac might have wished for her to be more skittish—to move like a prey ani-mal. But she was alone, obviously nervous. That would have to do to attract the wolf.

She made her way quickly across the open space, taking the concrete sidewalk from the dorms to the school building. She moved more quickly than he'd have preferred, just short of jogging, looking anxiously around her the whole time.

The werewolf wasn't going to go for such obvious bait, Cormac decided. But he wondered. It was losing control, that much was clear. Killing livestock was the first step. Attacking people was the next. It had to know it was losing control, so why stay here? The town was rural, but this spot was full of tempting targets—a hundred kids, easy pickings. He had to conclude that the monster just didn't care. Or the thing thought it could handle itself. And it was wrong.

Even if the werewolf was too smart to go after such an obvious target as the girl, Cormac was pretty sure the monster still had a bone to pick with him, so to speak. One way or another, the werewolf would make an appearance.

The girl was two-thirds of the way to the school building when he saw it, a shadow pouring across the lawn. It wasn't stalking; it had already targeted her and was running, ready to strike. Wolves hunted by running, smashing into their prey, which they knocked over as they anchored their jaws and teeth in its flesh. The girl wouldn't even see it happen. She might have enough time to scream.

No hesitation, Cormac stood, braced, aimed, and fired, all in the same motion, as reflexive as breathing.

The wolf fell and cried out.

Cormac walked toward it and fired again. The wolf flinched again. It rolled over itself in a chaos of fur, biting at its own flank, whining in pain.

The girl had stopped, frozen in fear or panic, hands to her face. Then she stepped forward, arm outstretched as if to comfort the monster.

"Get inside! Get inside right now!" Cormac yelled at her. She ran inside the dorm and slammed the door.

The silver ought to be traveling through the wolf's veins, ought to be poisoning its heart and killing it in slow agony. The beast looked to the sound of Cormac's voice and snarled, lips pulled away from gleaming teeth, hackles bristling. Then the wolf turned and ran.

A last burst of adrenaline, a final gasp before death. This thing wasn't going to go down so easy after all. But it was only a matter of time.

Cormac jogged after it as it ran, trailing drops of blood, to the church.

The wolf had slowed to a stumbling trot, limping badly, to the front steps of the church, where Father Patrick was waiting for it.

Cormac watched dumbfounded as the priest guided the injured wolf inside and closed the door behind them. He ran up the steps and stopped himself against the door, rattling the handle. Locked, the son of a bitch.

On the plus side, it was an old lock on an old wooden door, a latch and not a dead bolt. He stood back, put his shoulder to it, and rammed hard, and again. The wood splintered. The third time, the latch ripped out of the wood and he was inside.

A shaded electric light illuminated the altar area of the church, at the far end of a long aisle. Father Patrick and the werewolf had made it about halfway there. A trail of blood dripped unevenly along the hardwood floor from them to the door. Cormac stepped around it, hesitating at the last pew.

The wolf was gone. Father Patrick held Sister Hilda's body on his lap. Two bloody wounds were visible on her naked back, blackened from the poison. Dark streaks of silver-poisoned blood crawled up her back and down her legs, along the veins.

Cormac's hands flexed, ready to raise the rifle and aim at Father Patrick.

"She smelled you. Sunday, after Mass. She knew what you were and told me. Told me to be careful." His voice was stretched to breaking, but he held back the tears. He didn't look at Cormac but kept his gaze on the woman. "She controlled it for forty years. She took orders to help her control it, and it worked. The routine, the structure of this life—it worked for so long. I helped her, helped take care of her. But she was losing the fight, she knew she was losing. I suppose I should thank you for doing this before she hurt anyone. She isn't a killer. And she's with God now. This wasn't her fault."

What a story. And of course it wasn't her fault; it was never anyone's fault, was it?

"This is just God playing tricks, is it?" Cormac said, his voice flat, his patience thin. He just wanted to get out of here.

"God sends us obstacles," Father Patrick said. "It's up to us to overcome them. Like she did."

He'd killed a monster, Cormac reassured himself. He'd done the right thing, here. He knew it.

"I have to ask—are you infected, too? Has she ever bitten

you?" Cormac asked. He'd shoot the man right here if he said yes, if he even hesitated, if he gave the slightest hint that the werewolf had bitten him.

The priest shook his head and murmured, "No."

There were ways of telling for sure. Slice his skin with a regular knife and watch if it healed fast. Slice it with the silver-inlaid knife and watch if he died from it. But Father Patrick didn't have the wolfish look in his eyes. He didn't have the rage, the tension, as if he were holding something back. Cormac believed him and left him alone.

Cormac retreated from the school without saying anything to the girl. He'd already done a piss-poor job of covering his tracks; no need to make it worse. At dawn's light, he checked out of the motel and showed up on Harrison's doorstep.

He knocked on the front door and waited for Harrison to answer, which he did after a couple of minutes. His wife was looking over his shoulder, until he barked at her to leave them alone.

"Did you finally get it?" the rancher asked.

"Yeah, I got it."

"Who was it?"

"It doesn't matter. But you won't have any more problems."

"And where's your proof that you got it?"

"Talk to Father Patrick over at the church. He'll tell you."

Harrison frowned, plainly not happy with that idea. "Just a minute, then."

He went inside, leaving Cormac standing alone on the

porch. Didn't even invite him in for morning coffee. Mrs. Harrison would have invited him in, which was maybe why Mr. Harrison had ordered her away. Folks didn't like having Cormac around much more than they liked having the monsters. Two sides of the same coin in some ways, Cormac supposed. Though Sister Hilda never killed anyone, did she? And Cormac had. Over and over.

Harrison returned with a fat envelope to round out the job. He didn't hand it to Cormac so much as hold it out reluctantly, making Cormac take it from him.

"You can let your herd out now," Cormac said, instead of thanking a man like Harrison.

"Well. I'm glad the bastard's gone. I hope it died painful, I hope——"

"Shut up, Harrison," Cormac said, exhausted on a couple of levels. "Just—just shut up."

Tucking the blood money in his jacket, Cormac walked back to his Jeep, feeling the rancher's gaze on his back the whole time.

He drove away from Lamar, away from the morning sun, as fast as he could.

* * *

Carrie Vaughn is the author of the *New York Times* bestselling series about a werewolf named Kitty who hosts a talk radio advice show for the supernaturally disadvantaged. Recent volumes include *Kitty Raises Hell* and *Kitty's House of Horrors*. Cormac is a recurring character in the series. Carrie's first young adult novel,

Voices of Dragons, the rock climbing, jet fighters, alternate history with dragons book, is due out in 2010. She lives in Boulder, Colorado, with a fearsome miniature American Eskimo dog named Lily. Visit her at www.carrievaughn.com.

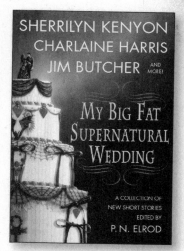
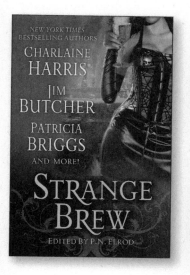